The Way Back To You

A Novel

Hayden Fox

Fox Cabin Publishing

DEDICATION

To my family for believing in me every step of the way. To my husband, thank you for chasing this dream with me. Of all the love stories I'll ever write, ours will always be my favorite.

To my daughter, the bravest person I know, thank you for teaching me how to be brave too.

To my mom, my very first supporter, thank you for always encouraging me to write and follow my dreams.

For all the people that believe in relationships that are built to last, hope that feels real, and love stories synonymous with home.

Content and Trigger Warnings

Dear Reader,

This book covers heavier themes and a few sensitive topics. I wrote it in part to deal with some of my own trauma, grief and mental health challenges. Please be mindful of the following trigger warnings while reading:

Adoption, bullying, homophobia, racism, addiction, alcoholism/alcohol abuse, drug abuse, gambling addiction, suicidal ideation, postpartum depression, discussion of abortion, depression & anxiety representation, PTSD, physical violence, physical abuse, open door romance/sexually explicit content, kidnapping, torture, car accident, hospitalization.

All my love,
Hayden Fox

PROLOGUE

"*K*ENDALL, DO YOU TAKE *Kai—wait, what's your middle name again, Kai?" Jenna leans in, her brow furrowed. She's shuffling back and forth on her feet holding a makeshift bouquet of wildflowers we picked from Mrs. Buchanan's garden. They were starting to wilt in the heat. It was a humid hazy summer day and we had spent most of it by the lake until we got bored. Now we were having an impromptu wedding ceremony for me and Kai. Jenna's idea.*

"I don't have one," he whispers, barely audible.

"Oh right. Kendall, do you take Kai Matsumoto to be your husband forever and ever? In sickness and in health, in good times and in bad?"

"I do," I say excitedly, squeezing his sweaty hands tighter.

"Kai Matsumoto, do you take Kendall Elyse James to be your wife forever and ever? In sickness and in health, in good times and in bad?"

"I think so," he murmurs, his eyes darting around and finally settling on my face. I smile at him and he smiles back, a real one. The one I feel like he saves just for me.

"You have to say I do Kai, or it's not real," Jenna chides with one hand perched on her hip.

"I do," he responds.

"Okay great. Kai, you may put the ring on Kendall's finger," Jenna tells him. He takes a red ring pop from his pocket and slides it onto my finger.

"Kendall, you may put the ring on Kai's finger." I mirror his actions with a blue ring pop.

"Okay. I now pronounce you husband and wife. Kai, you may kiss your bride!" Jenna announces with enthusiasm. Kai doesn't budge. I'm not even sure he's breathing. Jenna glances back and forth between us expectantly.

I take a small step towards a nervous, trembling Kai and whisper, "We don't have to kiss if you don't want to. It's okay. It's just for fun," I try to reassure him. But he still isn't moving and his face has gone rigid.

"No, we can. I want to," he replies, even though he looks like he'd rather stick his foot in a pool full of piranhas.

"Okay. How about I kiss you on the cheek?" I ask. He nods in agreement. I lean forward and place my lips on his flushed skin and the whole time, he remains perfectly still.

***

A FEW HOURS LATER, we're sitting on the front steps of my house, eating popsicles in silence and waiting for the fireworks to begin. I lean back against the metal railing and it cools my skin, a nice contrast to the humidity we've been fighting all day.

"You were brave today, Ken. You know when Jenna said it was time to kiss," he says before taking a bite from his melting patriotic flag. I chuckle while blue and red juice dribbles down his chin and falls to the ground.

"What do you mean?" I wonder, staring at him.

"I was too nervous," he admits.

"That's okay. You're brave too, Kai. There's a lot of things that scare you and you do them anyway."

"Like what?"

"Like marrying me and the kiss."

"Well, you kissed me," he points out.

"But were you scared?"

"Yes."

"And did we still do it?"

"Yeah."

"So that makes you brave," I decide.

"You think one day we'll get married for real?" he asks.

"I hope so. You're my favorite person. Well, you and Jenna."

"You're mine too," he answers. I notice he doesn't include Jenna in his list of favorite people. Just me.

"Come on, let's go. We don't want to miss the fireworks!" I yell and offer my sticky palm to him. We stand up and sprint across the lawn hand in hand, the last of our popsicles sloughing off to meet their end on the grass below our bare feet.

Chapter 1

Kai

"Hey, it's me. I need to see you. I saw you at my game last night, so I know you're in the area. Meet me at the Beech Street Diner at twelve, *please*. I just want to talk." I press the end call button and let the panic sink in. I stare at the date on my phone: January 11, 2020.

Three years. It's been three years since I've seen or talked to Kendall. Not for lack of trying. I had called, emailed, and written her letters but had never gotten any responses. Until last night. In the second period, down by a goal, I glanced past the puck looking to pass to Jax, and in the space of a millisecond, I spotted her beautiful face in the crowd. In insanely expensive seats no less. She'd always drawn me in like the compass of an arrow pulled north. My eyes snapped to her, registering her favorite green hoodie—before lowering to the child in her arms. It was almost like she wanted me to see her and the child she was holding. He looked maybe two years old but that couldn't be right. A jolt of recognition gripped my spine as I took in the entirety of his features. Kendall and I locked eyes, my deep brown to her swirl of hazel, and she froze. Half a second later, I got slammed into the wall so hard I couldn't breathe.

I woke up in the trainer's office convinced it had all been a dream. But he confirmed that I had actually been hit hard—hard enough to lose consciousness. And the only person who was able to distract me long enough to break my laser focus and obsessive need to win was her. Had she been real? God, I hoped she was.

Because the only thing I love more than hockey, than my career, than that feeling of freedom on the ice is Kendall James.

Chapter 2
Kai
2016

"A RE YOU SURE ABOUT this?" Jonah asks, gesturing to the tattoo I had selected. "You know you don't have to do this. You could just back out. Tell them you changed your mind." He leans over the glass display table at the front of the tattoo shop.

"Positive, it's the lesser of two evils," I reply, seeing as how the other option was shaving my head. I'm an attractive guy but I know my limits and that includes not being able to pull off being bald.

I had lost a stupid bet with my teammates that I could out drink our biggest defenseman, Mason. He was Hungarian, had almost one hundred pounds on me, and had been drinking since he was nine. I knew I would probably lose but that didn't stop me from trying. And while Jonah's right—I could just walk away—I would never hear the end of it from my teammates. Part of being a rookie means paying my dues, proving my worth, and showing that I'm a team player. If that means submitting myself to hazing tactics, grunt work, and following through with bets then so fucking be it. It's a small price to pay to be a starting player for the Boston Bucks my first year in the NHL.

"Okay man, whatever you say," he replies while making no attempt at all to hide his grin. Jonah leans his back against the counter and flips through a magazine while I take a seat in the chair.

"You didn't have to come, you know. I would have been just fine without you," I gripe, irritated I was spending my one day off in a tattoo parlor making a fool of myself. He may have claimed to come with me for moral support but I know he'd rather be here than with the rest of our teammates at the bar. Jonah and I had bonded during training camp this past summer and then became good friends both on and off the ice. If there's one person I'd allow to be here for this fuckery, it's him.

"And miss a front row seat to these shenanigans? Absolutely not," he responds smugly. While the tattoo artist starts on my back, I watch Jonah flirt shamelessly with the guy working at the counter. *Moral support my ass.* He asks about different designs that he probably never plans on getting with feigned curiosity, seeing as how he often referred to his body as a temple. All in an attempt to get this guy's number and I know he will. He always does.

Jonah had first come out to me as bisexual during preseason before he made the same announcement to our coach and team. My initial response was: "Okay, what do you want to do for dinner?" Which I think was pretty shocking to him. I followed that up by explaining it didn't change anything between us. He was still one of my closest friends and I supported him no matter what. To say that sentiment wasn't shared by the rest of the league is a colossal understatement. But the world of professional sports just hasn't evolved that much. Not in the seventies when Red Auerbach introduced the first Black starting five. Not after David Kopay came out as gay and certainly not now.

And Jonah was no exception. But he assured me the shit he got from some of our teammates and the media wasn't nearly as bad as what he suffered through in high school and college. He said he wasn't concerned about the critics and trolls because his reputation spoke for itself and he was right. Jonah Gibson could play his fucking ass off. He was fast, agile, always where our offense needed him to be and he could score. He had the kind of raw talent and innate athleticism that once made me wonder why he wasn't a first round draft pick. I know better now.

A few months ago, the media stopped commenting on his romantic conquests and sexual orientation and shifted the narrative to his game, his added value as a team member. They had no other choice because Jonah didn't give them one. Jonah didn't just make a difference, he made *the* difference, he closed the gap, and he was helping us win games. *A lot of games.* His performance eventually forced them to shut the fuck up and start paying attention. And I was proud to call him my friend.

Once the guy at the front counter leaves to attend to another customer, he sits down in a chair next to me clasping his hands behind his head.

"What's that one on your ribcage for? Is it a date?" he asks, pointing to my left side. I run my hands over my ribs debating whether to tell him the origin of this tattoo. Jonah had divulged a lot to me. He trusted me and I definitely trusted him. I could give him something.

Clearing my throat, I confess, "I got it for my ex, Kendall." He knows she's a touchy subject, so I hope he'll just drop it.

"Ah, the one who has you all broody and depressed, never wanting to leave your apartment?" he questions.

"That's the one," I respond reluctantly.

"It's a shame," the tattoo artist chimes in, apparently feeling bold.

"What is?" I turn my head over my shoulder to look at her.

"A handsome guy like you being wrecked over a girl. You seem nice too." She flashes a smile at me and it's then I notice how pretty she is. In a terrifying, intimidating sort of way. All dark features and sharp angles. *Is she flirting with me?* I glimpse at Jonah who waggles his eyebrows as if to say, *Yes, you idiot. She's flirting with you.*

"Thanks," I blurt out.

"Welcome. There. You're finished," she says as she wipes the tattoo and places a bandage over it. "So. Do you guys make a habit of getting tattoos when you lose bets?" she jokes while glancing from me to Jonah.

"I'm hoping not," I grumble and stand up from the chair, stretching my arms.

"Pity seems like it'd be incredibly lucrative for me," she teases. She gives me the instructions for tattoo care along with a card in case I have any questions. Wash carefully. Moisturize. Avoid direct sunlight and swimming. I stop her gently when she starts talking about obvious signs of infection.

"This isn't my first rodeo. I've had six before this. Thank you though. It looks great," I comment.

Right before we turn to walk out, she shouts, "Wait! Can I have the card back for one second?"

I hand it back to her, curiosity gnawing at me and watch as she scribbles something on it. "Here's my cell. In case you get tired of being broody and depressed," she explains with a gorgeous smile. "Or you lose any more bets."

I make eye contact with her and hold it for a few seconds, her auburn eyes burning into mine. *Fuck*. She was funny too. I hate to admit that I'm intrigued.

"Thanks," I smile.

Once we're outside, Jonah bumps his shoulder into mine.

"So, you gonna call her?" he questions. "She seems cool, hot too. And those tattoos? Pretty badass," he observes, rubbing his hands together.

"Yeah, probably not. She seems like the kind of girl you date and that's not what I'm looking for right now."

Not when I'm still a mess over Kendall leaving.

"She looks like the kind of girl that's *interested*. And who's to say she's not into casual hookups?" he challenges.

"Yeah, I guess. We'll see," I answer quietly. We make the rest of the brisk walk to the bar in silence, trying to outrun the December chill in the air. As soon as we open the door, I spot our group of loud boisterous teammates taking up three tables in the center. Zeke comes up to me and claps me on the shoulder.

"So, how'd it go, man? You go through with it?" he jests.

I turn around and lift up my shirt showcasing the clean white tattoo bandage. Jonah opens his phone to display the picture he took of the tattoo as proof. A bold black number 32 in the middle of a red heart. Mason, the defenseman's jersey number.

Chapter 3

Kendall

We arrive at music playgroup at our local library ten minutes late. I rush in the door, Akio in my arms, in one of Kai's old threadbare hoodies and black leggings. I could never force myself to get rid of this sweatshirt and no matter how many times I've washed it, it still carries the faint scent of *him*. Along with memories I don't want to think about but can't let go of either. Ms. Candace, the eccentric, overly enthusiastic teacher has already passed out instruments to the kids and their family members. Everyone is staring at us, but we're used to it by now, having never made it on time to playgroup.

"Oh, come in, come in," she says, welcoming us and clapping her hands together from her wooden rocking chair. "We were just getting started, Kendall. We're so happy you and Akio could join us today!"

I head over to the bench and drop our belongings while Akio toddles over to the group. His favorite instrument, the maracas, are clutched in another pair of chubby fists. I watch as Akio's lower lip begins to tremble. Ms. Candace hands him a chime, which he stares at with disdain. Before this evolves into a tantrum, I sit down on an unclaimed rug and pull him into my lap.

Shortly after Ms. Candace starts the music, Akio throws the instrument on the floor with a frustrated shout. He then crosses his arms and refuses to participate. He isn't the only feral two-and-a-half-year-old in the group. Lincoln, bless his heart, is currently licking the carpet in front of him and high energy Ava is running laps around her nanny, while shaking a tambourine above her head. And Maddox has not followed a single instruction that the teacher has given, and appears to be fast approaching a meltdown. To be fair, he is the youngest here. Luckily, Ms. Candace is kind *and* patient. She coaxes Akio out of my lap and tells him he can be her special helper for the next song if he uses the chime for the rest of this one. Eventually he comes around.

When the playgroup is finished, Veronica Leonne waltzes over to me, her daughter following close behind her, with what I know is going to be unsolicited advice. Veronica and her atrocious attitude, expensive athleisure outfits, perfectly blown out hair, and Pilates ass is the kind of mom that other moms band together to collectively hate. At least I imagine they would. I wouldn't know, seeing as how I don't have many mom friends. Christ, she is the last person I want to talk to right now. She clears her throat to announce her arrival, and it grates on my already frayed nerves.

"You know if you guys made it on time and came to the playgroup more consistently, I'm sure he would be a little better behaved," she tells me with a sneer, her glacial blue eyes narrowed at me. Somehow I resist the urge to roll my eyes all the way back into my head.

"Yeah, you're probably right. We just had a busy morning and his schedule was thrown off yesterday. I'm sure that's part of it." Wait, why was I explaining myself to this Lululemon bitch, who showed up to playgroup twenty minutes early looking like she just came from a high end salon?

"Yeah, I'm sure it's hard for you guys, you know, being a single mom and all," she responds, looking at me with what I think is pity. Fuck her.

"We're doing just fine."

"Good. Well, it was nice to see you guys," she says.

"Uh huh. You too," I mumble while I pick up Akio and hurry out the door. As we walk to the parking lot, I hear footsteps behind me. I palm the small canister of mace on my keychain just in case.

"Hey Kendall, right?" Maddox's mom says brightly, shifting him from one hip to the other.

"Yeah," I pause, staring at her. I really hope she wasn't here to scold me too. One can only take so much playgroup hostility.

"Don't pay any attention to Veronica. She used to give me crap about Maddox all the time. I've just learned to ignore her," she explains.

"Thanks. I appreciate that. Glad to hear I'm not the only one who's been victimized by her," I joke and hope it lands. "It's Emma, right?" I ask.

"Yup, Emma! And I'm sure you know this little heathen here is Maddox," she states, turning towards her son. "He's not always like this I swear."

"No explanation needed," I say, smiling at her. She looks like she wants to say something else and then she asks me something I was not expecting.

"Not sure how far you guys live from the library but maybe we could get the kids together for a play date if you wanted?"

"Sure, that sounds great. Want to give me your phone? I'll put my number in," I respond while putting Akio on the ground. "You can just shoot me a text so I know it's you."

"Okay cool," she replies, passing it over.

***

WE HAVE A LITTLE time to kill after leaving the library, so I decide to take Akio grocery shopping with me. We stop in the pasta aisle first and get some Kraft mac n' cheese and spaghetti.

"Cheese, cheese!" he shouts excitedly when I nod at him, giving him the silent go-ahead. He places it in the cart—or more like throws it.

We make our way over to the produce section and pick out bananas and apples. I notice an older woman near the strawberries openly staring at us and not being subtle about it. She starts pushing her cart towards us and up close, I realize she isn't as old as I initially thought she was.

"Um, can I help you?" I ask in bewilderment.

"I'm sorry. I was just wondering where you adopted your son from? He's so adorable," she purrs.

What in fresh hell?

"Excuse me?" I respond defensively, in utter shock.

"Your son," she repeats, nodding at him, "Isn't he adopted?" Apparently the universe was playing a joke at my expense today, testing me. I stare at Akio, who is very much biologically mine, and realize how much he resembles his father. This would actually be a great time for his dad to be here. But he isn't here and that's entirely on me. Akio continues to play with his red matchbox car oblivious to the uncomfortable situation we have now found ourselves in.

Someone glancing quickly between Akio and I would be hard pressed to believe we were related, that much I knew. I didn't like it but I accepted it. My hair, long dark corkscrew curls, with caramel highlights was lighter than his. My skin tone, a shade below almond, was much darker than his olive complexion. And while the color of our eyes were similar, they were still distinctly different. Mine, a combination of green, brown, and gold that most would call hazel, and seemed to shift based on the weather and my clothing choices. Akio's were a permanent and stunning forest green. The shape of Akio's face and the contours of his cheeks were an exact replica of Kai's. To the point where it was almost painful to look at him without remembering how much I loved his father. He had also acquired his father's dark shaggy hair, his serious contemplative gaze, and I always thought, his breathtaking smile. But I hadn't seen it in so long up close, it was hard to be certain. The woman clears her throat and I'm anchored back to this awkward moment. My rage incited by this woman's obscene, intrusive comment and perhaps my longing for everything that was Kai spurs me forward.

Fuck it.

I had today and tomorrow off. I've had two coffees already, and I was still fired up from my conversation with Veronica.

I have time for it today.

"I could see how you might think that," I begin while stepping in front of the shopping cart to shield Akio. "But if you look at the half-moons of his fingernails and the ridges of his hands, those are definitely mine. The way his mouth crinkles when he's happy and his gorgeous green eyes he inherited from me too."

I can tell the woman knows she's made a mistake but isn't sure how to course correct. Her cheeks start to redden as she looks from me to him with embarrassment. Good. She should be uncomfortable. And I don't feel one ounce of shame. I refuse to do mental gymnastics to protect her ego because honestly, fuck her feelings.

"I'm so sorry. I didn't mean to—"

"You know what else I hope he gets from me?" I ask rhetorically, cutting off her apology. She swallows.

"The confidence to stand up to ignorant, small-minded people, people who believe they are entitled to information because of their privilege and whiteness. It is incredibly insensitive and rude to make assumptions just because you can't see the physical similarities between us and more importantly, it's absolutely none of your fucking business."

"I—"

But I turn my back to her before I can hear her response and I push our cart away as fast as humanly possible. The fucking audacity of that woman, the brazenness. It wasn't the first time I've encountered micro aggressions or people just being assholes but it was the first time I've encountered it with Akio. Have people started speaking to me in Spanish because they assumed I was Latina? Yes. Have random strangers asked to touch my hair or if it was real, because to them I was foreign, or other? Also, yes. But never has anyone suggested that Akio and I weren't related even if their judgmental stares signaled that's exactly what they were thinking. And it fucking hurt. It made my momma heart bleed.

The overwhelming need society had to look at a person or people and be able to label them, define them, understand them in a way that made them comfortable was unbelievable. It wasn't even that she thought he was adopted. It was more that she felt she had the right to know. That she was entitled to our life story to satisfy her own curiosity. That she assumed we couldn't possibly be related to each other by blood. That she needed to be able to put us in a category, in a box that could be wrapped up tightly in a bow. Maybe it also struck a chord because I was a child of adoption and I'm sure my moms got looks and questions like that all the time while raising me.

As if my day couldn't get any worse, I glance at my phone and watch a call from an unknown number light up my screen. *Buzz buzz buzz.* Silent alarm bells start ringing in my head. I don't recognize the number but instinctually, I know it's him. *Buzz buzz buzz.* I let the call go to voicemail, my heart pounding like a steel drum. I was still on the other side of this—the side where he lived his life and I lived mine and they never *ever* intersected. And if I listen to his voicemail, I know with certainty that they would. After last night, there's no way I could retreat into my illusion of safety, a world where Kai and I coexisted independently. I had known this would be a possibility and yet I went anyway, guns blazing. Maybe my heart had recognized something my head wasn't ready to accept.

It was time to finally pull that trigger.

Akio has been asking recently about a dad, *his* dad. He knows our family looks different from others, even at his age. And I don't have answers for him, not any that make sense. Ultimately, Akio needs a father and he deserves to have Kai in his life. Even if I don't. After my last relationship ended in disaster, I realized there were some feelings that were too loud to ignore. It doesn't matter how much time has passed, Kai would never truly be out of my system.

Once we reach the car and I buckle Akio in his car seat—fighting with the tangled seatbelt like it's the universe's last *fuck you* for the day—I allow myself to listen to the message. He wants me to meet him at the diner *today*. Less than two hours from now.

Chapter 4

Kendall

I HAD TRIED. REALLY I had. I circled the block three times and almost pulled into the parking lot of the diner on my third time around. But I couldn't do it. Regret and shame had me in a chokehold and the threat of every burgeoning unknown hurtling towards me at once was enough to send me spiraling.

I wasn't ready to derail our entire lives. I'm not sure I ever will be. Our world is small but full. It is loud, messy, toys everywhere, *Cocomelon* on a fucking never ending loop. It's chaos but it's *ours*. Maybe one day we'd be open to more, more than just the two of us. More than hoping. I had come farther today than I ever have in the past. I had actually paid for a ticket and stayed for the entire game. I had listened to his voicemail for once without breaking down in tears. I had every intention of walking into that diner and facing my demons. But no matter how hard I try, I can't give myself that final push I need.

***

THREE DAYS LATER, I'M still a wreck from attending Kai's game and ghosting him after he asked me to meet up with him. I sigh as I scurry through the back door of Kip's restaurant, hopefully unnoticed, as I'm four minutes late for my shift. I yell, "Hey guys," into the kitchen cheerfully and get a few heys, a few winks, and a grunt from Sal, the ornery line cook who can't be bothered with pleasantries. I put my hair up in a quick bun while

I trot to the hostess stand. Once I've secured a pen, pad, and some oversized sticky menus, I scope out Amber.

"Ken, finally!" she shouts, her gaze connecting with mine at the counter.

"Sorry," I say, shoving the pen and pad in the black apron tied around my waist. "Traffic was horrendous," I grouse.

"It's fine, I appreciate you covering. Also, you can thank me in advance for the big tip you're going to get from nine and ten," she chirps while removing her apron. "Bunch of Neanderthal athletes with big pockets."

I look in the direction of my section and even from a distance, I can hear the racket and witness the scene they're making. Laughing, cursing, hollering. She isn't kidding; they're rowdy and obnoxious, likely already drunk. I'm definitely going to be getting a nice fat tip from that group, if I could manage not to be socially awkward for the next two hours.

Together, they took up two booths, and from the looks of them, all hulking muscle and broad shoulders, they could eat. But I don't pay enough attention. I'm listening to Amber prattle on about the tabs she closed out and how the rest of her shift went. I scan the list of specials quickly while she thanks me again and heads out the door. My mistake was not getting a closer look at the group crowding tables nine and ten. I shimmy up to them, light on my feet, eyes still on the specials.

"Hi, welcome to Kip's. I'll be your server tonight—" but my words catch in my throat. Because the man seated third one in from the left is Kai. *My Kai.*

"Well, hello there, gorgeous," a square jaw attached to a blonde head of curls muses. My mouth is open but no words come out. Like there's a hundred tabs open in my brain and they're all frozen. I'm left speechless by the sight of him. A few guys, I assume are his teammates, say something but I can't make it out. Their voices sound muffled like we're under water. I'm still stuck on *him.* The same brutally handsome man I fell in love with. The same midnight eyes, untamed dark waves, the same beautiful tan complexion that made people wonder—sometimes out loud—where he was from or what his race was. And the same perfect smile that cut straight through to my soul. Except he's not smiling, not anymore. His face is ashen, his lips downturned into a grimace, like he's just seen a ghost. I suppose he has. My throat feels dry and my head is a little fuzzy.

Am I going to pass out?

"Don't call her that," he warns blondie, his eyes locked on mine and his voice is just as deep and velvety smooth as I remember it. His voice could tame the most ruthless ocean. I don't think I realized how much I missed it until now. The timbre of it glides over my skin and caresses my heart. It reverberates throughout my chest and sinks its talons into my bones. It's not like I hadn't listened to his voicemails or heard him talk in interviews. But this, hearing him in person, seeing him in the flesh a foot away from me is different. It's throwing my entire limbic system into upheaval.

"Why? You don't even know her," he postures.

"Wait, Kendall? *You're Kendall?*" another unfairly attractive man asks in disbelief as he raises his pierced eyebrow. But I don't respond. Every word I could possibly utter gets trapped in my throat and blocked by an immovable wall of shock.

Every small yet distinct detail of him throttles me with startling force. One after the other. The smokey baritone of his voice. The intensity of his gaze. The sheer size of his hands that always seemed to engulf mine completely. That fucking scar that gives him an edge he certainly doesn't need and that pesky lock of hair that obscures his eyes. They all hit me in the gut and worsen the dull ache in my chest that I had been trying to extinguish for three years with no success.

"Fucking Christ, Jonah," Kai grits out. But I don't hear the rest of the conversation. I'm already sprinting to the staff bathroom trying to hide from this torturous seventh circle of hell I've stumbled into. This isn't happening. This is a nightmare I will wake up from. It has to be. I splash cool water on my face and force myself to breathe.

In through my nose, out through my mouth. In my nose, out my mouth. In, out, in, out. Fuck, this isn't working—

"Ken, it's me." His voice is soft and pleading from behind the thin door. "Can you please come out so we can talk for a second?" *Fuck.* I can't wait in here my entire shift. I have to face him one way or another.

"Just give me a minute," I respond but it comes out high pitched and a little deranged. I take what little time I have to collect myself and steady my breathing. As soon as I walk out of the bathroom, he takes a hesitant step toward me and reaches for me like a reflex, one built over years of being with someone. But I can't meet him where he's at. I have to meet him where I'm at, and that is utterly and completely terrified. I retreat a step instead and he winces like I caused him physical pain. It's almost imperceptible but I've spent most of my life learning him, reading him, *loving him,* so I know it's not the reaction he was hoping for. But I can't touch him. I can barely look him in the eyes. I know if I do, any resolve I have would crumble. The raw unhealed pieces of my heart would break all over again. Thankfully, he's so tall that the only thing at my eye level is the fraying string of his Boston Bucks sweatshirt.

"I called you the other night. I know you were at my game—"

"Kai, I can't do this right now. I'm working and I really need the tips," I whisper shakily. He runs his hands down his face in frustration.

"Yeah, and why is that, Kendall? Why exactly do you need the tips so badly?" he asks, pinning me with an intense stare.

He knows. He might not know everything, but he knows something is off.

"Kai, I can't. Not here. Please," I beg him. He looks hurt, confused, angry, all the things he should be.

"Fine, meet me tomorrow. The same place. Same time. Clearly there's things we need to talk about."

I have to do this. I have to give him some shred of hope or he probably won't leave. The frightening unknowns are happening now whether I want them to or not. The alluring possibility of *more* is standing right in front of me and for the first time, I want to reach out and take it.

"If I meet you tomorrow, you'll leave and let me get through the rest of my shift in peace?" I stipulate.

"Yes," he says, a small grin taking over his face. Jesus that *fucking grin* makes my heart stutter and my brain short out. That smile alone could level cities. "But don't think I won't come back if you stand me up again."

"Okay. Tomorrow," I confirm.

"Tomorrow," he repeats, moving closer to me and holding his hand out. I reluctantly place my palm in his and smother the urge to gasp because of how good it feels to be near him again. I already know I'm in over my fucking head. Before I can draw my hand away, he tugs me the slightest bit closer, leaning in. I forgot how large he was, how captivating his presence could be. How easy it was to be consumed by everything that was Kai. His breath warms my face, the scent of his cologne, woodsy and clean with a hint of spice. It overpowers the rational part of my brain and sends tingles skittering down my spine. "You look beautiful today by the way," he whispers in my ear and his stubble almost, *almost* tickles my cheek.

Dangerous. This is dangerous, my brain yells. And yet when he takes a step backwards and releases my hand, I have to fight the instinct to reach for him again.

Then this devastating, enchanting man walks away, like he didn't just land a lethal blow to my self-control and my rapidly beating heart. It's impossible to peel my eyes away from him as he says his goodbyes to his teammates and mumbles something to Jonah. Then he waltzes through the front door, confident and unbothered, and every female head swivels to his towering frame as he does.

Two hours later, their group of ten leaves and I can finally take a full breath. I start clearing their tables when I feel someone hovering behind me.

"Hey, sorry. I didn't mean to be creepy," he says as I turn around to face him. I recognize him from some of the articles I had read about the Bucks and my recent social media stalking. He's tall, not quite as tall as Kai, with warm light eyes, multiple piercings, and perfectly manicured short brown hair. He has a slight tan even though it's the dead of winter and rings adorn every finger. He is objectively, undeniably attractive and I get the sense he is someone who is very comfortable in his body.

What is it with these hockey guys? Is unlimited sex appeal a prerequisite to playing in the NHL?

He smiles awkwardly, his hand ringing the back of his neck.

"I'm Jonah by the way."

"I gathered that. I'm Kendall, but I suppose you already know that," I say while picking up used napkins and collecting plates.

"He would kill me if he found out I told you this but he never got over you, you know?" he says quietly.

"Somehow I doubt that," I scoff.

"I'm serious. He was a mess for a while. I think he just hides it better now." I remain silent so he keeps talking while I finish cleaning the table. "I'm probably overstepping and I don't know everything that happened with you two, but at the very least, he deserves closure. A conversation."

I close my eyes and pinch the bridge of my nose. "You don't know everything that happened between us. What I did, what I've done, it's unforgivable," I admit to this man who is basically a stranger.

"Maybe. Maybe not. There's only one way to find out though."

He's right: there is only one way to find out.

But will I survive it?

Chapter 5

Kai

A T EXACTLY 11:52, I pull into the parking lot of the homey diner promising the tri-state area's best waffles. I needed to get there and collect myself before she did, try and work out exactly what I'm going to say even though I have been agonizing over it into the early hours of the morning. I have so many questions for her that need answers. But I realize I don't know this Kendall anymore, this version of her at all. There's so much pain and distance separating us now that I'm starting to regret asking her to meet me here.

The Olympus Diner had an old school retro vibe, heightened by the weathered sticky jukebox tucked in the front corner, the metal tables, and large glass windows that spanned the entire front half of the restaurant. Kendall and I had come here for hundreds of dates, drunken late night food runs, and hungover brunches before, well before everything went to shit. This restaurant has been around far longer than we've been alive and is a staple in the surrounding community. I knew if I told her to meet me at the diner, I wouldn't have to specify.

I sit down in a small booth near the window, the red worn leather squeaking underneath my weight. I shift uncomfortably not knowing what to do with my hands, so I run them through my hair—realizing I hadn't even bothered to shower this morning. I was so preoccupied with the idea of seeing her and finally having her undivided attention, that basic hygiene hadn't crossed my mind. I probably look disheveled and unhinged, which is exactly how I feel.

An older waitress, probably in her sixties with graying hair pulled up tight in a bun and a stained white apron around her waist, stops by the table to ask if I need anything. I order a black coffee even though I know I'm not going to drink it. Not yet anyways. I've already suffered two panic attacks since seeing her yesterday and the last thing I need is caffeine buzzing in my veins during one of the most intense conversations of my life.

I glance at my watch, 12:02. Maybe she isn't even going to show up and all my panicking was for nothing. Maybe I already got my one shot and blew it yesterday when I cornered her at work.

And then like a fucking tidal wave, she comes crashing into the diner. She chats with the hostess briefly. I watch as she scans the restaurant for me, her hazel green eyes flicking from table to table, her dark curls bouncing around her face.

She's painfully beautiful, even more stunning than the day she left, the last time I saw her. *Really* saw her. Because yesterday was a fluke, an anomaly. A happy accident depending on who you ask. It probably never should have happened and yet I find myself thanking whatever god that exists that it did. Yesterday I didn't have the opportunity to appreciate her beauty because I was flustered and momentarily knocked off course. The mere sight of her had shaken me to my core. Today though, today I have the time to admire her and it nearly steals the breath from my lungs.

She locks eyes with me as she approaches the table, and something clenches around my heart. The hustle and bustle of the restaurant ceases to exist, all the noises and chatter fading into the background, as if her walking in could stop the entire world from spinning on its axis.

"Hi," she says. "Is it okay if I sit?"

"Hi, of course," the words tumble out of my mouth. "I wasn't sure if you would come after yesterday," I admit.

"Neither was I," she responds, fidgeting with a loose straw wrapper.

"I'm really happy you did," I reply, covering her hand with mine. It grants me a small smile, but she still pulls away. She's hesitant, guarded like she still hasn't fully committed to being here in this diner with me.

"So," I clear my throat, "Like I said, I saw you at the game the other night, right before I got my ass handed to me by the other team."

She looks down at her hands but doesn't say anything. I press on, figuring it's better to rip the Band-Aid straight off.

"You were holding a boy on your hip, smiling at him."

Still no response.

"Why does he look like me, Kendall? Why does he look like the perfect mix of both of us?" I ask sharply. Surely it had been a trick my mind was playing on me. I was exhausted from the game, crumbling underneath the pressure, my head conjuring things, seeing things that weren't there. Because the alternative, keeping a lie that big? That's so much worse.

I watch her swallow, but she won't meet my eyes. And I know instantly without her saying a word.

"Is he mine?" It comes out as barely more than a whisper.

"Yes. He's yours. His name is Akio." And I feel the world shifting beneath my feet, my heart starting to come apart at the seams.

"Why...how could you keep this from me?" I raise my voice, on the verge of yelling in this cozy diner with elderly couples and families surrounding us.

"I don't expect you to understand my reasons or my choices, but I was trying to protect you," she states as if that's some sort of rational explanation.

"Protect me? You have been hiding my son from me for two and a half years, Kendall. How the hell is that protecting me?" I demand.

It doesn't make any sense. Why hide him? Why lie about having the abortion and why is she telling me about him now? Pain, confusion, resentment all fight for space in my head. I never thought she was capable of this kind of betrayal. And I really want to hate her for it, for everything she's put me through. Every lie, every secret, every bit of darkness I succumbed to over the past couple years. Every time I put a bottle to my lips hoping to drown out the memory of her. I'm so fucking tempted to walk away from her without a second thought and never look back. But it's not just about me anymore. I owe it to myself and my son to get answers.

Holy.

Shit.

I.

Have.

A.

Son.

CHAPTER 6

KENDALL

2016

T o move forward, we need to go back, back to the beginning. Well, almost the beginning. There are some moments in life that serve as a demarcation, a line in the sand, when something so pivotal occurs that you categorize time into before and after that moment. This was one of those moments, so small yet so impactful I felt like time itself was frozen. I stare at the pregnancy test, tears sliding down my face and fear settling in my gut. The two pink lines are like a sledgehammer to my heart. Unable to accept what I already knew to be true before I peed on this stick, I chuck it in the small garbage can and sink down to the bathroom floor. I peel my knees up to my face and wrap my arms around my legs, letting loose uncontrollable sobs.

How did this happen? I mean, I know *how* it happened, I was familiar with basic biological processes. But we had been so careful. I was on birth control and if I had forgotten to take it, Kai would use condoms. Then I remember the day we found out Kai had been drafted to the NHL. We had a celebratory dinner with both our families. We went out for drinks with our small but close-knit group of college friends. We had both gotten so drunk we called an Uber to take us back to my apartment. Then Kai and I had celebrated privately on the table, in the shower, and again the next morning in my bed. We had clearly been too far gone to use any precautions. Fuck. I cry harder thinking about how I could possibly break this news to him when he had his whole future and career ahead of him. We both did. God, I love him so much and I know he loves me. We can figure this out. He'll know what to do. Everything will be fine.

Right?

Chapter 7

Kendall

H E WRINGS HIS HANDS and picks at his cuticles the same way he used to when he was younger. He's different in some ways, more assertive. He has a quiet confidence now and shadows in his eyes that weren't there three years ago. But I know there's bits and pieces of the old Kai in there too. The Kai I had known so well and loved even more. Like the way he gently touched my hand when I sat down, reassuring me without saying a word. Even if I didn't deserve it. He's still Kai—the same, but different. I wonder how he feels about me. Do I seem familiar and foreign to him at the same time? I wonder but don't ask—there's too many other things I'm thinking, feeling, desperately wanting to say but can't. Instead, I stare at a piece of the ripped leather booth behind Kai's shoulder and focus my attention there, willing myself to breathe in and out.

"I don't know what to say, Kai. I thought I was doing what was best for both of us. I couldn't be the reason your life and dreams were destroyed..." I clench my hands hard to try and stop the tears that are burning my eyes, my fingernails digging into my palms.

"I made an appointment. But in the end, I couldn't do it." I turn my head away from him needing to collect myself. I quickly wipe away a stray tear and continue "I knew he was meant to be in this world, and I was supposed to be his mom. I had made my choice as hard as it was, and I wasn't sure you would have made the same one." It was a half-truth, part of the story, but not the whole thing. He glares at me, his large, calloused hands in fists on the table. The temper I had only seen a few times starting to rise to the surface. The thing about Kai though, is he reserves his anger for people and situations that truly push him past a breaking point. The person on the receiving end usually deserves his fury. I know I did. I wait for the hurled insults, the hatred, the storm. But it never comes. Instead, I watch him carefully try to reel his frustration in the best he can. He tilts his head, studying me, contemplating.

Does he realize the regret has consumed me whole at this point, like a flesh-eating virus? Can he see right through every lie I've ever told him?

Of course he can. He was always good at that. Seeing me even when I didn't want to be seen. Whatever he was going to say, he thinks better of it.

He lets out a long sigh, head pressed against the booth and replies, "That's the thing, Ken. You took away all my choices when you broke my heart and cut me out of your life and I have spent every day of the last two years wondering what I did to deserve that, how I lost the love of my life." I can still see the pain and anguish I caused him; it's written all over his face. I'm unable to stop the tears now, knowing how much I had hurt both of us. It would be better if he hated me, if he couldn't stand to be in the same room as me. Anything would be better than this nightmare I've created.

"You didn't do anything wrong, Kai," I say, my voice trembling. "I'm so sorry," I sob. He immediately slides into the booth next to me, wrapping me up in his arms. Of course, his first instinct is to soothe me, protect me. I melt into his warm, solid chest and take comfort in the fact that his scent of pine, spice, and something achingly familiar hasn't changed.

"It's okay, it's okay," he whispers.

I shake my head and let out a garbled laugh, "No it's not. None of this is okay."

"It's not. But I think it will be."

We decide to finish our conversation privately and take his coffee and my tea to go. With my purse in one hand and earl grey tea in the other, I follow him to his car. Once we're both seated inside his black Audi, he ends the silence.

"I think we can take a break from the heavy for a while, if that's okay with you? Why don't you tell me what you've been up to, aside from working at Kip's."

He's offering me an out, a temporary reprieve from pouring gallons of salt into old wounds and I'm grateful for it.

"I only work at Kip's periodically because the tips are too good to pass up. Full time I work as a paralegal at a firm a few towns over. I'm trying to save up enough money for law school tuition, but putting away money has been...challenging with a two-and-a-half-year-old," I explain.

"Wait, back up, what happened to law school?" he wonders, confusion on his face. Right, because as far as he knew, I moved to North Carolina to attend law school. I gulp, embarrassed about all the lies I've intricately woven between us over the past couple years, lies intended to keep him far away from our life. And now here I am, sitting in his car. I've never been this close to someone and felt so far away at the same time. The history between us feels insurmountable and the baggage weighing us down is a noose around my throat. It's robbing me of oxygen.

What the hell am I thinking meeting up with him?

"I never went. I mean, I did move to North Carolina to live with my aunt for a while. But I never attended law school. It just didn't work out," I admit awkwardly.

"That would have been nice to know," he mutters under his breath, tightening his grip on the steering wheel.

"What do you mean?" my eyes flick to the wheel and back to him.

"Clearly there's a lot I don't know about you. Just forget it," he says sharply, clearly agitated.

"Yeah, I guess there is. I'm sorry, Kai..." I trail off quietly.

"It's fine...so Akio, is he in daycare?" he asks, quickly changing subjects.

"Yeah, three days a week. Then I'm usually home with him one day a week and he's with my mom another day." Trying to keep the conversation casual and upbeat, I say, "This wasn't the car I was expecting you to drive."

"What's not to like about the Audi?" he smirks, any hint of earlier frustration has disappeared from his face.

"It's a little loud for you, over the top," I observe. But something tells me he already knows that.

"Well, I am one of the highest paid players in the league."

"A little cocky, are we?" I joke and playfully roll my eyes.

He laughs, a deep rumble that I feel in my bones. I forgot how much I missed his laugh, his smile. The planes of his face, the scar that runs through his left eyebrow. His dark eyes that I could drown in. Everything about him really. He's still devastatingly handsome, that is not lost on me. I haven't been able to get his beautiful face out of my head for the last sixteen hours.

Who am I kidding, I haven't been able to get him out of my system in three years.

He's always been there, floating around my periphery, hiding in the darkest, forbidden corners of my mind. Tucked away but never forgotten. The sudden realization impales my chest like an ice pick. My memory of him, all my memories of us together didn't do him one ounce of justice.

"Not cocky, just stating facts." He grins. "Your hair is different, shorter," he adds, running a finger through a loose curl. That simple touch alone sends my head and heart into a tailspin.

"So is yours. It looks good." I don't know why I added that last part, the compliment. I certainly don't need to, but I *want* to. My therapist says I need to spend less time second guessing myself and more time trusting my gut. I blame the compliment that feels dangerously close to flirting on my gut.

"So, if you don't mind me asking, are you...seeing anyone?"

I know he's trying to tread carefully but curiosity seems to draw this question out of him.

I clasp my hands together in my lap, trying to decide how I want to respond.

"It's okay, Ken, you don't have to—"

I cut him off, "I want to. I've had two short term relationships since we broke up. Nothing serious. Again, hard to date with Akio, also significantly lowers the dating pool." I laugh half-heartedly. "What about you?" *Please say no, please say no.* I don't think I can handle hearing he is in a serious relationship. He purses his lips together, in deep thought.

"I don't want to lie to you. I've been with a lot of women...mostly in an attempt to get over you. A few short-term girlfriends. Nothing seemed to stick."

Oh, thank god. Relief floods my veins. My frantic heart nearly bursts out of my chest. Every part of me aches for him, aches for who we used to be together.

"Why don't you hate me, Kai? You should hate me and I would understand if you did."

"I wanted to. I tried to. I convinced myself that I did. But seeing you today, I know that's not true. This, us, Akio is more complicated than that. There's a lot of layers to it. I don't think that's how our story ends."

"Do you want to meet him? Akio?" I ask shakily.

"Yes, of course. I wanted to ask but didn't want to be presumptuous or push too hard. We have games the next two weeks up and down the East coast, so I'll be traveling. But how about when I get back? Would that be okay?"

"Sure," I reply.

"Do you have pictures of him on your phone?" he wonders.

I smirk. "Do I have pictures of him? I could fill up three phones with the pictures I have." I pull out my phone and scroll through my camera roll, tilting my phone in Kai's direction, "Here's us at the park. He loves the swings." He stares at my phone in admiration of his son, *our son.*

"You can scroll through more if you want. Most of my pictures are of him anyway." He continues going through pictures of Akio, smiling the entire time. At one point, I think I see tears forming in his eyes, but he quickly blinks them away. He hands my phone back to me.

"Thank you for showing me him and meeting with me today."

"Of course. You don't have to thank me, Kai. It was the least I could do after..." *After I broke your heart and betrayed your trust.*

After I went to great lengths to erase you from my life. I can't bring myself to finish the sentence out loud, so I don't. He nods silently. We exchange contact information before we part ways. I have to meet the babysitter—I told her I'd only be gone for two hours when I begged her last minute to watch Akio. Kai has an early afternoon practice to make, but he promises to get in touch with me as soon as he's home in two weeks.

I think about Kai the entire ride home, our past, our conversation, my head reeling with questions. As I pull into my apartment complex, I hear my phone vibrate with a text in the console beside me. Goosebumps prick my arms, and I know it's him without having to look.

> *I couldn't wait two weeks.*

> *Not when I've gone almost three years without you.*

> *I'm glad you didn't.*

I reread the text five times, a mixture of hope and excitement fluttering in my chest and it's promptly undercut by feelings of dread. Finally, the impact of what I had done weighs on me. What if this went spectacularly wrong? What if all this conversation did was make things worse? What if Kai meeting Akio was a terrible idea? But I don't let myself spiral any further. I refuse to resign us to failure before we even begin. Because that's what this feels like, a new beginning. I turn the key and cut the engine, staring at the Lego keychain with my son's name on it. I remember the only man who deserves all my love and attention is waiting for me inside.

Chapter 8

Kai

"**A**GAIN, RUN IT AGAIN!" Coach yells from the middle of the ice. "Not sure where your head is at today but it's not fucking here, Matsumoto!" Since I saw Kendall yesterday, I haven't been able to stop thinking about her. My head is in a million different places, none of which are here at practice.

I wanted to scream and tell her all the things I've been dying to say to her. I had this overwhelming urge to shake her by the shoulders and demand answers. But I didn't do any of that. I couldn't. Instead, I played the part of caring and empathetic ex-boyfriend against my better judgement. I listened to her. I made small talk. I even flirted with her for fucks sake. Like she hasn't been harboring a life altering secret. Like she didn't rip my heart from my chest, drag it over hot coals, and leave me to bleed out alone. But it was clear neither of us were ready for a deeper conversation. Just seeing each other, sitting across the table from her was enough of a shock. Reconnecting with Kendall after being deprived of her for so long felt like a punch to the gut. And at the same time, I felt like I could finally come up for air. This razor thin line between love and hate, passion and pain, are fucking with my head and my game.

I miss an easy pass and then two more. My shots are sloppy and most of them don't make it near the goal. I fuck up the last offensive play we run, a play I've done a hundred times perfectly. I breathe a sigh of relief when Coach finally blows the whistle. Everyone skates towards the locker room but I hear him bark from behind me, "Matsumoto, a minute?" I quickly turn around and skate over to him, knowing I'm about to be chewed out. He's tall but I still tower over him. He stares at me with his eyes narrowed and arms folded, his face unreadable. But I know he's pissed. I'd be pissed if I were coaching me right now too.

"What's going on with you? The last two games and then practice today? I haven't seen you this distracted in a long time," he notes. I know exactly what he's talking about. He means I haven't been this preoccupied since I first started on the team two years ago. When I had gotten myself into so much trouble with drinking, partying, and fights that my professional hockey career was almost over before it began. I take my gloves off and wipe beads of sweat from my forehead.

"It's nothing. I just have some family issues that I'm dealing with." I hope that's enough of an explanation. I don't really want to air my dirty laundry to him when I've barely processed the last twenty-four hours myself.

"Do I need to be concerned?" he presses.

"No, you don't," I answer, my tone flat and unflinching.

"Good, because we're approaching playoff season, and I need you with us one hundred and ten percent. Take care of it son, discreetly and quickly. Get your head right. Are we clear?"

"Crystal."

Usually, I could take the pain and anger I was feeling and put it aside when I stepped on the ice. I allowed myself to miss her at night, alone in my bed, or when I was sharing it with a stranger whose name I wouldn't remember in the morning. But aside from that, I tried not to let my brain wander too far into Kendall territory. That rabbit hole was too dark to climb out of. When I first joined the team, I harnessed that rage and loneliness. I let it feed that gnawing, insatiable hunger inside of me. It motivated me to become better. Unstoppable. A formidable opponent, and an even better leader. I wore that chip on my shoulder proudly, always playing like I had something to prove. Now it feels like the only person I have to prove something to is Kendall.

***

CLEAN, SHOWERED, AND CLOTHED, I sling my practice bag and gear over my shoulder and head to the parking lot. I step outside the arena doors and into the frigid January night. The brutal wind bites at my neck and stings the bruise forming underneath my eye. Fuck it's cold.

Get your head right, get your head right. Coach's words replay in my head on the long walk to my car. If only it were that easy. How could I do that when my head and heart are with her, *with them?*

I don't know how she managed to keep this from me for so long. I can't begin to understand why she thought I would be better off without them; that I wouldn't do anything but support her. And I'm so fucking angry with her, but I also know that the gaping hole that's been growing in my heart feels a little smaller right now. Every instinct that I tried to ignore drew me closer to her today inch by inch. Even in the depths of my rage, I still wanted to be near her. I guess that's what happens when you spend so much time wishing for someone you can't have. I wanted so badly to hug her before I left, to commit everything about her to memory. Just in case she slipped through my fingers again.

After I stuff everything in my trunk and crank up the heat, I snap a picture of my face and send it to her with the caption "rough practice".

She responds almost immediately.

Oof what happened?

Let's just say something has me distracted today.

Something or someone?

Someone, two in fact.

Someone has me distracted today too.

Glad I'm not the only one.

What are you two troublemakers up to?

Just finished bath time.

I'm trying to put him down for bed now

Can you send me a picture of him?

A few minutes later I feel my phone vibrate.

Sure

A selfie of her and Akio appears on my phone. As soon as I open the picture, I feel a distinct pang in my chest. I wish I could reach out and hold him, hug him, tell him how much I've missed him. But I can't do any of that, one because I'm not there and two because who the hell am I to him? I'm just some random guy he has never met before. This causes my chest to hurt a little more. I flip my phone facedown and clench my hands into fists. *What the actual fuck.* How is this going to work? I'm supposed to just step in after all this time and be his dad? Suddenly, I'm not in the mood to talk to her anymore.

***

I DON'T TYPICALLY GO out the night before a game or an early flight. But I made an exception for Aiden since he's only going to be in town for a few days and I haven't seen him in months. We planned to meet at Marty's, a low-key sports bar, and when I walk in, he's already half a beer deep scrolling through his phone. Large plasma screen TVs are plastered on every wall, flipping continuously through various hockey and basketball games. The general vibe is still calm, most of the patrons people just getting off work.

He stands up from the corner high top as soon as he spots me and brings me in for a hug.

"Good to see you man. It's been a minute."

"You too, Kenney. I see you didn't wait to start drinking," I nod toward his beer as I sit down.

"Sorry. It's been a long week. You don't mind if I drink right? I know you're sober but when you suggested Marty's, I figured it would be okay if—"

I interject before he can finish. "Relax, it's cool. I'm fine with people drinking around me. Me not drinking is more out of choice rather than necessity," I explain.

"Okay. Good. So, how you been and how'd you get that fucking shiner?"

"Practice was terrible and I played like shit. Not sure if you caught the end of the game Saturday but it was more of that. Evans got a cheap shot in today when I wasn't paying attention and I took a bow to the face."

"Well hopefully tomorrow night you'll get your shit together and you won't suck ass," he replies, taking a long swig of beer. If I had to guess, Aiden has money riding on our game tomorrow night in Philly. He works as a pharmaceutical sales rep and makes more money than he knows what to do with. It wouldn't be a stretch to assume the cobalt Maserati parked out front is his.

"Yeah maybe," I grumble noncommittally.

"Maybe?" he presses.

"I need to tell you something and I need you to not freak the fuck out about it okay?"

"Okay?" He arches his eyebrows and leans further towards me. Before I can unload everything that has happened between last night and today, a waitress appears at our side with a pen and pad in hand. She's cute, perky, and young with blonde hair and blue eyes. The kind of girl I would take home and wouldn't call again.

"What can I get you guys? Do you need a drink?" she asks, glancing at me and the half empty table in front of me.

"Just a club soda. Thanks," I reply harshly, barely making eye contact.

"That's it? Any food?" She looks between us. Aiden gets an order of wings and she begins making small talk with him, realizing I'm not in the mood to chat.

"Wait, do I know you from somewhere?" she inquires, staring back at me. "You have a very familiar face."

"Nope. Don't think so," I brush her off.

"He plays for the Boston Bucks. You've probably seen him on a billboard or two around here," Aiden supplies with a shit-eating grin, knowing full well I hate this kind of recognition. I go to great lengths to avoid it.

"That's it! I knew I recognized you. I'll get your orders right in, superstar," she muses, winking at me and flitting off to the kitchen. On any other night, I would flirt back, engage with her, make her feel special. Then do what I always do and have meaningless sex that will amount to nothing. But that was *before*. Before Kendall dropped a live grenade in my lap. Before I found out she doesn't hate me. Before, when I didn't have any hope that we would ever reconnect. Finally being able to talk in private again, I lean into the table.

"Listen, I saw Kendall at my game the other night and I met up with her today for coffee. She has a son and he's...he's mine," I stammer. I conveniently leave out the part about running into her yesterday, when I had to convince my body I wasn't being hunted by an apex predator.

"What the fuck, Kai, why didn't you lead with that? Elaborate please," he insists, his eyebrows nearly meeting his hairline.

"Remember when she broke up with me a little after I got drafted? Well, before that, we found out she was pregnant. I told her I would support her whatever her choice was. She wouldn't let me go to the clinic with her even though I begged her. She told me she had the abortion and basically cut off all communication with me a few weeks after that. But she never had it." It feels good to finally get it off my chest and tell someone, although Aiden was not the first person I imagined breaking this news to.

"Holy shit! Do you need me to intervene and ask her to homecoming again so you guys can get back together?" He makes light of the situation in a way only he can, in a way that only someone who has known you since childhood can. And humor is exactly what I need right now, that and something to take the fucking edge off.

"No, I think we'll manage without your help." I smirk.

"Seriously though that's fucking crazy. How are you feeling about it all? How are you doing with the news and seeing her?" He keeps bombarding me with question after question that I don't have answers to.

"I mean, she lied to me about something monumental for a long time and now I have a son. Things are messy with us...complicated." I acknowledge, wringing my hands together.

"Listen, I know things are..." he hesitates, choosing his words carefully, "...challenging right now. You are literally living in one of my worst nightmares—a girl from one of my *many* one night stands knocking on my door and telling me she's pregnant. But the difference is that this is Kendall, and if there are two people that can figure this out, it's you two. Honestly, I thought you guys would be married by now."

I sigh. "Me too. But I guess that's life, right? God laughs while we make plans."

"You don't believe in god," he states, cocking a brow.

"I don't, but someone has to be laughing at us while we sit on this spinning rock and try to make sense of everything."

"It'll be okay, you know," he replies.

"That's easy for you to say, you didn't just find out you have a child. What if I'm not cut out to be a dad?" I noticeably lower my voice to a whisper. You never know what dark corners press are lurking in these days and the last thing I need is rumors or versions of the truth about Kendall and Akio circulating right before playoffs.

"Kai, I've never seen you fail at anything. Being a dad won't be any different. Will you make mistakes? Sure. Will you have moments of doubt? Absolutely. But you are going to be a great fucking dad and you had a pretty good role model."

My dad was okay. He provided for us, made sure we had a roof over our head and everything we needed and then some. But as a doctor, he worked long hours and he wasn't around a lot. He never really cared to know who I was. He still doesn't—sometimes I think all he sees when he looks at me is raw athletic talent and ability. My worth directly proportional to how well I perform. I want it to be different with me and Akio. But now isn't the time to mention that. I've dumped enough on Aiden already.

"Thanks," I mutter. "So, speaking of women, are you settling down anytime soon or still living the bachelor life?"

He studies the back of his beer bottle while rolling it between his thumb and forefinger.

"You know I haven't had a serious girlfriend since Leah," he confirms without averting his eyes.

"Why do we always love the girls that break our hearts?" I wonder out loud more to myself than anyone else.

He snorts. "I don't know man. That's a loaded fucking question though."

"So, you think I should try and work it out with her?" I eye him anxiously, half expecting he'll tell me to cut my losses and move on.

"Look man, all I'm saying is if I had a second chance to fix things with Leah, I would. You have to decide if Kendall is worth it and I'm pretty sure she is."

I lift my glass of club soda in response, wishing it were a fucking beer, and tip it against his. "To the girls that broke our hearts."

***

L ATER THAT NIGHT, WHEN I'm in bed, I replay my conversation with Aiden in my head. I think about how my dad raised me with a cold unforgiving hand. All the trouble Aiden and

I used to get into mostly over Kendall. I spend a long time getting lost in forgotten memories, and start to worry that maybe I have no idea what it takes to be a father. Mine certainly didn't.

"Fighting, Kai? What is going on with you? You have tarnished your name, brought dishonor to this family, and probably turned away any scouts that might have been coming to watch you play this season. Colleges don't want to admit division one athletes that have records, Kai," my dad yells.

"I know, Dad. I know. I'm sorry," I plead.

"What happened between you and Aiden?" he demands, sitting down at the kitchen table and taking a swig of seltzer.

"He called Kendall a slut so I punched him and then he tackled me. And you know the rest."

"This kind of behavior is a disgrace, Kai. You know what we expect of you and you know damn well what the stakes are. You need to fix this mess," he instructs icily. His voice remains neutral this time, his words clipped. But it didn't matter because his word was law in this house. I knew exactly what he expected of me. Perfection. Anything else was considered unacceptable. I had stepped out of line for maybe the first time in my entire life. And while my dad's approval and love were unattainable, I still fought for scraps of them.

My mom chimes in, "While that is particularly vile of Aiden and he can be an arrogant little shit sometimes, fighting is not going to solve anything. We don't solve problems like that in this family," she explains matter of factly.

"Right, we sweep them under the rug instead," I grumble under my breath.

"What did you say?" my father presses, gripping the glass in his hand.

"Nothing," I respond.

"This could hurt your grades and your college prospects, and I don't think you want either of those things to happen. You are grounded indefinitely. You go to school, practice, home, that's it. You're going to ask for and complete any extra credit assignments in all your classes. And evenings will be spent doing homework. No

phone, no computer, no TV. No Kendall." My mom lays out the parameters of my punishment and of all the restrictions they make, the last one hits the hardest.

"Don't forget community service," I reply with a little too much snark.

"Do you think this is a game?" my dad questions, narrowing his eyes at me.

"We have worked our entire lives to make sure you have a bright future and every opportunity you could want. We raised you to be smart, hardworking, and empathetic. We didn't teach you to lash out or raise you to be violent," my mom cuts in, her words dripping with disappointment.

"I have always been the dutiful son and done whatever is asked of me. I have a 4.0 and I'm in three AP classes. I've started varsity in two sports since sophomore year. I am hardworking and empathetic. I made one mistake. It doesn't erase all the positive that I've done up until now. But it's exhausting trying to be perfect all the time," I explain slightly relieved.

"We don't expect you to be perfect, Kai, but we do expect you to make better choices than this," she counters.

"Well, I do feel like I've had to be perfect ever since..." my voice trails off and my throat feels thick.

"Ever since what?" my mom probes, looking concerned.

"Never mind. Forget it. I made a poor choice and I messed up. It won't happen again. I promise," I state feeling dejected.

"Good." She looks at my dad for reassurance, but he continues staring at his drink. Like he'll find answers about his failure of a son at the bottom of it. His silence cuts me deeper than his words. I quietly excuse myself from the table and head upstairs.

Chapter 9
Kendall
2016

I SIT ON MY bed with my head in my palms, Kai rubbing soothing circles on my back. I don't think I have any tears left but I want to cry knowing our lives—our futures—are ruined all because of one mistake. Kai, on the other hand, seems to be breathing steadily, perfectly calm, which makes me feel even more distressed. He takes my hand in his and squeezes it lovingly, reassuringly.

"It's going to be okay. We can figure this out. Our parents will help us. I'll withdraw from the draft temporarily—"

I pull away from him. "No, Kai. Absolutely not. You can't do that. You can't just put your whole future on hold. You've been working so hard for this." I feel the floodgates starting to open again and I know I can't let him do this. "Maybe there is a way out of this. I can get an abortion. Nothing has to change." I stare at him waiting for approval. He searches my eyes.

"Except that everything will change. Do you think we can come back from having an abortion? That's a pretty big loss."

"Do you think we can come back from having a child at 21 and 22? We're barely adults ourselves!" I shout frustrated with this situation and the fact that we're having this conversation at all. I've been going in circles with myself the past forty-eight hours, unable to think about anything else. And now Kai and I are talking in circles too, virtually incapable of arriving at an answer.

"That didn't come out right. I think we can come back from anything. We can survive anything together. But you specifically going through an abortion and living with that choice—can you do that? I'm not judging you and I will support whatever decision you make. I just want us—you—to be absolutely sure. I want to make the choice that is the best for both of us, especially you."

"There are no good choices here, Kai. Just two terrible ones," I concede.

Hours later, we're huddled in my bed together. He pulls me close to him, surrounding me with his love, his warmth. His strong steady embrace is enough to soothe me for now.

"Shh, it's going to be okay. Everything is going to be okay," he promises. I hear his words replay in my head like a mantra long after he falls asleep. I cling to them and hold on for dear life. And I know I have never felt safer. I've also never been more broken.

Chapter 10

Kai

I'M BACK IN MY hotel room alone after one of the worst games of the season and she is all I can think about. I climb into the bed slowly, all my muscles tight and on fire, and alternate between flipping through channels and scrolling through my socials. The media is already in a frenzy over tonight's game and I don't have the bandwidth to deal with it right now. It's almost 11:00, probably too late to call her...

Hey

Hey

How are you guys doing?

We're good. How are you?

How was your game tonight?

It fucking blew. I mean we played our asses off but they were just better, faster.

I know, I watched most of it.

You guys put up a good fight though

Wait, you watched the game?

I sit up staring at my phone waiting for her response. My stomach doing flip flops while I watch the text bubble that tells me she's typing.

Of course

A moment later I decide to call her. I need to hear her voice. Even if it's just for a second. I went too long getting nothing but silence from her that now I would take whatever I could get. I would settle for scraps of her as long as she is in my life. And it drives me crazy, makes me spiral in more ways than one. It makes me wonder how she did it. How she survived in the absence of us. Because I nearly died in the absence of her. It was like cutting off a limb and then trying to reprogram my body and mind to live without it. And I had almost succeeded, convinced myself that being alive without said limb was doable. That I could be happy like that, incomplete, but happy.

That was until I saw her four days ago.

And I knew instantly, like a shock to my system. I could never again settle for the "happy" I was without her.

Thankfully, she picks up on the second ring.

"Hey, is everything alright?" she asks, worried.

"Yeah, I just wanted to hear your voice. Is that okay?" I wonder, laying my head back against the pillow.

"Of course," there's a short pause then... "Can I tell you something without you getting angry?"

"It depends," I qualify, wondering what the hell she was about to say.

"Kai," she demands more forcefully.

"Fine, I'll do my best not to get angry," I relent. As if everything when it came to her these days didn't make me irrationally pissed off.

"It hurts to hear your voice and know you're so far away. I missed that...hearing your voice," she admits. The way she ends her sentence tells me there's more she wants to say. More she's holding back. And I want to ask her to say it. All of it. But I don't.

"I know what you mean," I agree after a long pause.

"When I left, I was so broken. I hated myself for what I did to us and I grieved for our relationship for so long..." She pauses. "I never stopped, actually. Losing you broke me entirely."

I built my entire life around Kendall, knew her before I even knew myself. And then I lost her. Just like that. And here she is, talking about *her* grief. I drowned in my fucking grief with no answers and no lifeline. Nothing. I find myself getting angrier.

"I spent a lot of my time infuriated with you. Pretending I hated you even though all I wanted was to make things work. I held out hope for a long time thinking you'd come back, that we'd figure it out. I thought if I could just talk to you, we could work it out. I even..." I begin.

"You even what?" she probes.

"Never mind. It's not important. Anyways... Here we are." I decide it best if I don't share *all* my feelings in one night. In one call.

"Here we are," she repeats. "What do we do now?"

God, what a loaded fucking question.

"Honestly. I have no idea," I admit. "Can I ask you something though?"

"Sure, fire away."

"Why the name Akio?"

"I knew you wanted your first son to be named after your uncle. I thought it would be nice. I'm sor—"

"No, it is," I interrupt. "I just don't understand. If you thought we were never going to see each other again, why would you do that?"

"Maybe part of me hoped we would," she answers.

"I love the name, Ken. I just wish I had been there for it. For all of it." The wounds start aching again.

I hear Akio crying in the background and I'm made acutely aware that our time on the phone is up.

"I have to go, Kai. Akio is stirring," Kendall explains.

"Okay. No problem. It was good to talk to you."

"You too. Goodnight, Kai."

"Night, Kendall." But for some reason, I hesitate to hang up the phone and so does she.

"Kai?" she asks.

"Yeah?"

"You can call me again if you want. If you want to talk while you're on the road. I mean, you don't have to…"

"Okay. I will," I promise. I want to. She must know that by now.

"Okay, bye," she says and ends the call.

Chapter 11

Kendall

I LOOK AROUND OUR apartment trying to game plan how I'm going to clean and keep an eye on Akio at the same time. Emma and Maddox are coming over later today for a play date and I so badly want to make a good impression. No one talks about how hard it is to form friendships as an adult and I've discovered firsthand how challenging and isolating it can be. Even harder than that is making friends and maintaining relationships after having a child. I had a small group of girlfriends in college but we barely stayed in touch. There were a couple yearly Facebook posts, the obligatory birthday text, and a few group chat exchanges but that was it.

My closest friend had been Kai up until a few years ago and Jenna had moved across the country shortly after Akio was born. Thankfully, now they're both in my life but those friendships operate differently than they used to. I desperately want some semblance of a social life and I want a few friends to show for it.

Begrudgingly, I set up Akio in his room with plenty of toys and his iPad. That should at least buy me a half hour if I'm lucky. I rush to tidy the kitchen, bathroom, and living room, stopping to put away books, loose toys, and the occasional stray Lego. I take a break to put him down for a nap and finish up dusting and cleaning as quietly as I can, holding onto the stillness for a little longer. Once he's up, I light a vanilla scented candle in the kitchen and set out snacks for the boys and Emma on the counter.

Am I trying too hard? I definitely am. Hopefully it pays off.

Twenty minutes later, Emma and Maddox are standing at our door. Maddox comes barreling in at full speed, leaving Akio looking alarmed and a little frightened.

"Hi, please come in. I'm so happy you guys could make it," I say to Emma.

"Thanks for having us," she responds as she hurries to trail her son.

"Should we let them play for a little?" I suggest. "I left some games and toys out next to the couch."

"Sure," she smiles. "It's so nice of you to have us over." She takes her coat off and helps Maddox wrestle out of his jacket. I offer to take them both and hang them over the back of a chair.

"Akio baby, can you show Maddox some of your toys?" I ask him. All I get is a hesitant nod in response. Once they start racing trucks next to each other, I turn to Emma. "Do you want anything to eat or drink? I have snacks in case you guys are hungry." I gesture to the chips and fruit platter on the counter.

"Oh my god, that's so sweet. You didn't have to go through all the trouble. But yes, I will definitely have chips," she says moving towards the counter. We sit at the table and start snacking while the boys play happily on the floor.

"So, do you have a lot of play dates?" I wonder. "We haven't really had time to do any recently."

"No, not really. It's hard to find time. I'm mostly raising him by myself. His father hasn't been great in that department and my mom lives almost an hour away. So, she helps when she can here and there but we don't see her as much as I would like to," she explains. "What about you guys? Does your family live close?" she asks, reaching for another chip.

"My moms live about 15 minutes away and we usually see them twice a week, which is nice."

"You're lucky that you have them," she comments.

"Yeah, we definitely are. I also work, so I don't know what I'd do if they weren't close by."

"Oh, what do you do?"

"I'm a paralegal at Porter and West. I always wanted to be a lawyer but my plans kind of took a backseat once he was born," I admit. I wasn't embarrassed about this, not exactly. My job paid the bills, it had good benefits and we were financially stable. But I was disappointed that I hadn't continued chasing my dreams.

"I get it. I work at a bank as a teller and part time manager. Probably not my first choice career but it pays the bills," she sighs.

"Exactly," I nod, happy someone understands at least a little of what single motherhood entails.

"What about Akio's father," she asks. "Is he around?"

"He wasn't up until recently," I whisper. Then I proceeded to explain the whole sordid story to her—how we grew up together, broke up shortly after I found out I was pregnant, and hadn't seen him in almost three years. That he hadn't known he had a son and now that he did, he would undoubtedly be part of our lives.

What I don't say is how excruciating it had been to try and forget about him. But you don't forget a man like Kai. Even at five years old, I knew that we belonged to each other in some special and incomprehensible way. When I met him, it was as if my heart seemed to whisper, *ah there you are, I've been looking for you,* like there was an invisible thread that had always connected us. And how do you muddle through losing someone like that? Someone you built your entire life around, someone who knew you before the world got their hands on you. How do you recover from that?

You don't. Not really. Not ever in my experience. You somehow pick up the shattered remains of your heart and will it to keep beating, to do the best it can. I naively thought the pain would be easier to carry as time went on but it turns out it was pretty damn heavy no matter how much time had passed. I don't admit that I allowed myself one simple kindness and that was saving every article about his career that I could find. I had folders of them by season—trade-deadline rumors, postgame scrums, breakdowns of his zone entries and faceoff percentages, all the little metrics people used to explain why he could tilt a game in one shift. I had just wanted one small connection to him that wasn't mangled or confusing or beyond repair. Something I could preserve and marvel at and call mine. No, I don't tell her all the twisted, convoluted details. Not yet anyways.

"Wow," she replies when I've finished.

"Yeah, I know, you probably think I'm terrible for not telling him, right?" I bite my lip, worried about her response.

"I think everyone has their reasons for doing things," she replies, her lips forming a thin line. "My history with my ex isn't exactly rose colored either," she explains. "He wasn't a very good person to me or to Maddox and it took a long time for me to figure out how to separate from him." She pauses, seemingly conflicted about her next words. "We lived in a shelter for a while and with my mom after we broke up. It took us some time to get on our feet," she looks down at her hands.

"I'm sorry," I say delicately. "That must have been very hard for both of you."

"It was."

She brings her gaze to mine but looks past me, through me, not at me. Almost like it's too painful to recount this part of her life and also make space for someone else's reaction to it. "But we're in a much better place now." Her eyes are watery and she swipes a finger under one of them, brushing away a tear. "Oh god, look at me blubbering the first chance I get to socialize with an actual adult. I didn't mean to dump all my drama on you," she shifts uncomfortably in her seat. And I know right away that Emma and I will be fast friends.

"You didn't. I wanted to know and I totally dumped my drama on you first," I comment and then we both break into laughter.

We spend so much time chatting and learning about each other that we don't realize Akio and Maddox had slipped off into his room. When we open Akio's bedroom door, my eyes go wide. There is crimson lipstick streaking the walls and smeared across his bedspread. Maddox is brandishing the tube of red lipstick like a weapon, preparing to strike again, while Akio shoves his hands into the mess on the comforter. I'm horrified but I can't help a laugh that bubbles up my throat and escapes my lips. When Emma steps in next to me, I think she is going to have a coronary. Her eyes widen as she slaps a hand over her mouth.

"Oh my god. Kendall, I'm so sorry." She squats down in front of Maddox and takes the lipstick from him. "Did you use this to write on the walls?" she asks in a firm but gentle voice. He nods.

I turn to Akio with my arms folded. "Did you both do this?" Tears start brimming in his eyes but he eventually responds, "Yes."

"We'll help you clean this up. I'm so sorry. He can be a handful sometimes," she admits, her voice tinged with embarrassment.

"It's okay. Honestly, we weren't really watching them that well," I say trying to ease her guilt.

"Right, but you have a pretty well behaved child. I have an outdoor pup who sometimes acts like the Tasmanian devil. This has Maddox written all over it. I feel terrible," she replies, blowing out a long breath.

After we've attempted to clean up the mess and I throw his bedding in the washer, we give the boys a *supervised* snack. Maddox hops around from the couch to the floor to his mom's lap while he munches on fruit. He moves so quickly and frequently I'm surprised he doesn't choke. Akio pops a few chips in his mouth and hums in contentment to himself on the chair next to me. They're quite different but they seem to get along, and so do Emma and I, which is great.

I just hope we can move past the great lipstick debacle of 2020.

Chapter 12

Kai

"**H**ELLO?" SHE CROAKS GROGGILY.

"Hey, did I wake you?" I wonder as I pace frantically around my hotel room.

"No, I'm just watching reruns of Gilmore girls, trying to fall asleep. Why, what's up?"

I take a deep breath and let it out slowly. "I need to say something, ask you something before I lose the nerve." I clench my fist together and unclench it, clench and unclench.

"Okay."

"Did I conjure up the five years we were together and our entire childhood before that? Did I imagine it? Every kiss, every touch, every laugh. Every time we were together and it felt like it meant something, everything. Every goddamn moment with you—"

"Kai, no," she says defensively, her tone sharp but certain.

I just need to dislodge some of this pain from my chest, exorcise some demons and maybe then I'll feel like I can breathe again, like I've regained some solid ground.

"Kendall, please let me get this out. Did I romanticize things? Did spending the rest of our lives together not mean the same thing to me that it did to you? Was I an idiot? What am I missing here? Because I'm really starting to feel like I'm insane. Either that or you didn't love me as much as I thought you did."

I sound angry and desperate. I'm clawing for answers but I don't fucking care. This is years of pent up frustration, anger, and resentment and this conversation is a long time coming; three years too late.

"Kai, I know you don't believe me but I loved you more than you could ever imagine." *Loved* as in past tense but I would worry about that later.

"Just not enough to stay, right?" I allege, resting my forehead against the wall.

"What am I supposed to say to that?" she asks but doesn't sound angry.

"You could start with the truth," I answer, venom in my tone.

"I was scared, Kai—"

"That's bullshit, Ken, and you know it. That's not a real answer. We were both terrified."

"Yes, but you didn't have to wear the evidence underneath your shirt. You didn't have to carry him for nine months. You didn't have to move back in with your parents or put your future on hold. So, I would say my fear looked a little different from yours."

"And whose fault is that?" I demand.

"Kai, you were able to live your life and pursue your career. I thought that's what you would have wanted."

"Yeah, well you have no idea what I would have wanted. You didn't ask. You just disappeared. And I would never have chosen to live my life without you in it."

"I know. That's exactly why I had to leave. Look, we can talk what ifs all day. We can talk about what we should have done, what I should have said. How I could have handled things differently. But we can't change anything. We'll never know which path was the right one, if different choices would have led to better outcomes. But we can try to move forward and make things right in this moment. All we have is what we choose to do now."

And she chose to find me, come back, tell me about our son. That has to count for something.

"I know," I whisper gently. She's quiet for a moment when I think we've come to an impasse.

"I was trying to protect you. Give you an out. At least I thought I was," she explains.

"Protect me…you keep saying that but I don't know what you're talking about. Protect me from what? What exactly has changed in the three years we were apart?" I realize my voice is climbing higher.

"Protect your career, your image. And the difference is that now you're here out of choice, because you want to be. Not out of guilt or because you felt trapped. I didn't want to spend the rest of my life worried you made a decision you'd regret, that you made a mistake with your back up against a wall."

"It was my decision to make and just so we're crystal fucking clear, I have only ever been with you out of love. Unconditional, all-consuming love." *That has never changed.* I swallow the lump forming in my throat. "The fact that you think I could ever feel trapped by you is absurd."

"I made a mistake and I thought I was doing the right thing at the time," she says with resignation.

It's now or never I think and then I let it fucking rip.

"I want you to know I'm always going to choose you. Then. Now. Every lifetime before this and after this, I'm going to choose you. In every hypothetical scenario and alternate universe. I would choose both of you in every lifetime that we're together," I confess and I mean it. Every single word. It's so quiet I'm certain she can hear my heart pounding through the phone.

"Kai, I…I don't know what to say," she says softly.

"You don't need to say anything. I needed you to hear it though. Just once." There's a silence between us that seems to stretch on forever.

"If I could go back and change things, I would. I would undo all the hurt I've caused you and if I had the opportunity to choose you, I would—of course, I would. You need to know that," she admits.

I had started the phone call hostile and frustrated, but I don't want to leave things like that. Not when all I really want is her. Despite all my complicated feelings, I can still sense the love we have for each other buried underneath years of damage. Maybe she could too.

"You do have that opportunity. Forget three years ago. I'm talking about right now."

"It's not that simple, Kai. The last three years didn't happen in a vacuum."

"Maybe it is that simple." *Maybe it's that simple if we want it to be, if we love each other enough.* I hear my teammates yelling from the hallway about hitting up a local bar to celebrate our win. But I don't want this conversation with her to end, not when we're finally getting somewhere.

"It's okay, Kai. It's getting late and it sounds like you need to go. You deserve to celebrate—you guys kicked their asses."

"Everyone is going to be out of their minds and I don't even drink anymore." There's a short pause.

"Oh, you don't?" she asks. "I didn't realize that."

"I stopped a little after I joined the Bucks. It just wasn't good for me," I admit, not really sure why I feel embarrassed.

"I'm sure you can still go and have a good time," she suggests.

"Fine. This conversation isn't over," I decide.

"For now it is. Go, have fun."

"Night, Ken"

"Night, Kai."

No more than twenty minutes later, I text her, hoping she is still up.

Hi

Hi

I miss you

I just got off the phone with you lol

And then a minute later

I miss you too

Can you send me a picture of you guys?

Sure, this pic is from earlier today.

He is passed out in her arms in his Spider-Man pajamas, holding a dinosaur stuffed animal and they're both lying on his bed. Also Spider-Man themed. She's smiling my favorite smile, the corners of her mouth upturned but her lips are pressed together. She looks exhausted but happy. I don't know what comes next. I'm not sure what will happen tomorrow or the day after that. But in this moment, both my head and heart are at ease regardless of the mountains Kendall and I still have to climb.

Chapter 13

Kai

2016

I OPEN MY EYES and scan my surroundings, not a goddamn clue where I am. My head feels heavy, pounding in time with the bass from the music. No, that can't be right. I'm not at the club anymore. The pounding is solely in my head because I'm experiencing a hangover from hell. My ears are ringing and my mouth feels like I swallowed shards of glass. Light streams in through a large window covered by curtains that definitely don't belong to me. I'm lying in a bed. I look down. *Naked?* Yup, definitely naked, my bottom half at least covered by a thin sheet.

Where the fuck am I? What time is it?

I wearily reach over in the bed looking for my phone but instead, I'm met with a giggle. *Shit.* Someone else is in this bed with me. I turn to look at a fully naked brunette, sitting up, back against fluffy white pillows scrolling on her phone.

"Shit. Uh, did we?" I ask, hoping she fills in the blanks.

"Yes, we did. A few times. I'm surprised you don't remember. Well, not that surprised. You were pretty shitfaced for a while. But you fucked like you were sober, don't worry," she explains without looking up from her phone. *How much did I drink last night?* I don't even remember leaving the club or the bar. Wherever we had been. I sure as hell don't remember picking her up or having sex with her, which is saying something because a woman like this would be hard to forget. Gorgeous face, full tits, luscious curves, and legs for days. But she's not Kendall.

"Got it. Where are we?" I wonder, swiping my hand down my face.

"A hotel room in Vancouver." Right, we had won our game last night against the Grizzlies. That's why I was out of my mind. I vaguely remember taking an Uber to a bar with my teammates and then having shots. A lot of shots. Everything else is blurry after that. The night swallowed in a sticky, drunken haze.

"Sorry, I don't remember much from last night," I admit sitting up and resting my arms on my knees.

"She really did a number on you, huh?" she asks, her eyes flicking to me, her face filled with pity.

"What are you talking about?" I reply with confusion.

"Your ex? You kept asking if you could call me Kendall. You wouldn't let it go so eventually I gave in. She must have really messed you up." That's the fucking understatement of the century. Just when I think this can't possibly get any worse. The last thing I need is some random chick I have no recollection of psychoanalyzing me while the room around me starts to spin.

"Yeah, sorry about that," I apologize and cover my face with my hands.

"That's okay. I need to get going anyways," she responds, seemingly unbothered. Mystery girl gets out of bed in search of her clothes, giving me a view of her stellar ass. *Jesus Christ*. I need to fucking reign it in. This is a new low for me. I don't even know her name. She slips on her skimpy excuse for underwear and pulls her hot pink mini dress over her head. She stands at the foot of the bed with her clutch and heels in hand, staring at me awkwardly. The fuck if I know what to say.

"I'm not going to bother giving you my number. I know you won't call me," she grins. "But you were an amazing lay. I sent you a request on Instagram. If you're ever in the Vancouver area again, you know how to find me. Nice meeting you, Kai," she smiles warmly before heading for the door.

"Yeah, you too," I call after her.

And as mysteriously as she appeared, she's gone.

I lie back and pull the covers over my face, hoping to sleep it off. As the day drags on, the previous night comes back to me in pieces and fragments. A final buzzer, a game winning shot.

Three assists. The crowd erupting with hysterical, manic energy. Everyone around me is hollering and cheering. I get swept up in the euphoria, the high of winning one of the most crucial games of the season. I forget for a second about Kendall and the damage she had done.

Later at the bar, I see a girl who looks so similar to her I have to do a double take. I nearly break my neck staring at her. Once I'm certain it isn't her, I return to the chaos of my teammates and their celebratory partying. But I'm no longer drinking to celebrate; I'm drinking to forget. To chase away memories that were ingrained in my head and imprinted on my heart.

The sound of her laugh that lives rent free in my mind. *Shot.* Her smile that feels like sunshine. *Shot.* The feeling of her beneath me, moving inside her, my body pinned to hers. *Double shot.* The kaleidoscope of colors that form her hazel eyes. *Shot.* The first day we met. *Shot.* Spring break in Cabo. *Double shot.* The look on her face when she told me she was pregnant. *Shot.* And before I know it, I'm too far gone. My only goal to erase her completely. At least for the night.

I'm certainly fucking paying for it today. But how long am I going to keep paying for it? The ghost of her that haunts me wherever I go, this sickness that feels like it's eating me alive, this incessant festering wound that refuses to heal. I'm quickly running out of options and out of vices. I could drink myself into an early grave, emerge unscathed from fights I instigated, rack up DUIs and sleep with my choice of women and it doesn't change a goddamn thing.

I still wake up wishing for the only person I can't have.

Chapter 14

Kendall

The next week goes by incredibly slow. The long hours at the legal firm drone on and I look forward to the one day I have off with Akio. He and I stick to our normal schedule and routines as if our world hasn't just imploded. As if I haven't spent the last few days texting Kai, talking to him on the phone whenever he has a spare minute, and getting my hopes up that maybe we could have a future together. I make it a priority to watch his games and he plays just as fiercely as he ever has. Of all of his professional hockey games, I've only missed a few.

The day before he's due to arrive home, my body starts buzzing with anticipation and excitement. The only thing I can think about is seeing Kai again, having him in my apartment, meeting Akio. Unable to calm my nerves, I decide to go for a run after work. Maybe that will help me clear my head and gain some clarity. Three miles in, I've worked up a sweat and managed to expel some of the nervous energy from my body. Cutting off Drake's angelic voice in the middle of "Make Me Proud" is an incoming phone call from Kai.

"Hello?" I say, almost completely out of breath. Apparently, I need to do more cardio.

"Hi, are you okay?" he pauses. "You sound...busy."

"Just a little winded—I'm out for a run, but it's okay. How are you?" I blurt out, stopping to sit on a nearby bench.

"Good, happy to be coming home tomorrow. How are you guys?"

"We're good. Nothing new here," I reply, moving the phone between my ear and shoulder so I can rub my gloved hands together.

"I'm wondering if tomorrow would be a good day to come over and meet Akio?" he asks hopefully. I can hear other guys, probably his teammates chatting and laughing in the background.

"I don't know if tomorrow will work but I'm off on Tuesday, if you want to come over then?" I suggest, realizing I'm twirling my hair as I talk to him. *What am I, twelve with a school girl crush?* Then I remember Kai was my first real crush. He was my first real everything.

"Sure. What time?"

"He usually naps from 12-2 give or take. So any time after two. Is that okay?"

"Yeah, that's perfect. I'll be there shortly after two." There's a long pause. "I'm excited to see you guys."

"Me too," I respond.

***

THE NEXT DAY, I'M a complete mess and Tuesday is no better. I spill coffee all over my shirt. I put orange juice in Akio's milk cup, and after realizing I've lost my phone charger, I find it in the freezer. I spend the roughly hour and a half that Akio is napping searching for the perfect outfit and attempting to make myself look cute. I settle for skinny jeans and what appears to be a clean enough eggplant sweater. Pearl earrings that Kai gave me for Christmas a few years ago complete the look. I pull my curls up into a tight bun and apply lip gloss and some mascara. I look in the mirror and shrug, thinking *this is as good as it's going to get* and then I remember Kai has seen me at my absolute worst.

Two minutes later, there's a knock on my door. I take three deep breaths before I open it and tell myself that everything will be okay, no matter what happens. And then I see him and realize my heart is most definitely not okay. It's rioting wildly in my chest about to lose control like a runaway freight train. He's standing in the doorway, a gorgeous bouquet in one hand and multiple shopping bags in the other, his charcoal eyes gleaming with something I can't quite put my finger on. Looking at him is like looking at the sun; he's that fucking beautiful. Mesmerizing really. He's living proof that god, the universe, whoever absolutely played favorites. With his chiseled jaw cut from glass, plush kissable lips, perfectly angled cheekbones, and the darkest eyes framed by thick luscious lashes. The kind that no man has any business having. I could get lost in his eyes no matter how many times I stare at them. And that jagged slice that cuts through his eyebrow, *what is it about that fucking scar that could bring me to my knees*? Maybe it's the reminder that in all his perfection, he's still perfectly imperfect. Still a little rough around the edges.

He's wearing a black wool peacoat over a navy button up with fitted jeans. His cheeks are flushed and his nose red from the cold. And he is still without question, the sexiest man I've ever met. I rake my eyes over him twice and before I can do it a third time, he smiles and says, "Can I come in or are you still busy checking me out?"

"Uh, yes. Please come in, come in." I laugh a shrill high-pitched laugh that I instantly regret. "Do you need help with any of this?" I ask, reaching for the bags.

"No, I've got it." He steps through the doorway and I lead him to the small kitchen.

"You can just put them on the table." He sets them down and moves toward me, wrapping me in a tender hug. God, he smells *amazing*.

"I wasn't checking you out, you know. I was…" I struggle to find any words because checking him out was exactly what I was doing. His voice, his scent, the feeling of being in his arms again, the thud of his heart beneath my ear—they are all melting my brain cells, turning me into a pile of wordless goo.

Jesus Christ, Kendall. Get it together.

"It's okay," he whispers against my temple. "I was doing the same thing to you."

I take a step back from him, finally peering into his midnight eyes and bite my bottom lip. "I spent more time than I'd like to admit getting ready today," I confess, feeling my cheeks start to heat up. I don't know why I tell him—but his admission that he was blatantly checking me out makes me feel like I can be honest and vulnerable with him.

"You look amazing. Are those the earrings I gave you for Christmas a while back?" he wonders, lightly caressing my ear. A rush travels through my body as the feeling of his fingers on my skin threatens to destabilize me. I'm not prepared for this. Him being in my world, in our space. Like it isn't both the easiest and hardest thing I've ever done. I'm not sure anything would have prepared me for him. His overwhelming presence, the comfort and familiarity of his touch, and these small, intimate moments that feel like they're happening in slow motion.

"Yes," I respond, beaming at him. He pulls his hand away, and I miss it immediately.

Nostalgia for what we used to be mixed with grief for what might have been start to pull on the strings of my heart. Something harder and unnamed, rough and raw reaches up to grip me by the throat and choke me up a bit. I can't be the only one feeling this way.

"Weird, this is weird, right?" I blurt out. His handsome smile starts to falter a bit.

"I'm going to need you to be more specific, Ken."

"This. Us. Being in the same room again, sharing a child, all of it. It's weird and hard…right?"

He rubs his palm over his mouth while he formulates an answer. "Yes, but I would take weird and hard any day, every day, if it means I get to see you again," he comments. The corners of his mouth turn up. "You don't have to be nervous with me, you know. It's still me. Still us. We've known each other since we were five."

At least we both agree this is uncomfortable. I rock on my feet, unsure what to do with my hands, my anxious energy and all my competing feelings. "But I have been nervous...all day. All week, if I'm being honest."

"Me too," he chuckles. "Just be your perfect, natural, gorgeous self. You do it so effortlessly, Ken." *Jesus Christ*. This man. He seems determined to make me fall in love with him all over again.

"Thanks, Kai."

Chapter 15

Kai

She's so achingly beautiful it feels like a fist squeezing my heart, an elastic band pulled tight around my chest. She begins shifting on her feet when I realize I've been staring at her wordlessly for far too long. But I can't help it. It's impossible to be in her presence and not admire her.

Looking to the table, I grab the arrangement and offer it to her. "These are for you."

"These are gorgeous. You didn't have to do that though."

"It's fine. I wanted to," I shrug.

Then, out of nowhere, a small human in Spider-Man pajamas appears at her side. It's like the whole world tilts on its axis; everything about this experience feels surreal. I know even while I'm inside of this moment that I will remember it with perfect clarity forever. The way he instinctively waddles over to Kendall, his tentativeness, his small hands, the sleep in his eyes. All of it is a core memory for me. The first time I met my *son*. I feel my heart expand the size of the universe to hold all the love I have for this boy I barely know but whom I instantly need the same way I need oxygen.

Is this what being a parent feels like? A love so full you feel like you can't breathe? Watching your heart walk around outside your body in the form of a miniature version of yourself?

It's striking how much Akio looks like both of us. His piercing green eyes and bright smile are without a doubt Kendall's, but so many things about him are undeniably me. His shaggy black hair, his reserved nature. He hides behind her leg and tugs at her jeans.

"Mama, come play," he pleads.

Kendall kneels down so she is at eye level with him and pulls him close to her chest. "Baby, remember I said we were having company? This is my friend, Kai. He's really excited to meet you. Can you say hi?" she says gently to him. Akio doesn't budge or make a peep, which is fine. To him, I'm a complete stranger.

She glances from him to me warily and cautions, "Sometimes he's a little slow to warm up."

"That's okay. So am I," I reply. And I like that he takes after me in that way.

He leans into Kendall, pushing his head against the side of her face, his little hands grasping her chin. It's the most adorable thing I've ever seen. The whole time he's sizing me up, trying to determine whether I'm someone he can trust. She whispers in his ear loud enough for me to hear.

"I think Kai might have some gifts for you. Maybe we should go check them out, yeah?" He cracks a small smile and nods his head the slightest bit. They walk over to the table hand in hand, Akio pushing up on his tiptoes to try and see what's in the bags. "How about we bring them into the living room so we have more room, okay?" she suggests. Another subtle nod from him. I follow them into the tiny, cozy living room that has an old denim couch sprinkled with mismatched pillows and a windowsill overgrown with different types of plants. The room is so unapologetically Kendall with loud, bright colors and boho decor. Kendall sits on the couch with Akio snuggled at her side and reaches into the first bag.

"I didn't really have time to wrap anything—sorry. I wasn't sure what he liked so I got a little of everything." I explain, sitting on the arm of the couch with hesitation. He reaches excitedly for the massive electronic T-Rex toy before she can get it out of the bag. He wastes no time rushing to the floor with it and trying out every feature.

We spend the next two hours playing with his dinosaur toys, coloring, making slime, and pretending to be bad guys while Akio chases us around the apartment as Spider-Man. It's the most fun I've had in a long time and it's the happiest I've felt in years.

When we finally settle down, Paw Patrol is Kendall's first choice when she reaches for the remote, and I immediately know why. Akio is snoring in her arms in minutes. I stare at them in disbelief. I thought I knew all the sides of Kendall, every version of her. But this version of her, as a mom, is quickly becoming my favorite. I'm in awe of her beauty, her heart, her love for him, and the way she makes being his parent look so easy. Like she was handpicked specifically for him. I hope I am too, that I could be the dad he needs me to be.

She stares back at me, a knowing look on her face. "You didn't have to get all those things, you know. He would have loved you even if you came empty handed—just because you're you."

"I know, but I wanted to. I've missed out on so much already...I just," I falter, every word in the English language escaping me.

"It's okay. I understand," she answers and gives my hand a gentle squeeze. She sits up, adjusting her and Akio.

"I think we need to wake him or else he's going to be a monster for dinner and bath time." She tenderly rubs his back as she carries him to the kitchen, his whole body melting into hers. And me, what am I doing other than disrupting the delicate balance of their two person ecosystem? I'm not sure if my intrusion is what they need in their lives. It seems like they were doing just fine before I came along, and suddenly, I feel like I can't breathe. I haven't had a panic attack in a while, but it feels like the beginning of one. My vision starts to blur at the edges and my heart beats erratically. I can feel my pulse in every available space of my body.

I quickly follow her to the kitchen and announce, "I'm going to step outside for a second. I think I need some air."

She looks at me with concern in her eyes as she places a sleepy Akio in his highchair.

I nearly sprint outside into the cold night air before giving her a chance to respond. I force myself to sit on the steps with my head between my legs and take a few calming breaths. *Fuck. I really need to get my shit together.* Tilting my head upward, I take a second to stare at the dark sky dotted with stars. I can't panic about the future yet when I haven't even had the chance to really talk to Kendall about everything. But not only am I confused about what exactly my role is here, I'm distraught that I've missed the beginning of Akio's life.

I feel gutted, robbed, like something has been stolen from me. *Because it has, hasn't it?*

Time, time. All this precious time. I should be furious, angry, seething. I should be foaming at the fucking mouth for an argument that would finally bring me some long-awaited answers. Something that would force all this to make sense. And I am mad but underneath all that is love. Anger, resentment, bitterness, those are all solid. Tangible. Something I can label and hold in my hands. I feel it everywhere. And every once in a while, it dissipates. But the ache I have for her in the deepest parts of my heart, that's fluid, constant, and unflinching. The need I have just to be near her is strengthened only by time and distance. It's harder to ignore and damn near impossible to quell. I can't silence that part of myself any longer and quite frankly, I don't want to.

Still, two and a half years. That's tough to swallow. That's time with him that I won't ever get back and I'm not sure how to forgive Kendall for that. If I even can.

When I walk back in the front door, Kendall rushes me, grasping my arms.

"Are you okay? I wasn't sure if you had left or not." She looks uneasy and I know she won't pry for an explanation, but she deserves one. It's strange and unnerving to feel like I'm exactly where I belong and at the same time, completely out of place.

"I'm okay. It's just a lot, you know. A lot to take in and process. I would never leave though," I reassure her.

"I'm sorry. I know this is a lot. It's a lot for me too. I think it's going well though," she admits.

"I can make my way out if you two are trying to have dinner alone. I don't want to intrude."

She looks at me with her brow quirked and a lopsided smile. "Don't be ridiculous, Kai. You aren't intruding. I want you here. We want you to have dinner with us. Although I have to warn you, I don't have a ton to offer. Akio will have his usual but we're stuck with whatever is left in the fridge," she opens the refrigerator door, scanning the top and bottom row. "Which is not much. Can I interest you in some pickles and leftover fried rice?" She laughs.

"Sounds amazing. Exactly what I was hoping for. Why don't we have fried rice as an appetizer, and I'll order us a pizza?" I propose.

"As long as it's from Marchettis," she stipulates.

I grin and tap my head with my index finger. "You read my mind." While I order us dinner, Kendall starts preparing Akio's "usual", chicken nuggets, boxed macaroni and cheese, and green beans. Before she can pour the frozen chicken nuggets on a sheet pan, I intervene, placing my hand on her wrist.

"Kendall, why don't you sit and I'll finish this. I doubt you have many meals where you aren't standing."

She glances from Akio to me. "Okay...are you sure?" she questions, hesitation in her voice.

"Yes. I'm sure. What if I have to make him dinner by myself one night? I'm not saying anytime soon. But I should at least know how to make his usual," I suggest, hoping she'll sit and relax for a little bit. I take the box of chicken nuggets out of her hand and continue pouring them on the pan. Akio chimes in with, "Cut, cut, cut," and I look to Kendall for translation purposes. She chuckles as she slides into the chair and explains.

"He's trying to tell you he wants you to cut up the nuggets really tiny and put them in his macaroni and cheese."

"Okay, got it. Cut them up and put them in the mac 'n cheese," I repeat, looking at Akio before adding, "Cut, cut, cut" for emphasis. I also offer a chopping motion with my hand, just in case. He squeals with laughter and claps his hands. The sound goes directly to my heart.

After dinner, Kendall takes Akio to his room to have some downtime before bed. When she comes out, I'm standing near the door, not entirely sure what to say. She senses it just like she always does and breaks the silence.

"Thank you for everything today, Kai. I'm so happy you came."

"Me too. I can't believe we made him. He's perfect, Kendall," I observe.

"I know," she smiles, her eyes brightening. *God that smile*, it rivals the moon and the stars. The Grand Canyon. The whole fucking universe. I wonder if she knows how it affects me. How it has haunted me for years. That all it takes is a simple tug of her lips to turn me into a giddy love struck teenager again. It makes me fucking *weak* and wrecks any sense of self-preservation I thought I had. I want so badly to kiss her and it takes every bit of restraint I have to remain locked in place.

"Do you ever look at him with so much love and pride and joy that you are overwhelmed? Like your heart could explode with how much you love him?"

"Only every day. Multiple times a day," she answers.

"Good, so that's a...typical parent feeling?" I wonder.

"Yup," she confirms, taking a few steps toward me. It's clear we're both unsure how to end this conversation, neither of us wanting to say goodbye.

"Listen, Ken. I need to say something and I don't know how you are going to take it."

"Okay, out with it. Just say what you need to say."

"I'm so fucking angry and confused about this whole situation and the things you have kept from me. But I don't know how to not love you." I hold my breath waiting for her response.

"So be angry and confused and whatever else you're feeling. Every emotion you have is valid and I don't blame you for them. But maybe when the dust has settled a bit, let's talk because there are things we need to figure out. Just please don't take it out on Akio. Blame me, be mad at me, but he deserves to see you and know you and learn how amazing you are and have you be a part of his life. I want him to have a relationship with you and I really hope it's not too late."

"It's not too late. But I need to know Ken, why now? Why wait three years?" I ask, my voice rising.

"I know I should have told you sooner. I know I wasted so much time. I was scared and so alone. I didn't know how to tell you and I wasn't sure you'd forgive me. Akio started asking about you—well, about his dad—recently and I knew it was time."

There's more she isn't saying. I can feel it, but I'm not going to push right now. Our emotions are running high enough today as it is. My need to feel my lips on hers is battling with my desire to flee this apartment and drink myself into oblivion.

"Okay Ken. I will be here as much as you want or allow me to be. But what about...us?" I ask, taking a step closer to her and then another, my breath mixing with hers now. *So much for restraint. It's currently dangling by a fucking thread.* She bites her bottom lip, glancing down at her hands and then slowly locks eyes with me.

"What about us?" she whispers.

I take her hands gently in mine. "What kind of relationship do you want us to have?"

She doesn't pull back or move away from me, which is a good sign. Instead, she leans into me, our noses nearly touching. "Would it be too forward to say I have no interest in a platonic relationship with you?" God, I love the way she always wears her heart on her sleeve. And as much as I want to hate her, I know I can't. Spending the day with them is proof enough. If anything, I hate that I can't hate her.

"Not at all," I smile. "But this is a very delicate situation, so I think we should take things slow. Is that okay?" Because the truth is I don't trust her to stay put, to not up and disappear when things get tough. I definitely don't trust her with my heart. Every time I think about how she shattered it into a million unrecognizable pieces, an anger I can't explain surges inside me. But then I see her smile, and every broken piece turns in her direction. I don't know how to reconcile the heartache that lingers and the fleeting glimpses of hope she offers. So, right now, I know the only thing that will help us heal and build trust is time.

"It's more than okay."

I touch my forehead to hers, a gesture that always served as an unspoken promise between us. *I love you, I support you, and I will be there for you however you need me to be.* I wrap my arms around her waist and breathe her in, her scent of coconut and vanilla enveloping me. My anger and frustration get lost in the absolute need to be as close to her as possible.

How many nights have I dreamed of having her back in my arms?

Holding her?

Touching her?

It feels wrong, criminal really, leaving her with just a kiss on the cheek and a hushed goodbye. When every cell in my body is screaming at me to kiss her, stay with her, to never let her go again. Like she's a grain of sand that can slip right through my fingers.

As soon as the front door closes behind me, I feel it. The vast emptiness. There's a Kendall and Akio shaped hole in my chest and I know every time I return home without them, I'll be returning without my heart. Because my purpose, my passion, my entire world could now be summarized in one word.

Them.

CHAPTER 16

KENDALL

But I don't know how to not love you.

I close the door behind Kai, white knuckling the knob and leaning against it for support. I keep replaying the conversation we just had. Today went infinitely better than I thought it would. *So why am I not relieved, overjoyed?* All the feelings for him I've tried to keep tucked away and just out of reach come rushing back in full force. Guilt and grief, love and hope. Complete adoration for this man I once thought I would marry. When he wasn't a part of our lives, I could keep him at arm's length. From a distance, he was merely someone I used to love. Even if I was lying to myself. But seeing him twice in two weeks, having him in my house is something else entirely. I can't fight the eventuality of him, of us any longer. I can't pretend that all my regrets are isolated to me and Akio anymore.

Watching Kai with him was almost too much to bear—I can't believe I have been depriving them both of a relationship with each other for so long. And for what, to protect myself? Because I was too scared of what the truth might do to us? What good had it accomplished except make us both miserable? If the guilt alone wasn't enough, the tension and chemistry between us is palpable, electric—threatening to take down all the walls I had carefully constructed around Akio and I.

But I don't know how to not love you.

I feel the throbbing pain of a cluster headache starting to take shape and begin massaging my temple. Realizing I need reinforcements, I pry open the fridge and pour myself a large glass of Rose. Sweet, buzzing relief hits me in minutes.

Just as the wine starts to warm me up from the inside out, I get an incoming text from him. I doubt he's even home yet.

I miss you both already

My heart.

My poor, stupid, defenseless heart that has *always* belonged to him.

I don't stand a chance.

Chapter 17

Kendall

This is too fucking nuanced and layered to try and disentangle. Too difficult to distill this thing between us down to its very essence. And yet when I try to do just that, it's actually quite simple, at least on its face. On the surface, we're two people who used to love each other a long time ago. And now we have a child together. For better or worse, we're tethered for life.

And what the hell are we supposed to do with that?

We aren't the first people to muddle our way through co-parenting. I'm not even really worried about what Kai would be like as a dad or trying to split time between the both of us. Kai was always meant to be a father—I know this in my bones. It's the things that lurk below the surface that worry me...like our complicated past and shared history. I'm more concerned about the way my heart starts to tap dance whenever he's around, the way my breath hitches whenever he hugs me, the pure weightlessness I feel when I earn a smile or laugh from him. Those feelings are dangerous. All consuming. Impossible to ignore. Because even if they're mutual, even if he feels the exact same way I do, I don't deserve the reciprocity. And I'm certain we could never work again, no matter how badly I want us to. I'm convinced I'm not worth the time, the effort, the eventual pain, and ultimately, the heartache. I haven't deserved him since the day I walked out on him.

And a darker smaller part of me, the part I always try and fail to silence, whispers, *You never deserved him in the first place.*

I need a second opinion on this entire situation. I need help navigating this mess I've created. I need, I need...I honestly have no clue what I need. But I think I know someone who will. The only other person I've known as long as I've known Kai is Jenna. The three of us used to be really close growing up. Until Kai and I started dating. Suddenly, a memory comes online, the first time Jenna ever gave me dating advice about Kai.

I know Kai disagreed with my answer just to get a rise out of me. I haven't talked to him in over a week and left all his texts on read. I just need some distance from him. I guess this is his way of trying to communicate with me. He would rather publicly argue than go without speaking.

I quickly follow after him when the bell rings and pull him aside.

"What the hell was that?" I demand, getting in his face.

"What?" he says. I wish he would wipe that smug look off his face.

"That. Coming at me in Whitheim's class. You hate him and that class and I have never seen you willingly raise your hand to answer a question," I shoot back, annoyed.

"I don't know what you're talking about."

"That's absolute bullshit."

"I asserted an opinion that was different from yours. I didn't come at you. But that hasn't ended well for me in the past."

Crossing my arms I respond, "What's that supposed to mean?"

"Having an idea or opinion that is different from yours or different than the one you want to hear."

"I can't do this with you right now," I decide.

"You approached me, Kendall," he states, his shadowed eyes zeroing in on me intensely.

Right as I turn to leave, he grabs my arm and spins me towards him. He is so close his breath tickles my lips. And all I can think about is kissing his stupid beautiful face. "We are going to do this right now. I'm sick of thinking about you and dreaming about you and wanting to talk to you but not being able to talk to you. It is killing me."

"Do you know how hard I have to work to actively stop my brain from thinking about you? Do you understand what it's like for me

to care about you as much as I do only to be rejected?" I practically yell. I can feel myself starting to lose my temper and I refuse to give him the satisfaction.

"I didn't reject you," he answers quietly.

"Well, you didn't want to be with me and you have never honestly told me how you feel. So, what would you call that?" I question, glaring at him.

"Well, I'm not rejecting you now," he explains. We're interrupted at the most inopportune time by Jenna.

"Are you two finally talking again?" she asks, gesturing between us.

"Barely," I respond through gritted teeth. Kai looks disappointed but not shocked. I can tell he's satisfied with himself having baited me into a conversation. But it's going to take a lot more than that to fix what is broken in our friendship. Relationship? Situationship? I don't even know anymore. But the charged energy between us is undeniable. I would gladly rip his face off along with his clothes.

"Okay. Come on, we're going to be late for practice. Later, Kai," she says as she tugs on my shirt. I don't bother with the pleasantries. We turn and head in the direction of the gym. I don't need to look over my shoulder to know he's staring at me. I can feel his eyes burning a hole in my back.

"What the hell was that about?" Jenna whispers and weaves her arm in mine as we walk away.

I sigh. "I don't know. He is trying to talk or work things out with us. But he's infuriating. All I've asked him for is space and he can't do that. He can't even admit that he has feelings for me, so I'm not quite sure where we stand."

"But you know that he does and he has basically done everything short of groveling. Isn't that enough?" she probes.

"If he feels for me what I feel for him, he needs to be able to say that—or at the very least, fight for me. Don't I deserve that? Whose side are you on?" I ask, slightly annoyed and already exhausted from this conversation.

"Listen, baby, I'm Switzerland in this scenario. You're both my best friends and I can't take sides. I hate that he hurt you. But I think *we all know how bad he feels about his mistakes. Is this about him declaring his love or about punishing him?" As frustrating as it is, I know Jenna is being honest and probably telling me things I'm not ready to hear yet.*

"He hurt me in a way that I never thought he would. I'm not ready to forgive him yet. I'm not ready to be friends with him again. Okay?" I respond, hoping she will drop it.

"Okay. All I'm saying is waiting for Kai to express his feelings might be futile. You know he has a hard time talking about things. But he does love you, you know, and he would do anything for you. Except leave you alone. That's probably a tough one for him to swallow. So maybe cut him a little slack?" she suggests gently. I'm sure it must be hard for her to get caught in the middle of this feud between us.

"I'll try. I just don't know how he feels or what he wants."

"Kendall, he has been in love with you since we were twelve and that is a hill I'm willing to die on. The three of us have been friends for how long and he has never once looked at me the way he looks at you. He has never been protective over me the way he is with you. Christ, he has never started fights with guys that wanted to hook up with me and there have been many. It always used to make me a little jealous but now I get it. Trust me on this. He may not be able to say it, but he shows it in his own ways all the time," she counters, like she had that argument locked and loaded.

After Akio finally goes down, I FaceTime her and within seconds, her beautiful sun kissed face pops up on my screen.

"I don't think I'll ever get used to the fact that you are now a brunette and have a better tan than me," I joke, plopping myself down on the couch.

"Yeah yeah," she laughs. "Where's my nephew. Already asleep?" she wonders.

"I just put him down. So, how are you? How's California?"

"I'm good. Work is busy. California is amazing. You guys should really come visit soon. How are you and Akio?"

"We're good. Same ol'. Listen...I met up with Kai a few weeks ago—"

"What?!" she exclaims.

"Just listen. He met Akio today and I'm like completely spinning out," I admit, not wasting any time.

"Okay, we'll revisit the fact that you guys met up and didn't tell me later," she says, raising her eyebrows. "How did it go today?"

"Really good. He's so good with him, Jenna, and he brought flowers and gifts."

"Well, of course he is. It's Kai, and he's his father," she responds while opening an unidentified snack out of view from the camera.

"Please keep your voice down." I warn. "Akio doesn't know yet. I'm not sure if he'll really understand or be confused."

"Shit, sorry. How did you introduce him?" she asks while munching on a carrot.

"As my friend..." Which wasn't exactly a lie but it wasn't the truth either. He had been my friend, my best friend, once.

"And is that what he is...your friend?" she presses.

"I don't know. All I know is ever since he reappeared in our lives, everything has been off kilter. I don't know what to do."

"Well, did you call me for comfort or advice?"

"Both?" It comes out more like a question than a statement.

"My honest opinion or the watered down version?"

Then all of a sudden, I hear her fiancé, Amir, shout from somewhere else in the apartment, "Be nice, Jenna!"

"I am being nice. I can be honest while being nice!" she challenges. "Anyways, you both have always loved each other. My guess is you still do. And judging by the look on your face, I know my assumption is correct," she grins. *Christ*. I wasn't even aware I was making a face. But this is good, ruthless honesty is what I need. This is why I called her. "Kai waited for you in high school for years. I'm sure he'll wait as long as it takes for you both to figure this out."

"What if he can't forgive me for...everything?" I grate my bottom lip with my teeth, tears forming in my eyes.

"He will, you know that. But you also have to give him the opportunity to do that. He can't forgive you if he doesn't know everything, if he doesn't have all the facts," she states, letting that comment sink in.

Fuck, I hate it when she's right.

"But I don't think that's what this is about. At least not entirely. At some point, you have to stop punishing yourself for decisions you made under duress when you were barely an adult. This is about whether you want to do the hard work with him and for him to repair things." She pauses. "Is that what you want?"

"Jesus, spoken like a true therapist."

"Not a licensed therapist yet but thank you. So, is that what you want?" she repeats herself.

"Unequivocally yes. What if that's not what he wants?"

"Somehow, I doubt that, Kendall. I don't think we'd be having this conversation if that were the case."

"I'm scared that it's all going to blow up in my face and worse, Akio will get attached to him and if things don't go well, I don't want him to get hurt," I admit.

"I know, but the only way out is through, babe. I don't want you to take this the wrong way, but what about couples counseling? It might be helpful, you know? You two have a lot of history and baggage to work through that might be better discussed with someone to help mediate, like a neutral third party?"

"Do you think he'd go for that? We're not even a couple."

"But you were once and maybe you will be again. My parents went to couples therapy before they got a divorce, so it obviously didn't work for them," she scoffs. "But I've seen it help improve a lot of relationships and marriages."

"Yeah maybe."

"Just think about it. See how the next couple weeks go and ask him if it's something he would be interested in," she suggests.

"Okay, thanks."

CHAPTER 18

KENDALL

"**W**HAT EXACTLY AM I looking at here, Jenna?" I ask while she's on speakerphone. Even though I know exactly what I'm looking at and it makes my stomach coil with tension and my body simmer with rage. It's a slightly blurry photograph of Kai and some gorgeous super model. I know she's a model because I'm almost positive I saw her on the cover of *Vogue* a few months ago. A tall brunette in a crimson peacoat that swallows her thin frame. Her long legs are on display in leather pants. They're walking out of what I assume is his apartment complex, their hands nearly brushing, a grin on both their faces. She's just close enough to him that it looks ambiguous. Maybe they spent the night together? Maybe they live in the same building and just happened to walk out at the same time?

Maybe maybe maybe. The maybes might just annihilate me.

"That is a photo of daddy dipshit with someone who obviously isn't you. And they look pretty cozy if you ask me."

"Yes, thank you, Jenna. I can see that," I observe. "It doesn't prove anything. It's also none of my business. He can do what he wants. He doesn't owe me an explanation."

So then why do I spend the next three hours giving him the cold shoulder, clipped answers, and the bare minimum of conversation?

"Are you okay?" he asks right before he leaves. His dark eyes are calculating, assessing.

"I'm fine," I lie. "I'm just a little tired," I respond, crossing my arms.

"Are you sure because you don't seem fine. You seem upset." He takes a step toward me and gently touches my arm. There was no point in continuing the charade; Kai knows me too well. My tells, my body language, my everything. And wasn't this an opportunity to start being honest with him? The thing I should have done from the start.

"I saw a tabloid photo today," I murmur, avoiding eye contact with him.

"Okay…" there are probably so many pictures and tabloids of him. I'm going to have to be more specific.

I sigh while pulling my phone out of my pocket and open the text thread I have with Jenna. Clicking on the photograph, I hand him my phone. He stares at it for a few seconds before returning his eyes to me.

"This was from a few weeks ago. It was a PR stunt coordinated by her publicist. We live in the same building and nothing happened between us, Ken." He's telling the truth. I know he is. Besides, he has no reason to lie. We aren't together and the picture is dated a week before I went to his game.

"It's fine, Kai. You are free to do what you want. You don't need to give me an explanation." He grins and I wish it didn't have the effect it always does.

"Are you jealous, Ken?" he wonders, moving a half a step closer to me.

"I wouldn't say that I enjoy this picture," I admit, leaning into his chest.

He brings his hand to my cheek, strokes it with his thumb. My stomach bottoms out, my pulse pounds. *Is he going to kiss me?*

"I need to hear you say it, Ken. I deserve that much, don't I?" he asks, his voice low, lethal, *dangerous*. I wonder if he realizes he leaned in closer, or maybe I have.

"Of course I'm jealous. I don't want to see you with other women," I reply harshly. He frames my face in his hand while he curls one arm around my waist. Holding me to him. Our hearts beating furiously. I want him to kiss me, more than I've ever wanted anything. I might lose my goddamn mind if he does. I'll self-destruct if he doesn't.

"Whatever you've seen in the tabloids, in magazines, on TV. None of that matters. Because the only person I haven't been able to get out of my head over the last three years is you. You are the one woman I can't stop thinking about. Always you. Only you," he explains. His forehead is against mine and we're both breathing hard. "I really want to kiss you right now. But we're taking things slow."

"We're taking things slow," I repeat before licking my lips. My heart skips a beat and then another.

Breathe, Kendall.

"And figuring out how to trust each other," he whispers. I'm intoxicated by his scent, the timbre of his voice, the broadness of his shoulders, and the comfort I feel whenever I'm in his arms. He laughs and it vibrates throughout my entire body before sinking deep into my core. He pulls me close to his chest and presses a kiss to my crown. "I'm going to leave before I do something reckless," he says, letting me go and moving towards the door. "Night, Ken."

"Night, Kai," I reply, biting my lip. He smiles that devastating smile and closes the door shut behind him. Which is probably for the best.

Because I want him *reckless*. I want him undone. In my head, on my skin, underneath my body. Infiltrating my defenses, worshipping my soul, and holding my heart in his hands. I want him any way I can have him. *Every way.*

And I know very well that I can't.

Chapter 19

Kendall

2016

THE THING I'VE DISCOVERED about lying is that it gets easier and easier the more you do it. The first lie you tell someone you love, the kind of lie you can't come back from, is the hardest. The other ones you tell to maintain the first, well, those are just a necessary means to an end. They seem to roll off your tongue effortlessly.

So, when I tell Kai I had the abortion but that I need space from him for a while, it nearly breaks me. In the five years we've been together, I have never lied to him, not about something this big or important. Sure, I've told small white lies over the years like any normal person. But I know this level of deceit is something we won't and can't recover from. That on the outside it appears purely malicious.

But to me it feels like protection. Compassion. *Mercy*.

Because I'm quite certain neither one of us are ready to have a child. Neither of us are prepared to completely blow up our lives. At least he can still have his. I try to rationalize it as steadfast devotion to helping him accomplish his dream. And at the end of the day, I have to be able to live with myself, put my head on a pillow, and make peace with my decisions. So, if I have to wrap up spineless betrayal in a pretty bow and call it a gift, then so be it.

He sits on my couch and he looks utterly devastated, worry and pain etched across his face.

"But this is temporary, right—just a short-term break?" he asks, his eyes scanning my face, digging for the truth. I stand in the doorway of the living room, barely able to look at him.

"Yes, of course," I lie. "I just need time to sort some things out, process everything. This has been really hard on me. I'm exhausted from all of it." I hug myself as my bottom lip starts to tremble uncontrollably.

"Okay, Ken, if that's what you want and what you need right now, I can give you space." He swallows and I know there is a but coming. "But you know how much I love you, right?" His gaze collides with mine, holding my heart hostage. "I can't picture my life without you and I don't want to. I fully intend on marrying you someday."

He had said this a few times before, but this time it feels different, more of a promise than an idea. We've discussed it a little over the past year. We know we want to spend the rest of our lives together but decided it would be best to wait until Kai's an established player in the league and I've graduated from law school. I considered us the lucky ones, one of those rare couples that have been together since high school. But those conversations feel so far away now, like our luck has finally run out.

I smile and force a mirthless laugh because otherwise, I'll cry and I don't know if I'll be able to stop. I'll break down and tell him the truth, that he is the single most important person in the world to me aside from this baby I'm carrying. That the last thing I want from him is space. That I need him the same way I need oxygen. That he is and always has been my person. That I can't picture my life without him either but now I have to and every word he says to me about our future is like another dagger to my heart.

He rises from the couch, closes the distance between us, and embraces me. His warmth and his scent invade my senses and I immediately feel safe and at peace in his arms.

How could I let my heart go?

How could I do this without him?

How? How? How?

Hot tears start streaming down my face knowing this is the last time I'll see him. I try brushing them away while he kisses my hair and squeezes me tighter.

"It's okay, Ken. It will be okay. I'll wait as long as you need me to. I'm not going anywhere," he finally says.

He isn't but I am. He doesn't know it yet, but I'm leaving in two weeks to stay with my aunt in North Carolina at least until the baby is born. If I stay here, if Kai and I are in the same state, there will be nothing preventing me from trying to make things work with him. I don't even know if the 700 miles between us will be enough to keep me away from him.

But I have to try.

CHAPTER 20

KAI

"HELLO? MISS ME ALREADY?" I joke as I pick up Kendall's phone call. We've been texting back and forth all morning, so I'm surprised to see her calling me.

"Kai? Where are you?" She sounds worried.

"About to leave practice, is everything—"

She cuts me off. "Can you come to the hospital? It's Akio. He had an allergic reaction and his throat started closing up," she explains frantically.

"Kendall, where are you guys? I'll leave right now."

"Rayfield Memorial. We're in the ED at the children's hospital." Fuck, I know Rayfield Memorial. I've been there a few times for injuries I got during games. It's almost a half hour away.

"I'll be there as soon as I can, Ken," I choke out as I sprint to my car.

"Okay, thanks."

It's an enormous feat trying to keep it together on my way to the hospital. My hands are covered in sweat, my heart thundering against my ribcage, and my brain keeps coming up with increasingly worse scenarios the closer I get to my destination. I stop at a four-way intersection three miles away from the hospital, and nearly clip another car, my mind somewhere far away. I pull over and park my car at the next gas station I see, realizing it's dangerous to drive like this. Which is ironic seeing as how I've driven in far worse conditions without any concern for the outcome.

My grip on the steering wheel tightens like a vise and I force myself to take three deep breaths, *in and out, in and out, in and out.* Nothing is going to happen to Akio. Everything is going to be fine. I just got them back.

The universe wouldn't be that cruel, would it?

***

THE WAITING AREA FOR the ED is pure chaos and stimulation overload. Kids sneezing and coughing, a toddler with vomit on his shirt. A teen or tween with what appears to be a broken wrist. Multiple other children with various illnesses waiting to be assessed. I approach the front desk and try to plaster on my most charming smile.

"Hi, I'm here to see—"

"Child's name please and date of birth" the receptionist demands in a no-nonsense tone.

"Akio Matsumoto, January 13, 2017."

"And are you related to the patient?" she asks briskly.

"Yes, I'm his father," I respond, simmering with fear and agitation.

"Can I see your ID please?"

"Sure," I open my wallet and hand her my driver's license. She reviews it carefully then gives it back to me.

"He's in room 203. It's straight back, fourth door on your left—you can stand by the doors over there and I'll buzz you in in a moment,"

"Thanks."

After she buzzes me in, I follow her instructions and find the correct hospital room. Kendall is curled up on the hospital bed with Akio and he seems okay, not in any immediate distress. She looks drained though. Instinctually, I wrap my arms around her and lightly kiss the top of her head. I give Akio a small wave and he smiles back at me with a sleepy grin from underneath Kendall's shoulder.

"Hi," I whisper. "How is he? How are you doing?"

"He's better now. We took an ambulance here, which was pretty scary and I think a little traumatizing for both of us. He's eaten strawberries before. I don't know what happened. But he had a few bites of one and I went to get something from the fridge and when I turned around his lips were swollen and he looked like he was having trouble breathing so I called 911. They stayed on the phone with me until they got to the apartment," she explains, tears welling in her eyes.

"I'm so sorry, Kendall—"

And just as I'm about to complete my thought, there's a brisk knock on the door followed by a stubby, balding man who appears to be in his early sixties. Without looking up from his notes, he announces, "I'm Doctor Larson, I'll be in charge of Kio's care and discharge planning today."

"His name is Akio," I state, emphasizing the vowel sound. Doctor Larson mispronouncing Akio's name was his first mistake.

"My apologies. You must be Akio's parents," he responds without a single hint of remorse, shaking both of our hands. My eyes quickly flick to my son, hoping he didn't hear the doctor declare me as his parent, but he is too wrapped up in his iPad to notice anything else. Kendall answers for us. "I'm his mother, Kendall. I just want to make sure he is going to be okay. He seems better now, still a little shaken up though."

"Your son is going to be just fine. The swelling has come down significantly. He appears to be acting normal. All of his vitals look good and stable. He can probably go home in a few hours."

"But he's eaten strawberries before, and he's never had a reaction. Is that typical?" she asks, lowering her voice and stepping around to the front of the hospital bed.

"Sometimes allergies come on seemingly out of nowhere. It's possible he has been allergic to strawberries in the past, but the reaction just might not have been as severe or even detectable. We are going to send you home with an EpiPen that can be used if something like this happens again. Additionally, it might be a good idea to let your family members, pediatrician, and any daycare providers know so they are aware of his allergies and how to treat his symptoms. I promise a good night's sleep and some extra snuggle time and he will be just fine."

"Okay, thank you so much. I appreciate it. Is there any way he could be discharged sooner rather than later? I have to work tomorrow."

"Unfortunately, we are short-staffed tonight and have a few traumas in the ER. But we will try to get you home as soon as we possibly can," he offers while listening to Akio's lungs with a stethoscope. Making Kendall and I feel like Akio was not high on his priority list was his second mistake.

"If there's nothing else..." he states, standing next to the hospital bed. I curl my knuckles into my palms to keep from grabbing him by his shirt.

"Actually, there is. I have it on good authority that the Boston Bucks make a generous yearly donation to this hospital. I also know a few of the acting board members personally. If you want that money to keep flowing and retain your job, I would suggest you get us discharged immediately," I snarl. Kendall scowls at me and I can't tell if she's angry or embarrassed.

"I don't take kindly to threats, Mr..." his voice trails off, and I know he's staring at me trying to place me, wondering why my racially ambiguous face seems so familiar.

"Matsumoto. Kai Matsumoto," I finish. He stands up a little straighter and deposits his pen in his jacket pocket and stethoscope around his neck.

"Ah yes, Mr. Matsumoto. Again, I will try to hurry things along, but I really don't have the power or ability to make this entire department more efficient. After all, this is a public hospital and patients will be treated and discharged based on the severity of their injuries and illnesses, and level of acuity. I suggest you all get comfortable."

As soon as he exits the room, Kendall pulls me into the bathroom by my arm. The harsh fluorescent lights flicker on and reveal a small toilet and sink.

"What the hell was that stunt?" she demands, eyebrows furrowed and her cheeks flushed. I forgot how cute she is when she's angry. For a second, I imagine what it would be like to kiss her with her back pressed against the door of this bathroom.

"Nothing, he was just pissing me off. I thought maybe some name recognition might get us out of here faster," I shrug trying to get rid of all the fantasies this forced proximity was planting in my head.

"He was actually pretty nice as far as pediatric doctors go. He's just doing his job."

"I know I was an asshole. I just feel like Akio deserves better and I didn't like that he said his name wrong. You know it happened to me all the time as a kid. I hate that shit."

"I know you do," she tuts.

"Wait, back up, what do you mean as far as pediatric doctors go? Has he been to the hospital a lot?" I ask, my head starting to spin, wondering what else I've missed in the past two years.

A panicked look spreads over her face as she chews on her bottom lip.

"I used to date a pediatric doctor that worked here. He didn't treat me very well to put it bluntly," she confesses.

"What do you mean he didn't treat you well?" I press, taking a step closer to her.

"Ugh, it was so long ago. I don't even want to think about it. He was just arrogant and belittling. He made sure I knew my place, which he considered to be far below him. Seeing as how I was just a paralegal, a single mom, and could barely afford my rent. And he was a hotshot doctor making well above six figures."

I slowly tilt her chin up towards my face, wanting her to hear every word I'm about to say. Her hazel eyes soften and focus on me; they're a lighter shade of green today with shimmering flecks of gold.

"Kendall, any guy who makes you feel like you are less than the fucking beautiful, intelligent, extraordinary gift that you are does not deserve your time, okay? And any guy that doesn't worship the fucking ground you walk on is a moron." She starts blushing, her tan cheeks turning a deep scarlet and I know I've made my point.

"It's fine, Kai, it was a long time ago. It's ancient history."

"No, Kendall, it's not fine."

"Yes, Kai, it is. I've gotten over it and so should you. Besides, it was never going to work with him anyways," she admits, inching closer to me, her arms brushing against my chest, her face so close I can feel her breath on my lips.

"Why?" I ask, my breath quickening.

"You know why."

"I'd like to hear you say it, Kendall," I respond, doubling down.

"Because I don't know how to not love you either."

"I know we are taking things slow but I'm having a very hard time restraining myself from kissing you in this hospital bathroom," I admit, allowing my knuckles to graze her cheek and cupping her face in my hand. Kendall had always been just out of my reach, out of my league, untouchable. Until she wasn't. Until I realized the attraction went both ways. Now here I am, feeling very much like my seventeen year old self, chasing after my first crush, like I still have something to prove. Begging her with everything I have to give me a chance, to stay, to cross that line with me again. The only difference is that now, we have more to lose.

Did she still taste like sweet sin? Would she still come undone when I flick my tongue against her pulse point? These are suddenly the only questions I need answers to.

"So, stop restraining—" I cut off her words with a kiss that's aggressive, feral, and completely *unrestrained*. I tilt her head back, needing more of her, and slip my tongue in her mouth greedily. She opens for me without hesitation, letting me explore her. It's enough to elicit a whimper from the back of her throat. *Fuck, I'm in trouble. This* is trouble. Her tongue slides against mine and this kiss feels like mistakes and promises, home and heartache. I grip her neck with one hand as my other hand snakes around her waist, pressing her chest flush to mine. Her fingers rake my hair while my hands start roaming the curves of her body, just as a moan escapes her lips.

"Mm, Kai," she murmurs, pulling away gently.

"Not done with you yet," I growl. I want nothing more than to reacquaint myself with the burning temptation of her body. I need to know what she likes now and exactly how she likes it. I want to relearn every whimper, every moan, every gasp and know I'm responsible for it, that I've earned it. I trace her jaw with my nose and proceed to kiss my way from her cheek all the way down to her collarbone. She shivers beneath my touch when my mouth lingers underneath her ear and melts back into me. *That's a resounding yes.*

"God, I missed you, miss the way you taste," I whisper against her skin. No woman has ever tasted as good as she does. Like summer and sunshine.

"Kai," she pleads while simultaneously placing her hand on my chest to stop me.

I sigh in exasperation, knowing this fantasy turned reality is about to be cut short.

"Yes, Kendall?"

"As much as I missed you and this, I really don't think we should do anything further in this hospital bathroom with Akio right behind the door." Her words tell one story while her eyes tell another. She wants this just as badly as I do. She presses her forehead to mine and gives me a light chaste kiss on the lips. "To be continued at a more appropriate time and location?" she rasps.

"To be continued." I repeat her words and place a kiss on her forehead, because at this point, I would do anything this woman asks.

Chapter 21

Kendall

Suddenly I'm transported in time back to senior year of high school. We're eighteen, in Kai's bed, sharing our first kiss. It's hands and heat, fire and passion. It's tangled limbs and wild hearts and inexperience. It's everything we feel but can't say. It's crossing a line we both know we can't come back from. He kisses me like he's been waiting his whole life and goddamn it if he doesn't make every second count.

When I think back on this moment years later, the versions vary but the end result is always the same. We kiss for the first time and it's nothing short of *magic*. I'll claim I made the first move because I told him not to stop when his fingers started dancing on my skin. He'll say he made the first move because he leaned in to kiss me. Either way, it's earth shattering, reality altering. A kiss to measure all others against. I had no way of knowing it at the time, but this kiss would set an impossible standard for every guy that came after him.

And then I'm firmly back in the present. I'm staring at Kai, my oldest friend and first love, his dark eyes shining down on me with an emotion I can't place. If it weren't for him hanging on to me so tightly, I would be struggling to remain upright. Somehow, I'm lucky enough to experience a second first kiss with him and I send a silent prayer to the universe that it's the last first kiss that I ever have. I hope against hope that whatever this beautiful broken thing is between us, that this time, it ends in forever. Because I want to keep him so badly it hurts. I want to keep him in a way that feels illegal. Unattainable. *Irrevocable.*

My lips tingle, my skin vibrating from his touch. I forgot how my body reacts to his like there's this undeniable magnetic pull between us. There's little stopping me from fucking him right here in this bathroom—other than Akio's presence less than five feet away. I have to exercise some sort of self-control before we do something we can't undo, right?

Right?

I step out of the bathroom and adjust my shirt, smoothing down my hair. Thankfully, Akio begs me to watch some videos with him, so I don't have to dissect the near mental breakdown I almost had. Hooking up with him here, now, would have been a lapse in sanity, a mistake. I'm just tired, overemotional, in need of comfort and Kai was there.

He keeps his hands to himself the rest of the time we're at the hospital. But he remains close, never leaving my side, like a shadow. He reminds me how fierce and loyal of a protector he is, that if only for tonight, we belong to each other.

***

WE DON'T END UP leaving the hospital until just after one. I know Kai can sense my exhaustion because he offers to drive us home in his car and I don't argue with him about it. Barely able to keep my eyes open and desperately needing my bed, I shuffle behind Kai as he carries a snoring Akio on his shoulder. Once we get to the car, I slide into the passenger seat while Kai puts Akio in the car seat. I lay my head back and blow out a tired breath.

"It's been a long day and tomorrow is going to be even longer at work," I say to no one in particular.

"You're not going to work tomorrow and neither am I," he tells me after he turns my car on.

"Kai, what are you talking about?" I turn to look at him incredulously. "I have to go to work and so do you, I imagine.

Besides, I'm getting low on sick days. I can't really afford to take a day off tomorrow," I explain, slightly embarrassed.

"We—but mostly you two—have been through a stressful experience and spent most of the night in the hospital. I think what we all need is to call in sick tomorrow and spend some time together. Get back to baseline."

"While that sounds great, not all of us have the flexibility or means to do that, Kai," I scoff, a little irritated that he suggested it so casually.

"Look, I wanted to wait to talk to you about this, but I might as well just tell you now. I want to set up a savings account and trust for Akio. I want to support him and you however I can. I guess what I'm trying to say is you can afford a sick day, if you want."

"That's very kind and generous, but I can't accept your money, Kai. It's too much," I say, pinching the bridge of my nose, willing myself not to cry. I have kept it together somehow all goddamn day and I am not going to fall apart now.

"I'm not taking no for an answer, Kendall. Isn't it exhausting being the sole provider for both of you? Don't you want things to be a little easier? I never want you guys to feel like you are struggling. Not when I can help."

"Of course it's exhausting. It's so much pressure trying to be everything for him by myself. Of course I want softness and ease and to be taken care of for once."

"Then let me take care of you, both of you. Please," he begs. His voice is a little softer but I know he's not going to give up on this.

"Fine. I'm only agreeing to this because I'm so tired and I physically and emotionally cannot have this argument right now. But I resent the fact that you think I can't take care of him. I'm doing the best I can with what I have." If he meant to bruise my ego or damage my pride, he certainly hit the mark. Somehow, I know he had nothing but the purest intentions but still, I'm frustrated. With my head back against the seat and my eyes growing heavy, I resign myself to this new reality. Where Akio has two loving and supportive parents in his corner. And I don't have to do everything alone.

"Kendall, come on, you know that's not it. I think you are doing an amazing job with him. I just want to help, okay?" he pleads, weaving his hand in mine. It's warm and comforting and somehow, the contrast of his rough palms rubbing circles against my soft skin soothes me to sleep.

***

I WAKE UP GROGGY and confused as to why I'm in Akio's bed with him and about fifteen stuffed animals. Pulling my phone out of my pocket, I realize it's 3:00 and that Kai must have carried us both in the house. Trying not to wake Akio, I slip my arm out from under him and tip toe out to the living room. Kai is sleeping open mouthed and snoring on the couch, with nothing more than one of Akio's tiny blankets. He must be freezing. It barely covers one of his arms. I kneel next to the couch and take his hand in mine, stroking it gently.

"Come on, you can't sleep on this couch. It's terribly uncomfortable," I say, urging him to get up. "Come to bed."

"Mm, are you sure, Ken?" he mumbles sleepily. "I'm fine here."

"Kai, you don't even have a blanket big enough to cover half your body and your back will be killing you tomorrow. I can't in good conscience let you sleep on this couch."

"Okay," he replies. I pull him by his hand leading him to my room and he follows me with both eyes still closed. We crawl into my bed and slip under the covers, him on the left, me on the right, and it feels so familiar, so us. But we aren't an us anymore—I'm not sure what we are to each other.

"Hey, Ken?" he whispers.

"Yes, Kai?"

"Do you sleep on the right side of the bed because..." *Because those are the spots we claimed when we first started sleeping together.*

Because that is where I fall asleep no matter what bed I'm in. Because the left has always been reserved for you. But he doesn't finish his sentence and neither do I.

Instead, I say "Goodnight, Kai. Sweet dreams."

"Sweet dreams, Ken," he whispers against my hair before pulling my body in closer to him, his chest molded to my back.

"Is this okay?" he murmurs.

"Yes, now go to sleep."

It's a few hours later when I wake up startled and relieved to find Kai next to me. He had come when I called. Some part of me knew he always would. He drove us home, he carried us inside. He stayed. He wasn't going anywhere even though I had deserted him all those years ago.

Wait, drove us home, in his car?

My brain and my heart scramble to come to terms with the fact that Kai, in all his goodness, must have installed a car seat unbeknownst to me, at some point between our reunion a few weeks ago and now. The realization grips my chest and tears sting the corners of my eyes.

I know I'm not worthy of his patience, his kindness, his devotion. But I love him for it anyways.

***

T**HE SUNLIGHT PEEKING THROUGH** my bedroom window wakes me up earlier than I would have liked. I feel something warm and hard behind me. No, someone, not something. Kai's rock solid body is spooning mine, his hand curled around my waist and his fingers just barely grazing my boob. He must feel me stirring, because he starts drawing lazy circles on my stomach sending delicious shivers down my spine. I forgot how good it feels to wake up next to him, share a bed with him, and live my life with him by my side.

"Careful, Kai, or it will be very difficult to take it slow," I warn.

His teeth graze my ear, and he kisses my neck tenderly. "So, do you want me to stop?" The only thing I offer is a shake of my head.

"If I feel you right now, how wet are you going to be for me?" he whispers seductively.

"Pretty sure I'm bone dry," I lie. It's a ridiculously absurd lie. I don't even know why I tell it. He laughs and it's deep and husky.

"Can I find out for myself?"

"Please do." His fingertips trail my torso and he plays with the hem of my lace underwear. They disappear underneath the thin material and I swear he's moving at a glacial pace just to torture me. He always enjoyed a good tease. Then he starts stroking me slowly, my core already throbbing for him. He slips one finger inside me, pulsating in and out while stroking my clit. He adds another finger, eliciting a deep moan from me.

"Bone dry, huh?" he says, pumping harder.

"Mhm," I murmur, reaching my hand back and tugging on his neck. My fingernails scrape his hair and my back arches off the bed. I angle myself towards him giving him more access to all of me, my body pleading for more of him.

"As much as I like fucking you with my fingers, I'd prefer to taste you," he grates out, capturing my mouth in his. I pull away, grasping his arm, shocked I'm even considering what he's asking.

"Kai, this is risky enough as it is. Akio could walk in at any moment and catch us. He'd probably be scarred for life!"

"Kendall, you're drenched and you're so close I can feel it." A pause. "It will take me less than a minute. Two minutes tops."

God, I forgot how cocky he could be sometimes—knowing he could get me to fold like a lawn chair with very little convincing. But he's right and we both know it.

"Okay," I hear myself say breathily and I know I'm entirely at his mercy.

He flips me over onto my back in one swift motion and yanks my underwear down with haste and hunger in his eyes. Kneeling at the edge of the bed, he slings both legs over his shoulders and plants tender kisses along each thigh, kneading them as he goes. I grip the sheet in my hands, feeling like I might combust.

"Kai, please," I beg. "I need you." He pauses for a moment and I'm certain I'm going to kill him.

"What's this scar on the inside of your thigh from?" He kisses and suckles the exact spot he's referring to and then pulls his head away so I have a better view.

"Akio and I were climbing a tree in the park and I fell and scraped the inside of my leg pretty bad."

"Hmm," he hums against me and the vibration of his mouth on my skin causes a descent into madness. "I didn't recognize it and I have every inch of you memorized," he admits. I know he did because I had every inch of him memorized too.

"That's very nice, Kai, but could we get back to what we were doing...please?"

"So eager, Ken," he chuckles and I can hear the arrogant smile in his voice. I give him a playful tug on his hair hoping it hastens his pace. His tongue swipes a line up my center and I moan.

He takes me in his mouth, sucking and licking, swirling his tongue in frenzied circles over my delicate bundle of nerves while he continues to fuck me with his fingers. I'm so close to shattering into a million pieces; I can feel the orgasm building in every cell of my body. Every touch branding me with heat and need. He flicks his tongue against my clit, bringing me higher and higher.

"Kai," I moan breathlessly. "I'm so close," I say, pulling on his hair and bucking against his mouth.

"I know baby, come for me." And I do. I'm an avalanche crashing down a mountain. I'm a flower bending towards the sun, basking in its warmth. Kai is the sun. He always has been. He might be torrential downpours and turbulent storm clouds to everyone else. But to me he felt like sunshine. A warm golden light poured through an open window.

I ride his face, shamelessly bucking and writhing as the orgasm washes over me and the shockwaves course through my body. His voice has haunted my dreams and a few of my nightmares for years.

Now here he is, in the flesh, bringing me to the brink and sending me careening over the edge, hoping he'll be there to catch me.

Even if I don't deserve it.

He kisses his way up my body slowly, gently, and I collapse in his arms. He presses a kiss to my forehead and then starts tugging his pants on over his boxers.

"Wait, I didn't get a chance to make you feel good, Kai. You know...return the favor."

He turns to me, a sly smirk on his face, and without warning, scoops me up and places me in his lap so I'm straddling him. He cups my face in his hands and stares at me like I'm the most beautiful thing he has ever seen. It's been so long since I've been looked at like that. But that's not really what floors me. That's not the thing that sinks its claws in. The truth is that it's been too long since *Kai* has looked at me like that. Like we have only ever belonged to each other. Like he would tear apart the world just to get to me. Like infinity days plus one wouldn't be enough time to hold the depths of his love, the sheer magnitude of it. I've never considered myself a romantic, but I come to the realization that everyone deserves a person in their life that looks at them the way Kai Matsumoto is looking at me right now. The way he has looked at me since we were seventeen.

"Just so you know, I plan to wreck and worship your body on every surface in this apartment and then when we're done with that, I plan on fucking you on every surface in my apartment. We'll have plenty of time and opportunities to make each other feel good. But today, I wanted you to have a release. I wanted to taste you come apart because it's so goddamn sexy and I know you needed it. Don't worry about me."

I wrap my arms around him and hug him, clinging to him like a baby koala. I can't believe I ever let this man go. I'm not entirely sure I can allow him to leave this bed now, let alone my apartment later. This man who always knows exactly what I need without me ever saying the words, who makes my body, heart, and soul ache for him.

"What's that for?" he asks, holding me tighter, embracing me with his massive arms and cradling my head.

"I just missed you so much. I missed being with you and I missed the way you make me feel and..." *Fuck*. I feel tears starting to wet the corners of my eyes.

"The earth-shattering orgasms?" he jokes.

I pull away from his chest, eyeing him questioningly, my hand planted firmly above his heart. He realizes his mistake almost immediately, his facial expression rearranging into one of worry and trepidation.

"Is that what this is about for you?" I ask, suddenly feeling stupid and self-conscious and a whole other host of emotions I can't pin down.

"Kendall, no. This is not just about hooking up or a quick fuck. It was just a joke," he sighs and places his hand over mine.

"This is about me winning you back. This is about making things work with you if that is what you want. This is about proving to you we are meant to be together despite all the shit life has thrown our way. This is about finally being able to go after what I want and I want you, I want your whole damn heart, Kendall. I want your complicated and your messy and all your fucking baggage, our baggage." He pauses for a second and I don't dare say anything, worried I'll ruin the moment. Ruin his perfect declaration of everything he has been holding on to all of these years. He caresses my bottom lip with the pad of his thumb and says softly, "The mind-blowing sex, all the times I get to hear you scream my name, the sounds you make in the dark just for me, the pieces of your soul that only I have access to—those things are just a bonus. The fortunate consequences of loving you."

I'm certain those words will be my undoing.

"I don't deserve you, Kai. Your understanding or your kindness. I don't deserve any of this. Not after what I did," I reply, wiping a stray tear from my cheek. Goddamn it, I really didn't want to cry in front of him—not yet anyways. He kisses away the tears on my face so slowly, like he's terrified I'll bolt at any sudden movements.

"Regardless of what you have done or what has happened in the past, you deserve happiness and love. We deserve a real chance. And when I say we, know I mean the three of us. Me, you, and Akio. We deserve the chance to be a family. I know you don't see that yet. But I have confidence that you will, that we'll get there."

I nod silently, unsure how to respond.

This isn't the same Kai who refused to let the mask slip, who couldn't bear the thought of wearing his heart on his sleeve. This isn't the shy anxiety ridden teenager who blacked out in large crowds and whenever he had to speak in public. No, this Kai is dripping with confidence and smooth words. He's willing to lay it all on the line because he knows the risk is worth the reward. This Kai has been burned and he doesn't want vengeance or closure even. He wants a future with me. *With us.* The one thing I'm not positive I can give him. But I desperately want to believe I can. That this future he's talking about isn't some ludicrous fantasy but something we can build together, piece by piece. Brick by brick. But to do, that we have to be willing to peel back the layers and expose the cracks in our foundation, the uncomfortable truths that landed us here in the first place. And I'm not sure either of us are ready to do that yet.

"I want all those things with you too, Kai, I just..." my voice is thick in my throat, all the words I want to say stuck there.

"I know," he squeezes my hand tightly. "It's going to take time and patience and work. But I'm not going anywhere and neither are you this time—if I have anything to say about it," he smiles wide, melting me into a thousand little pieces. "Now that that's settled, how bout we eat something. I'm thinking pancakes. How do you feel about that? Does Akio like pancakes?" he asks, tucking a stray curl behind my ear. "Also, if I'm intruding, let me know. If you two need the day to yourself that's fine."

"He loves pancakes, and I want you to stay, Kai. Spend the day with us," I clarify.

Spend forever with me. Spend a thousand lifetimes with me and then a thousand more. I don't want to go one more day without you being a permanent fixture in my life.

"And that's not just because I gave you a perfect ten out of ten orgasm?" he laughs and presses a soft kiss to my temple.

"It was a fifteen out of ten actually, and no, it's not just because of that. You're the better cook out of the two of us—or did you forget?" I quip and jab him with my finger. He wrestles me to the bed and starts tickling me relentlessly.

Chapter 22

Kai

After spending the morning decidedly not taking anything slow, I slip out of her bedroom in search of ingredients for pancakes. I find oil and enough pancake mix for one batch in the cabinets and eggs in the fridge. Which is honestly better than what I'd anticipated. Kendall never really liked to cook, that much hasn't changed.

I try to rummage around as quietly as possible for a mixing bowl, measuring cups, and utensils, hoping Kendall and Akio can rest for a little longer. Just as my head starts to drift back to her beautiful lust filled face and the sounds she makes when she's on the edge, I hear a shuffling sound behind me. I turn around to find Akio in his bedroom doorway, blankie in hand. He walks over to me warily and looks at everything I have laid out on the counter.

I crouch down to his eye level, hands on my knees. "Hey, Mommy is still resting. I thought maybe I could make us pancakes. Have you ever made them before?"

He shakes his head no.

"Do you want to help me?" I ask and only get a slight nod in return. This kid is certainly going to make me work for it—his love, attention, and trust. And I know he has me to thank for that. I wouldn't call myself unfriendly, but reserved, quiet, guarded—those are accurate descriptors. But I'm willing to put in the work and effort, whatever it takes. I'm more than ready to earn that title of Dad. I pull over a chair to the counter and help him stand on top of it.

"So first, we have to measure the mix. We'll pour it in this measuring cup." I pour in the correct amount, letting him hold the box and pour in a little too. His eyes widen as he does it and I detect the smallest hint of a smile on his face. Then I show him how to add the oil and crack the eggs into the mixing bowl, which is arguably his favorite part. He claps his hands in anticipation when I reach to get another egg from the carton.

"Do you want to try cracking some eggs in your own bowl with me?" He nods excitedly.

I get another small bowl out from the cabinet, break an egg into it demonstratively, and proceed to do one with him with my hands over his. Just as we pour the first two pancakes in the large skillet, I hear Kendall clear her throat behind me.

"So, what do we have here, chefs?" she asks, walking over to Akio and giving him a hug as she rests her chin on top of his head.

Akio shouts. "Eggs Mommy, eggs!"

She smiles at him and he grins back at her with pride, even if all he did was add more shells to the batter. She rubs her nose against his and laughs, "The *eggs* smell delicious. I'll get us some plates." Kendall sets the table for two and pulls his highchair up to the edge.

After I remove the last pancake from the pan and slip it onto my plate, we sit around the table together. Kendall tears his pancakes into bite size pieces and pours us all glasses of orange juice. She chuckles as Akio licks syrup and pancake crumbs off his fingers and then reaches for more. I watch her spear a piece of food with her fork and shove it in her mouth before smiling at me. She looks at me and tilts her head as if to say *what?*

"Do I have food on my face or something?" she asks, embarrassment blooming on her cheeks.

"No, you don't have food on your face, Ken...I'm just happy, that's all," I explain, knowing how I feel is much more than that. It's everything. All the pieces start to come together. I might as well be watching the sun rise for the first time. That's what this moment feels like, the gravity of it.

I could fall in love with this life.

In fact, I already am, and I have no idea how to stop it. I don't think I could even if I wanted to.

For the first time in my life, I feel whole. Content. Serene. All the chaos in my head is momentarily silenced. I know I'll be chasing this calm for the rest of my life and I'll do whatever I need to do to keep it.

***

"So..." I say, EDGING closer to the door but not quite feeling ready or willing to leave them. We spent the entire day together and I find myself starting to miss them before I've even walked out the door. I scratch at the back of my neck, hoping she'll know what to say after the last twenty-four hours that we've spent together.

"Thank you for coming to the hospital last night and staying with me, with us. It means a lot," she finally whispers, moving from the doorway to stand directly in front of me.

"Of course, I wouldn't want to be anywhere else. I loved spending the day with you guys. I just wish I didn't have to leave," I admit, eyeing her cautiously, trying to gauge her feelings.

"Me too, but I do think it's important for us to have some boundaries, especially with Akio until we figure out what this is," she gestures, pointing between us.

"So, no more sleepovers?" I joke, trying to hide my disappointment.

"As much as I enjoyed last night and this morning, I don't think we should have any more sleepovers. Not yet anyways. I don't want to confuse him. But that doesn't mean we can't spend time together, or go on dates..."

"Okay, dates. I can live with that for now," I answer, brushing my hand across her cheek. She leans into my touch and sighs, staring up at me, like there's a question on the tip of her lips.

"What about kissing you goodbye? Would that be pushing a boundary?" I ask, even though I already know the answer. And she's right. We should be setting boundaries to protect Akio. We shouldn't be rushing into anything. But I can't help how much

I want her in my life, how much I need her to be mine again. The smart thing to do, the safest thing, would be to maintain some type of friendship until we have a better handle on things. But the way she's looking at me tells me she's feeling this too, like all caution and restraint have effectively been thrown out the window. The embers that were stoked when we first reconnected weeks ago, now being fanned into scorching hot flames.

"Yes, but it doesn't change the fact that I want you to," she answers. Thankfully I'm not feeling smart or safe right now. I don't hesitate or give her a chance to change her mind. I grasp her face in my hands and bring her mouth to mine. She tastes warm and sweet. She kisses me back lovingly, longingly, her hands twining around my neck. It's a promise and a declaration of all the unsaid words between us.

This kiss feels like I've finally been able to come *home*.

She pulls back slightly and I really wish she hadn't. She slides her arms down so they're no longer clasping my neck and I immediately miss her warmth, her touch.

"Kai, I don't know how to do this. How to be us again with all the history and baggage between us," she concedes. Her confession stings a little but it's not surprising.

"Me either, but I think we muddle through until we figure things out. Until we figure out how to be us again. But Kendall?"

"Yes?"

"You know we'll never be the us we were before all this happened. That version of us is long gone," I acknowledge and I hate saying the words but I know I have to.

"I'm painfully aware, Kai and I know it's my fault," she responds through gritted teeth, her eyes looking everywhere but my face.

"No, that's not what I mean. I'm not trying to place blame right now. What I mean is we were young, naïve...we were practically kids." I pause, taking the time to coil my arm around her waist and pull her to me, so close I can feel her heart hammering out of her chest. Our noses brush and she looks up at me through thick dark lashes, relaxing in my arms.

"We may not be able to have the same relationship we had before, but maybe we can have something better, something stronger because we had to work so fucking hard for it. To find our way back to each other. But I want that. I want to find my way back to you. Because make no mistake, Kendall, there is no part of me that ever wanted to let you go in the first place."

She kisses me again, crashing her mouth to mine and stealing the breath from my lungs, obliterating any rational thoughts I had about maintaining boundaries or playing it safe or whatever the fuck. And I know she feels the same way. She doesn't have to say it.

Chapter 23

Kai

I CHECK MY PHONE and there is an unread text from Aiden.

hey man, how are you feeling about your next game?

Pretty good, their offense isn't as strong as ours and

it's a rebuilding year for them

Why?

just wondering. I might have something cooking for this game and a few others

could you be any more vague?

I placed some bets on your game in Rochester

And D.C.

> *WTF man you know I can't be involved in any shit like that.*

> *I know I know. I'm not asking you to do anything other than bring your A game*

> *And score at least one goal…*

When I don't respond, he continues and something about his tone sounds eager. Desperate even.

> *When have I ever asked you for anything?*

> *goodbye Aiden*

> *I'm deleting this thread*

Aiden would always question me from time to time about games I had coming up and I know he likes to gamble, along with dabbling in drugs and overindulging in alcohol—but this feels different. He has never asked for specific outcomes before and I always keep our conversations general, never giving him anything tangible he could latch on to. I love Aiden and he's one of my closest friends, even and especially after all the shit we've been through. But I have no dreams of losing my career, not when I worked my ass off to get it.

My brain drifts back to the first time I realized Aiden's life was far from perfect. It's two weeks after we beat the shit out of each other over Kendall and right before I realized I had been punishing him for something that wasn't his fault.

"So…" he says.

"So. Kendall wants us to resolve things. Whatever that means." I respond and take a drink of my iced tea, condensation droplets forming on the outside of the glass.

"Yeah, I know. Listen, I'm sorry I called her a slut and all the other things I said about her this year." He looks down at his

paper plate, rolling a piece of uneaten crust between his thumb and forefinger.

"I'm sorry I broke your nose," I affirm, looking directly at him.

He pops the piece of crust in his mouth and wipes the grease off his hands with a flimsy napkin. "Lucky for me girls find bruises and a crooked nose endearing," he grins, and I think that's going to be the end of the conversation. But he presses on, undeterred.

"Seriously though, can I ask you something, Kai?"

"Sure, fire away," I reply.

"Why do you hate me so much?"

Why do I hate him so much? What is it about him that makes me so adversarial, makes me want to bash his fucking head in almost every time we talk? I'm not even sure how to answer his question. Somewhere along the way, all the squabbles and arguments blended together and the root of this rivalry became muddied.

"I feel like it's mutual hatred, don't you think?" I try to play it off as a joke, but it just makes me sound like even more of an asshole.

"I don't know. I feel like you came back to school after your accident and I was public enemy number one. I just followed suit. But I never had any real reason to hate you," he confesses and it sounds raw, honest.

"I don't know if you remember but the day of the accident, I was supposed to get a ride home from the game...with you."

"Oh." He pauses. I can tell he's rolling over that statement in his head, picking it apart.

"So, you blame me then for the accident, your mom?" he questions.

I shrug. "I needed someone to blame other than myself." I admit, peering down at my hands.

"Wow, that's fucked up man," he finally says.

"I know..." I trail off, realizing how stupid and juvenile it all sounds out loud.

"I get it. I'll be the villain in your story if you need me to be, but I think we both know terrible shit happens to good people all the time, and there isn't usually a reason or an explanation. That's just life."

"Yeah, what terrible things have happened in your life, golden boy?" I inquire, slightly ticked off, but starting to warm up to the idea of not hating him.

"Is that what you think?" he scoffs. "My life is great and everything is wrapped in a perfect fucking bow?"

"I guess," I mumble, shrugging my shoulders.

"Well, after your accident, my mom was in rehab for two years and it almost destroyed my family," he explains in a hushed tone.

"Fuck, Aiden. I'm sorry. I didn't know."

"Well, why would you? You stopped talking to me. I mean things are different now, better. She's been sober for almost six years. But it doesn't take away the feeling of always waiting for the other shoe to drop."

Another phone notification pulls me out of my memory but I make a mental note to check on him soon. Something about this text exchange feels off, maybe he's got himself in too deep with gambling or maybe he owes someone money. Maybe I'm overthinking it. Aiden is a grown adult and he can take care of himself. But it doesn't change the unsettling feeling in my stomach or the cold dread slithering up my spine.

CHAPTER 24

KENDALL

THE NIGHT AKIO WENT to the emergency room was the last and only time Kai stayed over. But he's been visiting twice a week for a while now, always bringing thoughtful elaborate gifts for Akio and flowers for me. Sometimes he'll switch it up and bring me coffee exactly the way I like it, or groceries, which is his gentle way of telling me the fridge is too barren. But the important thing is that he's here consistently, without fail for Akio, and a part of me hopes he's here for me too. I'm not sure why I expected anything less. Kai has always been sturdy, dependable, solid. I'm the one who broke his heart and disappeared.

We sneak kisses and lingering hugs that I always wish would turn into more whenever Akio is out of sight. But we never let it go farther than that, even though I desperately want to. Slowly, days turn into weeks and weeks turn into a month and we find ourselves falling into a steady rhythm. It's been easy acclimating ourselves to life with Kai, especially when Akio adores him. So, I know how painful it will be to try to revert back to life without him.

I quickly shake that thought from my head, my fingers hovering over my phone, trying to muster up enough courage to ask Kai out on an official date. I don't know what I'm so scared of. This is the same Kai I used to trick or treat with, the Kai who took my virginity, the Kai whose house I used to have dinner at a million times growing up. The same Kai who came to Pride every year with me and my moms, that I dated for almost five years. But suddenly, I'm nervous, even though I know he won't say no. I know it'll be a resounding yes, but still, my palms are sweating and

my pulse is pounding like a jackhammer. After going back and
forth with myself for days about it, I send off a text to him before
I can chicken out.

Hi

Hey

So I've been thinking would you want to go
on a date this week?

More than anything

I've been meaning to ask you

my schedule has just been nonstop

that's okay

I know sometimes it's hard for you to make
the first move

Kidding

No you're not.

But you're right, it is

So you finally admit it?

Admit what?

I made the original first move

Our first kiss

I KISSED YOU

But if that's what it takes to seal this date then yes Kendall

YOU made the first move

I'm not talking about our first hookup,

I'm talking about our sham wedding

in third grade

Fine. You got me there

Yeah I know

You drive me crazy

in the best possible way

I'm taking that as a compliment

Good, you should

So our date…

How about coffee on Thursday at Milo's?

Sounds good. I'll pick you up

What about Thursday though that's usually my day to see Akio but I have practice at 6

What about this weekend can you come over to see him then?

I have a game Saturday but Sunday I can come over.

I'll make you both dinner

Sounds perfect

CHAPTER 25

KAI

I STARE AT THE contact on my phone, my thumb frozen over the call button. I hadn't spoken to Ryo in a few months. Which was unusual for us. But he had been on sabbatical, trying to figure out his life in Thailand. And I didn't want to bother him with my shit—he had enough of his own problems at the moment. But this situation with Kendall and Akio is complicated and difficult to navigate and I know I need another opinion on it. *Fuck*.

It rings three times before he picks up.

"Hey, long time no talk, baby brother, what's up?" he sounds chipper, almost too chipper. Nothing like how he sounded two months ago when he dropped out of medical school on the verge of a nervous breakdown.

"Hey, how are you?" I wonder.

"I'm okay, been trying to get outside as much as I can. Learning how to surf, getting to know some locals. Ducking dad's calls. It's been good. I'm good," he says and I almost believe him. "How are things with you?"

"I'm okay. Listen, I need to tell you something, okay?"

"Okay..."

"Kendall is kind of back in my life now and she has a son...he's mine. I have a son."

"Oh my god. Okay. Okay. Wait, what the hell do you mean she has a son? How are you just finding out about this now?"

So, I explain the whole story to him and he lets me. He doesn't interrupt or ask questions. He doesn't supply judgement. He gives me the space I need to share this part of my life with him and perhaps the space I need to process it. He's kind, patient, considerate, the way I knew he would be.

"I don't know what to do. I mean, I know I want to try and I want to be in Akio's life but..."

"But she hurt you and lied to you," he finishes.

"Yeah," I admit.

"I mean, this is Kendall we're talking about. She's family for god sake. If she lied about Akio, kept this from you, she probably had a really good reason. I'm not saying just trust her again. I'm not saying forgive her but...It's Kendall."

"Yeah I know," I reply.

"What does your gut say?"

"My gut says we aren't done."

CHAPTER 26

KENDALL

HERE'S THE THING. THE cynics, the critics claim chivalry is dead, that all the good ones are already taken. Those people have never met Kai Matsumoto. Those people have never been on a first date with him. Or in my case, a second first date with him.

He shows up at my apartment with flowers, because of course he has flowers, and that gorgeous smile that does stupid, crazy, beautiful things to my heart. His entire presence sets me off kilter and causes my chest to constrict. The smell of his cologne, woodsy with a hint of spice, the way he moves with quiet grace and confidence, the way he looks at me like I alone am tethering him to this earth. I have to check my pulse to make sure I am, in fact, still breathing. He asks all the right questions, compliments my outfit, holds the door open for me. Stares at me once, twice, *three* times like he can't believe I'm real. And I remember all the little, insignificant, subtle reasons I fell in love with him alongside all the obvious ones.

And isn't that what love is? All the invisible things, the million nuances, that when added up and taken together make someone you can't stand to live without.

***

THE WALK FROM MY apartment complex to his car is short but cold. The gray February day frozen and biting at our skin. Kai curls a protective arm around me, tucking me into his side as we hurry through the parking lot and I'm grateful he can still read me like an open book. Once we get in the car, we sit in comfortable silence broken up by easy smiles and stolen glances. He takes my hand in his, interlacing our fingers and the car suddenly feels like it's a thousand degrees inside. The toasty heated seats, his presence, and the feel of his skin against mine sets my nerves on fire and thaws my frigid body.

How is it that we're this close and still not close enough?

He gets off the exit and all at once, I'm struck by reminders of our youth; the nostalgia for simpler times caresses me like a gentle hug. We pass by familiar streets and restaurants. Hyde park where we spent hours as kids running around, playing, climbing trees, and getting dirt under our fingernails. Jefferson's, the convenience store Kai's dad always used to send him and his brother to for miscellaneous supplies and tools. I've tried to erase his dad from my memories. I don't want them to be tainted by pain. But so much of Kai and his family are ingrained in my childhood. Some places have been demolished, restored, renovated, while other buildings remain untouched by time or circumstance. And I start to believe if a town can survive like this, growing and evolving, adapting and changing, bearing witness to both heartache and hope, yet still retain its unshakeable foundation, the very essence that makes it uniquely and distinctly what it is—if a town can survive this way, maybe we can too. Maybe this thing we used to call us is salvageable after all.

Kai parks the car and quickly skirts around to the passenger side to hold my door open for me. He ushers me inside, his hand resting on the small of my back. It's electrifying, taking root somewhere deep in my body. We walk in the front door of the café and my senses are flooded with the smell of freshly brewed coffee and sugary pastries.

In the back, we find a table tucked into the corner, away from prying eyes. I slide into my chair first and just as he's about to sit down, he surprises me by pulling it to the right. Before I can register his movements, he huffs, "Fuck this, the whole point of going on a date is being able to do things like this." He sits down next to me, his face centimeters from mine, and without the distance of a table separating us, all bets are off. It's more intimate, romantic, and he's so close I can smell his aftershave. He leans in, invading my space and intertwines our hands, his legs knocking against mine underneath the table. Pressing a soft kiss to my temple, he grazes the curve of my ear with his mouth.

"Not being this close to you on a daily basis is absolute fucking torture," he whispers.

Fuck. I don't know what I expected him to say but it definitely wasn't that. I feel my face heating up, my cheeks burning red. *How did he manage to turn my insides to mush and my core molten with just one sentence?*

"Agreed," is all I can choke out and it's strangled. *Agreed? That's the best response I can think of?* He smiles a devilishly handsome smile.

"It's fun making you a little nervous."

"I'm not nervous," I respond but it's completely unconvincing.

"Uh huh," he laughs.

"Fine, maybe I'm just a little flustered."

"Well, it's nice not being the only one for once."

"You mean I've ruffled the professional hockey player worth millions? I find that hard to believe." I pause and then add, "You're the bravest person I know, Kai."

"Not when it comes to you. You fucking terrify me—you always have. It's one of the things I love about you." He still knows exactly what to say and do to make me come undone and I don't know what to make of that. I shift forward wanting to be as close to him as possible, leaning into his chest. If I get any closer, I might as well be in his lap.

"So, I realized there's some things I need to tell you. You know the night you stayed over after Akio was in the hospital? You told me the next day that you never wanted to let me go. I know I have no right to ask this of you, but I really need you to believe me when I say I never wanted to let you go either. It was one of the hardest things I've ever had to do."

I watch him swallow, his eyes never leaving mine.

"If you didn't want to let me go, then why did you? And please don't give me some spiel about protecting me. Because I know it's more than that, that isn't the only reason you left," he says, pain and confusion twisting his features. And there it is, the burning question that's been lingering around us like smoke for the past two months. The one I always knew and feared he'd ask. It sits at the table like an extra person between us and I don't even know how to broach the subject. I can't go there with him, not yet.

"I'm not sure that question is exactly first date material, but I need you to trust me that when I'm ready to talk about it, I will." Because it's not just one question. It's all of them. All the ones that matter anyways.

Why did I break his heart?
Why did I leave without saying goodbye?
Why did I lie about the abortion?
Why didn't I trust what we had?

I can barely answer those questions for myself, never mind for him. But I need to, I want to. He deserves that much.

"Okay," he answers.

"Okay? You believe me?"

"Yeah, Kendall, I do, and I know that whatever happened, whatever I did to make you feel like we couldn't be together, I'll never make that mistake again," he says solemnly.

"Kai, listen to me very carefully. You didn't do anything. I fucked up and I made the biggest mistake of my life leaving you and I've regretted it every day since. Nothing I say now can erase what I've done but hopefully everything will make sense in time."

"I hope so too."

We spend the rest of our coffee date falling into easy conversation, holding hands and straddling the thin line between kissing and making out. Every so often, I have to remind myself we are in a public place and not in the privacy of my apartment or his car. I pull back slightly from a kiss that I wish would turn into more with a mixture of relief and disappointment. Relieved we haven't yet made any mistakes we can't come back from and disappointed because all the things I want to do to him, with him cannot be done in the company of other people.

I can feel his hot breath on my neck. Picture my hands trailing his muscled back, moving down to his torso to feel his abs carved from stone. I imagine his lips tracing my skin, his touch making me delirious with pleasure. Our bodies are molded together, moving in sync—

"Ken?" His voice snaps me out of the fantasy and his deep eyes searching my face ground me. I steel myself ready to answer his question I know is coming.

"What's wrong?" he asks quietly, skimming his thumb over mine. I swallow and will myself to calm down, to continue breathing in and out slowly.

"It's just... it's so hard because I want to do this right. I want to take things slow, but it's hard to do that when we already know what it's like to give ourselves entirely to each other. To be all in. Does that make sense?" I whisper, hoping my rambling makes sense to him.

"Yeah, it does. I think you're scared. Scared of what this could be. Scared to make a mistake. Scared that things will go wrong—or worse, they'll go right. But I'll tell you a secret. I'm scared too, and I know that we're going to figure this out."

"When did you get so wise?" I smirk.

"I don't know but can I let you in on another secret?" he asks, a smile tugging at his lips.

"Do I have a choice?" I joke.

"I'm going to ignore that," he says, his face turning more serious. "But honestly, Ken, we're going to make mistakes. It's inevitable. We just can't let them ruin us this time, okay?"

"That sounds more like a hard truth than a secret," I observe.

"Tomato, tomato," he quips, looking thoroughly satisfied with himself.

Kai leaves the table to put in our order. He saunters over to the counter and it's hard not to stare at him while he does—he's just so easy to look at. His broad frame, his muscular build, and that smile that gives me heart palpitations. And I know I'm not the only one ogling him. The cute blonde behind the counter laughs and twirls her hair around her index finger as she talks to him. Everyone in this café is probably wondering what someone like him is doing with someone like me. I'm self-assured enough to know he only has eyes for me, but smart enough to realize every female in here would donate a non-vital organ just to be with him. In his orbit.

If I didn't know him any better, I would be incredibly intimidated by his near Herculean body. His face that suggests he's the offspring of Hawaiian gods, a byproduct of superior genes. But I do know him better. I've known him since I was five. So, I know he's not a god among men—he just resembles one. The same way I know he hates melon. That he's allergic to mushrooms. That when he sneezes, it's always three times. That he sometimes gets disabling panic attacks and loathes public speaking. That he's a textbook introvert who has been forced to act like an extrovert his entire life. So instead of being threatened by his beauty, I accept it for what it is, a small facet of who *he* is. Knowing that underneath the broodiness, the stunning armor, the facade of unwavering confidence, there's a human who bleeds just like the rest of us. And it's this immutable fact that endears him to me even more.

He returns a few minutes later with his hands full and a tray piled with delicious food and steaming mugs of coffee. It takes me a second to realize he remembered all my favorite things.

"So, that's one blueberry scone, one chocolate chip muffin, a bacon egg and cheese on a cheddar bagel to split, my coffee, and your abomination that you call coffee," he rattles.

"A peppermint white chocolate latte extra whip?" I wonder, beaming at him with excitement.

"Uh huh," he replies, setting the tray down on the table.

"I don't even drink coffee for the caffeine anymore. It's just part of my personality at this point," I remark, causing a deep throaty chuckle to escape Kai's mouth.

"You remembered..." I trail off, glancing from the food to him.

"Well, yeah, you love scones, but their blueberry is your favorite and we got lucky. It was the last one. And we always used to split an egg sandwich, you know, offset the sweet with the savory. Shit, did I forget something? Did I do something wrong? I kind of just went for it. It was stupid to assume you still like all the same things—" he suddenly looks flustered, worried. It's adorable. Laughable even that this flawless human specimen would be nervous around me, but I revel in it all the same. I take his rough hand in mine.

"No, Kai, it's perfect." *You're perfect*, I want to say but I don't. I can't. The words sit in my throat, coating my tongue like honey. And I can't seem to force them out. Instead, I cup his face, my fingers tracing his bottom lip, and kiss him softly.

CHAPTER 27

KENDALL

A s soon as we leave Milo's, Kai starts fidgeting. I'm not sure why he paused, why we aren't moving towards his car, especially when it's 18 degrees outside.

"So, I kind of have a surprise. I know you thought Milo's was our date but I decided to extend it and take you somewhere special. I hope that's okay." He stares at me, waiting for my answer.

"Yeah, that's fine, but where are we going?" I ask confused, my bones rattling from the gust of wind. He looks both ways before crossing the street and then pulls me by my gloved hand.

"I can't tell you. It's a surprise. Now close your eyes!"

I take a few steps and follow him blindly, trying to keep up with his large strides. Finally, we stop and he says, "Okay, you can look now."

I'm standing in front of K.J. Mason bookshop, an old brick building wedged in between a barbershop and an antique store. A small white sign hanging inside the door reads *closed* in bold red lettering. Another paper inside one of the windowpanes lists their hours. I blink at him and tilt my head.

"I think it's closed. They're only open 8:30-2:00 today."

He smirks and holds the door open for me. "I think they made an exception for us."

"Kai, what are you—" but I can't finish my thought. I'm transfixed by the scene in front of me. The main overhead lights of the bookstore are off, but there are a few smaller lamps turned on and fairy lights strung across the ceiling, in addition to the electronic candles that are sitting on every shelf and flat surface. There are two massive bean bags that could probably fit four people leaning up against the back shelf of books, complete with plush blankets and colorful pillows. And directly in front of me is a circular table adorned in white linen, rose petals, and votive candles with chairs on either side. The table is set for two.

I've been in this bookstore before, many times. I know exactly what the interior looks like. He did this, all of this for me. I can feel him behind me, his thick stubble tickling my cheek. As he wraps his arms around my waist, I cover my mouth to stifle my gasp and tears. I lean into him, letting him embrace me. Letting myself have this moment.

"Kai, how did you do this? When did you do this?" I whisper, still slightly in shock.

"I talked to the owner of the bookstore. I convinced him to let me use it for the price of what it would cost to open and maintain operations for the day. I set all this up late last night and this morning. We can hang out and look at books and the best part is you can take home whatever books you want. As many as you want. On me. We're having dinner delivered to us here. I can only stay until 5:30 but you can stay as long as you want. There will be a car here to take you home when you're ready," he replies, nuzzling my neck. "So, what do you think. Do you like it?"

"I don't even know what to say. I love it," I stammer, turning to him and sliding my hands up his chest and around his neck. "This is the most thoughtful thing anyone has ever done for me, Kai," I admit.

"I would do anything for you," he says, glancing at my lips before his eyes flicker back up to meet mine. And before I have time to talk myself out of it, I'm bringing his face down to mine, kissing him with intensity and hunger and pushing him backwards until his boots meet the edge of the industrial sized bean bag.

"Sit."

He does as instructed, pulling me on top of him. We start laughing as our bodies collide and as soon as his hands touch my skin, it's like it's been set ablaze, something predatory and primal unleashed. Both of our jackets hit the floor and we don't have time to think. Everything we do next is purely reactionary, trying to make up for years of lost time.

He's unzipping my jeans, his hand sliding underneath my shirt and across my rib cage, under my bra to cup my peaked nipple. I nip at his neck, my teeth grazing the sensitive skin on his throat, while I roll my hips against his jeans. He's already thick and erect. The material separating his hard cock from my wet, pleading center is at the same time too much and not enough. I ache to feel him inside me again, to be full of him almost to the point of pain. To have nothing separating our bodies, except the space between our heartbeats. My hands move frantically as I attempt to remove his belt. I'm trying and failing to think of a reason, any reason not to do this with him right now. But need and longing and carnal attraction win out over any sort of rational thinking.

"Ken," he breathes and a switch in my brain flips on. One of us has come to their senses, *thank god*. We stop kissing, both of us breathing hard. He leans his head against the bookshelf, his hands gripping my thighs and his face seems torn.

"I don't think we should do this here. I mean, I'm sure there's cameras in here and we haven't been together like this..." he trails off.

"It's okay, you're right. We got ahead of ourselves. This was probably not the best idea. I don't know what I was thinking," I murmur, sliding off his lap and fumbling around for my shirt. I find it and pull it over my head, suddenly feeling embarrassed.

CHAPTER 28

KAI

*F*UCK. I DON'T EVEN know how I summoned the willpower to stop this. She wanted me. She still wants me just as much as I want her. I'm walking a thin line between restraint and insanity. I need her legs hooked around my waist, her nails sinking into my flesh, need to hear her screaming my name. I need to feel her body detonate with pleasure because of how much she wants this and how undeniably perfect we are together.

But more importantly, more than anything I need her to *stay*. And she needs to stay for the right reasons. There's about one hundred ways for this to go wrong and only one way it could go right. No matter how good she looks straddling my lap, in her black lace bra, her eyes scorching with pure desire. I can't risk scaring her off with something she might regret hours later. And we can't have sex for the first time in three years in a bookstore. I had to draw a line somewhere and now that I have, I feel like I ruined our date.

"Ken, look at me. It's not that I don't want to do this with you. Believe me, I do. I just think it should be somewhere more meaningful and private, okay? Especially if we're trying to take things slow and do this right," I explain, tilting her chin up and repeating her own words back to her. She flinches out of my grasp.

"Right, because your career doesn't need a scandal, and nothing screams scandal like sex with your ex-girlfriend and mother of your child in the middle of a bookstore."

"Woah, Ken, what's happening? That's not it—"

"Are you embarrassed of me? Of us?" she demands, eyes wide. She looks like she might start crying. *Fuck, this is not going how I planned.*

"What? Of course not. How could you think that?" I gently take her hands and hold them in mine. "Whatever it is, we can talk about it. Talk to me."

She plops down next to me on the bean bag so we're sitting shoulder to shoulder. She doesn't say anything for a while and then finally blows out a breath through pursed lips.

"I know you're right. Of course you're right. We obviously can't have sex in a bookstore. We just haven't really talked about what this is and I know you try to keep your private life separate from hockey." She pauses to look down at her chipped nails. "I guess I'm worried that you're embarrassed of me or our baggage. I know I'm not like the other girls you've dated or been with the past couple years, so I get it." She says the last part so quietly I can barely hear her. I've never seen her like this—so small, so unsure of herself.

"Kendall, I have always considered myself lucky. Lucky enough to grow up next door to you, lucky you took me under your wing and became my best friend. Lucky you gave me a chance. Lucky that you somehow fell in love with me. And now I know I'm really fucking lucky because we are getting a second shot at this. I could never be embarrassed of you when you and Akio are the single best thing that has ever happened to me. And for the record, there is absolutely no comparison between you and any other woman I've been with because none of them were you." I explain, pulling her to my chest and stroking her hair.

"So, you aren't trying to hide us, this?" She gestures between us.

"You and Akio mean so much to me. Everything else is small details, background noise. If I'm being protective or cautious, it's because I don't want you both to be thrust into the spotlight or your lives to change unnecessarily. At least not yet. So right now, I think it's best to keep this in our little bubble. What do you think?"

What I don't say is that I'm terrified of putting a label, any label on this because what if it all goes to shit again? If we don't name it, don't put any pressure on it, we could just be us for a little longer.

"Okay, but what is this? What are we doing?" I can hear her silent question, all the things she's afraid to say. *Can we mend what she broke? What are we to each other now, after everything that happened?*

And what is she if not my entire world, my reason for breathing, every thought I've had since she walked back into my life? I'm falling in love with her all over again, that's so painfully obvious to me. But we haven't even scraped the surface of the most difficult conversations we need to have. And the more time I spend with her and Akio, the harder it is to not have those conversations, to not know. But hopefully, my patience will pay off because I deserve some answers before handing over my heart to her again.

I let out a deep sigh and decide to go with a version of the truth, "We're figuring it out the best we can. Taking it day by day."

***

TWO CANDLES SIT BETWEEN us on the table, lighting up her face with an ethereal glow. Staring at her leaves me breathless. It always has. That much hasn't changed. It makes me wonder why she chose me all those years ago. Why she kept choosing me. But I guess all that matters is that she did.

I watch her stab a pillow of lobster ravioli and delicately pop it into her mouth. A smile plays on her lips and I could have sworn I heard her make a sound that could only be described as something between a hum and a moan. She eyes me, carefully holding my gaze.

"Why are you staring at me like that?" she asks.

"Because I love making you happy and it's clear you're very very happy right now based on the little song and dance you do after every bite of ravioli." She laughs and the sound nearly swallows me whole.

"I didn't even realize I still did that. That's embarrassing."

"On anyone else maybe. But on you it's adorable."

Her cheeks flush and she says, "Thank you I guess?" in between bites.

"You're welcome," I say with a grin. "I'm surprised you haven't asked me for any of my short rib yet. I saved some specifically for you."

"I don't want any short rib actually." God, she's so stubborn, immovable at times. She's going to make me force her hand.

"More for me," I say, slowly moving one of the last bites to my mouth.

"Okay fine. I do want to try it," she concedes. I lean over the table and feed her the last piece on my plate.

"Oh my god, that's good," she moans again and I have to tell my dick to chill the hell out.

"Aren't you happy I saved it for you?"

"Mhm," she says as sauce drips down her face. She uses the back of her hand to wipe it away and then licks her fingertips, savoring every last decadent drop. I didn't know eating could be sexy. But I guess very little isn't sexy when it comes to her. Getting up, I take her hands and start pulling her to her feet and towards my chair.

"Kai, what are you doing?"

"I missed you. You weren't close enough," I explain, planting her on my lap. She tucks her head into my neck and the soft curls of her hair provide me with a much needed pillow.

"You're right. This is much better," she decides. I hum in agreement. "Akio would have loved that short rib. It was so good," she says curling into my chest.

"Yeah?" I wonder, realizing there's still so much I don't know about my son. "I don't know many toddlers who would eat short rib."

"He can be picky but lately he has been into short rib, meat-loaf, and steak. But it has to be slathered in something," she chuckles.

"That makes sense; he's a kid after my own heart."

"I can't believe you remembered all my yapping about my dream dates when we were in undergrad. That's impressive, Kai, and really sweet," she admits happily.

"There's very little I could forget about you. Speaking of old memories, do you remember the pact we made in high school?" I ask.

"Of course," she smiles. "Why?" she asks, staring up at me.

"I think we should make a pact again."

"I think we're a little past that, don't you think?" she scoffs.

"I don't mean a virginity pact. I mean we decide not to have sex until we've figured things out, worked on this. Until we trust each other more. Besides, sex was never our issue, if you recall," I say, burying my nose in her hair. *God, she smells good.*

"Okay, yeah, maybe you're right. We were pretty good at that aspect of our relationship. Sex complicates things and we need to try to uncomplicate things." She's taking this better than I thought she would.

"But what about hooking up, doing other things...is that al-lowed for the duration of this pact?" she wonders, her hazel eyes gleaming with mischief.

"I think everything else aside from fucking is on the table. What do you think?"

"Let's do it."

It's either one of the smartest decisions or the dumbest deci-sions I've ever made, I can't tell. I suppose there's still time for it to be both.

The rest of our date goes smoothly. Kendall seems happier, lighter, like some weight has been lifted after our conversations. We spend the next two hours laughing and talking about nothing and everything. She curls up next to me with her arms full of books and a grin plastered on her face and I'm certain that I want to make all her dream dates come true. No matter how ridiculous or outlandish they might seem. Because seeing her this happy, making her smile is a drug I'll never be able to quit.

CHAPTER 29

KAI

2011

JUST AS SHE REACHES for my float again, I pull her hand closer, wrap my arm around her waist, and bring her in for a hug. I missed having her this close to me all summer. I hold her against my chest as she wriggles and laughs and I realize I will never get tired of that sound—her laughing. She unsuccessfully tries to free herself but I eventually let her perch on the end of my float. She stares at me, head cocked to the side.

"Why are you looking at me like that?" I ask.

"I don't know, you seem different," she shrugs.

"Different how?"

"I don't know. More mature maybe, or older?" Not at all what I expected her to say.

"Oh okay."

She continues to stare at me silently as she kicks her feet in the murky water. She giggles and pulls her feet out to avoid the minnows.

"Listen, Ken, I'm sorry I was being weird before about camp. I was embarrassed and I just wanted to not have to think about it anymore."

"It's okay, Kai. I'm sorry I made you tell me. I knew something was bothering you. We don't have to talk about it anymore if you don't want to."

"That's it? You're just going to drop it, captain of the debate team?"

"Yeah, I'm just going to drop it...for *now*." For now is the best I'm going to get from her.

"I should probably tell you the rest."

"What do you mean the rest? What are you talking about?"

I wring my hands together. "I got into a fight at camp too—" I start to explain.

"Excuse me, what? Why didn't you lead with that, Kai? Who are you and what did you do with my gentle giant? Tell me everything. Do not leave out any details," she demands eagerly.

"The guys all know me and you are close. That we live on the same street, we hang out all the time. One night, Aiden snuck in some alcohol and we all got pretty drunk. I didn't want to but they kind of forced us. They started asking if we were together and why we hung out all the time if we weren't fucking. I kept saying we were just best friends. But Aiden wouldn't leave it alone. Then he said, 'She's smoking hot. If you won't fuck her, I will. Ass like that I doubt she's a virgin,' and that's when I punched him. That's pretty much it."

She stares at me, eyes wide like saucers. "Holy shit, Kai. I can't believe you did that. Aiden's a douchebag anyways. I've always said he could use a swift punch in the face."

"I know you have."

"Thanks for protecting my honor," she quips.

"I wasn't trying to protect your honor. I just wanted him to stop running his mouth. He was being a disrespectful asshole."

"I know. Thank you. He's also wrong. I've got a great ass and I'm still a virgin."

I can feel my cheeks heat up at Kendall's mention of the word virgin. But I'm not really sure what to say and I know she can sense my hesitation.

"To which you say...so am I. If only to make me feel better," she continues.

"I don't have the confidence to talk to girls much less sleep with one," I admit.

"Bullshit, Kai. We talk all the time," she challenges.

"That's different. You're my best friend. Talking with you is easy. Besides, I don't have to do a lot of the talking with you," I say jokingly.

"Oh, shut up, Kai! How about we make a pact?"

"What kind of pact?" I ask, intrigued.

"If neither of us have had sex by the end of senior year, we do the deed. With each other."

"You're serious?" I press, eyebrows raised and very skeptical of this plan.

"Deadly," she responds, her warm hazel eyes locked on mine. Ken never backed down from a challenge—that and she was true to her word. Both of those things make me hesitate. But not for long.

"Okay fine," I hear myself say against my better judgment and shake her hand with a smile.

Little did I know we wouldn't even make it until the end of the school year. That we would both lose our virginity when she snuck into my room during our senior year ski trip. I had no idea that what we'd do would irrevocably alter my DNA and brain chemistry, giving our relationship legs and claws, definition and depth. It was sweet and fleeting but it also felt infinite, like forever. She gave me the kind of divine salvation and brutal vulnerability that is only ever true of your first love.

Kendall was my first and after that, I knew I wanted her to be my only.

CHAPTER 30

KENDALL

I T'S NOTHING AND EVERYTHING. It's such a simple thing, really, him making dinner, taking care of us, showing up. I have half a mind to pinch myself and make sure he's real and not some dream I'm going to wake up from.

Kai is standing over the tiny stove in my kitchen stirring gnocchi or tortellini. Whatever it is, it smells amazing. He's even wearing my *Breaking Bad* apron that says "Let's cook" for fuck's sake, an apron that I have never once put to good use. Until now. He looks good, really good cooking for us in my kitchen. Like he-is-the-only-thing-I-want-for-dessert good. But I shut that part of my brain off, remembering the conversation we had on our date. *No sex until we trust each other.* God knows when that will be.

He turns around to look at us and smiles, some of his dark hair falling in his eyes. Akio and I continue to make "ingredients" for dinner out of Play-Doh and it's in this moment that I wish I hadn't waited so long to let Kai into our life. Because it's becoming more and more clear that he belongs here, with us. Perhaps he always has. I hope he knows that, that he can feel it too.

After dinner, Kai suggests getting craft hot cocoa from one of the cafés down the street. They have all sorts of signature drinks like a gigantic hot chocolate that comes with an actual s'more on top of it. It's late, we're all stuffed from the delicious meal Kai made, and by the time we get home, it will be past Akio's bedtime and he will be all hopped up on sugar. I try my best to reason with them, but my attempts are futile and I'm outnumbered. Akio's pleading face alone would be enough to sway me. But both of them together? It's a done deal.

A half hour later, Kai is putting in our order at Cocoa Loco while Akio and I find a cozy table. As soon as we sit down and rest our backs on the metal chairs, I spot a familiar face approaching us at a clip. *Fuck*. Doctor Beckett, well, Julian Beckett to me. At least he used to be.

Julian Charles Beckett III reeks of privilege and belongs to a family that comes from old money. Filthy rich, one percent kind of money. The kind that easily paid for his undergraduate tuition and shelled out hundreds of thousands of dollars for med school. He and I are not the same; we don't lead similar lives. And even if we could, there was one major barrier in our way. And yet, I stayed with him for months longer than I should have.

Hindsight, I guess.

Julian is dreamy in the way 90s teenage heartthrob Heath Ledger was dreamy. Golden locks, always perfectly coiffed, arresting crystal blue eyes, a strong sharp jaw, and the kind of dazzling smile that makes your core tighten. Not to mention he has the charm and ego to back it up. I'm sure he'll make some woman very happy one day but it won't be me. Because for all that he could offer, for all that he was, he still *wasn't* Kai.

"Kendall, hey," he says warmly.

"Hi," I respond a little too loudly. My eyes flick nervously to Kai and thankfully, his back is still facing us. Panic starts to bloom in my chest, especially since I didn't exactly tell Kai the truth about Julian. I get up to hug him at the same time he bends down to place a kiss on my cheek and I wish right then I could die of embarrassment. He smiles politely, ignoring my awkwardness. Julian looks, well, he looks great. And, I, of course, look like a frazzled, exhausted mother of a two-year-old.

"So, how are things? How are you guys?" he asks standing straight, hands in the pockets of what are no doubt very expensive jeans.

"We're good, everything is good. How are you?" Just as he starts to respond, Kai appears with our drinks, setting them down on the table and interrupting our less-than-ideal exchange.

"Uh, Julian this is...my...well, this is Kai." I stumble over my words with a mixture of nerves and uncertainty. *Because honestly, what the hell are we even and how are we supposed to explain it to people?*

Kai glances uncomfortably from me to him and finally extends his hand.

"Ah, Kai, I'm Julian, nice to meet you," he says with way more enthusiasm than I would expect from an ex-boyfriend.

"How do you two know each other?" Kai asks deliberately, although I suspect he already knows the answer.

"We know each other from the hospital. I had Akio as a patient once or twice," he explains with an easy grin, conveniently leaving out the part where we dated for five months. But why would he do that? Why come to my rescue when our breakup was less than amicable?

"Anyways, it was good to see you guys, Kendall. Enjoy your hot chocolates. Nice to meet you, Kai," he turns and walks back towards his table, where a beautiful brunette is waiting for him.

***

"S O, THAT'S YOUR EX." A statement, not a question.

"That's my ex," I confirm, hoping we can blow past this awkward encounter, knowing I would never be that lucky.

"The arrogant doctor?" he presses, crinkling his brows.

"Yupp. Listen, can we please not talk about this now? We had such a great day together. Let's talk about it later or preferably never," I plead.

"Fine, later, but I need the abridged version now," he concedes. His face is a portrait of nonchalance, but his tone is unrelenting.

"Fine," I huff. "The SparkNotes version is that he wanted more than I could give him. And ultimately, we just didn't want the same things."

CHAPTER 31

KAI

IN BETWEEN GIVING AKIO sips of his hot chocolate and making small talk with Kendall, I watch Julian out of the corner of my eye. He's cool, calm, collected. Not a hair out of place. I can't believe I almost lost her to him. This self-absorbed prick who clearly didn't appreciate Kendall and the rare fucking gift that she is. Suddenly, jealousy and white-hot anger have hijacked my body. He makes a move to go to the bathroom and I realize that's my opening.

"I'll be right back." I say to Kendall and Akio standing quickly, my body vibrating with tension. When I open the door, Julian's already at a sink marveling at himself in the mirror. I stand at the sink next to his and pretend to wash my hands. He moves to turn around, but I grip his arm before he does, forcing him to face me.

"Listen man, I don't know what happened with you two. But I know she deserved better." He rips his arm from my grasp and stares at me for a beat, assessing. He takes a step forward so that we're eye to eye.

"What are you talking about?" he asks, looking alarmed.

"She said you were condescending and egotistical and didn't treat her well," I explain. He grunts, taking a step backwards and leaning against the counter. He crosses his arms like this is amusing to him, like he knows something I don't.

"I may very well be all those things from time to time. But I assure you that's not why we broke up," he responds casually.

"What do you mean?" I demand.

"I mean, Kendall hasn't told you everything. She's good at that—omitting important details to people she cares about. We broke up because there were three of us in that relationship. Me, Kendall, and you."

"Me?" I ask, even more confused than I was a minute ago.

"Our relationship couldn't survive you, the baggage you two had. The absolute chokehold you had on her. But seeing you two together today…it makes sense. I see it. It's like the universe intervened to finally give me closure."

"See what?"

"What you two have. No one else ever stood a chance with her. Not even me. A charming, handsome, pediatric surgeon," he smirks. This is where a smarter, more evolved guy would have walked away and ended the conversation. But he just had to have the last fucking word. Regardless of what it cost him—his ego, his pride, his date that was no doubt wondering where he was by now. "Oh, and Kai, she may have faked her feelings for me at the end, but there are some things she definitely *didn't* fake, like how much she loves my tongue," he says glaring at me.

The thought of this asshole's mouth anywhere near her body has me seeing red. My rage starts to boil over and it takes less than a millisecond for my flying, curled fist to connect with his face. I hit him with precision and strength—hard enough to cause serious pain but not hard enough to break anything. He stumbles backwards bringing his hand to his mouth and when he pulls it away, there's bright red blood dripping from his thumb.

"Fuck. A little sensitive about our mutual love interest, huh bro?" he asks, baiting me.

Did this guy have a fucking death wish? I advance towards him, quickly grabbing his arm and pinning it behind his back. With his face shoved against the paper towel dispenser, I twist his arm a little more for good measure.

"Okay, okay," he pleads desperately, spittle flying from his lips.

"If you say another fucking word about her or ever come near her again, I will break every one of your fucking fingers slowly and make it look like an accident. And I'm pretty sure you need those to eat *bro,*" I warn.

"You made your point. I deserved that," he concedes.

I back away from him, easing up the slightest bit and he walks out the door as quickly as possible, tail between his legs.

Chapter 32

Kendall

Kai returns from the bathroom looking like he wants to punch someone. And based on Julian's busted lip and the way he scurried out of the café without so much as making eye contact with the three of us, I'm not entirely sure he didn't.

He's quiet on the drive back to my apartment. I know we are on a freight train that is fast approaching a fight, I can feel it. And yet I have no inclination to throw myself in front of the train to stop its inevitable demise. Which is okay. We need to clear the air. Let things hurt and breathe a little bit. This is a fight I know we need to have. There are some things that are more painful not to share with him and my history with Julian is one of them.

After I put Akio down for the night and make sure his sound machine is on, I lightly pad out to the living room. Kai is sitting on the couch head back and eyes closed. He has a bag of frozen peas resting on his right hand. I sit down next to him gently.

"What happened?" His eyes flutter open and he props himself up with his arms on his knees, his hands clasped together tightly.

"You aren't going to like it," he declares, laying the bag of peas on the table.

"Well I need to hear it anyways," I say, folding my arms across my chest.

"He was running his idiotic mouth about you and I ensured he wouldn't do that again."

"How?" I implore.

"I think you know how," he answers, his tone neutral as if all he did was flick an annoying fly off of his shoulder. I assumed him and Julian had gotten in some sort of altercation. I had put two and two together, but part of me was hoping I was wrong.

"Kai Matsumoto, you can't just go around threatening and punching my ex-boyfriends because they piss you off."

He shrugs. "I've done a lot more for a lot less. And I don't know what to tell you. You know how I get with you."

I do know how he gets. In fourth grade, when girls made fun of me for having two moms, he helped me put fire ants in their lunchbox. In seventh grade, when Becca Hightower started bullying me about my hair, he conveniently spit gum in hers and made it look like an accident. And senior year, when Aiden Kenney called me a slut at homecoming, Kai beat the shit out of him. He has little tolerance for people who don't treat me well. He is also overprotective to a fault. That's the way it's always been and I kind of love that about him. I'm pissed...but also a little turned on.

I let out a huff of frustration.

"You mean like a territorial caveman?" I ask and Kai snorts in response. "Even if he deserved it, you could have been the bigger person and walked away."

"I was. I allowed him to keep his precious surgeon fingers after he talked about fucking you with his tongue. He's lucky all he got was a warning," he explains sharply, his eyes focused intensely on mine.

That leaves me speechless.

"This isn't about me being jealous or you having sex with him, *good sex* apparently. This is about whatever happened between you two that you conveniently lied about. So, what really happened?" *Fuck. There's no way out of this now.*

"He was arrogant and cocky and all those things you'd expect of a surgeon. At least at first. But the more I got to know him, the more I saw a different side of him. I'll spare you the nitty gritty details but the longer we dated, the harder it was to deny he was actually a really good person who deserved better than me, someone who wasn't all the way in."

"What do you mean?"

"He fell in love with me. He wanted a long-term relationship. He wanted us to move forward in the same direction. He wanted more than I was willing to give him," I clarify.

"Okay, those all seem like good things, Ken," he observes. I don't miss the way he grinds his teeth together in irritation.

"I wanted all of those things too, Kai. Just not with him."

His eyes soften, heavy with understanding and recognition.

"So, it was messy and complicated with Julian. I think the hardest part was that he fell in love with me knowing I was in love with someone else. Knowing that would likely never change," I confess.

Things had gone poorly with Julian at the end. I'm mature enough to admit that now and accept it was mostly my fault. My relationship with him had lasted longer than I ever thought it would and I didn't know how to love Julian, to be emotionally available to him without letting go of Kai. More importantly, I didn't want to let go of him.

"Why didn't you just tell me the truth?" he asks, frustration and pain gripping his face.

"The first and only time we talked about him I was too embarrassed to admit we broke up because of all of my complicated feelings for you. It just didn't feel like the time to discuss it."

"Did you love him?" he whispers quietly.

"Kai—"

"Did any part of you love him?" he presses harder and I hear his silent plea. *Did you ever love him the way you loved me?*

"No. Kai. Absolutely not. But a part of me wanted to try. I felt like I could have maybe if things had been different. And that scared me."

"When did you break up?"

"Eight months ago."

"If you've known how you felt about me since then, why did it take you this long to find me, to confront me?"

"I was scared you'd reject me, that you'd never forgive me. Fight me for custody—"

"Ken, I would never do that."

I take his hand in mine and squeeze it tightly. "I know that now Kai, I do."

"So, what changed? You came to my game."

"I realized I was more scared of losing you forever than I was of you hating me."

Chapter 33

Kai

I PULL MY HAND back from hers and swipe it down my face in exasperation.

"I think I just need some time with this, Ken. It's a lot," I explain, not really knowing what else to say. Sometimes it feels like everything between us is too complicated, too heavy, like we have so many odds stacked against us. Julian I can deal with but her continuing to lie to me after what we've been through is harder to stomach. Am I ever going to be able to fully trust her again?

"Okay. I mean, I thought you'd be relieved once you understood why it could never work between me and him." I'm far from relieved. I mean, am I happy she didn't end up with some douchebag doctor? Of course. But the person I loved, the only person I've ever loved, is still keeping secrets from me and that feels pretty fucking shitty.

"I am, it's just—"

"You would have preferred me and him rode off together into the sunset and lived happily ever after?" she asks, laying the sarcasm on thick.

"No, Kendall. I would have preferred to not have met the guy you almost fell in love with tonight and then realize I was lied to again." I volley back with a little more hostility.

"Kai, the operative term here is almost. I feel like you're missing the most important part of what I'm telling you."

"Kendall, the most important part to me is that you withheld the truth *again*. I really couldn't care less about the reasons. We didn't talk or see each other for almost three years and I don't know about you, but it was fucking torture for me," I explain, pressing the heels of my palms into my eyes and standing up. I start pacing in front of the couch trying to keep my anger in check. "I would rather stick my foot in a vat of acid than lose you again like that. And the entire time you were keeping our son from me, so excuse me if I can't take any more fucking dishonesty from you."

"I'm trying to be honest now," she whispers.

"Yeah, well, you're three years too late for that," I fire back without even thinking. *Fuck.* I regret it as soon as I say it. It's a low blow and an immature one at that.

"I deserved that," she answers quietly.

"No, you didn't. I'm sorry. I didn't mean that." I sigh. I glance at her apologetically, my hands clasped behind my head. "In the spirit of honesty, I need to tell you something and you aren't going to like this either." We were already unearthing secrets and emptying our closets of skeletons. I'd rather her find out now, while we were facing conflict than be blindsided by it in a few months. And as must as I hate to admit it, I'm angry with her, and part of me wants her to know what it feels like to be so broken.

"Okay..."

"After you left, when I knew it was over for good, I got really drunk and I hooked up with someone," I explain, knowing this is going to be the final nail in the coffin. This fight can only get worse from here.

"Okay who?" she demands.

"Allison," I whisper.

"Allison Greer? You fucked Allison fucking Greer?! Are you serious, Kai? The one person I begged you to stay away from!" she's yelling now as she stands up from the couch. I'm fairly certain if she were a cartoon character she'd have smoke pluming from her ears. I knew she'd be pissed, what I don't understand is why. What exactly is her deal with Allison?

"Kendall, please let me explain. It was months after you left. I was hurt and pissed off and I just wanted the pain to go away. I wanted to forget about it for a night. And I think part of me wanted to hurt you too." In my defense, it sounded much better in my head.

"So, you had revenge sex with Allison Greer?" she balks.

"Yeah, and I regretted it immediately after. I don't even remember it," I say, my words laced with embarrassment and shame. "Listen, I think we both need some time to cool off. I'm going back to my apartment," I decide and grab my keys from the counter.

I have reached my limit of this god-awful argument and somehow, I'm in the wrong for fucking Allison almost two years ago? When *she* was the one broke up with *me* and then disappeared without so much as a phone call. I turn back to look at her and there are tears welling in her eyes. *Shit, not exactly how I expected tonight to end.* I'm pissed but I still care about her and I never want to be the reason she cries. Before I know what I'm doing, I sweep her up in my arms and bury my nose in her curls.

"I'm not going anywhere, okay? We're not repeating past mistakes. I just need a little time." She lets out a sob and stares up at me, her glistening eyes searching mine.

"How did you know?"

"Because I know how much reassurance means to you and how fragile this thing is between us still. I know what it is to miss you, to need you, and not have the slightest idea if you'll ever come back to me. I may be angry but I still want you to feel safe with me, feel like you can trust me to weather everything and anything with you. Because I will."

"Kai, you are the one that deserves reassurance right now. I fucked up again and I'm so sorry. Starting right now, there is full disclosure between us. There is nothing I want more than to earn your trust and make you feel safe too."

I hope she can keep those promises, that what she says now is the truth. Because I really want to fucking believe her even if the past has taught me not to. I kiss her on the forehead and hug her tightly before walking out the door.

CHAPTER 34

KENDALL

2011

I HEAR OTHER GIRLS entering the bathroom and when I realize it's Allison and Bianca, I quickly peel my legs up to my chest and sit on the toilet as quietly as possible. I almost drop my backpack on the floor but catch it just in time.

Allison Greer is our high school's reigning queen bee and she knows it. All the guys want to date her and all the girls want to be her, despite her cruelty and the ability to cut you with a single glance. I fall somewhere in between, hating her but also wishing I had her gorgeous looks.

"You know she's going to homecoming with Aiden, even though she's technically dating Kai?" Bianca asks while applying lip gloss. *Me. They're talking about me.*

"I mean, Aiden can do what he wants. We broke up two months ago and he's overrated anyways. Kendall can have my leftovers," Allison responds. I watch through the small slit where the stall connects to the door. Bianca pauses and shifts her body towards Allison.

"I thought you were like in love with him and shit?" Bianca challenges with skepticism while waving her pink tube of lip gloss in the air.

"Yeah, that's old news. Besides, the only reason they're both trying to get in her pants is because they want to know what it's like to fuck a Black girl, and since she's the prettiest of the limited options..." Allison lets Bianca fill in the blanks.

Bianca laughs but it sounds rehearsed and then says, "I'm pretty sure you can't say stuff like that." I always knew I liked

Bianca. Maybe because she's the only girl ballsy enough to stand up to Allison.

"Why? It's true," Allison answers, defending her nasty comment while applying a thick layer of mascara.

"I don't know. It's kind of racist," Bianca observes, calling her on her shit.

"Whatever. I'll see you later? I can't be late for fifth again or I'll get a detention."

"Later," Bianca replies.

Somehow, I hold in my tears until I'm certain both girls have exited the bathroom. I let my backpack fall to the ground with a thud. I know wholeheartedly what Allison said about Kai was false but it still hurts. I had no idea about Aiden but I don't care as much about him. I'm not *in love* with Aiden. But Kai's a different story. His opinion means everything to me. And the implication still fucking irks me and simultaneously makes me want to ugly cry into a gallon of ice cream for days. This notion that the only reason a guy would want to be with me is out of sheer curiosity. That I'm not enough on my own, pretty enough, popular enough, *white* enough.

I spent a lot of time building myself up over the years, honing my confidence, trying to fit in everywhere and consequently feeling like I didn't belong anywhere. Not with my handful of classmates that were also Black or mixed and not with my family members who were all white. The only people I feel like I belong to and with are Kai and Jenna, and that's taken nearly a decade. I spent almost four years of high school trying to outperform all my peers just so I felt like I, too, truly deserved to be there. And now I'm in the running for salutatorian. I made sure I was outspoken but not too strong willed, athletic yet humble, confident but not cocky and I tried my best to get along with everyone.

I've done everything right. And yet it isn't enough. I still come up short. I know what Allison said is untrue but a small part of me believes it anyway.

I allow myself ten minutes to cry in the bathroom. Then I wipe my eyes with the rough one ply toilet paper that scratches more than it soothes, check my face in the camera of my cell phone, and stand up. What's that thing people say, the best revenge is living a good life? And I know I will. I also know people like Allison, that enjoy tearing other people down for sport, that are vicious and brutal simply because they can be—people like that usually peak in high school.

Chapter 35

Kendall

I CAN'T FOCUS, CAN'T concentrate. I watch the hands on the metal clock above my desk tick on slowly. They might as well be taunting me.

Kai and I haven't spoken in over 48 hours, which is the longest we've gone without talking since I met with him at the diner in January. I have two and a half hours left at the firm and I'm going to need every minute to complete the brief I've been working on all week. But my head keeps drifting back to *him*. The fight we had, the words he said, the confessions that were made. I'm still reeling over the fact that he fucked Allison Greer. Allison was everything I could never be in high school, the perfect compilation of all the physical characteristics I secretly coveted. Shiny golden hair, a tiny pert nose, contoured cheekbones, stunning ocean blue eyes and most importantly, she was white. She was a goddamn walking, talking, breathing Barbie doll. And I realize that it isn't even actually about Kai. I had essentially disappeared and left him heartbroken; he had every right to go seeking comfort and an escape. It's more about my perceived flaws, my shortcomings that I haven't closely examined in years. My old wounds that I was still licking. It's that burning question that keeps me up at night.

Am I enough?

I don't blame him for being furious at me. Of course he doesn't trust me. Why would he? And Kai has always been the jealous type; I can't fault him for that either. He doesn't want to think about the guys that I've been with since we broke up any more than I want to think about the women he slept with. And there were many. But how do we move past our history that isn't with each other? How do we learn to trust each other again? Maybe Jenna was right, maybe we did need to try counseling. The more I pick apart every detail of the fight we had, the more I realize it's me who needs to fix this. I have to earn back his trust for as long as it takes or else we will never have a chance at being in a real relationship.

***

I MAKE MY PLANS for the night. I get Akio's overnight bag packed, change him into his dinosaur pajamas—anything Spider-Man related is all in the growing dirty laundry pile—and drive him over to my moms'. I'm at Kai's apartment by 8:00 that evening, willing to do everything and anything to make this right. It's a little jarring since I've never been here before. The valet parking, marble floor, and glass interior scream luxury and power. And the differences between this place and my 1200 square foot shoebox are abundantly clear.

Upon arrival, I tell the doorman who I'm here to see and wait to be approved as a visitor. I then take an elevator to his floor and request to be buzzed in over the intercom system. The silver doors slide open with a whoosh, and Kai, all 6 foot 4 inches of him, are standing in front of me in navy sweats and a grey t-shirt. The form fitting Nike shirt clings to his torso, highlighting his toned, muscular body and leaving his strong, tattooed arms on display. His jet black hair is still a little wet and tousled and there's a small ghost of a smile on his lips. How he manages to look downright irresistible even in gym clothes is beyond my comprehension.

"Hi," I say, a little flustered by the sight of him. "I came to talk, I hope that's okay. But if you still need more space, I can leave…" I really hope he doesn't need more time and space. The last 48 hours alone have been agonizing.

"No, it's okay," he replies, smiling, but it doesn't quite reach his eyes. "I missed you and I want to talk."

"Good. I missed you too," I admit. I take a step toward him and he embraces me in a crushing hug that soothes my soul and allows me to breathe again. He curls his arms around my back, pressing me tighter to him as I burrow myself in the crook of his neck. He cradles my head in one hand and holds me close to him with the other.

Home.

The scent of his cologne, his touch that's tender yet strong, the way I fit perfectly in his arms, and his unfairly gorgeous face that makes my heart skip a beat. All of it is home to me. And I think if I can package up this feeling, bottle it, and save it forever, I would. Because I never want to know what it's like to miss him again.

"Come on," he replies, tugging me forward and bringing me deeper into his apartment. "Let's talk." He takes my hand and leads me over to his black leather couch that's situated in front of a TV nearly the whole size of the wall. We both sit and he mutes the basketball game that's currently on.

"Can I go first?" I question. "There's just a lot I need to say."

"Sure," he nods.

"I am so fucking sorry for keeping things from you and I know that simply apologizing won't make up for that. I know you don't trust me yet and you shouldn't. I haven't earned it and the fact that I left and didn't contact you for three years doesn't exactly instill trust in me either." I look up at him, my gaze connecting with his. Willing him to believe the words I'm about to say. "But I will spend the rest of my life making it up to you and proving to you that you can. From now on, whatever you ask me, I will answer honestly. I don't want there to be any secrets between us. I'm not running from this ever again. But I do want you to keep an open mind about something."

"About what?" he wonders.

I chew on my lip nervously. "I think we should go to couples counseling," I explain, internally holding my breath.

"Okay."

"Okay? Really?" I ask in disbelief. "I did not think it would be that easy," I acknowledge, feeling relieved that he's on board.

"I've been going to a therapist since I was a kid and you know how I feel about it. If it will help us get closer and work through things, then yes, of course I'll do it."

Right. The accident, his panic attacks, his anxiety—all things he went to therapy for.

"I don't really know what I did in this life to deserve you, Kai," I admit. And I mean it. This isn't the first time I've uttered those words to him and I'm positive it won't be the last.

"I don't know what I did to deserve you either, Ken," he responds.

"Yeah, yeah," I joke.

"I'm serious," he notes. "Can I ask you something though?"

"You're wondering about Allison, right?" I supply so he doesn't have to.

"Yeah."

So, I tell him the whole ugly truth, the embarrassing past. All the insults and snide comments she made about me over the years. The things I don't want to dredge up but he deserves to hear regardless. I explain how her words had shaped me in ways that were unseeable, unknowable until now, that she had cut me in ways that lingered. I start tearing up a little towards the end and he pulls me close to him. So close I can hear his heart thumping against his ribs and the rhythmical cycle of his breathing.

"I'm so sorry, Ken. I knew you didn't get along with her, but I didn't really know all the details. You never told me that," he states, weaving his hand through mine. Which is probably the weirdest part of the whole thing, seeing as how we told each other everything. At least in high school.

"I know. I was insecure and embarrassed and part of me be-lieved some of the things she said..." I reply quietly.

"Kendall, I wish you had told me this in high school or college so I could call bullshit on everything she said to you and about you. But now will just have to do."

"What do you mean?" I ask, looking up at him and marveling at his ability to comfort and calm me.

"Allison was jealous of you and her family is made up of right wing nutjobs by the way," he clarifies. I mean, I knew her family was comprised of blatant racists but I highly doubt she was ever jealous of me.

"Uh huh, I'm sure. You don't have to say that just to make me feel better, Kai." He sits up and brackets my face with one hand.

"I'm not saying it just to make you feel better. I'm saying it because it's true," he admits. "Every guy in our senior class wanted a chance with you and it has nothing to do with the fact that you are Black. It's because you are a knockout and because you're *you*. Full fucking stop. You're gorgeous, and you're smart, and fucking fearless. You were like the nastiest gymnast, I don't even know how you did some of the things you did. You make everyone feel special and lucky to be around you. You're caring and empathetic and you see people for all that they are and all that they could be. You're this beautiful bright light with a huge heart. As if all that wasn't enough, you have an ass that doesn't quit. Allison was just a pretty face, no substance, no depth, no redeeming qualities. Not to mention she was evil incarnate. You were and are so much more than that." I don't bother with a response. I don't have any words. I just move my lips over his.

Thank you thank you thank you my heart chants silently.

When we stop to break the kiss, I'm overheating, dizzy, and completely relieved. I stare at him for a moment and try to fathom how I ever walked away from him. From this. The absolute love of my life.

"An ass that doesn't quit, huh?" I ask, smiling like a giddy teenager.

"Yup," he replies, pinching my ass and causing me to squeal.

"Can we just agree to let our history and people we've been with when we broke up go? Wipe the slate clean? I mean, there are other things we need to discuss, but as far as hookups and partners go, the only person I'm concerned about is you."

"Agreed. In terms of our dating history, let's start fresh. The only thing that matters is us," he responds.

"Just so we're absolutely clear—the sex with Julian, with other guys was nothing compared to what we have." I clear my throat "Had. It was nothing and it meant nothing."

"Oh sweet, innocent Kendall. Trust me, I know," he muses, smirking at me. God that *smirk* makes me want to do primal, truly unhinged things to him.

"You do?" I wonder.

"Yeah, I do. Because I've been searching for three years for someone to make me feel something, anything close to a fraction of what we have together. So far, no dice."

He gives me *the look*, the one that pulls his lips into a devilishly handsome smile and I can feel flames licking at my core. He kisses me then and it's all demanding, wanting, taking. We're making up for years that we could have been doing this with each other, for time spent with the wrong people. It tastes like broken promises and fractured hearts. Truth and honesty. It's layered with jealousy and possession and *mine mine mine*. It's us. It's everything.

When he pulls away, I whimper in protest. But he responds by placing me in his lap, my legs wrapping around his waist. He grips my neck with his hand gently, slowly pulling down the sleeve of my sweater to expose my shoulder. I feel heat searing my body, shivers sliding down my spine.

"Allison doesn't matter. Julian doesn't matter. No one else matters." He pauses to place a kiss on my neck and another on my collarbone. "All that matters is us, how you feel when you come on *my* tongue," his voice is a whisper and a caress.

"Fuck, Kai, if the goal is for us to not have sex, you really shouldn't say things like that," I reply.

"Baby, we don't need to have sex for me to make you come. In fact, I'm pretty sure if I feel you right now you are going to be ready for me," he says, making slow, intoxicating circles with his tongue along the column of my throat and caressing my hip. *Holy shit.*

"I am," I breathe. Though I'm not sure how I'm stringing words together. "Fuck, that feels so good, Kai," I practically moan, carnal need coursing through my veins.

"Is that what you want?" he asks, nipping my earlobe.

"Huh?" I respond, confused and a little dizzy. He laughs and pulls back to face me.

"I said is that what you want?" he repeats, kissing me senseless and capturing my bottom lip between his teeth.

God, why is that the sexiest fucking thing he's ever done? Oh right, because it's Kai, my ex-boyfriend, (current boyfriend?) and father of my child. Everything he does is hot, especially since we're banned from having sex. Maybe it's because I haven't had mind blowing sex in years. The sex with Julian was good, but it wasn't Kai. Only Kai could crack my heart and my soul wide open and make me come back, begging for more.

Every time.

Only him.

"I want you to do less talking with that mouth."

"What else?"

"I want you to fuck me with it," I demand, surprising myself. I don't just want him, I need him. I need his tongue sliding over every inch of my body more than I need my next fucking breath. I need to lose myself in him, drown myself in him. I'm starved for this man.

"Kendall, just so you know, another guy will never have their hands, mouth, or cock anywhere near you," he says, his hands gliding over my hips to stroke my back. "The only guy that is going to be worshipping your magnificent body is me. So, if you don't want that, say the word."

"I only want you," I rasp, breathless and lightheaded.

"If you let me, I promise to make you come so hard you forget your own name, you forget any guy that ever thought he deserved you," he says, heat flaring in his eyes causing my nerve endings to bristle.

Then he carries me to his bedroom and makes good on every single promise.

***

A HANDFUL OF ORGASMS later, we're lying in Kai's California king, me snuggled up to his side watching reruns of *The
Office*. He strokes my hair with one hand and draws small circles
on my thigh with the other. It feels like a dream and a memory
even though I've never had it, never lived it. I'm caught somewhere
in between deja vu and heaven. And it feels so good, so right, so
perfect.

CHAPTER 36

KAI

I TURN MY FACE towards her and brush a kiss against her forehead. This has to be what dreams are made of. Kendall in my bed after feeling her come apart on my tongue—not once, not twice, but three times. And god, she tastes so fucking good, like she's made for me. My own personal brand of euphoria. She's wearing my old Red Sox t-shirt, her nipples just barely visible, and her beautiful, tanned ass on full display. Her drugging kisses remind me how much I've missed her the past two days and her sweet, effervescent laugh vibrates against my chest.

"Kai, the magic you work with your mouth and fingers never ceases to amaze me," she whispers, and immediately, my cock springs to attention.

"I know," I respond with confidence but bordering on arrogance. She hits me playfully but before she can pull her hand back, I bring her palm to my face and kiss it lightly, followed by a kiss to the inside of her wrist. She presses into me, her soft curves against my hard edges and I start worshipping the spot underneath her earlobe I know she loves. "This shirt looks amazing on you but it would look even better off of you," I whisper into her neck. She lets out a soft moan that has me hard in seconds. She's so fucking sexy, beautiful, and mine. All mine.

It takes every ounce of willpower I have not to tear her clothes off and fuck her into oblivion. Distraction. I need a distraction and I need it right fucking now. Somehow, I manage to pry my lips from her skin and shift my body so that I'm peering down at her.

I tilt her chin towards me and brush her cheek with my thumb. "Are you hungry by any chance?" I ask, knowing the answer to this question is always yes.

"Yes. Thank god you asked. I'm starving," she admits, rising up to sit on her knees. "I didn't want to seem too eager, but I barely had time to eat dinner before rushing Akio to my moms' and then coming here," she responds.

"I knew you'd be ravenous after a night of lovemaking," I joke.

"I am ravenous," she chuckles. "We've burned a lot of calories tonight. What are you in the mood for?"

"I'm good with whatever you want, Ken."

"Okay. But are you sure? I mean, it's getting kind of late. Maybe I should get going," she suggests.

"No," I say quickly and probably louder than necessary. "I mean, if you want to go that's fine, if you'd be more comfortable at your apartment. But I want you to stay."

"Good. I want to stay. Sleeping without you for years..." she hesitates "I hated it."

Fuck it. We've already crossed so many lines tonight, what's one more?

"I want you to stay. Not just tonight, or tomorrow, or the next couple weeks. I want you to stay with me permanently. Being apart from you and Akio night after night just feels wrong," I explain, sitting up.

A million emotions cross her face before she finally speaks. "What are you saying, Kai?" she implores, her voice climbing a few octaves.

"I'm saying I want you both to move in with me."

"So, let me get this straight, we are taking things slow but you want me and our son to move in with you?" she asks incredulously, both hands plastered to her temples.

"I mean, when you put it like that, it sounds insane," I admit, laying my head back against the headboard. "But I know you must feel it too, that pull for all of us to be together in one place..." I say, moving my hands up and down her thighs in a soothing motion. It's a fantasy, a far-fetched dream. I know that but it doesn't mean it's impossible. She proceeds to dive face first into a pillow and let out a dramatic groan.

"Of course I feel it, Kai. But we can't just move in together. Akio doesn't even know you're his father yet. Let's think about this realistically and logistically. There are a lot of things we need to do before we commit to making a life transition that big. We just aren't there yet."

I sigh, realizing she's right but the disappointment sits heavy on my chest.

"I know, I just miss you both so much when I'm not with you." She scoots closer to me, leans over, and cradles my face in both her hands.

"We miss you too," she pauses to place a kiss on my lips. "It's not a no, okay? It's a not yet," she explains, and her serious penetrating gaze gives me a small kernel of hope. "Repeat it, Kai. I need you to understand that I'm all in. I'm not rushing things and I'm not doing anything that would harm this relationship again. If that means waiting to move in together until we're both on the same page and Akio is well adjusted, then so be it." I look at her and I know I can't argue with her logic or her reasoning. This is the right call even if it feels like a loss.

"It's not a no, it's a not yet," I echo solemnly.

"But I want you to keep asking, okay?" she continues cautiously, threading her fingers through mine.

"What do you mean?" I stare at her, trying to read her expression.

"I want you to keep asking. I mean, not every day and probably not for a while. But I want you to keep asking. Because eventually, it's going to be a yes."

I had already waited three excruciating years for her. I could wait until eventually came around. Even if it felt wrong, even if that tugging in my chest got stronger and louder. I would wait forever for them.

"Where is he tonight by the way? I miss him," I admit.

"I dropped him off with my moms' before I came here," she replies. "He fell asleep on the way there so hopefully he sleeps okay for them tonight."

"Is he a good sleeper typically?" I wonder. God there's been so much that I missed. It felt suffocating at times. All the more reason to have them here at my apartment with me.

"For the most part, sometimes he'll wake up crying from a bad dream or he's inconsolable when he's sick. But aside from that he sleeps through the night."

"What else? Fill me in on everything. What does he like? Is he a picky eater? What is he into right now?"

"He's a little quieter than most kids. I imagine he's exactly like you were at that age. He's an observer, very curious and pays close attention to his surroundings. I don't think we ever have to worry about stranger danger with him. You know he loves superheroes, Spider-Man, dinosaurs. Anything involving Paw Patrol. He's really into opening and closing doors and drawers right now. That's like this thing. He's kind of picky but he'll also try new foods every once in a while. Like a few weeks ago he started eating mango and avocado." She pauses for a second and I take everything in. "What else...oh his best friend at the moment is Maddox. They are total opposites, but it works. We met him and his mom at library play group. You should come sometime if you can."

"Okay, I will," I respond, delighted.

"You will?"

"Of course. I'd love to."

Chapter 37

Kendall

"WHAT?" I ASK AS he looks down at me with a thoughtful, contemplative gaze. I'm curled up against his chest, my legs resting in his lap, his arms tightly wrapped around me. Leftover Styrofoam takeout containers and fortune cookie wrappers are strewn across the coffee table in front of us.

"Nothing, you're just so fucking beautiful I have to remind myself to breathe sometimes," he responds cupping my face in his hands and I melt into his touch.

"Yeah, yeah," I mutter, incapable of accepting this compliment or any compliment for that matter. "You give all the girls that line?" I ask, picking imaginary lint from the bottom of my shirt.

He sits up, shifting his body towards me and resting on his elbow. "No, I don't. And it's not a line if it's true," he says sternly.

"Okay," I tip my chin in defiance. "Give me one example where you thought I was so pretty you couldn't breathe," I challenge, completely unprepared for his answer.

"Senior year homecoming. Before we even started dating," he replies without missing a beat. "You came to my house in that black silk dress, your hair was up but there were a few curls hanging by your face. You were wearing your silver bracelet from your grandmother and I remember thinking, *Holy shit, I'm going to have a panic attack because of how gorgeous she is.* In my head, I had to count back from twenty to catch my breath."

I'm staring at him slack jawed, but he keeps on going.

"Cabo spring break, when we were juniors. We fucked in the hot tub twice, the shower multiple times, but my favorite was the beach right by our villa. We were still a little tipsy from day drinking and you had a mischievous look in your eyes on the way home from dinner. You somehow convinced me that sex on the beach was an amazing idea, and you were right. Like always. I laid you down on a towel in the sand, your hair fanned out around you. Your skin was soft and radiant and your cheeks a little sunburnt. I couldn't stop staring at you. I never wanted to freeze a moment in time so badly. And god your smile, it filled me up. *I wanted to drown in it, bask in its warmth forever.* I loved that you were smiling like that for me, because of me. I deliberately took my time. I wanted to memorize every inch of you."

And apparently, he had. I'm working hard to fight back tears at this point.

I remember that day vividly. It happened exactly like he said. And somehow with the waves crashing at our feet and the trees overhead rustling in the breeze, the air thick and hot with possibilities and him undressing me with his eyes, drinking me in like he had never seen me naked before, it felt like our very first time all over again. Like this perfect slice of paradise had been carved out specifically for us.

"Why?" I ask, terrified of the answer yet hanging on his every word.

"Because even then I knew what I was looking at. I knew I was staring at my future—that I was trying to memorize my wife."

"Kai…" but what could I possibly say to that? I'm not sure I have any words.

"You want me to keep going? I could, all night. How about when you first wake up and you're so goddamn grumpy, it's dangerous to talk to you before you've had a cup of coffee. Your crazy curls everywhere, usually a little spit in the corner of your mouth, wearing nothing but baggy clothes and no makeup. Even and especially then you are the most beautiful creature I have ever seen."

"Kai," I choke out.

"Kendall," he utters my name like a plea and a promise. Then he delicately brushes my knuckles across his lips.

"Why are you crying?" he whispers. Because he *sees* me. Because he sees through my hardened exterior to the person I am underneath. He knows me in ways that no one else can. Even now, after everything. Sometimes I feel like he knows me better than I know myself, unearthing truths I have only whispered in the deepest recesses of my mind. Because he remembers everything about us, every perfect and imperfect detail of our relationship—even when it's been agonizing. And here I am, rifling through his private thoughts, holding them hostage because I'm too fucking insecure.

"Kai, you're just," I turn away and shake my head, unable to look at him. "You're too damn good for this world. You're pure and honest and so fucking genuine. And I want to be the kind of person that deserves you," I explain, hesitant to go any further.

"I don't know if I'd call myself pure," he laughs. "And you do deserve me. We are good for each other," he replies in a way that tells me I've lost this argument.

"Maybe," I say. "I guess I wasn't expecting everything you said either. I had assumed you probably tried to forget about us, the good and the bad."

"I figured it was better to live with the ghost of you than pretend we never happened. I mean, for the record, I did try to forget, a lot. But..."

"But?" I pry.

"You're impossible to forget," he concedes.

I could give him something, this much at least.

"So are you, and I'm sorry. That you had to do that. And for how much I hurt you."

"It's okay. We're here now. That's what matters,"

Kai understands that *my* unique love languages are reassurance and words of affirmation and he's incredibly fluent in both. He's the only person that can make me feel like I'm both the most stunning and most important person in the room.

Kai knows that for me, to be loved is to feel beautiful and worthy—because it's taken my whole fucking life to convince myself I've earned that privilege. And some days, I still fall short of both.

But not tonight.

Tonight, I have Kai. And the curve of his smile and the creases of his eyes make my heart twist and flip and ache all at once. And this man thinks I'm *breathtaking*. Tonight, I deserve his love, adoration, and kind words.

Self-loathing can wait until tomorrow.

Chapter 38

KENDALL

"Good morning, beautiful," he greets me, pulling my hair away from my neck and replacing it with a soft, seductive kiss. He curls his arms around me, one slipping underneath the bottom of my shirt and the other banded across my chest. His touch leaves goosebumps in its wake. *God, the things I would do to wake up every morning like this.*

"Morning handsome," I reply, turning towards him. I take him in—in all his early morning glory—his mussed up hair, his sweats hanging low on his hips, the V of his lower abdominals disappearing into the waistband of his boxers, and his absolutely ripped abs. I want to lick the dip and peak of every single one. *For fuck's sake.* I have to stop or there's no way I'll make it out of this apartment on time. But instead, I move closer to him, my traitorous body heating up. He takes a second to scan the length of me with dark hooded eyes.

"Ken, you know this is like one of my top three fantasies," he whispers, his voice low and gruff, as he fists the bottom of my shirt in his hand.

"What is?" I ask innocently.

"You in my kitchen, making us coffee, wearing my old t-shirt and looking sexy as fuck. The morning after we've spent the entire night doing everything but fucking," he breathes into my hair, his lips skimming my jawline. "Even though that is all I want to do," he slides his hand over my ass to palm my hip.

"Kai, we made a pact, remember?" I grin. "It was your idea. And we need to cool it if I want any chance of picking up our son and making it to work on time, okay?" I respond.

"I can't help it," he says, laying his forehead against mine and lacing my hands together behind his neck. He presses his body into me, his hard, thick cock against my throbbing center and I nearly faint at the contact. "You're here and you aren't a mirage or a hallucination. You. Are. Here. I've been deprived of you for too long and now that I have you...I can't get enough of you," he explains with punishing, bruising kisses. "What can I say? I'm an animal. I can't be tamed. I'm insatiable when it comes to you," he insists, his teeth scraping over his bottom lip.

"Maybe I don't want you tamed," I reply, smiling against his mouth. Then we're moving. He lifts me up at the waist and places me on the edge of the counter. He tugs my hips towards him, sliding his hand down, past my underwear to soothe my aching clit. There's no teasing going on, no time wasted.

Thank fucking god.

"Fuck, Ken, is all of this for me?" he asks, plunging his fingers into me at a torturously slow pace, giving me the most delicious pleasure only he can provide.

"It's all for you. Every time," I pant, breathless.

"Do you think about me when you're fucking yourself?" he asks while working his thumb in tandem with his fingers. *God his hands... that mouth should come with a fucking warning label.*

"Yes." How could I possibly think of anyone else when he's the only thing my body craves.

"What do you want?" he rasps.

"You," is all I can manage. *Harder. Deeper. Faster. Everywhere.* But you is the only thing that comes out.

As if he can hear my thoughts, he drags his chin down my chest, along my stomach, pushing the hem of the T-shirt upwards with both hands to give him better access. He pauses to trail featherlight kisses along my hip bone and my whole body shudders. Then he starts removing my underwear.

With. His. Teeth.

Once they're on the floor, he replaces his fingers with his mouth and my brain short circuits. He sucks and licks and swirls, his teeth sliding over my clit, winding my body tighter, pulling me closer to the edge. I bury my fingers in his hair and tug as he flicks his tongue against me. I'm scrabbling, clawing for any semblance of control, even though it's an illusion. *I am his.* My body, my heart, all of it belongs to him. He's ravenous. And I love being devoured by him.

"Fuck, Ken. I could live forever with my head between your legs," he growls from somewhere far away, his voice sounds like it's coming to me through static. My feet are planted on his back, heels digging into his trap muscles. I grip the counter hard, bracing for impact as I buck my hips against his mouth again and again—chasing the sweetest euphoria I can only get from him.

"That seems highly impractical," I reply, although how I'm forming words is unclear. His tongue and his mouth take me higher and higher, every nerve ending firing in rapid succession until the pressure builds and the waves crescendo. The orgasm breaks me into a thousand tiny pieces of pure bliss. I don't just come, I fucking *detonate.*

Heaven isn't a place. It's Kai Matsumoto on his knees, with his head between my legs, worshipping me without restraint. His tongue merciless, his mouth unyielding like it's his fucking birthright. Kai, the single flame after I've been doused in kerosene. And he has turned me into a raging inferno of lust, desire and pure unbridled, biological need.

I let myself collapse, my back falling on the cool granite countertop. I cover my face with one arm and try to slow my breathing. But that attempt is short lived because Kai folds himself over my body, his hands braced on either side of my head. He's kissing me everywhere and the orgasm that has started to wane has now been kicked into overdrive.

"God, Ken, you're so fucking sexy, so beautiful when you come for me." *Kiss.* "I love the sounds you make when you're on the edge." *Kiss.* "I love every inch of your body." *Kiss.* "I love how fucking drenched you are for me," he says, reaching his hands down to sink his fingers into me again. *Kiss.* And this time, I don't just feel his touch on my skin, I feel it everywhere. Like he's kissing my very soul.

"Kai," I gasp in desperation. He lifts the pad of his thumb to his mouth and sucks.

"And how good you fucking taste." Jesus, he's got me on the brink again, his words turning me nuclear in a matter of seconds. Surely, I'm not about to have my fifth orgasm in less than 24 hours. Not that I'm complaining. Raging insatiable need has me feral for him as I reach for his boxers.

"Why are there still this many layers of clothes separating us?" I ask as I unleash his massive erection. I bring him closer to me, sliding his tip across my entrance and my body quivers with anticipation.

"I have no fucking clue," he groans with pleasure.

"You're the only person who does this to me, Kai, the only one who makes me feel like this. One touch and I'm burning for you, one kiss and I fucking melt. But I need to know I'm the only one for you too."

"It's only you, Ken. Always you. It has only ever been you," he promises, his voice low and soft. "And I fully intend on keeping you this time."

Within seconds, my shirt is off, and I shove his sweats and boxers to the ground with my feet. He carries me somewhere. Where we're going, I don't care as long as he doesn't stop. My legs are hitched around his waist, my pebbled nipples pressed against his firm chest and we're a tangle of limbs and hands, clashing tongues and teeth. Our mouths colliding over and over. My back meets a wall and then we're moving again. We bump into something and I hear a crash as a decorative vase lands on the ground in a million pieces.

"I hated that vase anyways," he mumbles and goes right back to ravaging my body. I think we're headed to his bed again but he stops in front of his shower, placing me on my feet.

"Kai, what are we doing?"

"We are going to get as close to fucking as we can without actually doing that and then we're going to shower," he decides with a smirk that makes me weak. "You know, kill two birds with one stone," he suggests.

"Okay," I oblige.

The shower is gigantic, all glass and marble, with intricate gray hexagonal tiles lining the floor and a rainfall shower head mounted on the ceiling. Not to mention a built-in seat and something tells me we'll be needing it. He turns the shower on and picks me up with ease, one hand twined around my waist and the other feeling the temperature of the water. Once it's warm enough, he carries me inside and pins me to the wall with all of him. *Yes yes yes.* He starts rocking his hips and thrusting his cock against me slowly, in a perfect rhythm as the water washes over us. My grip tightens in his hair as the friction between us intensifies. I bite his shoulder and arch my back, pleading, begging for more of him. The feel of him slick and wet and hard against me causes me to unravel. I cross my feet at his back, pushing him impossibly closer to me.

"More," I whimper. He reaches his hand between us, massaging my hypersensitive clit and giving me the exact pressure I need. I forget every word in the English language as I cling to him for dear life. I dig my nails into his skin harder as the pressure builds. My body is strung tighter and tighter, like a rubber band about to snap, and then I see the universe explode. I tilt my head back and let the orgasm crash over me in wave after wave, liquefying my bones, stealing my breath, and ridding me of my sanity.

When I finally take a moment to look at him, I realize how lucky I truly am. He's so fucking beautiful. The water drips off his hair in rivulets, sliding down his expertly sculpted muscles. His chest glistens with beads of water. Sweat and heat radiate off his glorious body while steam billows around us. He raises his tattooed forearms to cage my head in and stares back at me, his darkened eyes glazed with lust. One pull of his scarred eyebrow does me in. This man deserves to be worshipped, every inch of him.

I extricate myself from his body, planting my feet on the ground and proceed to kiss my way down his torso. I lick a path back up his body and it's infinitely better than I imagined. Then I'm standing in front of him, my hands on his chest, pushing him backwards until his thighs meet the bench.

I kneel in front of him and take my time licking him from the base all the way to tip, eliciting a deep guttural groan from him.

"Fuck, Ken," he growls. "That feels so good." I smile up at him deviously, clench his ass in my hands, and take him all the way to the back of my throat, tears pricking at my eyes. I'm so deliriously full of him and I fucking love it. I start slow, giving him long lazy strokes and then circle his crown with the tip of my tongue. He wraps my hair around his fist and tugs, his breath coming in short, ragged pants. I want to feel him let go, lose control. I want everything he's willing to give me. I move faster as his thrusts get sloppy, his movements more erratic, and I know he's close. His body violently clenches, every muscle rigid, a groan erupting from his throat. Moments later, he finds his release as water rains down on us. And I swallow every last drop.

If the not fucking him is this good, having sex might kill me.

Chapter 39

Kendall

I ARRIVE AT MY moms' small ranch style house almost twenty minutes later than I said I would. Which means Akio is going to be late for daycare drop off and I am just barely going to make it to work for 9:00. Even with the chaotic start to the morning, I'm feeling more relaxed and refreshed than I have in a long time. I guess multiple orgasms will do that to you. I ran out of Kai's apartment with a piece of toast in one hand and a to go coffee in the other. I'm certain my shirt is on inside out and I still can't help but smile as I rush into the foyer. I'm reaching down to fix my clothes when I discover Kai left me two early morning parting gifts in the form of red, angry hickeys. One on my collarbone and one on my left breast. I cover both by yanking my shirt up as high as it can go and folding my arms tightly across my chest.

God, I'm so fucked.

"Hey, sorry I'm late," I shout into the abyss of the kitchen. "Traffic was terrible," I lie.

My mom is standing at the oversized double sink washing dishes. "Traffic, huh?" she asks.

"Yes, that among other things," I mumble as I kiss her on the cheek. She shoots me a look of skepticism, and I can tell she's unconvinced. My other mom is playing with Akio at the kitchen table that is littered with Legos. He runs into my arms excitedly as soon as he sees me.

"Mama! Missed you!" he exclaims, wrapping his little arms around my leg.

"I missed you too, baby," I respond, smothering his head and cheek with kisses. "We got to get going though, so we aren't late for drop off," I explain, hoping my moms are finished pestering me about my night.

"Hi, Mom," I say, leaning down to kiss the top of her head while she continues picking up Legos.

"Hi, honey, how was your night?" she asks.

"It was good. A lot of fun," I respond, intentionally vague.

"Ken, you've never been a very good liar. And you've only asked us to watch Akio overnight when you have a *date*," she whispers. "Not to mention your shirt is on inside out," she indicates, raising her eyebrows. "So, I'll ask you again, how was your night?"

"Fuck," I mutter underneath my breath.

What am I supposed to say, I spent the last 24 hours being absolutely wrecked by Kai, in the best possible way? No, I have to handle this with care, finesse, and impeccable timing. My relationship with Kai is still fraught with tension and filled with unknowns, but the relationship our family had with the Matsumotos was effectively severed once I decided to raise Akio by myself. And everyone including me has paid for it dearly.

"Listen, you're right. I was with a guy and it's pretty serious. But I don't have time to talk about this right now. How about we come over for dinner later and we can talk about it then, okay?" I ask, trying to buy myself some time. Any time at all would be preferable to explaining to them right now that Kai and I have gotten back together. Or whatever it is we're doing. That after vowing not to contact him, and asking them to cut ties with his family, I had been the one to reach out to him. *God, this is not going to go well.*

The drive to daycare is twelve minutes. Akio spends most of it talking about the pancake situation from earlier this morning.

"Grandma said one handful of blueberries but I did two."

"And?"

"She used the big voice."

"Yikes." I glance at him in the rearview. "What else?"

He thinks about it for two seconds. "Can we get a fish?"

"No."

"A small one."

"Still no."

He sighs deeply and stares out the window for the rest of the drive. I fix his backpack straps at drop-off, kiss his forehead, and he's already gone, running inside wearing his favorite Spiderman shoes.

I sit in the parking lot longer than I need to.

My phone buzzes.

> How's your morning?

Kai. I smile before I can stop myself.

> Just dropped Akio off. He wants a fish now.

> Get the fish.

> I'm not getting the fish.

I see the text bubble that tells me he's typing pop up and then disappear a few times.

> What if I kept it at my apartment?

> Saves you the headache and he can still have the fish

> You would do that?

> You're never home…

> Of course I would and I have a housekeeper

> Maybe

I laugh alone in my car and pull out into traffic.

Work keeps me busy most of the morning. I'll take any distraction to stop me from thinking about how I'm going to break the news to my moms this evening. By mid-afternoon, I've rehearsed eleven versions of what I'm going to say and scrapped all of them. Kai texts once more around 2pm, a photo of a coffee cup, no caption, and I stare at it longer than I should before putting my phone face down.

The truth. Nothing else. Just the truth. That's all I've got.

***

WE'RE BACK AT MY moms' house seated around the large oak kitchen table. Akio is sleeping in his room that's been completely designed for him. I brought over a pizza and cannolis from their favorite restaurant, hoping it would put them in a good enough mood to soften the blow of my news.

My mom bites into a cannoli, powdered sugar exploding and falling on her plate. She grabs a napkin from the center of the table and starts to prod.

"So, this guy, who is he? Where'd you meet him?" she questions. And even after perseverating all day, trying to figure how to best deliver this information, and triaging the situation with Jenna, I'm still terrified of their reactions. The fallout. What happens after this admission—because these are words that can't be unsaid, unheard once they're out there in the open.

"It's Kai," I whisper quietly, holding my breath as if that could possibly help me. I glance back and forth between both of them. My mom drops her dessert abruptly and her face is lethally serious.

"What do you mean *it's Kai*?" she asks, anger and shock creasing the edges of her voice.

"I knew it!" Mommy chimes in. I give her a pointed glare that screams *what the fuck, Mom, you aren't helping*.

"We reconnected a few months ago." I clear my throat. Water. I need water. I take a sip from my glass slowly, hoping it will cure my inability to string words together. "And we've been spending a lot of time together. The three of us," I respond, treading carefully.

"You mean to tell me that you and Kai, Akio's *father*, have been together for months and this is the first we're hearing about it? Why?" she asks, noticeably raising her voice.

"I mean, it was new at first. We weren't exactly sure what we were doing and if it would turn into anything. We have a lot of history and things to work out still..." It's clear to me and probably them that I haven't thought this through. This is very obviously a mistake. But I have looked at it from every single angle and considered the consequences. And the one conclusion I keep coming back to is that I have to tell them. They would find out about Kai one way or another and I wanted it to be on my terms.

"We're well aware," she snaps, leaning back in her chair and folding her arms across her chest. "You told us before he was even born that you wanted to raise Akio without Kai for a lot of reasons—"

"I know," I interject, wary of where this conversation is headed.

"And we supported you without question. Even if we didn't agree with your choice."

"Maybe we should all just take a beat," Mommy suggests, her eyes moving back and forth between us.

"No, it's time she heard this. Running away from your problems, moving to North Carolina, breaking up with Kai and lying to him. Perhaps none of those things were the right choices even if they felt like your only options at the time."

Jesus Christ. How could she so callously rattle off my deepest regrets like they don't haunt me every day of my life? The three slices of pizza I ate sit in my stomach like a brick, weighed down by anxiety and guilt.

"That's not fair," I observe.

"Maybe not but it's the truth. You made difficult choices and now it might be time to accept that they might have had very serious, negative repercussions. You aren't the only person who sacrificed something in this family, Kendall," she presses.

My anger at myself, the situation, the pain I've caused the people in my life and the stifling unfairness of it all boils over and spills out in pure rage.

"You don't think I know how much I fucked up? You don't think I realize what I've lost, what I might never be able to fix?" I seethe, hot tears burning my eyes.

"Kendall," Mommy says gently like she's trying to approach a wild animal. "Let's all just take a moment," she suggests.

I sigh in defeat and frustration, swiping my hands down my face to try and regain my composure. "I never wanted your lives to change irreparably because of my mistakes," I choke out on the verge of crying. "I didn't know what else to do," my voice cracks on the last word.

"I want to be super clear. I might be frustrated and a little disappointed, but I have never thought of Akio as a mistake." Mom softens her voice the slightest bit. "We love him and adore him. Just as much as we love you."

"May I?" Mommy asks, always the emotional buffer. I nod at her through barely restrained tears and Mom remains silent.

"When everything happened, when you found out you were pregnant and decided to raise Akio alone, it felt like all of us lost so much, especially you. And I think we all hoped that it would turn out okay." She pauses to take my hand in hers gently. "But honey, we know how much losing him changed you and broke you. We saw it. And when you came home, it was like you were a different person. That fire, that independence, that tenacity you once had were all muted. I knew all those pieces of you were still there, just buried underneath a lot of pain. So, I think what we want most is for you to be happy, to be whole, for you to live a bold, beautiful, unapologetic life. We just don't want you to lose any more pieces of yourself. Okay?"

I'm ugly crying now, tears falling down my face. Because they saw too much and at the same time not enough. Because they had witnessed all the ugly, rotten parts of me that I had tried to disguise and mold into something resembling resilience. The way good parents often do. Because they want the version of me that I was before all this had happened. They longed for their daughter that had incredible dreams and a bright future. And god dammit, so did I. I ached for the innocence that came with not knowing what it was like to lose the love of your life. The person whose absence was so painful, whose loss so devastating it felt like the air had been ripped from my lungs. I yearned for the ease of surrendering to happiness and light before I knew the lure of darkness and depression.

Both my moms have tears in their eyes too. I get up from the chair and crush Mommy with a hug and shortly after, all three of us are embracing each other.

"I don't want to lose any more pieces of myself either," I sob. "But I think the only way for me to live my version of a bold beautiful life is to do that with Kai. I have to try. I have to know one way or the other or I will never be happy," I admit. They accept this quietly and both bob their heads in agreement.

"I'm sorry," I press on. "I know I haven't exactly lived up to your expectations of me." It's all coming out now, everything. All my fears and insecurities. Every thought I had formulated when I first got pregnant but couldn't put into words. There's no other option. It's a cleanse, a reckoning, a reset button for our family. I didn't know how badly I needed it until this very moment.

"Is that what you believe? That we think you failed?"

"Well, I'm not a lawyer." I reply, sniffling. "I didn't go to grad school and I'm barely making ends meet while supporting Akio and me. So, if that isn't failing, what would you call it?"

"Living. Surviving. Figuring it out. You haven't failed by any measure or stretch of the imagination, Kendall."

I let out a long sigh. "I also haven't told you everything," I concede.

"What do you mean?" she asks, leaning forward in her chair. So, I tell them the *thing*. The only thing that might close the chasm between what I did and where we are now. The weight that's been sitting on my chest for almost three years. I explain how Kai's dad had cornered me when I was at my most vulnerable and forced me into an impossible position. That he had taken advantage of the fact that I was confused and powerless. How ultimately, he added to the list of reasons I felt like my only options were an abortion or raising Akio without Kai. I tell them the whole story from start to finish. Only stopping to refill wine glasses and take out a carton of ice cream to pacify the ever-growing shitstorm I had created.

"That son of a bitch," Mom barks. "I'll kill him."

"I don't even know what to say," Mommy says, her mouth agape. "How could he do this? We were friends with them for decades!"

"I know, he was just being protective of Kai," I respond.

"That's not an excuse for this kind of behavior, Kendall. Does Kai know?"

"No, but I think I have to tell him, sooner rather than later."

"Is this part of the reason you wanted to move and break off contact with Kai?" Mom asks, her brows knit together tightly. I nod, my gaze swinging between both of them. There's an understanding there, a confirmation. I don't want them to press me anymore on the subject and thankfully, they don't.

Shortly after this, we retire to the couch, everyone in need of a good distraction. My moms sit down on either end and I nestle myself in between them. Mommy grabs the remote off the coffee table and starts an episode of Gilmore Girls.

"Gilmore girls, wine, and a gallon of ice cream can cure a multitude of ills," she observes digging into the open container of moose tracks. "Thank you for coming to my Ted Talk."

"Aren't you full of inspirational wisdom," Mom quips, leaning back against the couch. I laugh quietly to myself while wiping the remnants of my salt stained tears from my face. I bring a spoonful of ice cream to my lips and finally, I can breathe a sigh of relief. A thousand pound weight has been lifted off of my shoulders.

Now I just have to tell Kai.

***

I LEAVE MY MOMS' house the next day with a box of mementos I forgot had even existed. They urged me to take it home with me now that they know about everything. They claimed it was finally time to dig into the past and they're probably right. I peer into the box. Friendship bracelets Kai, Jenna, and I had made in second grade. My senior prom corsage. Letters Kai had written me after I left for North Carolina, a framed picture of us at our college graduation, and an old sweatshirt of his. My mom had tried to give me the letters while I was still pregnant with Akio. I refused to open them then. I couldn't. It would only have made things harder.

Now when I try to bring my trembling fingers to tear open the envelopes, I still can't do it. Fear, regret, and shame all morph together to form a lump that perches in my throat. I hastily shove the letters back in the plastic crate and return my hands to the steering wheel.

I have to manage one fire at a time and I doubt what I need after last night is reading hate mail from Kai. I would read them eventually. But not now. Because the horrible, unfortunate truth is that Kai couldn't despise the person I was back then any more than I despised myself.

Chapter 40

Kendall

2016

It's been a week since I took the pregnancy test and we're no closer to making a decision we can both live with. Except that Kai thinks we are. I told him I was going to the clinic, that I had made an appointment. And I did, but I'm not entirely sure I can go through with it.

Can I do this and somehow move on with my life?

Will I regret it?

Will the pain consume me until there's nothing left?

I have biological parents out there somewhere who decided to keep me and eventually put me up for adoption. Wasn't that better than what I'm now considering? But the thought of this child growing up in a different family, always wondering why they weren't wanted, living a life that's supposed to be with me and Kai—I can't quite stomach that either.

Kai and I fought all morning. All he wants is to drive me to the appointment and I keep refusing. Probably because deep down, I know my heart won't let me do it. Then he rushed out early for practice and something about the way we left things makes me uneasy. Like this is something our relationship won't survive.

Seated at my kitchen table, I let the warmth and steam from my coffee surround me. Then I hear a brisk knock on my door. I undo the lock and deadbolt to find Mr. Matsumoto, Kai's dad, standing on the front porch.

What the hell is he doing here? How does he even know where I live? He's carrying an umbrella and shuffling back and forth from one foot to the other.

"Hi, Kendall, can I come in?" he asks, closing the umbrella and fastening the clasp.

"Sure," I reply, holding my front door open for him. He has light blue scrubs on underneath his jacket and white sneakers. He clearly just finished a shift at the hospital and came straight here. He seems tired and on edge, like he'd rather be anywhere but in my apartment.

"Is everything okay? What are you doing here?" I question, worried, as if my day could get any more stressful.

"I don't want to take up too much of your time—so I'll be brief. I know about the pregnancy, the baby." I feel my knees buckle, the ground beneath my feet unsteady.

"H-how?" I stammer, not sure how I'm putting words together.

"It doesn't matter how I found out, what matters is what you plan to do about it," he says, his tone sharp, his words clipped. I can't believe we're having this conversation.

"I'm supposed to go to the clinic today. Have you talked to Kai about this at all? I feel uncomfortable discussing this with you when—"

He cuts me off. "No, and he doesn't know I'm here. He's not even aware that I know about the *situation* and I'd like to keep it that way."

"Okay. So why exactly are you here?"

"To ensure Kai's future stays intact. This kind of thing, this kind of scandal could ruin his career before it even starts. I think we both know you are too young to raise a child on your own. I'm hoping we both want what's best for him—for both of you," he explains.

"And what is that? What do you want from me?" I demand, starting to sense where this conversation is going.

"I want you to have it taken care of, discretely. I'll help cover the cost and then some. Or have the baby and use the money to start over. But either way, leave Kai out of it."

I ball my hands into fists, rage threatening to take over. "And if I don't?" I counter.

"Ultimately, the choice is up to you. But if you love him, you won't destroy his future or his career," he postures.

"Get out," I yell through gritted teeth, my hands trembling.

"Please, Kendall, think about my offer—"

"You have a lot of nerve coming here behind Kai's back and trying to bribe me to have an abortion!" I shriek. I clasp my elbows with my hands and fight back tears in an attempt to keep all my emotions from spilling over at once. "I wonder what he would think if he knew you thought so little of him, of me, of our relationship. Kai always described you as cold and callous, said you were a difficult person to understand and even harder to love. But I defended you, tried to give you the benefit of the doubt. But I get it now, what he meant."

He stares at me in disbelief, his face haunted and devoid of color as his defenses slowly start to come down. I don't know if it's embarrassment or shame. I realize I might have gone a step too far, but I don't care. Neither of us says anything for a few seconds.

He sighs, his features softening. "Kendall, you've always been like family to us. Just think about what I'm saying. You're young, smart, you have so much potential. You can still be a lawyer and Kai can still play in the NHL. Neither of you should have to give up the things that you've been working your whole life to achieve."

I glare at him.

"Except each other, right?" I ask coldly. "This has been the hardest day on top of the most difficult week of my life and your presence here has made it infinitely worse. You don't have to worry. I'll have it taken care of without your money. Now please get the hell out of my apartment." He looks like he wants to say something else but doesn't. Thankfully, he leaves without another word and I slam the door shut behind him. I feel sick to my stomach and not from morning sickness and not because my boyfriend's father just tried to buy my compliance. But because I know at my core there's some truth to his father's words.

This wasn't the first time Takura expressed concerns about our relationship or the first time he meddled when he probably shouldn't have. But it's the first time it leaves me feeling wrecked and hollow. The only things left are dread, rage, and impossible choices.

Getting drafted straight out of college to the NHL is a pipe dream and he might never get an opportunity like this again. I can't let him risk his future for me, everything he's been working relentlessly for. I peel back the curtain covering my small dining room window and watch his dad slowly walk away from my apartment, get in his SUV, and drive off. I feel humiliated and dehumanized. But I have more clarity than I've had in a long time. The events of the past week, more notably today, have illuminated three simple truths for me.

I love Kai.

I'm having this baby.

To protect him, I need to do the hardest thing I have ever had to do and let him go.

CHAPTER 41

KENDALL

2014

I'M LYING IN THE threadbare woven hammock that's stationed between two sprawling oak trees in the backyard of our summer cottage. It's warm but getting cooler out as the ocean breeze sweeps over me. Kai and I are in Cape Cod vacationing with both our families, the summer after sophomore year of college. It's the only time of year Kai is granted a break from his demanding hockey schedule. We spend our nights laughing, kissing, holding each other, touching to the extent that we can with both our parents a few doors down. We spend our days soaking up the sun, swimming, filling up on ice cream and exploring North Truro.

His father's low authoritative voice carries over to me. I stop and close the book I'm reading to listen. I don't think they know I'm back here.

"You know you're going to have to get even more serious about hockey, Kai. You can't afford to have any distractions," he informs him.

"I don't. You know my schedule, my routine. I barely have time for anything else," Kai argues.

"Except Kendall," Takura indicates, leaving something unspoken.

"Dad, I don't want to talk about this again. Our relationship is none of your business. She's also not a distraction. She's..."

I'm what?

"Maybe not yet. But she will be. I'm not saying you two shouldn't be together, just that now might not be the right time. I just think you need to keep your priorities straight—"

"I know, Dad," Kai cuts him off. "I am. You don't have to worry about it."

"Well, I am going to worry about it. There's zero room for error, Kai. You don't have the luxury of being able to afford fuck ups or mistakes. When people who look like us try to achieve greatness, we have to work twice as hard for the same amount or sometimes half of the appreciation and accolades."

The way they're talking about this makes it seem like they have this conversation a lot. Suddenly I don't want to keep eavesdropping. I get up from the hammock as inconspicuously as possible and start speedwalking somewhere. Anywhere to get away from what I just heard.

But Kai wouldn't do that, would he? Break up with me. Discard me like garbage and forget about us? Would he sacrifice our relationship for the sake of his career? I didn't think so but now I'm not so sure. Kai's life has to be controlled, organized, disciplined with tight schedules and strict food regimens. Daily workouts that leave him exhausted and that's on top of practices and games. That's the cost of playing at a collegiate level. And getting drafted, playing in the NHL, would require even more of him. Everything. I am throwing all of that off balance. I'm chaos and unpredictability. Not intentionally. But just the fact that he's in a serious long-term relationship is enough. He's forced to carve out time he doesn't have. Time that can be better spent preparing for his career.

Am I a welcome face after long days? A reprieve from the pressure of his grueling athletic commitments and rigorous course load? I don't know anymore. I've always thought I make his life better, enhance it. The way he enhances mine. But maybe all I am is a distraction he can't afford. One more thing he has to devote energy to, that he probably doesn't have. And just like that, the seeds of doubt are planted in my heart, watered with insecurities and uncertainty. Words spoken into existence by his father that before were only soft whispers in my head. This makes it real. Threatening.

It becomes a wild insatiable beast in my chest, snarling and scraping, thrashing with hunger, and yearning to escape. Ready to feast on the parts of me I don't quite know how to love or nurture yet.

For the first time, I wonder whether Kai's future—neatly outlined, clearly defined, and laid out for him before he could even walk—if maybe that future doesn't include me at all.

Chapter 42

Kai

Two weeks. It's been two weeks since Kendall slept over and we've already reverted back to horny lovesick teenagers again. If I'm not with her, I'm thinking about her and when I'm with her, I'm trying my hardest to get her alone and remove as much clothing as possible. Practice, games, and visits with Akio and Ken eat up most of my time. Which doesn't leave a lot of room for anything else.

Realizing I haven't heard from Aiden in a while, I drop by his apartment on my one free afternoon in weeks. Whoever opens his door is the most haggard, unhinged version of him I have ever met. A gaunt, pale face I almost don't recognize peers back at me. His hair sticks up in random places, bones peek out from underneath his skin, and his eyes are red rimmed and glassy. And somehow, he smells worse than he looks, which is pretty fucking bad. Like he hasn't bothered to shower in days.

"What are you doing here?" he mutters, hand gripped firmly on the door that's barely open. Which I assume is intentional—if this is how he looks, I'm a little terrified to see the rest of his apartment.

"Nice to see you too, asshole," I remark with a smirk. "You realize it's like two in the afternoon, right?"

"Yeah, so?" he grumbles.

"Don't you have work or something?" I ask suspiciously.

"It's a work from home day, what's it to you?" he scoffs.

"Nothing," I shrug. "I just came over to see if you wanted to hang or grab dinner or something. Maybe catch the beginning of March madness?" I ask hopefully.

"Tonight's not a good night, Kai. I've got a lot of work to catch up on," he replies and it's obvious it's a blatant lie.

"Okay, what about—"

"I'll text you when I'm free, okay? Sorry man. Tonight won't work," he repeats, closing the door in my face.

What the fuck just happened?

I'm tempted to knock on his door again and force him to tell me what the hell is going on. But the state he's in doesn't exactly scream stable. I doubt he'd listen to what I have to say right now anyway. I text Kendall on the way to my car, needing someone else to weigh in on this.

> Hey, random question. Have you talked to Aiden recently?

> No why?

> I was just at his apartment and he was being really fucking weird

> Weird how?

> Idk he seemed out of it

> Drugs maybe?

> Yeah I haven't talked to him in a while.

> Jenna still keeps in touch with him though. Maybe ask her?

> Okay. Good idea

Thirty seconds later, Jenna's chipper yet threatening voice answers my call, right as I open my car door.

"Hey stranger, to what do I owe the pleasure? You better not be fucking things up already with Ken."

"Hey, Jenna. No, things are good with me and Ken. How are you?" I ask, attempting to make small talk.

"Things are good. Amir and I are doing well. California is gorgeous and sunny and about as perfect as you'd expect it to be in early March. But let's cut the bullshit. I haven't talked to you in ages. So, what's up? Spill the tea, my guy."

I sigh, resting my head against the steering wheel. "I was wondering if you've heard from Aiden recently?" There's a pause so long I begin to wonder if she hung up on me.

"Why?" Her tone shifts from bright and cheery to deeply concerned in a matter of seconds.

"I don't know. Things just seem off with him lately. I was just at his apartment and he was acting really fucking weird," I reply. I didn't even really know how to explain his behavior and what I just witnessed, but it definitely was out of character for Aiden.

"Look, I'm not sure if I should be the one to tell you this. But I guess if you're calling me, you probably already know." I hear chatter in the background and then it suddenly goes quiet, like she's moved to somewhere more secluded and private. "Aiden was in California last year for work. He stayed with Amir and I for a day and he didn't leave on great terms."

"What do you mean?"

"I mean the morning before his flight, he asked me for a loan and I honestly thought he was joking at first. But he wasn't. He told me he needed the money and that he would pay me back," she explains.

"Did he say what it was for? I'm assuming you didn't give him the loan."

"Ah, beauty and brains," she jokes. "I didn't give him the loan. But I had a feeling he was in trouble. I didn't have that kind of money to blow without a guarantee I would get it back. I mean, I've loaned him money once or twice but never this much," she admits, her tone somber.

"How much did he ask you for?" I wonder.

"Five thousand dollars," she answers quietly. I realize with sobering clarity that this is way worse than I thought it was. Fear settles in my gut while cold dread slithers across my skin.

I mutter a string of expletives under my breath. "What do you think it is? Drugs? Gambling?"

"I think it's probably both. And I think he's in over his fucking head, Kai." I can tell by her tone that she's serious, that she's already come to terms with the gravity of the situation. But then why wasn't she freaking out like I was?

"Fuck. So, what do we do? How do we help him?" I ask, panicked.

"I don't think we can. Not yet anyways. Not until he's ready to accept help. You of all people should know you can't save someone that doesn't want to save themselves," she answers firmly.

"What are you talking about?" I demand, confused about the detour this conversation had taken.

"Kai..."

"Jenna..."

She sighs heavily. "I know you stopped drinking your first year on the Bucks. Kendall told me."

"So? What does that have to do with Aiden? I'm not an alcoholic. This isn't the same thing," I respond defensively.

"Maybe not. But I saw the headlines. Your very public fall from grace. It seems like you were trying to drink yourself out of a tough spot, or maybe into an even worse one—"

"Are you nearing the point, Jenna?" I interject.

"Yes Kai," she says curtly. "The fact remains that you decided to stop drinking and you're still sober. But would you have listened to anyone if they asked you to stop drinking? Aside from Ken?" It's a question, but she asks it with such unwavering certainty that it sounds like an accusation. And we both know that she's right, that she's got me. Because I was in such a fucked up place at the time, that nothing would have stopped my downward trajectory, aside from the threat of losing my career. Aside from hitting rock fucking bottom. Which for me, was a DUI that almost got me killed.

"No, probably not," I murmur.

"Exactly. You had to decide for yourself that you wanted to dig yourself out of that hole. That has to come first. Otherwise, best efforts, good intentions, interventions, rehab—none of it is going to stick."

"So, you're saying there's nothing we can do? We just have to sit back and watch while he spirals and self-destructs?"

"I'm saying you can try talking to him, an intervention. Maybe reach out to his parents? But I wouldn't get your hopes up."

"Okay," I respond, feeling defeated.

"And Kai? I'm proud of you for digging yourself out of that hole. I'm proud of you for a lot of things. I don't think I ever told you that. Becoming a professional hockey player is no small feat. Losing her wasn't small either. I know that."

"Thanks. I appreciate it."

"I'm sorry I wasn't there for you more when Ken left and everything happened. I should have been. That was shitty of me," she admits.

"It's okay," I pause. "Did you know about Akio?"

"Yeah. But it wasn't my secret to share. I had to respect her choice," she reasons.

"I know...you're going to make a great therapist, Jenna."

"Thanks," she chirps. "I got to get going, Kai. Keep in touch, okay?"

"Okay. You too."

The line goes dead and I reflect on how blunt and honest that conversation had been. Exactly like Jenna. But also cathartic in a way I didn't even realize I needed.

Last I knew, she was studying to be a licensed marriage and family therapist, undoubtedly spurred by her parents' ugly divorce when we were in high school. She's going to be a damn good one. That phone call makes me realize how much I've missed her over the past couple years. It feels good to finally have the band back together. Kind of.

But Aiden is a whole different beast, one I don't feel confident I can tackle on my own. Or at all. I thought this conversation would be illuminating and it was, but not in the way I had hoped. I wanted to walk away with concrete solutions, something I could do. But now all I have is more questions and crippling anxiety. I feel the familiar hum of it buzzing underneath my skin. It seeps into my chest and starts expanding like a balloon ready to burst. A frantic, crazed energy that's itching to be released.

I'm terrified that the only person who can help Aiden now has already given up.

Chapter 43

Kai

2017

THE LAST THING I remember is crashing through a guardrail. That and the explosive impact of the airbag. The harsh beeping of monitors, the presence of an IV bag, and the pain radiating up my side and across my ribs tell me I'm most definitely not in my bed. I'm in a hospital, groggy and confused, trying to put the pieces of the previous night together.

I turn over to my right side and wince with pain. My mom is asleep in her wheelchair, tightly grasping my arm. God she must have been so terrified.

How could I have done something like this to her, to my family again? What the fuck was I thinking?

I guess I hadn't been. I've been reacting for months. Drinking, partying, gambling, getting in fights, all in an attempt to distance myself from her. The real pain that still hasn't faded. My mom hears me shuffling in the bed and opens her eyes.

"Oh my god, Kai. You're awake," her voice is soft yet strained. I doubt she was able to get any sleep in the position she's in. "How are you feeling?" she asks while squeezing my hand.

"Like absolute shit," I reply. "Mom, I'm so—"

But I don't get the chance to apologize, beg for forgiveness, tell her I have finally come to my senses. A tall female doctor walks in directly followed by my father. Her bright fiery hair is pulled in a tight bun, her green eyes scanning me with cursory judgement. I know what it looks like. Another idiotic, juvenile professional athlete, who thinks he's invincible and none of the rules apply to him, on his way to a second DUI charge. Worse, I know what it actually is. Me on the verge of ruining my career because I can't seem to get my shit together. I'm fucking pathetic.

"Kai, how are you feeling?" she greets me but it doesn't carry any warmth.

"Kind of terrible."

"Yeah, I would expect so. Your car collided head on with a tree on Glendale. You were unconscious when the paramedics showed up. The window shattered so you do have some lacerations on your arms and face from that. Thankfully, you were wearing your seatbelt and the airbag deployed, so you'll have some residual bruising. You also have a few fractured ribs, but aside from that, you should be fully recovered in a couple weeks."

"Was there anyone..." *Jesus, how do I ask this?* "Did I hurt anyone?" I'm so fucking embarrassed. I'm so angry at myself I want to scream, curl up into this hospital bed until it swallows me whole. I feel tears collecting in the corner of my eyes but I push them down.

"No, it doesn't seem there were any other cars or people around at the time. The police are going to want to question you and get your statement though. They'll be waiting outside when you're ready." My dad is hovering in the corner, his arm on my mom's shoulder glaring at me. His face is cold, hard, impatient. Fuck, he's going to kill me. He's never going to speak to me again.

I swallow, my mouth dry and gritty, and look away from them. "Okay. How soon will I be able to play again?" I wonder.

"We're going to keep you another night for observation. But you don't appear to have a concussion or anything else that might require an extensive stay here. I'd say a few weeks and once those ribs are healed you can be cleared to play."

"Okay. Thank you, I appreciate it."

"A word of advice?" I nod. "If you are going to be drinking that heavily, it is imperative you do not get behind a wheel. You could have died or killed someone else. You are very lucky to be alive," she pauses, taking in my reaction. Then she continues, her voice quieter. "There are a lot of great mental health resources and addiction services available at this hospital. I'd be happy to make a referral or recommendation if you need one," she smiles politely.

"Thank you."

"Thank you, Farrah, that was helpful. I think Kai could use some rest now though," my father remarks, effectively shutting her up and shooing her out the door. Of course my father knows her by name. He worked here as a surgeon early on in his career.

"Dad, I'm really sorry," my voice cracks on the last word. He holds his hand up as if to say enough.

"This is the last time we will speak of this foolishness. You've been given everything, *everything*, and you choose to squander it. Why? I would have killed for the opportunities you have," he fumes. "The Bucks director of PR is already spinning a story, controlling the narrative so you come out of this looking relatively decent. The team lawyers have gotten the charges dropped. All you have to do is your part, which is to stop fucking up. You think you can manage that?" he snaps. My mom stares at him in shock but remains silent. Good. I deserve his wrath, his anger.

There's something wrong with me. I'm not right, I want to say. And the longer it goes on, the harder it is to admit it, to try and resolve it.

I open my mouth to say something but nothing comes out. The conversation has spiraled so out of control I have no idea how to get it back. I have a few bruises and scrapes but over time, those will heal. I haven't killed anyone but I could have. I've forced my mom to endure the aftermath of another traumatic car accident. And I'm just getting another slap on the wrist.

How long can I narrowly evade death? How many times can I tempt fate and be rewarded for it?

This isn't me. This isn't who I am, or at least it isn't who I want to be. I don't willingly endanger myself and other people out of pure stupidity. I'm blowing up my life and watching as the pieces scatter like ash around me. I have to fix this. Now. Today. Yesterday.

I've been selfish, immature, and reckless. Not to mention my deplorable behavior won't change one goddamn thing.

It has to stop.

Chapter 44

Kendall

I pick my head up off the couch and that simple movement alone is excruciating. I peek at my phone, even though the brightness of my screen adds to my overall discomfort. It's only 9:00 but somehow it feels like it's three in the morning. Akio is probably already asleep at my moms' house.

They called earlier to see if we wanted to come to dinner. When I answered my phone, I was already running a 101 fever and sounded pretty fucking terrible. After I coughed for the first minute of the conversation, they offered to take Akio for the weekend and would not take no for an answer. Which is for the best. I'm quite certain I'm approaching death, or something eerily similar. My head is heavy, like it's been stuffed with cotton, my throat hoarse and sore, my nose won't stop running, and my chest is burning from all the coughing fits. Small things like moving from my bed to the couch take an astronomical amount of energy. But the couch is prime real estate, situated directly in front of the TV. And the only thing distracting me from the prison that is currently my body, is reruns of *The Office*.

An incoming call that makes my head vibrate with pain interrupts me from my obligatory illness related wallowing. It's Kai. I let it go to voicemail and start drafting a text to him, but before I can send it, he calls again.

"Hello?" I croak.

"Ken? What's wrong?" His voice is coated with concern.

"I was just about to" *cough* "text you" *cough* "I think I have the flu."

"Shit. You sound awful. Is Akio sick too?"

I turn over onto my side and let the phone balance precari-ously on my cheek. Holding it up to my ear is too much effort.

"No. My moms' took him for the weekend so I could get some rest."

"Okay, but who is taking care of you?" he asks, which is such a Kai thing for him to say.

"I'm fine," *cough*. "My moms brought me soup, and I have some leftover cold medicine from the last time we were sick." At least I think I do. My thoughts are starting to become hazy, and slightly incoherent.

"Ken," he insists, "I'm coming over. The flu has been bad this year. A lot of people have gone to the hospital—"

I close my eyes, starting to nod off. "Kai, I'm fine, I'll be okay. I swear." I think he's about to pressure me into letting him come over, when I hear a chirping sound that seems too close to be coming from outside. I watch horrified as a flurry of wings and feathers zip across my ceiling.

What the fuck? Am I hallucinating? Am I that sick?

"Kai, I have to go. I think there's a bird...or something in my apartment," I explain and abruptly hang up on him. I somehow peel myself from my indented hole on the couch and poke my head above the cushion. There is indeed a small brown bird sitting on my dining room chair.

"Hey there little guy," I say in my most non-threatening voice, which he doesn't seem to appreciate. He immediately takes off and flies straight into my kitchen cabinets. I lay back down in my cozy nest of blankets and used tissues to pull out my phone and Google animal control.

Is that even who I call in this situation?

But I have depleted my energy reserves for the entire day. Before I can ponder my current predicament any further, my eyes flutter closed and I drift off into a peaceful, birdless sleep.

***

W HEN I WAKE UP, I'm in my bed. At least I think it's my bed. I lean over to turn on the lamp that's on my nightstand, confirming that I'm definitely in my room. Even the tiniest bit of light burns my retinas and adds to the throbbing at the base of my skull. I switch it back off wondering how I ever made it to my bed, when I hear a deep voice coming from outside my room.

"If you're here to kill me, know I have the flu," I shout into the hallway hoarsely. Kai appears in my bedroom doorway, dressed in Boston Bucks athletic gear, his inky black hair unruly underneath his hat.

Did he still remember that a backwards hat was my weakness, my kryptonite? God, I need to get a grip.

And of course he's grinning as he leans against the doorframe. Fucking grinning, and it's absolutely diabolical. I'm on my deathbed and here he is, looking like he effortlessly rolled out of a GQ spread. He's so devastatingly handsome it's comical. But I'm beyond caring. The part of me that would be mortified to have Kai witness me at my lowest, sickest, hot dumpster fire self, had been desecrated along with my dignity when I had mono my junior year of college.

"I might actually kill you if you don't let me start taking care of you," he counters, his tone playful.

"What are you doing here?" I ask, exasperated and confused.

"I was already on my way when you said you had the flu," he explains. "But the bird in the apartment was the real selling point for me," he smiles. Just seeing it has me feeling the slightest bit better.

"Right," I say, fighting against the pressure building in my head. "I think I may have fallen asleep after the bird...So, I wasn't hallucinating?"

He moves to sit down at the foot of the bed. "You were not hallucinating. I did get him out though. I just got off the phone with your landlord—"

"Wait what? What do you mean you got him out? How?" I attempt to lift my head off the pillow and quickly realize it's not doable.

"I read online that if you leave a window or door open, eventually they'll fly out. I also gave him a little bit of a nudge with a broom. After like thirty minutes he finally went into the hallway. I called your landlord to let him know it's his problem now."

"How—" his face breaks into a smile again.

"Your landlord's number is on the side of your fridge," he comments. He lifts the blanket, taking both of my feet in his lap, and then starts massaging them. He moves his thumbs over the arch in smooth circular motions, applying just the right amount of pressure, and it feels amazing.

"Thank you, Kai. You didn't have to—god, that feels good," I groan, interrupting my own thoughts.

"I did have to and it was nothing. You know I'm not leaving. So just let me take care of you, Ken," he responds.

"Fine," I relent. "But I feel like you should keep your distance. You have important games coming up. Maybe don't stay longer than necessary?" I suggest.

"Kendall, I'm staying for as long as you need me, okay? I'll be fine, you know my immune system. Now close your eyes, lay your head back, and let me massage your feet," he insists.

I wake up two times throughout the night. Once to Kai stroking my hair while he scrolls on his phone. I'm positive I hear him murmur something like *go back to sleep, beautiful*, but my feverish brain cannot be trusted. The next time I'm starving because I haven't eaten in almost eighteen hours. I get up in search of a snack but Kai guides me with a gentle hand back to bed. He returns five minutes later with toast and chicken noodle soup, which is somehow the perfect temperature. He spoon feeds it to me like I'm a goddamn baby bird. And it's at this moment that I find myself feeling so grateful and relieved that he came. I know in my bones that this is what it is to be truly loved and taken care of by Kai. That he always shows up and is fiercely loyal to the people he cares about. I also realize, not for the first time, that I probably don't deserve him.

But I want to be the person who does. I want to keep him anyways. And I know it's not just the illness talking.

Chapter 45

Kendall

The next morning, there's a split second, a small fragment of time where I forget I'm sick. That tiny innocuous sliver between sleep and awake. But reality hits me hard when I realize my clothes are sticky or possibly wet? I also can't stop shivering despite being under a thick down comforter. With maximum effort, I sit up against my headboard, still bundled underneath the blanket.

"Kai?" I call and then start coughing. I hear him shuffling in the living room, his heavy footsteps moving across the floor.

"Hey, you okay? How ya feeling?" he asks with a yawn, still half asleep. He's wearing nothing but his black Calvin's, his hair is disheveled, and his deliciously sculpted muscles are on full display. His tribal tattoos twist and swirl around his biceps and smaller ones caress his chest and torso. Beckoning me to touch them, run my hands over them. Not to mention, he has a semi straining against the inside of his boxers. I'm being tortured, I have to be. This is some sick sort of cruel and unusual punishment. But for what? I don't know. I pay my taxes, I go to church. *Once a year.* Still, I'm not really sure what I did to deserve this.

"I think my fever is spiking." *Cough.* "I'm freezing and sweaty and I feel like I can't get warm enough," *cough*. He walks over to the side of the bed resting the back of his hand on my forehead.

"You feel clammy and you're burning up," he observes. "Let's get you into a nice cool bath."

My eyes pop open. "I really don't think that's necessary. I'll just stay here and shiver it out," I object while shaking my head. "Plus, you know how I feel about baths."

He gives me a lopsided smile. "Yes, I know. In the words of Schmidt, 'bathtubs are medieval filth cauldrons.' But you're still taking one," he informs me while he begins unraveling the blanket.

"How about a cold shower?" I bargain.

"Fine. I'll go start it," he says and makes his way down the hall. When he comes back, I'm sitting up in bed, my feet slung over the side, with my eyes closed. I've made no progress in the removal of my clothes.

"Part of me wishes you didn't have to see me like this. But the delirious part of me simply doesn't care," I whisper.

"I want to be with you no matter how you look. I want to see you even when you're sick or in pain or hurting," he pauses to peel my sweaty t-shirt from my body, lifting it over my head. "And I want to be the one to take care of you, to put you back together. I love all the parts of you—not just the parts that are convenient or easy, Kendall."

I swallow loudly and with difficulty while my heart starts galloping in my chest. I skip right over his blatant admission. He said he loves all the parts of me. Not that he loves *me* or that he's *in love with me.* That's an important distinction, I think. I can't be sure, but my muddy swampland of a brain is screaming at me to not touch this live grenade right now.

"I know, Kai, I appreciate it," I say while sheepishly crossing my arms over my bare chest. He moves his hands to my underwear and pulls them down delicately. His rough palms trail the back of my thighs and calves until suddenly, I'm sitting in front of him completely naked. My clothes are in a damp pile on the floor. And I think this is the most vulnerable I've ever been in front of him. I feel totally exposed and of course he knows, because he is always dialed into me and what I need. He scoops me up with one arm under my legs and the other bracing my back and I wrap my arms around his neck.

He kisses my temple softly as he carries me to the bathroom. "I've seen you sick, lonely, depressed, miserable. I've seen you hungover and overcome with grief. I've seen everything, Ken, and you have never stopped being beautiful," he whispers into my hair. A strangled laugh escapes my throat. I'm coughing, sneezing, and sweating my way to death's doorstep and Kai does not bat an eyelash. He doesn't even flinch. He just does what needs to be done.

"I probably look like the grim reaper, Kai. And I'm quite positive I smell worse. I sweat the bed for Christ sake."

"Good thing we're showering then."

He sets me down in the bathtub and the water is alarmingly cold at first, pricking my skin like ice. But after a few seconds, I adjust and it feels heavenly on my face and the rest of my body. This shower might actually revive me. I wait for him to make his way out but he doesn't move. Instead, he sits down on the edge of the tub as I blink at him. "Tilt your head back," he instructs and starts lathering my hair with shampoo. I sigh in response. After that he does my body, running a soapy washcloth over my tired, aching muscles with care and attention. He leaves almost no part of me untouched and his calloused hands caressing my skin are shockingly gentle. His touch soothes and comforts me, so much so that I let loose a strained whimper when he finishes. This is one of the most sensual experiences of my life—if only I didn't feel like I'd been flattened by an eighteen wheeler.

"This is nice," I mutter, resting my head on my arm and my arm against the ledge of the bath.

"It is," he admits, kissing my forehead. He leans over me to turn the knob of the shower faucet off.

"Maybe we could do it again...when I don't feel like absolute shit."

"I think we can make that happen," he replies while helping me stand up. Then he wraps me in a fluffy towel and I'm in his arms once again.

CHAPTER 46

KAI

AFTER GETTING KENDALL IN some dry clothes and tucking her in under the covers, I let her rest for a few hours. She seems slightly better, a little more lucid than yesterday. When I first got here last night, she was in rough shape. My heart stuttered in my chest when I saw her sleeping on the couch covered in discarded tissues. She looked so small and frail. Kendall's not good at letting people take care of her, at needing others, or relying on them. I've learned that lesson many times over the years.

My first instinct was to go to her but then the bird swooped overhead and my priorities shifted. I carried her to her room then I got to work on removing the wild animal.

Since then, I've taken care of her, cleaned and disinfected her apartment, ordered groceries, and made sure she stays hydrated and fed. I don't have anywhere to be until my game at 7:00, so I want to help her as much as I can before that. After I cook breakfast, scroll on my phone for an hour, read the three magazines I found, and tidy Akio's room, I'm feeling antsy.

I'm poking around her apartment in search of books, when I discover an old stack of newspapers and magazine articles. There's a pile firmly wedged in the back of a drawer that I have to yank out. The first one by the *Boston Post* is dated October 14, 2016. I could never forget that date because it's permanently seared into my brain. It's the day I played my first professional hockey game. The headline reads *"Rookie Kai Matsumoto makes waves in the Boston Bucks first game of the season."*

I remember that game, the entire day so clearly. How nervous I was, how anxious I felt. The chanting and cheering of the crowd vibrating through my body. The energy in the stands and the giant expanse of the arena was like nothing I had ever felt before. I also remember wishing she was there to experience it with me. And I guess in a way she was.

I scan the other snippets and articles she saved. They're all about me—my performance, my games, every highlight and loss. There are articles about playoffs and exclusive features from interviews I'd given. It's a curated catalogue of my entire athletic career so far. I can't believe she kept all of these.

Why the fuck do I have the overwhelming urge to cry and send my fist through a wall?

At one point, I thought I was the only one of us in unbearable pain. I assumed that she eventually gave up on us and I just ceased to exist for her. That couldn't be further from the truth.

We never stopped existing for each other.

***

T HE DAYS BLUR TOGETHER. Kendall sleeps a lot and I let her, checking in every few hours, keeping her fed and hydrated. I leave for my game and come back. We order Mexican takeout and eat it on her couch with bad television on in the background. Slowly, the color starts coming back to her face. But those clippings sit in the back of my mind the whole time, patient and waiting.

Five days later, when Kendall is almost fully recovered, I garner the nerve to ask her about what I found. She's curled into my side, my head resting on top of hers, and I don't want to ruin this moment. But I don't think I can wait any longer.

"Ken?" I whisper, lowering the TV volume.

"Yeah?" She shifts beside me.

"We need to talk about something," I reply. I look down at her and her face blanches, but she sits up responsively.

"Okay. This feels like a sitting up conversation," she notes, unease in her voice.

"Yeah, it probably is," I say looking down at my hands. "It's nothing bad. I just know I won't be able to relax until we talk about it."

"Okay," she whispers.

"The second day you were sick, I was searching your apartment for a book while you were sleeping. But I found a bunch of newspapers and magazine clippings, and they were all about me…" I trail off.

She nods, understanding taking hold of her features. Her lips form a thin line and at first, I think she's angry.

"You went through my things?" But if anything, she seems curious and maybe slightly disappointed.

"I didn't mean to. I was just looking for something to pass the time." I turn to look at her but her arms are crossed and she refuses to meet my gaze. "I stumbled on it by accident. I swear. But I just want to know why you kept all those things."

She sits back against her headboard and peels her knees up to her chest, curling her arms around them.

"I just need a second, Kai. To gather my thoughts," she finally explains. She starts talking but she still isn't looking at me, almost like it's too painful. "I wanted to feel close to you even when I couldn't actually be close to you," she sighs. "I wanted so badly to be there with you. You have no idea how much I missed you. And I couldn't stop myself from admiring you from afar either. I've tried to watch almost every game. I wanted to support you however I could."

I hear the subtext, everything she can't say. She still wanted some small piece of me to be hers and she wanted to share these moments with me any way she could. I don't think she gets it, that she fully understands. I have never not been hers. I have always belonged to her and as far as I'm concerned, she has always been mine. Every beat of my heart belongs to this beautiful, crazy, infuriating woman. But I don't say any of that.

Instead, I deflect, trying to defuse the tension. "Couldn't stop yourself from admiring me, huh?"

"Don't even give me that," she tuts. "We both know you're twice as irresistible on the ice as you are off of it. Sometimes I think you were born to play this sport, handcrafted by the hockey gods to unleash violent perfection," she comments. I was born to play hockey, yes, but I was also born to love her. Surely, she must see that.

"Thanks, Ken," I smirk.

She offers me a small smile. "It wasn't just about that though. I didn't know if I would ever see you again and I wanted Akio to know who you were and be able to truly grasp your greatness. I wanted him to understand how amazing you are," she admits.

"I get it, Ken—"

"I don't think you do," she cuts me off, shaking her head. "That first game you played. I watched the entire thing. I couldn't take my eyes off of you. You were magnetic and explosive. Dwyer got MVP and it was well deserved with the shutout. But anyone who was paying attention could see you were made for this. That you were the unicorn player the Bucks had been missing. It was one of the best games of your entire career and you only got stronger and better from there. I was so fucking proud of you. I *am* proud of you and I'm so sorry I wasn't there," she says, a tear sliding down her face. "But I want to be there now. I want to support you."

Kendall had always been my biggest supporter, my best friend, and confidant. She had been there for it all, since we were kids. She attended almost every game I had in high school and college and would send me inspirational quotes and messages when some other aspect of life pulled her away from me—if only for a moment. She made me protein packed breakfasts and lunches when we were inseparable, our last year of undergrad. She knew when I needed space and when I needed to be talked off a ledge. She helped me get through panic attacks when I felt like the pressure I was under was suffocating me. And I guess when you love someone enough, unconditionally, fully, you learn how to nurture their hopes and dreams. When you're in a meaning-ful, committed relationship—that for all intents and purposes is heading in the direction of forever—that's what happens. Your dreams become their dreams and theirs become yours. I wanted so badly to have that with her again. I wanted us to pursue our goals together and build a life we were proud of, for us and for Akio. For years I had fantasized about her being fully back in my corner and now that she was, or at least wanted to be, I felt *unstoppable*. But that didn't change her lived experience, and I knew her perception of things was being clouded by guilt and pain.

"Come here," I say, pulling her into my lap. I breathe in her scent and bury my face in her neck. Her coconut body wash and the faint hint of vanilla in her hair are instantly calming. "Shh, it's okay. Everything is going to be okay. We're here now," I murmur.

It's not that I wasn't expecting this confession, but it feels so fucking good to finally hear it out loud. That I wasn't alone in wanting to feel close to her, that I wasn't the only one affected by our catastrophic breakup and separation. All that to say, she had missed me in the same debilitating way I had missed her, and another piece of this confusing puzzle slides into place.

I don't say anything else. I just cradle her tightly against my chest while her tears fall.

Hours later, we're in separate beds, in separate apartments, in different cities. We might as well be a world away from each other. When I can't stop tossing and turning and my chest is aching from missing them, I send her a text. I want to solidify everything we talked about today. And ultimately, I want more than just the flimsy promise of the immediate future. But this version of Kendall is like a stray cat, skittish and easily spooked. One sudden move or wrong decision would send her running, even if she claims otherwise. I'm lucky she didn't disappear when I prematurely asked her to move in with me. Time and patience have been my allies in trying to repair everything that's broken between us. I know I have to start small and bide my time.

I'd love that

But what about everything I missed?

You've been with me every step of the way.

And like you said we can't go back and change things.

But we can try to move forward and take advantage of the time we have now.

CHAPTER 47

KENDALL

AFTER MUSIC PLAYGROUP, EMMA and I are giving each other the play by play of our weekends. The boys are occupying themselves with toys in the kid's section. After Emma tells me about her birthday weekend from hell, I explain how Kai took care of me when I was sick. That's all I really have to report—my weekend was uneventful to say the least.

"You're lucky, Kendall. They don't make guys like him anymore you know," she says. Seeing as how she spent the weekend suffering with her terrible ex-husband and his narcissistic family, I do not take her comment lightly. Her ex is the epitome of *if he wanted to he would*. If he wanted to get better, he would. If he wanted to work through the issues in their marriage he would. If he wanted to treat her with kindness and compassion he would. But he didn't. He doesn't. He's an arrogant bastard, who—on more than one occasion—has been verbally and physically abusive to her. And I know even without using her relationship as a comparison that Kai is the exception, an outlier. He's one in a million. It's evident in his words, his touch, and the way he looks at me. Even in especially hard moments, he has always treated my heart with care. He isn't perfect but he's perfect *for me*. Flawed but still whole. And that's the kind of love Emma deserves. She absolutely deserves better than the very little her ex had to offer.

"They really really don't," I respond, sitting in the red velvet chair across from her.

"Excuse me, I don't mean to barge in on your conversation, but are you talking about Kai as in Kai Matsumoto? The professional hockey player?" Veronica asks and I already know the words that follow will be dripping with venom. That and I'll be unlikely to forget them.

"Yes, we are. But with all due respect, Veronica, this is a private conversation," I reply flippantly. Emma and I try to angle our bodies away from her but she stalks closer instead.

"Well then maybe you shouldn't be having it in a public place," she sneers. "I was just surprised to hear you're dating him, that's all. You aren't really his type." *God, I wish I could slap that smug look off her face.*

"And why is that?" I bristle, simmering with rage and disbelief.

"I mean everyone knows he's a notorious fuckboy who doesn't do monogamy. And the last serious relationship he had was with a super model. I should know, Leighton's practically family."

"Right." I mean, what else could I say? Our relationship isn't a secret but it isn't exactly public knowledge either. But I can't understand why I feel like I even owe her an explanation. And she isn't entirely wrong, the slate of women he'd been with while we were broken up were painfully beautiful, devastatingly gorgeous, and sex personified.

"I mean no offense, Kendall, you're very pretty but you're not exactly a supermodel," she observes snidely.

"Yeah, imagine a handsome professional athlete dating a mere mortal like me, who's at worst a California 5 and at best a Boston 7," I scoff. But our relationship doesn't need defining and it certainly doesn't require an explanation—not to her of all people.

Still, her words reverberate throughout my head and rattle around in my skull hours after I leave the library. Not to mention I keep getting tripped up on that name. Leighton. *Leighton, Leighton. Why did that name sound so fucking familiar?*

After Akio falls asleep, I type in the name into Instagram. I choose the second certified Leighton, Leighton Carraway, and everything clicks into place. The ball of unease churning in my gut starts to solidify.

CHAPTER 48

KENDALL

2017

I PROMISED MYSELF WHEN I agreed to help my parents move that I wouldn't even contemplate reaching out to Kai or walking over to his house unannounced. Yet here I am, sitting in the driveway of what used to be my childhood home and I'm glued to the spot. I've been in my car staring at the garage through my windshield for the past twenty minutes. Stuck between the desire to flee this place that holds so many happy memories of Kai and I and the gut wrenching, soul crushing ache to talk to him.

Moments later, a car, *his car*, pulls into his parents' driveway across the street. My mind is made up. If this isn't divine, cosmic intervention, I have no idea what it is. I duck quickly so he can't catch me stalking him and slink into my back seat. When my head resurfaces, my heart drops into my stomach. Kai exits his brand new BMW but he isn't alone. Shortly after, a gorgeous, slender woman emerges from the passenger side. They walk into his parents' house, his arm casually slung around her shoulder and my breath catches in my throat.

Fuckkkkk. He's dating? He has a girlfriend, one that is so serious she's meeting his parents? I've deliberately stayed off of social media so that I wouldn't have news of his post breakup life thrown in my face at every turn. Every once in a while, a story or tabloid would pop up about him leaving a hotel or bar with a new woman. But that is not what this is. What I've just witnessed seemed unfathomable up until now.

I can't breathe. I'm suffocating inside my tiny shitbox of a car. This is not how I fucking die, I refuse. I shove open the rear door violently and gasp, taking a deep lungful of crisp fall air.

I have to get closer. I have to see for myself what this relationship is or isn't. I creep along the edge of my car, low to the ground, and move quickly to the large oak tree in our front yard. I cross the street with haste and sprint to Kai's sleek SUV, careful not to set off his alarm. It's just a few more feet and then I'm positioned in front of the hedges that line their wide dining room window.

God, am I really doing this? Am I really this desperate and heartbroken? I feel so stupid, so incredibly immature and yet I can't prevent myself from looking, from needing to know.

I raise my head a millimeter and chance a look into the dining room. They're all in the kitchen, picking on appetizers and talking. Kai's dad opens a bottle of wine, offering it to Kai and his date, and I cringe internally. I can't hear Kai's response but I see his jaw tick—he looks bothered, frustrated. The way he typically is when he interacts with his dad. If she notices, she doesn't give anything away. His date accepts the glass of wine with a smile, while she laughs at a remark Anela, Kai's mom, makes. Kai goes back to studying something intensely on his phone, completely ignoring the conversation happening around him.

Maybe he isn't as into her as I thought?

But that notion dies a quick death when she lovingly wraps her petite arms around his waist and rests her head on his chest. He responds by giving her a kiss on the cheek and I have to stifle the urge to vomit. *Mine*, my whole body wants to scream. *Mine*, my splintered soul sobs. But he isn't mine and he hasn't been for a while.

My heart is eviscerated all over again. Like it's been thrown into a den of vipers and dealt a series of fang toothed blows. I sink into the grass and fold into myself. Next to my feet lies a large, jagged rock. It feels cool and heavy in my palm. I probably won't even need one this big to break the window.

What the fuck, Kendall?

What is wrong with you?

I set the rock aside and allow the heaving sobs to consume my body. I broke up with him. I walked away. I set him free. I wanted him to be happy, to be able to live his life.

So then why can't I accept this?

A half hour ago, I was ready to break down his door, beg him to hear me out, and ask for his forgiveness. Over the course of the last several months, I've come to accept I made a terrible, likely unforgivable mistake. But the position I'm in now is excruciating, impossible to navigate, and also, entirely my own fault. I'm in a miserable bed of my own fucking making. I can't come running back to him when he finally seems happy for the first time in a year.

There's a large part of me that wants to just be done with it once and for all, to finally and truly let him go. But a small part of me—the part that's trying to stop me from crawling into another black pit of despair—knows I should fight for him. I barely made it out of the throes of postpartum depression with my life. I can't go back there, to that cold, bleak place filled with darkness, unable to take care of myself and Akio. Where everything feels impossible and my life isn't my own. I'm finally starting to feel like myself again, like I'm back on solid ground. With help from a healthy dose of SSRIs and an incredible therapist. I can't let myself drown again. I'm positive I won't be able to claw myself out of that hole—where hope goes to die—a second time. I need that tiny spark of hope now more than ever, even if it proves futile. I place my hand on my chest directly over my heart. It's still beating and that's enough. I'm still here, still alive. I use that knowledge to ground myself and calm my breathing.

Maybe they'll break up and I'll have another chance to make things right. Maybe there's still time.

But two months later, when he and Leighton eventually call it quits, it doesn't really matter. Not anymore. And nothing changes then either. By then, all the courage I thought I had gained along the way vanishes. And my opportunity to tell him everything, to come clean, disappears with it.

CHAPTER 49

KENDALL

I BRING MY UNEASE, snowball of anxiety, and all my deeply rooted insecurities with me to our first couple's therapy session. I wish I could say I checked them at the door, that I can go into this clear eyed with confidence and grace. In short, I want to win at therapy. But I'm sure my own personal therapist and many others would say winning is not the point. So here I am, with all my pain and all my fucking demons. And I'm hoping that after all is said and done, when the storm has passed and every ugly rock has been turned over, he still decides to choose me. That he wants me anyways. Us. Our love and our beautiful, tragic mess. Does that make me selfish? Maybe. But I also know now that no matter what, whatever happens, I am done not choosing him.

Caught up in all of this, our rubble and decay is Akio. The one person who links us together even if everything else falls apart. He's with Emma and Maddox right now at the aquarium. I know he's fine, I know he's probably having fun but still I worry about him.

Did I dress him warm enough this morning? Was he cranky from skipping a nap? Did he eat enough of a snack? Was he still upset about us leaving? He had begged to come with us because he loves spending time together, just the three of us. And the look on his face when I said goodbye and hugged him tight pulled on the strings of my heart. He's grown to love Kai over the past few months and it terrifies me. *Because what if it doesn't work out, what would become of the three of us then?*

We're sitting across from Magdalena Arroyo, a licensed marriage and family therapist. She's tall and slender, with frizzy salt and pepper waves that skim her shoulders. She's wearing a teal knitted sweater draped over a black tank top and the whole ensemble is tucked into high waisted bell bottoms. Her ankle-length mustard boots and turquoise rings somehow complement the outfit. She's giving whimsical, hippie vibes. Magdalena could definitely be someone's fun aunt or a middle school art teacher and somehow it just *works* for her. She's perched on a velvet green chair that looks incredibly uncomfortable, with her legs crossed, and my first thought is *I love her*. My second thought is I want to be her. Exuding warmth and kindness, effortlessly chic, clearly comfortable in her own skin and unapologetically herself. You know that feeling when you really want to impress your therapist but also kind of want to be friends with them? That feeling has decidedly taken over.

She lobs us a few easy questions first, small talk, the weather, nothing too invasive. Once we've discussed those, she smiles warmly, her brown eyes glancing back and forth between us.

"So, you both are here for marriage counseling, but I noticed neither of you are wearing rings. Are you married?" she asks.

"No—"

"No, we're not married. Yet," Kai says like its fact, an inevitability. I pin him with a look and I know my cheeks are flushed with embarrassment.

"I was going to start differently but this is *interesting*," she comments while jotting down a note. "Could you say a little more about that, Kai?"

"Sure," he replies, sitting up a little straighter. "When we first started dating—"

"Which was when?" she interjects.

"About seven years ago; we were both in high school. At the end of senior year, I told Ken in no uncertain terms that I was going to marry her someday. And that feeling hasn't changed, not for me at least." *Jesus fucking Christ, right for the jugular.*

"Kendall, how does that make you feel? Could you respond to what Kai just said?"

Could I? How do I even begin?

"It makes me feel guilty and terrified and hopeful. I don't feel like I deserve his love or commitment to us. And honestly, I didn't realize it was still an option for us...marriage, I mean."

"Let's unpack that a bit, shall we?" *I think the fuck not.* "Why exactly do you feel undeserving of his love?" I feel dread crawling up my chest, my throat clogging with emotion. I realize I have two options here. I can gut myself like a fish or answer her question vaguely, enough that it gets her off my back, at least temporarily.

"A lot has happened between us." I swallow. "Before we re-connected a few months ago, we hadn't been together for almost three years and I was the reason for that. I hurt him," I pause, trying to gauge his mood. But he remains stoic, unflappable. "I hurt both of us a lot," I trudge on. And then because I'm nothing if not a people pleaser, I say, "If it's all the same to you, I'd rather not go there quite yet. Our breakup. But I know I'll have to open up about that eventually, you know, get to the meat and potatoes of everything," I concede. She takes a second to examine me.

"Kendall, you don't have to divulge anything in here that you don't want to or aren't comfortable sharing. What matters is that you both are willing to put in the effort, time, and work to improve and strengthen your relationship. I don't think either of you would be here if you weren't already committed to doing just that. As far as the more difficult topics go, I'm comfortable with letting things unfold naturally. I'm sure we'll cover a lot of ground in the next couple weeks. Why don't you tell me how and when you two met?"

Bless her heart. I could kiss her.

"Well, that's easy. We grew up next door to each other. He moved into the house across the street from mine when I was five. We've been best friends ever since, at least for most of that time." She nods while writing down notes.

"And what was that like growing up together, living across the street from your best friend?" she asks, looking between both of us.

"The best. It was amazing," Kai answers before I can. "I'm incredibly lucky she was my neighbor," he notes, smiling at me.

"And why is that?" she wonders.

"I was a shy kid; making friends wasn't easy for me. Kendall became my friend instantly, took me under her wing. She always had my back and I never felt like I had to try to be anyone other than myself with her," he admits. At this I smile back. It's wide and toothy and impossible to contain.

Kai has weaknesses and insecurities just like any other guy, but unlike most other men, he faces them head on, acknowledging them, weaponizing them, and spinning them into gold. He knows how to make up for what he lacks and how to grow in the dark, untended places that need love and sunlight. Kai is beautiful, god is he beautiful. But what makes him irresistible in my opinion, and sometimes hard to look away from, is his tender heart and emotional vulnerability.

He recounts our history on Sycamore Lane together fondly. Summers spent at the lake, under the stars, being at each other's houses more often than our own, begging our parents to sign us up for the same sports and extracurricular activities. Just so we didn't have to spend any additional time without each other. I fill her in on our awkward teenage years, the trio formed between Kai, Jenna and I, middle school dances, summers spent vacationing with both our families.

"So, you two became very close friends it sounds like. When did your relationship evolve from platonic to romantic?"

"The summer before our senior year of high school," I answer.

"That may have been when it started for Kendall, but I had been harboring a very large crush on her since seventh grade. I think I knew I loved her before I even knew what love was," he laughs. I feel tears brimming my eyes but for some reason, I don't let them fall.

"That's a long time to wait for someone. Grades seven through eleven?" She blows a breath out her mouth. "You must have been very patient."

"I was. She was also worth the wait." *Does this man know he is single-handedly helping me repair my inner child? Is he aware that my love language was built by him, for him, around him?*

Magdalena's calm voice cuts through my inner monologue. "So, making the transition from friends to romantic partners, what was that like?"

"Easy and hard. Amazing and terrifying," I respond as honestly as I can. Kai nods his head and I know at least on this we agree.

"Can you say a little more about that, Kendall?"

"We were both terrified that being together would ruin our friendship and that was a big risk."

"But one that you both deemed important enough to take?" she hedges and we both nod.

"Looking back now, knowing everything you know now. Do you still think it was worth the risk? Put differently, if you could go back in time and not fall for each other, make it so that you never ended up together, would you?"

"The question is irrelevant, because there is no way I could know him and not fall in love with him," I say, a tear finally escaping and sliding down my cheek. "The thought of not experiencing what it's like to love and be loved by him is too painful to even conceive. But to answer your question more accurately, this portion of us, our beginning, no I wouldn't change a single thing about that."

Kai takes my hand in his and replies, "Me either."

"It looks like that's all the time we have for today. I feel like we've laid some really great groundwork here," she responds.

Damn, she's good. *Too* good. We leave her office and I feel both heavier and lighter than when I first arrived over an hour ago. The sweet spot of cognitive behavior therapy I suppose. For the first time, I'm somewhat hopeful that maybe we can heal all the things that need mending.

***

W HEN WE'RE BACK IN Kai's car, I turn to look at him and he kisses me on the forehead.

"That went well I think, right?" he comments, and I can't tell if it's a question or a statement.

"I think so." I look down to where I've interlocked our fingers. "I didn't know about all of that when we were kids. I mean, I knew you had a hard time making friends at your old school but that was kind of the extent of my knowledge." He sighs and lays another kiss on my knuckles.

"I didn't exactly run around advertising it either. And I don't even think I knew how to articulate it until now. But I knew if I could win you over, convince someone like you to be friends with me, maybe I'd have a fighting chance, maybe school here wouldn't be as bad as I thought. And I was right. I could be myself. Shy, introverted, anxious. I had permission to be terrified because you were fucking fearless and eventually that made me want to be fearless too."

God, I wish I could see myself through his eyes. I don't even remember the last time I felt fearless, brave, sure of myself.

"Kai?"

"Hmm?" he murmurs, piercing me with a thoughtful gaze.

"I'm pretty sure I loved you before I knew what love was too. It just took me a little longer to catch up to the realization," I admit.

He smiles. "I know, Ken."

CHAPTER 50

KAI

2011

KENDALL IS WEARING AN aqua dress that barely covers her ass and high heels. She has her hair pinned up out of her face in a high ponytail. She looks like a model. She also looks like we are getting in trouble tonight, sending me a mischievous grin as soon as she hops in the car. Kendall reaches from the passenger side and cranks the volume all the way up.

"Are you kidding me, Ken? Let's at least try not to get caught," I snap and turn the volume down to a whisper.

"Can you lighten up? It's the last two weeks of summer break. We just want to have some fun."

"I know I know, I'm just not pumped to be hanging out with the whole football team again," I reply.

Jenna raises her eyebrows "Why? You're on the team. Don't you hang out with them like all the time?"

Kendall thankfully changes the subject by announcing she has alcohol to pregame with. Ten minutes and four nips later, I pull my dad's old Toyota highlander into what is arguably one of the biggest driveways I've ever seen. By the time we walk up to the huge oak front door, both Ken and Jenna are a little tipsy. *Great.* Now I have to worry about getting caught drinking, sneaking out, *and* being responsible for not one but *two* drunk girls. I extend my arm to knock on the front door, but Kendall quickly grabs my hand and pulls it down.

"What are you doing? This is a party. Just walk in," she scoffs.

Shortly after we arrive, I find Kendall in the den playing a drinking game with Jenna and a few other people. She stumbles a little after she takes her beer pong shot. I'm still nursing my first drink, mostly for appearances. I walk over to her and whisper, "Maybe you wanna take it easy there, Ken."

"Maybe you want to try and have some fun, Kai. I'm fine, besides, I'm perfecting my aim." I ignore the fact that she's slurring and the fact that she smells amazing. Sin, salvation, and something undeniably sweet.

"Fine, let me help you then." I position myself behind her, put her arm under mine, pull back her hand, and let the ball go with the flick of our wrists. My face is so close to hers I can smell her shampoo. Coconut and vanilla.

"Yes!" she yells as we sink it. "Careful Kai, you might make me wonder if you're flirting with me," she muses.

"Your aim is terrible. I'm helping you if anything. Unless you intend to lose this beer pong game, big mouth?" I challenge. Kendall has been known to be a sour loser, but right now, she's probably too drunk to care.

"Uh hello!?" Jenna shouts, annoyed as she steps in between us. "She has a perfectly good beer pong partner right here. If you want to play so bad Kai, get next." I back away from the table with my hands up.

"Just trying to help you guys win," I mumble.

I decide to hide out in the kitchen, hoping the only people who talk to me are drunk and in search of food rather than a conversation. Unfortunately, the kitchen is massive and can accommodate just as many people as the den. Logan seemingly appears out of nowhere and claps me on the back.

"Hey man, I thought you weren't coming?"

"I wasn't. Somehow Ken talked me into it," I respond and take a sip of my beer.

"She talked you into it or she asked and you couldn't say no to her? What's the deal with you guys anyways?" he interrogates.

"There is no deal. We're friends."

"Uh huh," he grins. "Friends don't look at each other the way you look at her, man."

"What do you mean? How do I look at her?" I ask.

"Like she's the fucking sun and we're all just in her orbit," he replies. Logan doesn't seem that drunk yet so I know he's serious. He's also pretty observant.

"Fuck off, Loge, you're just mad I don't look at you like that," I reply jokingly.

"Whatever, it ain't rocket science, my guy. Just ask her out. Or don't. I don't really care. But if you don't ask her out, someone else will," he shrugs, takes a swig of his red solo cup, and meanders into the living room.

It doesn't take long before I see Kendall stumbling on the stairs behind Jenna. I push past drunk people and manage to make it to the landing just as she slurs, "I feel like I'm going to be sick."

"Come on, Ken, this is a huge house. There has to be at least four more bathrooms in it." I tug her away from Jenna and lead her down the long hallway.

By the time we find a bathroom that isn't occupied by people vomiting or hooking up, Kendall looks sleepy. As soon as I close the bathroom door, she collapses on the cool white tiles in a drunken heap. She attempts to take off her shoes but can't adjust the clasp.

"I got it, Ken, just lay down." I gently take her heels off and place them neatly at her feet. I take the towel that's hanging on the rack and put it under her head.

"Thanks, Kai," she whispers.

"For what?"

"For always looking out for me."

"It's no big deal, I don't mind."

She murmurs something I can't make out. I lie down next to her, close enough to hear her breathing but not close enough that we're touching. She snuggles in next to me and puts her hand on my chest.

"You wanna know a secret?" she mumbles, sleep distorting her voice. If possible, it's even sexier.

"I thought we didn't keep any secrets from each other," I reply.

"You know earlier when we made our little pact?"

"Uh huh," I say, wondering where this is going.

"I was secretly hoping you'd still be a virgin by the end of senior year. I guess that's kind of selfish though."

What. The. Fuck?

"Night, Kai, sweet dreams," she whispers.

She falls asleep before I can tell her I was hoping the same thing.

I wake up surprised to find my arm looped around Ken's waist. I'm even more surprised when I realize she's not wearing anything except a thong and a bra. I know Ken likes to sleep naked, but I'm mentally unprepared for this scenario. I've had dreams in which the thing that is currently happening happens, but right now, this feels like a cruel nightmare. If someone walks in this bathroom, they are definitely going to think we slept together.

"I can feel you overthinking, Kai. Just go back to sleep for a little." She leans over to look at her phone. "It's only 6 am."

I rub my hands over my eyes and down my face, exasperated. "It's kind of hard when you aren't wearing any clothes."

"I don't think that's the only thing that's hard. Is your phone in your pants or are you just happy to see me?" she quirks. Of course she knows. Her back and her ass are pressed up right against my crotch.

"Give me a break, Kendall. You're wearing dental floss for underwear. A guy can only summon so much willpower," I reply as I tear my hand away from her waist.

"You can leave your hand, Kai. I like it there and you're keeping me warm," she says and moves in closer to me. I reluctantly settle my left hand underneath her rib cage and the sound of her breathing lulls me back to sleep.

Two hours later, I'm woken up by her snoring like a chainsaw. How can someone who is so pretty make such terrible noises?

"Wake up, Ken," I say and nudge her. She scares herself awake and wipes a bit of drool from her lip. She looks beautiful even hungover.

"What time is it?" She asks.

"8:15. We should probably find Jenna and get out of here." I look down at my feet, trying to avoid looking at her chest.

"Okay, let me put the rest of my clothes on first."

I sit up and put my hands on my knees, trying hard to distract myself while she gets dressed.

"You know, if someone came in here, they'd probably think we slept together."

"We did sleep together, Kai," she replies.

"You know what I mean," I say, annoyed.

"So what? Let them think we had sex. We know we didn't. And if we did, what would be so bad about that?"

"Other than ruining twelve years of friendship?"

"Kai, we're never going to stop being friends. Stop being ridiculous and stop overthinking. We went to a party and we had fun, okay?"

"Okay, but I'm not admitting I had any fun."

"Got it, Kai. There was no fun had by you," she smirks. "Why do you care so much about what people think anyways?" she questions as she slides her heels back on.

"I don't know. Thinking about what people think of me makes me really nervous. I feel like everyone is always judging me," I explain.

"Isn't that exhausting?"

"What?"

"Trying to be perfect for everyone else."

"Yeah, but I'm not brave like you, Ken. I can't just do and say whatever I want, consequences be damned."

"Kai, I have two moms and I don't look like either of them. And I'm the only Black girl on the gymnastics team. If I started to care too much about what people think, I'd drive myself crazy. It's not a luxury I can afford. And you are brave," she clarifies.

"No. I'm not."

"Yes, you are. Remember when your sister lost her kitten and you spent the whole day searching the neighborhood for it? You climbed a tree to get it out, even though you are deathly afraid of heights. You were her hero—that's brave. And when you had to give your presentation in Mrs. Palmer's class about the forgotten cities. You were so nervous you were vomiting like the whole week before it was due. You made me listen to it a million times and I did because I knew you hated public speaking. Then you gave your presentation, and you crushed it. And you came to this party with me because I asked you to, and you didn't have the heart to say no. Even though all the dickheads on the team made you sleep outside naked at camp. That's sweet and brave."

"I don't know if any of those things are brave."

"Yes, they are, Kai. Your brave just isn't as loud as mine and that's okay. It doesn't have to be. Come on," she says and extends her hand to help me up off the floor. "Let's get Jenna and then get something to eat. I'm starving."

CHAPTER 51

KAI

2011

THAT EVENING WE DECIDE to spend the night in and stuff our faces with greasy delicious food that would soak up any residual alcohol.

"Delivery order for Kendall?" I joke as I walk through her back door. Lucy runs up to greet me, wagging her tail. She sniffs me and inspects the bags excitedly.

"Fuck yes, Kai! I don't think you'd make a very good delivery man though. Pretty sure breaking and entering is frowned upon when delivering food."

"Well, lucky for you, I'm not breaking and entering since I practically live here and have a spare key. I also come bearing gifts," I respond.

"What else did you get?" she asks as I start opening our take-out boxes.

"Provisions."

"What kind of provisions?" She takes the brown paper bag from my hands and dumps out its contents on the kitchen table. Ibuprofen, chocolate, and a heating pad. She looks mortified. I knew this was a bad idea.

"You said you had cramps, and I didn't want you to be in pain or anything..." My voice trails off as I try to explain my way out of this embarrassing situation. I'm in unfamiliar territory here. Thankfully Kendall doesn't make me feel worse about it.

"That's really sweet, Kai," she states, a flush creeping up her neck.

"It's no big deal. I just didn't want to hear you complaining all night," I tease.

"Yeah yeah. Let's eat. Did you by any chance get—"

"Extra chipotle aioli? Obviously. It should be at the bottom of the bag."

"This is why we're best friends," she comments, snagging a French fry and tossing it in her mouth.

Best friends. So maybe she doesn't want me to make a move. Jenna's probably wrong. But what if she's right? I wouldn't put it past Jenna to bait me into something just to make me look like an idiot. If there is anyone who enjoys seeing me embarrassed more than Ken, it's Jenna. Two hours later, I'm running out of time to make a choice. We're on our third episode of *The Office* and that's usually when Kendall falls asleep. She's lying with her head on my chest, feet stretched out towards the end of the couch cuddling a blue fleece blanket. My arm is resting on the pillow behind her and it would be easy enough to curl my arm around her or hold her hand.

"Kai, I can feel you overthinking. What's up?"

Dammit. How does she always know?

"Nothing. What do you mean you can feel me overthinking?"

"You get inside your head too much. I can literally feel your energy and it feels stressy. Plus, your heart is pounding."

"Sometimes it's scary how well you know me."

"It really is. What are you thinking about?"

"Holding your hand," I blurt out awkwardly.

"So, stop stressing about it and just do it already." Without hesitation, I thread my fingers through hers and she nuzzles her head under my chin.

"Isn't this better than torturing yourself all night?"

"Will you just shut up, Kendall?" I say grinning.

I comb her hair with my fingers until my eyelids get heavy and fall asleep to the sound of her cute little snores.

I wake up and check my phone, 11:15. Shit, my parents will be wondering where I am. I sit up from the couch as quietly as I can, trying not to disturb Kendall.

"Kai, don't go. I hate sleeping in this house alone." She's killing me. She could have asked me for anything right now, and I'm confident I would say yes.

"How about we go upstairs? I'll wait to leave until you fall back asleep, or your moms get home," I suggest.

"Mmmkay," she whispers sleepily.

I follow her up the stairs, which is the wrong choice. She's wearing a cropped t-shirt and tight black leggings that grip her thighs and waist in all the right places. She falls into bed and immediately starts stripping her clothing.

"Uhh," I start to protest while fiddling with my hands.

"Relax, Kai. I'll put on a shirt and shorts now that I know how nervous my sleep attire makes you. Besides, I doubt my moms want to come home and find me sleeping with you sans clothes, best friends or not."

I tug at the back of my neck with my hand worriedly. "What do you mean not?"

"I don't know, do best friends fall asleep together holding hands?"

"Maybe."

"Okay," she scoffs.

"What?"

"Do best friends get each other *provisions* to help with their period?" she demands a little louder. She sounds angry. I'm not even sure what I did.

"I don't know, I was just trying to be nice. I would do it for Amy if she needed it too," I reply.

"Right, because that's how you think of me, like a sister?" she snaps.

"Kendall, we're both tired. I'm sure your moms will be home any minute. I should just go home."

"Nice deflection, Kai."

"Ken," I say quietly.

"Whatever. Just go home. I'll see you tomorrow for the tag sale I guess."

I have officially fucked up. I run through the scenario a million times as I walk back to my house. Kendall and I rarely fight—but this feels like a fight to me. I should have just kept my mouth shut. Why did I listen to Jenna? Freaking Jenna always has to stir the pot and keep things interesting. But I would deal with her later. One problem at a time. Things were so simple before I started daydreaming about Kendall and punching guys on the team for wanting to sleep with her. They are messy now. The lines are blurred. We had made a pact. She's the only person who gets me. Like really gets me and still chooses to hang out with me. I don't think whatever this is or could be is worth jeopardizing our friendship.

CHAPTER 52

KAI

THERAPY HAS BEEN ILLUMINATING, at least for me. It would be all too easy to get caught up solely on the snags and mistakes made in the past couple years without acknowledging the first seventeen before that. Our childhood and the five years we were together were nothing short of perfection. But I know eventually we'll have to break down and analyze where we went wrong. Examine the fallout and the parts we played in it. We have a lot of complicated terrain to traverse, but if today's session is any indication, I know we will come out of it stronger.

When we get back to Kendall's apartment, I convince her to take the evening and do something for herself. I decide to take Akio for ice cream, our first solo outing together. Kendall bends down to hug and kiss him before she leaves and my heart squeezes.

"I love you baby," she coos.

"Love you too, Mama," he says while practically crushing her neck with a hug. She rises and turns to me.

"Well, I guess I'm off. I shouldn't be longer than two hours. You guys will be okay?" she asks.

"Yes, Ken. We'll be fine. I will send you constant updates," I promise, grasping her arms in my hands. She gives me a peck on the lips and smiles against my mouth.

"Okay, thanks for doing this, Kai. I'll see you guys later."

"We'll see you later," I kiss her back. "I promise to tire him out so bedtime is a breeze."

"You really know how to sweet talk a girl, Kai," she responds, walking out the door.

Ten minutes later, Akio is safely placed in his car seat that looks a little ridiculous contrasted with the sleek leather interior of my Audi. Once I triple check all the straps are tightened and he's secure, I slide into the driver's seat. I realize this is the first time I've driven with him alone and it's a little destabilizing. But it's also exciting to have this time to bond with him.

"Who wants ice cream?" I ask emphatically.

"Meeee!" Akio yells from the back seat. I watch in the car mirror as he plays with one of his Spider-Man toys and I drive 15 below the speed limit the entire way to the ice cream shop. I carry him on one hip into the store while he chants something that closely resembles *ice cream,* but I'm not entirely sure. We open the front door and the bell overhead dings. The scent of sugar, vanilla, and waffle cone waft over to me, instantly transporting me back to my childhood. Every school event, sports game, and accomplishment growing up was celebrated at Rocco's. I'm thrilled to share this tradition with Akio.

While we wait in line, I pick him up so he can see all the flavors and I read a few of them off slowly. "Vanilla, chocolate, peanut butter, mint chocolate chip...hmm, I think I'm going to get mint chocolate chip. What about you?" I ask, turning my head to him.

He smiles and claps. "Mint chip! Mint chip!"

"Okay, are you sure, bud?" I don't want him to copy my order just to be disappointed. Especially if he wants something a little more palatable for a toddler. But then I realize maybe he's always liked this flavor and maybe he does because I do. Maybe ice cream preferences are a weirdly inherited trait. Stranger things have happened. He nods his head enthusiastically.

"Two mint chocolate chips in a cone please," I say to the gangly teenager behind the counter.

When it's our turn to pay, I put Akio on the ground to retrieve my wallet and he slips his tiny hand in my free one. He waits quietly, humming to himself and observing everything happening around him. I give the woman at the register a twenty and tell her to keep the change.

"Thanks so much, that's very generous. And your son is adorable," she replies.

We sit at a round table shoved into the front corner of the store and eat our ice creams together. Half of his drips down his face and onto his bright blue and yellow rugby shirt, the other half melting in the cone. I try to get ahead of it by cleaning him up with napkins and wipes every couple minutes, but I guess this is life with a toddler. Active chaos and a never-ending mess at all times.

A warm fuzzy feeling seeps into my chest as he beams at me with delight, ice cream in his hair and smeared across his eyebrows. *How did he manage to get ice cream there?*

But that cozy feeling starts to dissipate when he looks at me and says, "Thanks Kai Kai." Because that's who I am to him. I'm Kai Kai, his mom's "good friend," a welcome face at their apartment, and a man who has infiltrated their lives cautiously but not completely. And I want to be more than that. I want to be his dad and I want him to know he's *my son*. It hits me like a sudden violent force. I know Kendall wants to handle this delicately and doesn't want to confuse him. This situation, *our* situation is complicated and difficult to explain, especially to someone his age. But I also feel like it's time he knows, even if he doesn't fully understand.

I just hope Kendall can empathize with me. I'm not confident in my ability to reign in this overwhelming paternal instinct. It's washing over me like a hurricane. I want to be both protector and provider for them and the drive to love him and guide him is all encompassing. It's ready to leave destruction in its wake, but like storms often do, it's also poised to bring a renewed sense of clarity.

I hope it's the latter.

***

LATER, AFTER AKIO HAS had a bath and is asleep in his room, I broach the subject with Kendall.

"We had a great time today. He loved it," I comment. "I wanted to ask you about something though."

"Okay." She sets her phone down in her lap and shifts towards me on the couch.

"I think we should tell him who I am, Ken. Who I really am, even if he doesn't quite get it yet," I explain nervously. Her eyes go wide and I don't miss the look of alarm spreading across her face.

"Okay...you don't think it's a little soon?" she asks, biting her lip anxiously.

"I think that if it were up to me, he would have known who I was a long time ago. But our situation is unconventional to say the least."

"It's definitely unconventional," she agrees but I know she's worried, unsure of how to respond. "Can I think about it, sit on it for a little?" she wonders.

"Of course. We don't have to decide or figure it out right now. It's just something I think we should start thinking about." It wasn't the reaction I was hoping for, but it was better than shutting me down. And then because I apparently hadn't purged enough of my feelings in therapy already, I bring up another sensitive subject. "Do your moms know we're back together? I've just been thinking maybe it's time to tell my parents."

"They know. I told them recently," she answers, but her mood has shifted from curious and open minded to visibly on edge. She starts picking the edge of her cuticles while she stares down at her hands.

"Okay. How did they take it?" I ask. I grasp one of her hands in mine in an attempt to disrupt her spiraling.

She snorts. "They were shocked but ultimately, they understood. They never blamed you or anything, Kai. They know the choices I made were mine and mine alone. And they never stopped caring about you when we broke up. I think they're happy you are back in our lives, it just caught them off guard," she explains.

"Well, that's good. Hopefully my parents will have a similar reaction. My mom was devastated when you broke up with me. She loved you like a daughter."

"I know. I loved them too, Kai," she says quietly.

And I let this sit between us for a few minutes. Because when we broke up, it wasn't just about us. We threw a wedge in a decades-long friendship between our parents. When we separated, the yearly vacations together stopped as did the monthly dinners with both of our families. Both her parents and mine took sides and obviously they both chose their own children. But maybe if we can heal, we could have something like that again. All of us. Because whether our parents like it or not, regardless of whether they approve, Kendall, Akio, and I are family already.

Kendall's words break through my wandering thoughts. "Remember when our parents first found out we were dating in high school? God, we thought we were so sneaky. Meanwhile, our moms and Mrs. Carlisle had all been scheming behind our backs." She laughs. This particular memory causes me to chuckle too, before bringing her face to mine for a kiss.

CHAPTER 53

KENDALL

2011

I'M SITTING ON KAI'S lap while he slips his hands underneath my shirt and places hot open mouthed kisses along my neck.

"Kai," I whisper, "We're going to get caught."

He smiles against my skin and replies, "So tell me to stop," while sinking his hand deeper into my hip.

"Stopping would be cruel." Something in my brain prevents me from doing that and instead, I tug on the hair at the nape of his neck and kiss him harder. He skims the top of my underwear with his fingers, dragging them slowly with intention. A tease. I'm fairly certain we'll end up naked in my bed if we don't stop. Footsteps coming up the stairs send our hookup session crashing to an abrupt halt. *Shit.* My mom must have gotten home early from work. I jump off of him, landing on my bed and adjust my shirt just as she opens the door.

"Hey guys..." she trails off looking from me to Kai. "Just wondering if you're joining us for dinner, Kai?" she asks, confusion marring her features.

"Um sure. Thanks, Mrs. James," he responds awkwardly.

My mom steps further into the room and pushes the door all the way open. "How's the project going?"

"Good. We've been hard at work," I answer, stretching the truth a bit and Kai's face turns bright red. *I mean we had been working hard on some things.*

"What's it on?" she inquires.

"What?" I ask, confused. Apparently Kai's soft pillowy lips and his large, eager, well-traveled hands have melted a few of my brain cells.

"What are you doing your project on?"

Shit shit. Our project.

"We're analyzing the ending of Macbeth," I say. Which isn't a total lie. We did have to analyze and eventually write a paper about the ending of Macbeth. That just isn't what we were doing when my mom walked in.

"Okay, well, let me know if you guys need anything. Dinner's at 6." She closes the door and both Kai and I start laughing uncontrollably.

"We have to stop sneaking around," I say and grab his hand.

"But it's so much fun," he responds, kissing my cheek.

No more than five minutes later, my mom yells at us from downstairs "Kendall, Kai, could you come down here for a minute?"

We hurry downstairs impatiently, knowing we've likely been found out. It's not like we could keep this from them forever. My mom hovers over the island, arms folded and lips pursed in a thin line.

"Sit," she states and nods toward the stools opposite her. "Is there something you want to tell me, Ken?" She stares at me pointedly while Kai and I both take a seat.

"Like what?" I ask, trying to fumble my way through this.

Is it better to own up to this or dig myself deeper?

"Like why I walked into the room and you and Kai appeared to be doing anything other than studying. How long has this been going on for?" she questions and I know I can't fake my way out of this conversation.

"Mom, I—" I start to plead. But she cuts me off.

"How long?" she demands.

"On and off since the end of the summer," I explain quietly, fidgeting with the hem of my shirt.

"I'm actually a little relieved. I thought you were going to say since last year," she sighs.

"Okay so...you aren't mad?" I wonder.

"I'm mad you two have been sneaking around behind our backs and clearly lying to us. But I'm not mad you guys are together. *Are* you guys together?" she asks curiously, leaning forward on the island.

"Yes," I reply. "We're dating." I glance at Kai and he is beaming despite the amount of shit we have managed to get ourselves in.

"My next question is, and Kai, hunny, I'm sorry you are here for this—are you guys sexually active and if you are, are you being safe?" I don't have to look at Kai to know his usual porcelain face has now turned beet red.

"We haven't had sex, but when we do, we will definitely be safe," I promise.

"Okay, *when* not *if*. So maybe this conversation is more timely than I thought. Kai, of course I can't tell you what to do here but I would highly suggest you use condoms and other protective methods. Kendall, I think we should make an OBGYN appointment and consider birth control options if that is what you want. But that is more your mother's realm of expertise, not mine. That is also not a discussion we need to have in front of Kai."

"You're really okay with this?" I ask, slightly taken aback. My moms are pretty progressive but I'm still surprised.

"I'm okay with it as long as you both keep up your grades and athletic commitments and stop sneaking around. And most importantly, you both need to be good to each other and be safe. Just so we are perfectly clear, I'm forty-eight but I'm not trying to raise grandchildren anytime soon."

I don't think I have ever been more embarrassed and relieved at the same time.

"Okay. I'm really sorry we didn't tell you guys sooner and that we've been sneaking around. But I'm glad you guys know and are okay with it."

"Why wouldn't we be okay with it? You two have been friends forever and we love Kai like family. There is no one we would trust to take care of you and be good to you more than him. But you guys were friends first and you've been close for a very long time. So please be gentle and kind with each other's hearts."

As if that hasn't been the exact dilemma we've been dealing with for the past two months. Kai feels my trepidation and gently intertwines his hand with mine underneath the counter.

"I care about Kendall a lot. I promise I will always treat her with kindness and respect, Mrs. James," he explains and I know he means every word.

"I know you will, Kai. If there is anyone I would have picked for Kendall to date it would be you. No contest. And just so you know, I texted your mom about my little discovery, and she knows we've talked about it. I'm not sure it will save you from another similar conversation with your parents, but it might." My mom smiles and winks at Kai hopefully.

"Did she seem mad?" he asks, worry bleeding into his voice.

"I don't think she is mad necessarily. Probably disappointed that you kept this from her and your dad. But truthfully, me, your mom, and Mrs. Carlisle had a bet about when you guys would start dating. Your mom won," my mom confesses.

"A bet!" we both say in unison.

"Yeah, your mom thought it would be some time this year. She thought you would be hesitant, cautious, and look at the situation from every angle. I assumed last year and Mrs. Carlisle is very surprised you two held out this long," she explains.

Kai and I start laughing. It's funny the way things work out. How everyone knew we belonged together long before we did. Like there has always been an invisible tether connecting us to each other. Maybe that's what our love story is about, its roots anyways. We aren't just childhood friends turned high school sweethearts, a cliche cautionary tale. Our story is unwavering friendship that grew and grew until it morphed into something new and different, beautiful and unbreakable.

Chapter 54

Kai

I GET THE CALL at 4:30 in the morning, when most of the world is still sleeping. I check my phone with tired eyes, because if someone is calling this early, it can't be with good news.

Fuck. It's my publicist.

"Hello?" I answer gruffly, tendrils of unease roiling around my stomach.

"Hey, Kai, sorry to wake you. But this is kind of important," Stephanie replies curtly. "And I wanted your take before it went to print." Stephanie is all business and no nonsense. If I didn't know her any better, I would say she suffered from an undeserving power trip. But she bosses us Boston Bucks players around like we're petulant children in need of a scold or good backhand. Stephanie does her job and she does it well, and right now, I appreciate her ability to cut through the bullshit and get directly to the point.

"It's fine, Steph, what's going on?" I ask, trying and failing to smooth the edge of alarm in my voice.

"A mildly reputable magazine snapped pictures of you getting ice cream the other day with...a boy." A short pause. "That is presumably your son?" she asks. She knows the truth but I can tell she's waiting for me to confirm it.

"Yes, he's my son," I respond, sitting up and swinging my feet over the edge of the bed. I have a terrible feeling I should be upright for the rest of this conversation.

"So, the magazine plans on publishing the picture tomorrow with the tagline *Boston Bucks former bachelor has secret son.*

Fuck. Fuck. *Fuckkkk.*

I can feel my heart pounding in my ears, bile and stomach acid threatening to make its way up my throat. I'm not super concerned about my reputation—that has been trashed and rehabbed more times than I can count. But I'm worried about my parents' reactions and Kendall and Akio's privacy. I release a long sigh.

"What are my options here, Steph?" I run my hands through my hair repeatedly like it could soothe me.

"Well, you could pay to make it go away. That would probably be the easiest option, path of least resistance and all. You could ask them to kill it in exchange for an exclusive, all access interview with you. Or you could just say fuck it and let the vultures in. If it's not them today it will be someone else tomorrow," she explains nonchalantly, like it isn't my future or anyone else's on the line here.

"Right," I mutter.

"But something tells me this situation was kept a secret for a reason, one you probably aren't particularly ready to share with the world just yet, hmm?"

"You're right. Tell them to kill it in exchange for whatever kind of access they want...I don't want this coming out. Not yet. I need to at least talk to her first and my family."

"Her?" she pries. And I know it's not out of curiosity, at least not entirely. She very much wants and needs to stay ahead of the story.

"My girlfriend," I clear my throat awkwardly. "His mother."

"Ah. I'll try my best to keep a lid on it for now. But sharks are in the water and they're circling. Someone is going to leak this probably sooner than you would like. I just wanted you to be in the loop."

"Thanks, Steph. Let me know what they say," I respond and end the call.

Before I get out of bed, I make another call to Kendall. I'm anxious to hear what she has to say about all this. I explain the situation with the magazine to her as calmly and quickly as I can. And she assuages any guilt I might have felt about it, the way only she can. She tells me that eventually both our families are going to know and so is the press and everyone else. She said ultimately the choice is up to me but she knows the terms and conditions, what she signed up for dating a professional athlete. We both agree that we want to protect Akio as much as possible and control the narrative but we aren't going to chase away every single story that comes up. Eventually, the world will find out about our past and our present and that's okay.

I want them to. I want everyone to know they're mine.

***

A WEEK LATER, I tell my parents and my younger sister about Kendall and Akio during our monthly *mandatory* family dinner. My mom looks shocked and my dad seems a little pale, like he's going to be ill. My sister, however, is ecstatic.

"This is so cool! So, I'm an aunt now?" she asks enthusiastically, her black bob swishing from side to side as she glances from my parents to me.

"Yeah, I guess you are," I answer, reaching over and ruffling her hair. She might be an aunt but she's still my younger sister and the baby of the family.

"So..." My mom eyes me carefully. "Did she give you an explanation for all this? The lying, moving away, keeping *your son* a secret?" she asks, trying to mask her emotions but her frustration surfaces anyways.

"It's complicated, Mom. She was young, we both were. I had just been drafted and there is still a lot of stuff we need to figure out," I respond, taking a large gulp of water.

"I'm sorry," Amy interrupts. "I think it's really cool you have a son but don't we all think it's a little fucked up she hid this from you?" she says while shoveling broccoli into her mouth. And while tact isn't her strong suit, I know she said what everyone else at the table is thinking.

"Amy, language!" Mom chides but my sister just rolls her eyes in defiance.

"Yeah, it isn't exactly ideal," I admit. "But like I said, it's complicated. We're trying to work on things and we're going to couple's therapy together."

"Well, that's good right? That's a good thing," My mom notes and I nod in agreement. "I just worry about you, Kai. I know how hard it was when you two broke up," she says softly. And I can see the concern in her eyes, in the pinch of her brow and the hardness of her features. What she's really asking is *will you be okay if things don't work out this time? Can you recover from that?* And I know she's right to be worried because I am too. About all the what ifs and the what nows, and the multiple balls Kendall and I are both trying to carefully juggle and keep in the air.

"I know, Mom. I think this time will be different."

God I really fucking hope I'm right. I don't think I can survive being wrong.

"So, when do we get to meet him, our grandson?" my mom inquires, excitement bleeding into her voice.

"We're taking things very slow, so not just yet. But hopefully soon."

"Okay. I can't wait," she replies, covering my hand with hers.

"Me either!" Amy chimes in.

My dad remains silent throughout the entire dinner, quietly moving food around his plate but never eating it. Which isn't out of character for him. He's quiet and reserved by nature. But his silence is suffocating and the complete lack of a verbal reaction makes me want to scream. As much as my relationship with my father is strained, I still crave his approval. Before we get up from the table, he excuses himself to his office.

Is he angry? Confused? Shocked?

I'm not sure what his fucking deal is but he needs to be on board with this.

"He'll come around," my mom says, reading the expression on my face. "He just needs a little time." But some shred of awareness unfurling in my gut tells me this isn't about time or patience or waiting for the shock to wear off.

A half hour later, Amy and I are supposed to be doing the dishes together. But like usual, she's leaning against the kitchen island scrolling through her phone while I do all the work. She wanders into the den and leaves me alone with my thoughts. Which admittedly is dangerous. My mom's soft voice and my dad's authoritative one drift out to me from his office. I put down the dish I'm working on and creep closer to the door, trying not to let my heavy footsteps and lumbering frame give me away. I feel like I'm fucking 16 again, eavesdropping on my parents, instead of just entering the room like an adult.

"You don't think this all seems a little strange, a little bizarre? She disappeared for years and now she returns at the height of his career with a toddler she claims is his?" my dad asks viciously. His words slice deep and sharp.

"I mean strange, yes. But what are you suggesting exactly...that Akio isn't his? That this is a ploy by her somehow? I find that highly unlikely," she replies. And I can picture the skeptical irritated glare she's giving him, in an attempt to reconcile the romantic she married with the harsh words and utter bullshit he's spewing. Because of course Akio is mine and there is no way Kendall is using me. I'm certain of that. But if my dad believes that then maybe he's more cynical than I thought.

"I know you're probably right. I'm just worried about him. He was so devastated over her. It seems odd is all. I don't think I'm wrong in wanting to be cautious. In wanting *him* to be cautious."

But his remark doesn't feel honest or genuine. It seems forced, performative. And what I want to know is *why the hell is he choosing to put on a performance now? When has he ever given one singular fuck about my happiness or what I want?*

My career? He's heavily invested in that. My stats? Definitely. My net worth? Sure. But the things that make me tick, the things that bring me pleasure outside of hockey—he never gave any in- dication that he cares about those. I'm not an idiot, I know my father loves me in his own unique fucked up way. Sometimes that looked like pushing me too hard, for too long as a kid. Sometimes that looks like freezing me out when I make a mistake. Cold indifference other times. It feels like love bordering on hate. So I should be grateful for this concern, his protectiveness. But I'm not. I can't move past my knee jerk reaction to believe the worst in him. I can't shake the nagging feeling that something is off.

Why does he suddenly care about my relationship or lack thereof with Kendall? He has seen me at my lowest. He has watched me fall apart over her and barely put myself back together. He witnessed me turn into a miserable, depressed husk of the person I once was. And he never said one fucking word to me about her or our breakup. I carefully tiptoe to the den, kiss Amy on the head, and grab my keys, heading to the door.

"Tell Mom and Dad I had to go, okay? Love you."

"Okay. Love you," she echoes.

I can't stand outside that door any longer listening to them, knowing every word my father said makes my skin crawl with rage and distrust that I can't exactly place.

Later when I roll over the situation in my brain, I realize my dad's initial reaction, unlike my mom's, wasn't shock or surprise. It was pure unadulterated terror.

CHAPTER 55

KENDALL

I DIDN'T WANT KAI's parents learning the truth about Akio, especially his dad. I nearly shit myself when he informed me that he had told them. I was even more worried about Kai learning things I'd kept hidden and buried for so long. But more than anything I'm scared of losing him. Again. And I know resolutely, like a bone deep ache, I can't keep him and continue to withhold the truth.

He doesn't bring up how the conversation went with his parents and I don't ask. I'm hoping I can avoid it for as long as possible. But I know there's an expiration date on my lies. Lies of omission, but lies nonetheless.

Our next two sessions with Magdalena go well. Or at least I think they do. Therapy is easy and hard, confusing and yet sometimes so simple. Full of paradoxes and ambiguity. So much time spent trying to reach an undefinable target and an unquantifiable goal. Because how do you know what to hold on to and what to let go of? How do you decide which battles are worth fighting? And how do you know when you've healed? You don't, I guess, is what I've learned. The pain just gets easier to carry, more manageable. And I suppose that's all we can ask for.

During our sessions, we discuss our relationship and what it looks like now. We also hash out the issue of dating someone constantly in the public eye, explaining to Akio who his father is, and what that means for the three of us. She encourages us to tell him when we're ready and gives us helpful language and tools to use with him.

On a Thursday night, after we've all had dinner together and finished our bath routine, we decide to do exactly that.

"Hey baby, can you come here for a second?" I say to Akio. "Kai and I want to talk to you about something." Kai moves over a little on the small bed, making room for Akio to sit between us. I pull Akio close to me while he continues to play with his toy car.

"So, you know how Mommy, Kai, and you have been spending a lot of time together? We have dinner and breakfast sometimes and we go to the park and get ice cream together?"

"Yeah," he nods rapidly without looking away from the toy.

"And you know that Mommy loves you so much and so does Kai?"

"Mhm," he replies, staring at me with love and so much trust.

God, why does it feel like my heart is falling into my stomach? Like nothing will ever be the same after this. There's an iron fist squeezing my chest and the anxiety is so visceral I'm worried I might pass out.

"Well, before you were born, Kai and Mommy were together for a really long time. We were best friends. And we loved each other so much that eventually, we had you. I'm your mommy, and I will *always* be your mommy, but Kai is your daddy, honey. And I think we're going to be spending a lot more time together. Would you like that?"

"Yeah!" he yells enthusiastically bouncing up and down on the bed.

And so it ended up being easier in a lot of ways than I thought it would be. After our discussion, Akio carries on playing before it's time for bed. We read him a story, we kiss him goodnight, and we tuck him in. Just like we do almost every night. Just like I have every night for the past two and a half years. So much has changed and yet so much hasn't. And isn't that how it always goes with kids? They're much stronger, more resilient, and understanding than we give them credit for. His little world has been rocked, permanently altered and he can't fully grasp it yet. But when he does, we'll be ready.

CHAPTER 56

KAI

"So, I THINK WE'VE done some really good work in the last few weeks. What I want to talk about now is the damage of the breakup. How it affected each of you when you weren't together. Okay?" Magdalena asks in her gentle, calm, reassuring tone.

Kendall nods, the curls of her bun bouncing against her head but I can tell she's nervous. I don't know if she's aware that her hands are shaking. I take one of them in mine and say her name. She locks eyes with me and I see a flicker of something that I can't name cross her face.

Pain? Guilt? Regret?

"It's okay," I tell her. *No matter what happens, we are going to be okay.* "I can go first," I say. "I was devastated. Fucking shattered when we broke up. I was so confused about what had happened or what I did. And I was just so angry with her."

"Kendall, how does that make you feel? What Kai just said?" she prods.

"I feel terrible. Like a really terrible fucking person. The last thing I wanted was to hurt him. And he had every right to be angry with me. I was angry with myself," she admits.

"What exactly were you angry at yourself for?" she wonders. Kendall wipes a tear starting to slide down her gorgeous bronze face and Magdalena hands her the tissue box.

"For making the wrong decisions out of fear and not being able to stand by them," Kendall replies.

"Okay. And Kai, what did your life look like when you broke up? How did you deal with that?" she asks, turning her head to me.

"Well, at first, I tried calling her, texting her, writing her letters. But when those went unanswered, I resorted to drinking, fighting, sleeping around. Anything I could to numb the pain. Looking back, I think I was very depressed and didn't know how to handle that exactly."

"Hmm," Magdalena murmurs. "And did you blame Kendall for this behavior, these choices?" I know Kendall already blames herself for so much. I don't want her to bear this burden too. I swallow and answer hesitantly.

"Yeah, I did."

"Do you still?"

God, this is…I don't even have words for what it feels like. Peeling back the layers of skin on a barely healed wound. Ripping down a decades' old house that once seemed sturdy to expose the rot, necrosis, and mold festering underneath.

"No, I don't. Every decision I made back then was overshadowed with intense pain I didn't know how to quiet. But I had agency. I was an adult. I had freedom to make decisions. But I do still get upset about the way it was handled. It always felt unresolved. She just kind of disappeared. No closure. Nothing. That was the worst. The not knowing, the hope." Because the hope for me back then was dangerous.

"Kendall, what about you? Did you feel like you had closure back then?"

"I mean, there wasn't really a way to have closure when I just up and left. I stopped communicating with him and we broke up under false pretenses. I told Kai it was a temporary break not a breakup. So, of course things were always left unsaid. Unfinished," Kendall explains.

"And how do they feel now? Are there things that still need closure that still feel unresolved?" she asks, glancing between the both of us.

"I don't think we'd be here if we didn't need closure or answers," Kendall says truthfully. I nod in agreement while smoothing my thumb over her fingers.

"Okay. Fair enough." Magdalena smiles. "Kendall, how did the breakup impact you?"

"That's a difficult question to answer," she replies quietly. "I was young and pregnant and confused. I felt so fucking alone. And I knew it was my own fault. But while I was pregnant, it was easy to focus just on being pregnant. After Akio was born, it got harder. I missed Kai a lot and trying to be a mom without him amplified those feelings. I felt like a piece of me had died. Shortly after I brought him home from the hospital, I started to panic. I knew I had made a mistake leaving Kai and I knew I couldn't do this without him. I also just didn't feel ready to be a parent. I was ill-prepared. I felt like I was failing Akio, failing myself. Everyone."

She pauses for a few seconds trying to get a handle on her emotions. She tucks a few curls behind her ear. "A few weeks after he was born, I was lying down in my bed trying to get a few seconds of rest while Akio was sleeping. I just needed a fucking break from his screeching, bloodcurdling wails," she glances down at her hands while she recounts this. I don't need to be looking at her to know how guilty and ashamed she feels; the pain rolls off her in waves. She takes a deep breath and carries on shakily. "From him needing so much of me all the time. Just a few moments of silence and relief. And I realized I didn't want to get out of bed again. I didn't want to do anything. And I didn't for three days. I didn't eat, I didn't shower, I didn't rock or hold or feed Akio. I didn't comfort him when he cried, or let him know I was there. I just slept. I fucking failed him. And that's when I knew something was wrong."

Chapter 57

Kendall

2017

DRIP DRIP DRIP.

I don't remember a lot about this time. Mostly because I had retreated so far inside of myself that I can't. I refuse to. A trauma response, my brain trying to protect itself maybe. But I remember the drip of the leaky faucet in my small apartment, my first apartment with Akio. I remember my moms dragging me out of bed and to the bathroom, helping me get undressed, and forcing me to wash myself after days of not bathing. Days of sitting in my own filth, my own stench, my own inner turmoil. Darkness and misery and intrusive thoughts swallowing me up like a black hole.

The burden and pressure of being a parent to this tiny little human has cracked me, broken me somehow in places I didn't know existed. To the point of inaction. I'm frozen, sinking in quicksand with no way out. Too scared to move forward and I can't go back. Trapped in a life I don't want and never asked for. Everything is about him now, my whole universe is him. My world has gotten very very small almost overnight, and so have I. I feel so obsolete and so alone that I fade into the background of my life.

I'm not even sure I can actually *do* this. That I'm cut out to be a mom.

"Ken, we need to try and brush out your hair, okay honey? It's really tangled," Mommy says but she sounds like she is somewhere far away. And I feel numb. Untethered. Disconnected from my body. I mean I'm here and I'm breathing and I'm going through the motions, barely. But withering away until I crumble into dust also sounds like a very good option. And she's talking to me like I'm a child.

Why is she doing that? Why can't I get my voice to work? I don't look at her but I nod. She helps me sit down in the tub. I'm no longer wearing my ratty t-shirt and stained sweatpants. They must have helped me change into a sports bra and athletic shorts at some point. I bring my hand to the top of my head. My hair is wild, greasy, and disgusting. I'm embarrassed that I've let it get this bad, but not embarrassed enough to do anything about it. It hasn't been brushed in days and it's starting to mat together and dread in some places. My mom drenches my hair, pouring water over it from a large pitcher the way she used to when I was little. She lathers it with conditioner and starts trying to work the knots and tangles out. She's pulling and tugging with a brush, trying to untangle some of them by hand. I don't wince, don't flinch, don't utter a word. Even though it hurts. Because I want this pain—I need this pain. I'm aching for anything that might make me feel like myself, anything that would make me feel alive again.

I've migrated so far from the person I used to be, I don't even recognize myself. The person staring back at me in the mirror these days can't possibly be me. This disheveled woman with chaotic hair and spit up caked to her shirt. She has pale purple bags under her bloodshot eyes and dried spit in the corner of her mouth and she reeks of desperation and bone deep exhaustion. She looks more like a ghost of my former self. I'm sure I'm an apparition floating around, meandering in and out of someone else's life, one that certainly doesn't belong to me.

She pulls on my hair hard and I'm brought back to this moment and reminded with overwhelming terror that this *is* my life now. Endless crying and sleepless nights and poopy diapers and warming up bottles and trying to breastfeed and navigating a pumping schedule. It's shushing him until my lips feel numb and rocking him until my shoulder throbs and everyone telling me I should be so *happy*. And all my aunts asking, "Don't you just love being a mom?" And telling me to "cherish the newborn stage because it goes by so fast." It makes me want to revolt, recoil, run away. I want to scream and cry and claw at my roots and pick at my cuticles until they bleed because I don't love any of it. And I'm starting to panic out of fear that I never will.

My mom's successful a few times but after a half hour, she sighs.

"Ken, I think we have to go to a salon. Like the one you used to go to that specializes in curly hair. Have a professional look at this. They'll probably do a better job than I will," she suggests.

"No," I shake my head vehemently. "I'm not leaving the house." I'm barely keeping my shit together in this apartment. If you can even call what I'm doing keeping my shit together. I don't want to think about what would happen when I set foot in polite society.

"Okay. Well, the only other option is to get the knots out that I can. The ones I can't we'll have to cut. Are you sure you want to do that?" She's looking straight at me, sitting on her knees outside the tub, her brown eyes locked on mine. I only nod in response.

Drip drip drip.

God, the sound of that fucking faucet. It's driving me insane. I want to smash it to pieces, rip it out of the wall. I grip the side of the tub tighter and grind my teeth together in irritation. The drip is all I can hear, all I can feel or think about. It's also the only thing securing me to reality at the moment. So, I let it go.

My mom trudges on, releasing some knots and restoring a few parts of my hair back to its former state. Every so often, I hear a snip of scissors and feel a delicate handful of hair on my legs. What were once beautiful, springy, vivacious curls fall to the bottom of the tub in thick matted clumps as silent tears roll down my face. I hear my mom say, "Okay, I think I'm done. You are going to have to get it fixed by a salon eventually though, Kendall."

I watch in horror, unable to say anything, as my hair swirls down the drain of the tub and disappears. It feels like my former life, and every shred of happiness I have ever had evaporates along with it.

Chapter 58

Kendall

"You had postpartum depression." Magdalena says. A statement not a question.

"Yes, I had severe postpartum depression. That and a whole lot of fucking grief. I mean a doctor just hands you this small, pink, wriggling bundle of flesh and you're just supposed to say thank you and you're expected to keep it alive and happy? That's kind of fucking nuts," I scoff. I don't look at him but I can feel Kai smiling next to me. "And no one talks about that. How wild and beautiful and terrifying that is. How motherhood rips you wide fucking open, leaving your heart vulnerable and exposed, just to see how and if you put yourself back together again. No one tells you how hard it is to give up everything that you are to become someone's mom." I sniffle.

"Perhaps if people talked about it more often, less people would become mothers," she acknowledges.

"Probably," I agree.

"But not you," she observes.

"But not me."

"And how does that make you feel? How does being a mom *now* feel?"

"Still terrifying," I admit. *Because are you even a parent if you aren't scared, worried about every decision that falls on their little shoulders?* "I still have no idea what I'm doing half the time. But I do love it and I love Akio more than anything. I'm very happy and lucky to be his mom."

"Going back to what you said before about grief and sacri-fices... Can I ask about some of the things you were grieving? What are some of the things you had to give up?"

She's good. We're in the thick of it now. I'm in the trenches baring my fucking soul. I've been cut open, my entrails laid across the table for everyone to see. I just hope it's enough.

"I was grieving the life I had before I was a parent. I missed Kai so fucking fiercely and I was grieving our relationship too. And I knew that my dreams would look different. I just hadn't expected it to annihilate me. I really thought I had ruined my life. That I was an imposter of a mother. I questioned if I loved Akio enough, if I was enough for him. I thought that every choice I made was wrong. I felt wrong. I went to a very dark place."

"Can I ask how you got out of that dark place? Did you have a support system to help you with Akio?"

I force a smile. "I had my moms. They helped me with Akio and encouraged me to get support for my mental health. I started seeing a therapist who specialized in postpartum depression. It was slow and painstaking and difficult but six months later, I started feeling a little better, like I had a better handle on being a mom," I explain. Magdalena shifts her body to Kai now, I assume trying to gauge his emotional reaction. I haven't really looked at him since I started word vomiting about this traumatic part of my life. I'm not sure I want to.

"Kai, how does this part of Kendall's story make you feel?" she asks him. Unwillingly, I turn to him and see tears brimming his eyes; his features are soft but there's a distinct look of distress on his face. Out of all the things I have said in these sessions so far, this confession cut the deepest. I realize that now. This isn't the nick of a small unremarkable blade. This is a knife twisting in your gut, a dagger to the chest to carve out an already bleeding heart.

Fatal. Damning. Irrevocable.

This will be the secret or one of the secrets that break the camel's back. I'm sure of it. And really, how many can one person take?

"I wish I could have been there. I wish I could have helped," he says choking up. "To know you were in so much pain feels awful. Like my heart fucking hurts hearing this."

I start tearing up again too because what else can I do? What else are we supposed to do with our heartache except release it, share it with those closest to us, and try to forge something better out of it?

"I'm so sorry, Kai. I don't want to put you through any more pain. I know you would have done everything you could if you were there. None of this is on you, okay? None of it," I reply, my voice unwavering, trying to reassure him.

"The hell it's not," but there's no edge to his voice. It's all quiet desperation, pleading, achingly tender. "I can't live without you, Ken. I don't want to. Okay? I can't. There is no me without you," he says with a shaky breath, a tear sliding down his face.

"I know, Kai. I know. Me either. But I'm not in that place anymore." I squeeze his hand in an attempt to ground him and slow his breathing. I can tell he's panicking, spiraling, his brain putting pieces together he's never seen until now. My eyes meet his dark smoldering ones. They are burning with vulnerability and concern, and I see the moment he steps back from the ledge.

"Okay," he replies. For a moment, I think that might be the end of our time—it feels like we've been here for hours. Then Magdalena turns back to me.

"Kendall, do you blame yourself for your pain and your grief? For Kai's?" she asks. I want to laugh wildly, hysterically because of how absurd the question is.

Who else is there to blame but myself?

"Yes," I choke out. "Of course I do."

"Can you forgive yourself?"

"I don't know," I say, squirming on the couch.

"Okay, we can work on that together. What about a conversation with your younger self? Could you do that?" she presses. God, I hate exercises like this. They always feel so fucking awkward and forced. But I also know sometimes they're necessary so I reluctantly oblige her request.

"I guess?" I respond.

"If you could talk to her now, your younger self, what would you tell her, what would you say to her?"

"I would tell her that even though you feel like you can't do it, that you don't know how to be a mom, you can and you will figure it out. That eventually you find a groove and a rhythm and Akio's smile brightens every day and his laughter becomes your favorite sound." I'm sobbing and hiccupping now but I fight through it. "I would forgive her for not feeling like she was enough, for not feeling ready, for not bonding with him immediately. I would tell her she is so much stronger than she thinks she is. That there is so much beauty and wonderful things waiting for her on the other side of the pain. That you and Kai find your way back to each other and everything will be okay."

"I also want you to tell her thank you. To thank her for being who you needed to survive at that time, okay? I want you to send her kindness and gratitude. I don't ever want you to forget the lessons that she taught you. But I do want you to know if you're ready, if she no longer serves you, you can choose to let her go. That version of you."

"Okay. I'll try."

"What do you two need from each other in this moment? Is there anything you need to hear from each other?" Magdalena asks both of us.

Kai turns to me slowly. "Kendall, I need to know that you're okay and that if you ever feel like you're in a dark place again, you'll tell me so I can help you."

"I'm okay, Kai. I promise. And if I get into a bad headspace again, I'll be open with you about it. I do think a lot of it was situational and I know I'm in a much better place now."

"What about you, Kendall? Is there anything you need from Kai?"

I swallow. "I know what I need to hear but I can't ask for it and I sure as hell don't deserve it," I admit. I can feel Kai move closer to me on the couch, his hand grasping mine.

"Ken, I forgive you. And honestly, I think a piece of me for-gave you a long time ago. I'm not mad, I'm not angry. I'm not bitter over it anymore. We're okay. We're better than okay because now I know how we got here."

"Before our session ends, is there anything else you want or need to share about that time in your life?" Magdalena asks us.

Kai clears his throat. "Who I was back then, the things I did. That wasn't me. I mean it was but it was also pain, grief. I was trying so hard not to feel those things. It's in no way a reflection of how I felt about you," he concedes.

"And how did you feel about her? If you could use one word?" Magdalena prompts him.

"Love," he answers immediately.

It's not an admission. Not exactly. But it's pretty fucking close. It's a very simple answer to a terribly complicated question. I've never yearned to hear three little words more. I have never wanted to hear them less. I'm standing on the edge of a cliff, everything I've ever wanted in my life and with Kai at the bottom. But I'm not sure I'll survive the jump, this incredible leap of faith. It's jumping and hoping to god we land on solid ground this time, that our newly built foundation could survive the impact. Not that it matters; I'm already falling for him or perhaps back in love with him. But how honest is that really? Because to fall back in love with him, it implies I fell out of it to begin with. And the simple truth is that I *never* stopped loving him. Not for a second.

"Kendall, what about you? Anything else you feel needs to be said?" she presses.

I turn my body towards him and take his hand in mine. "Kai, if I could go back and fix things, I would. I know I nearly ruined years of friendship and five years of love. Love that we built and worked hard for and cultivated together. I know that. I wouldn't change everything because Akio was going to come whether we were prepared for him or not and we weren't prepared," I smile. "But blowing us up, reducing us to ash, running away. I wouldn't make that choice again. I would fight for us. I'm so sorry that I wasn't brave enough before, that I hurt you like that."

***

EVERY ONCE IN A while, there are things that don't get addressed in therapy. Things that we leave unsaid and unknown. And most of the time, we let them go because we don't want to beat a dead horse. We don't want to push harder than we already have. For Kai, I could sense the not knowing was gnawing at him.

A few days later, while Akio is napping and we're lying in bed together, he asks me something I suspect has been eating at him for years. He's sitting up on his side, his head resting on his elbow, staring at me in a way I don't know I'll ever get used to.

"Ken, I need to know something," he comments while he traces the lines of my palm and I hear the trepidation in his voice. "You said you missed me a few days ago. That you realized shortly after you left that you had made a mistake. Did you ever think about coming back and telling me the truth sooner?" *I see the hope in his face. I can feel the breath he is holding. The only thing I can be is honest here.*

"Of course I did. Every day. I went to your house once and I planned on begging for forgiveness and telling you everything. But I saw you with your girlfriend at the time and I just couldn't do it. I lost the nerve," I confess. Saying it out loud, reliving the whole thing years later almost feels worse than the actual experience. He looks relieved though and he deserves that. Relief. Comfort. *Peace.* I'm starting to understand I do too.

"My girlfriend?" he asks, trying to work something out in his head.

"Leighton? The supermodel? The leggy blonde bombshell?" All incredibly obvious, accurate identifiers. Not to mention she's a woman that I imagine would be hard to forget. But it's abundantly clear he's still trying to remember who I'm talking about. And it hits me that the stock I put in their relationship was not the same as his.

"Oh right. She's just someone I dated to get my parents and teammates off my back. They knew I was miserable over our breakup," he responds nonchalantly.

"But I saw you guys together…" I trail off.

But what did I really see? A happy couple or just the image Kai had needed to portray to the world?

"Kendall, you saw someone I dated once and she happened to be one of many girls I slept with to keep a lid on my pain. It was a mask. A distraction to get you out of my head, which clearly didn't work by the way," he smiles. "I don't even remember being with her because all I could think about at that time was you."

How could I have been so wrong? How many nights had I laid awake crying over what I witnessed in that kitchen? Wondering if the beginning of him and Leighton signaled the end of me and Kai. Distraught over what I would never have with him. So much fucking time wasted. And isn't that what it all boiled down to in the end? Time. Time Kai would never get back with Akio. Time Kai and I could never reclaim. All we have left is what we choose to do with our time now.

And I'm not about to spend one more second not making the most of it.

CHAPTER 59

KENDALL

Sure. Akio is coming just for the game and I'll drop him off at the sitters if we get dinner or anything after

What time is the game?

4

Okay cool

There's one more thing…

Okay…

How do you feel about going on a blind date with one of his teammates after the game?

It'd be a group outing but he has a teammate I think could be good for you.

Please don't hate me

I don't hate you. I am a little intrigued.

What's his name?

Jax

Jesus of course he has a sexy name

You won't regret this!! I promise

> *You swindled me Kendall.*

> *You had ulterior motives for this game.*

> *It will be worth it.*

I DECIDE TO DOUBLE down and send her a very attractive picture of Jax from one of his social media profiles.

> *Fuck me*

> *That's the idea*

> *He's like male model attractive…*

> *And you're about to have yourself a hot girl spring*

> *and hot girl summer okay?*

> *You're welcome*

Kai and I had discussed the idea of going to his game this upcoming weekend. But something about Akio and I attending alone, being in the spotlight feels a little too exposed, too real. I just want to have fun and enjoy watching Kai without any additional pressure. I figure having Emma come with us would alleviate some of that. I've also asked Kai a few times to set Emma up with one of his friends or teammates. This feels like a golden opportunity that I can't pass up. Kai has met Emma twice now and he's unnervingly adept at reading people. I trust him when he says Jax is a genuine person and that he could be a really good match for her.

Two days later, we're sitting in a VIP skybox with a few other players' families and it feels surreal. The drinks are flowing as we snack on various deep fried appetizers and finger food. The energy of the crowd is anxious, excited, hopeful. And honestly, so am I.

I've watched so many of his games on my small television in our apartment or from the screen of my iPhone. But this is different. This is how it always should have been. Him on the ice and us in the stands. I'm so incredibly proud of him and I'm honored that he wants us here to support him.

"There he is!" I practically scream, pointing him out to Emma and Akio. "You gotta yell for him real loud, Akio, okay?" I say. He shakes his head up and down emphatically, a wide grin spreading across his face.

"Yay, Kai Kai!" Akio yelps excitedly. I also make a point to show Emma exactly where Jax is on the ice. She shoves me with her shoulder but I see her cheeks redden along with the hint of a smile.

God, I forgot how good he looks all suited up in his gear. His eyes are focused, serious, determined while he moves with speed and precision. He's a predator on the ice and he has the merciless wrath of one too. Over time, Kai's muscles have been cut and strengthened to deliver dominance and perfection. His impressively large body is only made bigger by all of his pads. He takes his cage off, some wisps of hair already plastered to his forehead, and smiles at me, a big goofy boyish grin. He then proceeds to wave his stick in the air. Like we aren't close enough to know exactly where he is at all times. I hear a loud whistle before Kai blows us a dramatic kiss and skates off.

Then the game begins.

Akio has pressed his face against the glass of the VIP skybox, totally captivated by the game taking place in front of him.

"Right there!" he says beaming, eyes wide. "That's Kai Kai!" Kai glides across the ice like he's made for it—fluid, fast, controlled. Number 23. No matter how hard I tried, I could never forget that number or the man wearing it. The back of his jersey, the way he moves on the ice is as familiar as his voice. And playing hockey is like breathing for him. Easy. Effortless. The stick might as well be an extension of his arm.

He swoops in front of the net, gets a pass from the wing, and—GOAL. The arena erupts with manic frenzied energy.

Lights flash, a horn blares and Akio jumps in my arms, unable to contain his excitement. We watch Kai skate past the glass, and for a split second, he glances up—eyes searching the skybox. I don't know if he sees us, if he feels how loud we're cheering for him, but my heart bursts at the thought anyway.

CHAPTER 60

KAI

THE ARENA HUMS WITH bodies packed shoulder to shoulder, their energy electric and infectious. The smell of popcorn, cold air, and rubber mingle together in that way that only exists inside a rink. Sticks clatter. Someone takes a hit twenty feet to my left and the crowd surges.

People always talk about the sound. The deafening volume of the crowd, the clang of the puck off the post, the sharp hiss of blades scraping against ice. And the unmistakable thud of heavy bodies into boards. But tonight, all that is drowned out by the momentary silence and peace I feel when I spot them. I look up into the stands and my eyes are instantly drawn to them like an unescapable magnetic force.

Upper level. Second box from the right. Kendall's wearing that long olive coat that sits right above her knees. Her hair's up in a tight bun, a few curls around her face—her go-to style. And in her arms—hands and nose pushed to the glass—is Akio. *Our son.* He's wearing a jersey with my number on it, 23. It's the smallest size they had but it still hangs from his tiny frame, draping over his shoulders and legs.

She points to me and waves, trying to show Akio and Emma exactly where I am. When he makes the realization, he starts waving furiously. Kendall and Akio are here for me and it means everything. I wave back and blow them a kiss and I couldn't care less about the shit I'm going to get for it later in the locker room.

***

C OACH BARKS ORDERS FROM somewhere behind me but I don't catch them. The only thing I can see is their faces. She's radiating warmth, love, and pure joy. Kendall looks ecstatic in a way I haven't seen in a long time, their smiles bright and contagious.

I blink and turn around with considerable effort, focusing my energy and attention back to the face off. It's the third period of the game and we're tied. Four minutes remain on the clock.

It's the kind of shift that feels inevitable when everything clicks, when your edges are sharp and your reads are a half-second faster than everyone else's. I've put in ten thousand hours to make four minutes look effortless.

No pressure or anything.

Once I win the draw, it's automatic, seamless, muscle memory. I pass to Jonah on my left, thunder down the side, and rush the net. I know this game—its pace, its rhythm—like the back of my hand, like I know the sound of her voice or the shape of Akio's smile. They're all tattooed on my heart.

When I get the puck back in my possession, I don't even have to think about it. I send it flying past the goalie and into the net. The goal light flares red and the horn swallows the entire arena whole. The glass shakes. The ice vibrates beneath my skates.

GOAL.

My teammates attack me, rioting and yelling, sticks knocking against helmets and pads.

I've played one of the best games of my fucking life and we won. It's no surprise I played my ass off. I wanted to make both Kendall and Akio proud. I also hope this marks the first of many games they'll attend.

The locker room is loud and hot. It smells like sweat and adrenaline and the sharp bite of athletic tape. Gear hits the floor in heavy chunks. Someone's got music blasting from a phone shoved inside a helmet.

"You were on fire tonight, Matsumoto," Jonah comments, snapping a towel on my back. "What's the move, we celebrating?" he asks, eyebrows raised.

"Fuck yes. I think we're all going to dinner at La Vela. Like 8ish? I'm sure some people will hit the bar after."

"I'll meet you guys there," he replies before making his way into the shower.

"So, La Vela? At 8?" Jax wonders skeptically.

"Yupp."

"And I'm supposed to be meeting one of Kendall's friends?" he asks, lowering his voice to a hush.

"Uh huh." I pause, furrowing my brows. "What, are you nervous, 48? I don't think I've ever met a girl you couldn't charm, Brandi."

"Yeah, well charming them is one thing. Dating is another," he grumbles.

"It'll be fine. Don't worry. It's casual. Okay? And Emma is super cool, down to earth." I catch his gaze and he still looks slightly concerned. *Okay, definitely nervous.* "But maybe have a drink or two before. Liquid courage never hurts," I suggest lightly. He nods but I'm not entirely convinced he heard me.

Chapter 61

Kendall

B Y THE FINAL BUZZER, Kai scores one more goal, and the Bucks take the win 3–2. But it's not the numbers that linger—it's Kai. He's a force to be reckoned with. He's ruthlessly developed his craft to unleash brutal perfection on his opponents.

Every. Single. Game.

Kai plays hockey the same way he walks through life. Confident. Purposeful. Ambitious. Cutthroat in his pursuit of success. And deeply deeply passionate.

He's devoted his entire life to this game and in return, it's given him everything. Kai has such an intense love and appreciation for this sport. I just hope he knows how proud I am. Not just of his accomplishments, his career, his fame. But the kind of father he's becoming. The strength of his character, and his steadfast commitment to Akio and me.

All of it.

When the game ends, Akio looks up at me, flushed and glowing.

"More game, Mama?" he says. I know what he's asking. *Can we come to more games?* I smile and brush my nose against his.

"We'll see, baby," I reply hesitantly, with caution, but in my head, I can already see it. The gears have been put in motion. More wins, more highs. More exhilarating nights exactly like this one. More moments where Akio falls in love with Kai, where he idolizes him like he hung the moon, the stars, the whole goddamn sky. And maybe for the first time, I can see a future where the three of us are a family. Not just in theory, not dealing in hypotheticals. Not some far-fetched fantasy.

For real.

***

WE ARRIVE AT LA Vela shortly after 8. It's an upscale, Michelin-starred, Italian restaurant. The kind that has valet parking and a coat check. Kai and a few of his teammates reserved multiple tables in the back room for all of us. Apparently, the Boston Bucks are beloved regulars here. I drive with Kai and Emma decides to meet us there since she has to get home to Maddox after dinner. Kai takes my hand and threads his fingers through mine as we enter the restaurant. It reeks of opulence, expensive wine, and the slight hint of cigar smoke.

I lean into him and whisper, "I'm so fucking proud of you, Kai. That game was amazing."

"Thanks, Ken," he murmurs, brushing a kiss against my hair.

As we make our way to the back room, we pass soaring arched windows and crisp white tables shadowed by flickering candle-light. Situated all the way in the corner is a gold-accented marble bar and one lone bartender. Behind him, only premier alcohol and top shelf liquor. La Vela is sophisticated, elegant, and also slightly romantic? Which confuses me a bit. But Kai warned me on the drive over that most of the game winning debauchery takes place *after* dinner.

Emma beats us there so she is already sitting at the oversized circular booth talking with Jonah, Jax, and another team member. Well, talking might be too strong a word to describe what Jax is doing. He looks uncomfortable, like he is in actual pain sitting between Jonah and Emma.

Fuck, I hope I didn't read this entire situation wrong.

"Hey guys," I say sliding into the brown leather booth to sit on the other side of Emma. Kai scoots in next to me. We get head nods from the guys and Emma gives me a sweet, welcoming smile. Hopefully that's a good sign. It doesn't seem like she needs rescuing from Jax. At least not yet. Soon we're all chatting, laughing, sharing small plates and rehashing the incredible game they'd just played. There are wine glasses and plates littered across the table amid garlic bread, bacon wrapped scallops, and panna cotta.

"Kai, how many assists did you have tonight?" Jonah asks, his mouth full of bread.

"One," Kai answers modestly.

"Two goals and one assist, what a fucking game! Guess that means you have to come to every one now, Kendall," Jonah replies, throwing a wink my way.

"Guess so," I smile.

I look over every so often to see Jax and Emma in a conversation of their own. And they both seem interested. The guys continue to talk shop, shouting across the table. Eventually, Jax gets up to go to the bathroom and I can't help it; I need to know what her first impression is. I nudge her with my arm slightly to get her attention.

"So, what do you think of Jax so far?" I pester, wiggling my eyebrows playfully.

"He's a little quiet. But nice. Definitely easy to look at," she comments.

"Well, you can't seem to stop talking so maybe that's a good thing?" I joke. She rolls her bright green eyes but laughs anyway.

"Maybe. I can't really tell if he's into me at all," she whispers. "He's tough to read. But it's clear Kai is into you despite what Veronica says."

I didn't really think anyone could hear us. That and I figured they were absorbed in their own conversations about hockey. But Kai chimes in without missing a beat.

"Who is Veronica and what did she say?" he demands.

"It's nothing, Kai. just forget we even brought it up," I respond, shooting Emma a look that screams *please drop this*.

"Ken," he pushes and I just know like a dog with a bone he is not going to let this go.

"Veronica is a snarky mom at playgroup that enjoys cutting us all down for sport," I respond, taking a generous bite of garlic bread.

"And..." he's waiting for the rest of the story. The details.

"And she said that I wasn't exactly your type because I'm not a supermodel," I say quietly. "It's not a big deal, Kai. Honestly."

"If you could just excuse us for one minute," Kai says to the rest of the table, extending his hand to me and rising. He drags me out of the booth and to the single bathroom in the dim hallway.

"What, what are you—" but before I can finish my sentence, he pulls me in through the doorway with him. Flicking the lock shut with a click. The walls of the bathroom are a deep maroon red. Bamboo vases on neatly arranged shelves hold delicate white flowers. I hear Ed Sheeran filter in from the restaurant and suddenly, I'm in a fever dream. Kai's smooth lips are on mine, soft and appraising. Sweet and spicy. I don't stop to question it. I'm pulled under like a riptide. He grips my thighs, picks me up like I weigh nothing, and my legs wrap around his waist of their own accord. He sets me on the counter, bracing my jaw with one of his expansive hands. His mouth breaks away from mine, but I can still feel his heat everywhere.

"Why didn't you tell me about cunty Veronica and her vitriol?" He's smirking despite the edge of seriousness in his voice. But it's impossibly hard to think when he's this close to me.

"Um, the same reason I didn't tell you about Allison in high school," I reply more breathily than I intended. He brushes a stray hair out of my face and pins me with a stare. He can be so fucking intense at times.

"Because you were embarrassed or because you believed her jealous rantings?" he asks.

"Both," I sigh. "I didn't feel the need to correct her and I didn't really want to fight her in the middle of a public library either." At this, his mouth turns up.

"So, even after all we've been through together, what we undoubtedly have, knowing how helplessly attracted to you I am, you still let shit like this eat at you? Why?" He doesn't seem mad, not entirely. More irritated, impatient even.

"Because she's right!" I nearly shout. "Almost all the girls you have been with after me have been flawless, ten out of ten, supermodels. It's no surprise I'm not a supermodel, Kai. It's just a fact. The objective truth. I'm not in the same league as them. I'm not even sure we're playing the same game."

Then he smirks—fucking smirks. That smile could heal me, I'm sure of it. It's gotten me through some of the toughest days of my life and I'm pretty sure that handsome grin is what led to me getting pregnant in the first place. "You are absolutely not in the same league as them, Ken. You're in your own fucking league. You could bring me to my knees with your smile alone." He moves closer to me, his hand caressing my hip through the thin fabric of my shirt. He kisses my forehead, my eyelids and my cheeks in reverence, his lips a whisper over my skin. "You know how many times I've dreamed of your beautiful face? Your delicious mouth? You are every fucking fantasy that I will ever want, that I'll ever need. And you're better than a fantasy because you're real."

He takes my hand and moves it to his jeans where I can already feel his marble length. We've never done anything like this before—been so desperate for each other we hooked up in a restaurant bathroom, where people could easily hear us. But I can sense we aren't leaving until he's made his point and I really fucking want him to. He gently presses his forehead to mine and rocks his hips against my hand.

"Does this feel like you aren't my type?" he rasps. His words sound like he swallowed gravel.

"N-no," I stammer.

"Jesus, these fucking hips," he hisses, kneading them with his hands and tracing the top of my underwear with his thumb. "You know how many times I've thought about taking you from behind and holding onto these hips for dear life?" He's kissing my neck now, whispering sweet depraved filthy promises into my skin. I want to beg him to do every single one of them. He moves his hands to my back and slides them into my skintight jeans to palm my ass. "This sexy round ass I could sink my teeth into."

I'm so fucking turned on and he's barely touched me, my body strung so unbelievably tight I'm sure I would come from a slight breeze. I know what he's doing. Trying to make me understand that he's attracted to gorgeous women but I'm the pinnacle of that attraction. That I'm sexy and perfect and stunning in my own right. And so help me, I want to believe him.

"These curls, this hair. You know how much I love it?" He whispers into my temple, lightly grasping some in his hand and tilting my head towards him. "How tempted I am to wrap my fists around it while your mouth is otherwise occupied?" *Jesus Christ.* His dirty mouth and words of adoration are enough to unravel me.

"Your body is torturous, Ken. It drives me wild." He pauses to run his thumb over my sternum. A gentle caress. A question. I don't bother answering, I just cover his hand with mine and move it underneath my bra. He groans into my neck like every manner of self-restraint is becoming impossible. "These amazing tits fit perfectly in my hand," he says as he rubs and kneads my nipple. "And my mouth," he whispers in my ear. "May I?"

"Mhm," I whimper, not even sure if it's intelligible.

"Words, Ken, I need words, baby," he chuckles. It's raspy and deep. I feel it at the base of my spine, where it melts into my core and sparks a flame.

"Yes," I grate out while he pulls down my black silk shirt along with my bra to expose my breasts. He's sucking, licking, nipping at me, his teeth grazing the most sensitive area of my flesh. And I'm borderline embarrassed at the sounds I'm making, writhing and wet with need, completely at the mercy of his mouth. Potent desire anchors my lips back to his. Raw lust buzzes and hums underneath our skin, burning and crackling and exploding to life between us. He pulls away slightly, both of us breathing hard and heavy. I'm panting like a goddamn dog in heat.

"We don't have to do this here. I just need you to understand how much I want you. That you're the only person I want. You can tell me to stop at any time," he whispers.

"Don't you fucking dare."

I can't tell him to stop. I don't want him to. Not when he unbuttons my jeans, not when he pulls my thong to the side and teases my entrance. And certainly not when he plunges two fingers into my slick wet heat so fucking slowly. I grasp onto his arm and moan into the alcove between his neck and shoulder. Like it could anchor me here and tether me to this moment. I'll die if he stops, I'll combust if he doesn't. The stretch, the fit, the feel of his fingers inside me curling to stroke the place I need him most—are all enough to send me hurtling to the precipice of oblivion.

"God, Ken you're so fucking wet and tight. I need to see you come. Please," he pushes in deeper and faster while I chase the delicious friction at the base of his palm. I'm flying. Floating. *Soaring*. My breath hitches when he tilts his hand, adding more pressure to my throbbing clit. I buck my hips against him faster as desperate breathy moans escape my lips.

"Fuck, Ken, that's so hot. I could come just watching you." My arms curl around his upper back, my nails digging into his shoulders. He plays me like a well-tuned instrument. I'm his religion, my body the altar at which he worships.

"Kai—" and then I shatter around him, my walls quake with pure ecstasy. His fingers are knuckle deep inside of me in the middle of a restaurant bathroom. It's hands down the hottest experience of my entire life. He muffles my cries of pleasure with a kiss and it's so easy to lose myself in him, in us. I rest my head against his chest, breathing hard.

I'm boneless, mindless, speechless.

Then he kisses my forehead and takes my face in his hands. His smokey eyes pierce me with love and longing. Hope and affection. He looks at me like I'm everything and in this moment, I know I am.

"You're so fucking beautiful, Ken. Perfection. I hope you get it now. My type starts and ends with you."

And I do get it. I really really do. His words wrap around me and settle in my chest, burrow in my soul. This has been about pleasure and desire but it's also about me standing so fucking certain in my truth and his that I never doubt it again. It isn't that he doesn't make me feel desired, wanted, *loved*. He does. It's my own inner critic and loud voices that make me question things. Not anymore. Hopefully never again if I can help it. I'm drunk on the fucking power. Dizzy and delirious from the intoxicating pleasure that is Kai.

I feel victorious. Sexy. Unhinged. I also have the overwhelming, delightful thought that Veronica can go fuck herself. That anyone who ever makes me feel small, insignificant, or insecure again can go fuck themselves. And I suspect—no, I *know*—that's been Kai's intent all along.

Chapter 62

Kai

S o much for debauchery happening after dinner. I've just come dangerously close to submitting to my base instincts, throwing caution to the wind and fucking Kendall hard and fast against the bathroom door of La Vela. I don't have much of an excuse—I'm not even drunk. Although I might as well be coasting on a high after feeling Kendall come apart in my arms and listening to her needy cries of pleasure. Still, I have no explanation for my behavior, for needing to defile her in between courses, where the rest of the team could probably hear us. Other than the fact that I can't take one more second of her doubting herself. She leaves first. I take a few moments to collect myself so I don't come in my hand like a horny fucking teenager. I don't want this to be reciprocal, not tonight. I want this to be entirely about her—what she needs but can't ask for.

When we make our way back to the table, it's apparent the air in the room has shifted. Like the temperature has suddenly dropped a few degrees cooler. Looking to the corner near the small bar, I can see why. Emma is there with a man who towers over her and definitely isn't Jax. But Jax' eyes are glued to her from across the room, cataloging her every move. The man Emma is talking to is agitated and drunk. He yells something in her face, getting entirely too close, and she takes a step back from him. But she doesn't get very far; he grabs her elbow aggressively and drags her back towards him.

"Who is that?" I say to Kendall as both our eyes follow Emma and the spectacle that's unfolding.

"That's her ex-husband, Trent. He's an asshole and he's been abusive to her. I have no idea why he's even here," Kendall explains and she sounds slightly worried. We're about to sit back down at the table when Jax quickly rises and makes his way over to them in three quick strides.

"I think it's time for you to leave," I hear him say low. His voice is lethal, definitive. It leaves no room for argument.

"Yeah, and who the fuck are you? Are you fucking her?" Trent slurs loudly, unsteady on his feet. Jax moves closer to Trent, encroaching on his space and instinctively positioning himself in front of Emma. There's absolutely no way this can end well.

"I'm the guy who is going to put you in the fucking ground if you put your hands on her again without her permission," Jax replies. *Fuck*. Somewhere in between appetizers and watching Kendall have one of the hottest orgasms of her life, things have deteriorated. This disagreement, lovers quarrel, whatever the fuck it is is about to spiral into an altercation. I can feel it. Jax has that searing, hungry, unforgiving look in his eyes. The one he gets before jumping into a fight on the ice. He's very close to losing his grip. Trent laughs in Jax' face and tries to sidestep him to return to Emma, which is certainly not his smartest move. Jax' defensive instincts are second to none. I watch his self-restraint vanish like smoke and I know Trent's belligerent ass is fucked. Before I can blink, Jax drags her pathetic ex out the back door by the scruff of his shirt. I follow close behind him with Jonah on my heels.

Against all odds and gravity, Trent wriggles out of Jax's hold, stands up, and puffs his chest out.

"WHAT THE FUCK MAN," Trent spits. "I'm just trying to have a little fun with my girl. I'm sure you know how much fun she can be." Jax right fist crunches into Trent's face a millisecond later.

"FUCKK!" Trent howls in pain as he brings his hand to his cheek. He strides towards Jax with fury in his eyes, but he doesn't get very far. Jax pummels him at the waist and tackles him to the ground with ease. Jonah and I let him get one more punch in before we drag him off of Trent. He needs that hand as a defender and we also need him not to get arrested tonight.

Jax is writhing, trying to break free of our hold, anger seeping from every pore. *I'd have to be restrained too if someone ran their mouth about Kendall like that.*

"If you ever come near her again, you'll regret it," Jax threatens.

"Yeah okay man. Whatever you say," Trent snaps but he sounds defeated and he looks a little worse for wear. I doubt he'll try reaching Emma again tonight. Bright red blood drips down his chin, from a gash above his lip and a mottled purple bruise is already forming around his left eye. He pushes up from the ground and hobbles down the street away from us.

Chapter 63

Kendall

THE NIGHT KIND OF fell apart after the fight between Jax and Trent. I don't even know that I would call it a fight. Jax got two good shots in before Kai, Jonah, and their other teammates were on him trying to break it up. Not to mention, Trent was way too drunk to defend himself. Even if he wasn't, Jax would have still beat the shit out of him. There's a reason he's the Bucks best defenseman. Given that the Boston Bucks are a high-profile NHL team, constantly in the public eye, it wouldn't have been wise for Jax to continue pummeling him. A fact Jonah reminded him of after he sunk a right hook to Trent's face.

As far as I'm concerned, Trent got a much needed ass kicking and Jax did everyone else a public service. But really, it's not my opinion that matters, it's Emma's and I feel terrible for putting her in this position. Apparently, Trent, the walking red flag that he is, was stalking Emma's Instagram stories even though she blocked him on all of her social media platforms. He saw that we were at the Bucks game and snippets from the beginning of the night at La Vela. Then the drunk angry idiot decided to come confront her. Maybe Jax' presence will deter him from doing it again, maybe it will add fuel to the fire. I have a dreadful sinking feeling—like lead attached to my feet—that Trent is not easily deterred. Not when it comes to Emma.

Emma is sitting at the kitchen table, a glass of water clutched in her hand. Her eyes are a little red and swollen from crying. I insisted she stay at my apartment with Kai, Akio, and me, given how shaken up she is. I definitely don't want her driving to see Maddox alone. She fights me on it before calling her mom to tell her she will stop by to pick up Maddox in the morning. Based on her mom's reaction, this isn't the first time something like this has happened. And my intuition tells me he's done much worse than this before. I don't have to ask.

"Are you okay?" I finally whisper as I settle down in the seat across from her. I've never been in a situation like this and I don't know what else to say. There's no handbook for when your best friend gets harassed by her abusive ex-husband, while on a date with someone you set her up with. But I really wish there was.

"Not really," she replies. "I haven't felt like that in a long time." She pauses. "Scared of him, scared for myself and the people around me. I'm so fucking embarrassed that you had to see that. That Jax had to deal with that," she admits wearily.

"Em, why are you embarrassed? You didn't do anything wrong."

"I'm ashamed that I let him treat me like that for so long. That I let it go on for years and that tonight, other people witnessed it." Her head is in her hands now. "I spent so long trying to get out from under his grip, his drinking, his mistakes. And things were better for a while. But somehow, I ended up right back here with him breaking me down and me letting him."

"Em, I don't think you are repeating cycles or patterns. I think Trent is a psychotic asshole who showed up unannounced, cornered you, and preyed on the fact that you'd be in public."

"Yeah, I guess," she murmurs, biting her lip. "Trent may be a dick but he's not stupid. Well, not entirely," she observes, looking down at her hands.

"I don't want to pry but is there more to this than you're telling me?" I hedge. "Because all of this kind of seems like Trent's fault."

She blows out a long breath and doesn't answer me for a few moments. "I've blocked him, his phone number. He doesn't have access to my social media accounts or at least he shouldn't. But sometimes he tries to contact me on burner phones. And I just wanted to have one fucking night to myself, to have fun," she sighs. "And unfortunately with Trent, it's easier on everyone involved to respond to him, pacify him. Rather than ignore him. I thought if I gave him a few updates about Maddox, he would leave me alone. But instead, he showed up at La Vela. I'm really sorry, Ken."

"Please don't apologize. I still don't think you did anything wrong. I thought you were going to be pissed at me because of Jax. I also hate that you were going through this alone for so long. I'm here for whatever you guys need, you know that, right?"

"Of course I do. Wait, what do you mean? Why would I be pissed at you because of Jax?"

"I don't know, maybe if I hadn't set you guys up none of this would have happened."

"Trust me, Ken. It would have sooner or later. I can't escape him forever. I just need to figure out how to deal with him better without him becoming a petulant, angry, manchild. And honestly, the fact that Jax stood up for me, having only known me for two hours was kind of hot. It only made me like him more."

"So, what you're saying is thank you Kendall, you are an expert matchmaker?" I joke, trying to bring some levity to the conversation.

"You're pushing it, Ken," she laughs. I get up and move to her side of the table and wrap her in a bear hug, my chin resting on top of her dirty blonde hair. I squeeze her small frame tightly, hoping she can feel how much I love and care about her. Sometimes people come into our lives that we wish we had met much sooner. So we could spend more time with them, know them longer. Emma is one of those people.

"Fuck Trent," I whisper and kiss the top of her head. "You deserve so much better. You deserve every good thing that is coming to you."

"Yeah, you're right. Fuck him," she replies.

CHAPTER 64

KAI

2016

I SQUIRM IN MY seat that's far too small for my body as I wait for the people ahead of me on the plane to exit. The scent of stale coffee and food linger in the air like fog, making my stomach even more uneasy. I'm itching to get off the flight, eager to say the words I've been reciting for three hours to the one person that I know needs to hear them. I'm also terrified of what will happen when I find her, but even more scared of what will happen if I don't.

I move through the airport baggage claim and exit to find the bustling pick-up lane where I'm supposed to meet my Uber. I'm overdressed and fucking sweating. It's frigid in New England right now. But North Carolina is warm, welcoming, 57 degrees and partially sunny. A slight breeze sweeps my face, but it does nothing to cool me down or calm my nerves. I wish I could say I'm visiting North Carolina for the first time for pleasure, but it's for closure. This is my Hail Mary, my last-ditch effort, my final attempt to right whatever the hell had gone so wrong between Kendall and me.

I check local coffee shops, bookstores, museums, restaurants, and art galleries in Durham first. Places I know Kendall would likely be drawn to. The majority of them are small holes in the wall, that most people wouldn't give a second glance. But Kendall isn't most people. She has a knack for finding the beauty in forgotten, overlooked things. Having virtually no luck at any of those, I make my way to Duke.

It's stunning, pristine, and meticulously cared for even in winter. The sprawling lawns, gothic architecture, and lush greenery draw me in instantly. No wonder Kendall fell in love with this place when she first came to visit in eighth grade. It's unique and beautiful exactly like her. I stroll around campus, and into a few different buildings hoping to see her face, the one that's been plaguing my dreams.

After two and a half hours of searching for her with no success, I stop to sit on a bench and clear my head. She has to be here somewhere. If she's enrolled in fall semester classes, then she has to be somewhere on this campus. The dorms, an apartment building, a lecture hall, a dining hall. Somewhere. My phone buzzing in my pocket interrupts my anxiety ridden thoughts.

"Hey, Dad, I can't really—"

But his deep demanding voice cuts me off. "Kai? I was just at your apartment hoping to catch up with you after practice. Are you going to be home soon?" he asks briskly. So typical of my father. He doesn't even have the decency to ask how I'm doing.

"No, Dad. I'm not going to be home soon. I'm not even in Boston," I sigh, running my hands through my hair. It feels thick and a little greasy.

When is the last time I showered?

"What do you mean you *aren't* in Boston? You didn't go to practice today?" he huffs disapprovingly.

"I'm in North Carolina," I reply. I tilt my chin up to the sky, pinching the bridge of my nose as I wait for my dad's response.

"What the hell are you doing in North Carolina when you should be at practice, Kai? You do recall you are an important contributing member of the NHL now, right?" God he can be such a condescending prick.

"It's nothing, Dad. I'm flying back tomorrow morning and I'll be home in time for practice," I say flatly. I don't have the time or patience for him right now.

"It sure as hell isn't nothing if you are flying off on a whim and missing practice," he barks. "I thought you were done partying and fucking around. I thought you were ready to lock in and get your head right. You said you were going to be focused. You *need* to be focused, Kai."

"I am. I'm trying. There's just some things I need to do."

"Is this about Kendall?" He says her name like it's an annoyance, an inconvenience rather than the love of my fucking life.

"Yeah."

"Okay."

"Okay?" That's it. No follow up, no questions. Nothing. He's a piece of fucking work. The least he can do is pretend to give a shit.

"Yeah, okay. Just," there's a brief pause. "You know what, never mind." I'm holding my breath waiting for him to say something, anything that would indicate he cares about this major disruption to my life. This hole in my heart I've been trying to fill with so many things that all eventually added up to nothing. But I know by now he isn't going to.

"Listen, I got to go. Thanks for the wellness check. I'll talk to you later," I say, hanging up on him. I'm already preparing myself for the inevitable, for what happens when this doesn't work. If I can't find Kendall. The moment I have to force myself to move on without her. I can't deal with my dad's bullshit and his need to control everything and everyone around him on top of it. It feels like the walls are closing in on me, my world collapsing around me. If there is one person who knows what that is like, who has been there, who can help me see my way through it, it's my mom. She picks up on the second ring.

"Hello?"

"Hey, mom."

"Hey, Kai, is everything okay? Are you with your dad?" she asks.

"No. I just talked to him though." I pause. "I'm in North Carolina."

"You're in North Carolina..." she repeats.

"Yup."

"Because?"

I take a deep breath. "Because I thought maybe I could find her," I clarify.

"Ah okay. You thought you would fly down there, find her, make a grand gesture, and right all the wrongs?" she offers.

I laugh dryly. "Yeah, I mean it sounds kind of ridiculous when you put it like that," I admit.

"Not ridiculous. I know how much she meant to you, means to you. You guys were each other's first loves. You were together for almost six years. That's longer than most people's marriages last nowadays. That's not nothing, Kai."

No, it isn't. In fact, to me, it feels like everything. *She* feels like everything.

"Not you and dad though. You guys have been happily married for what? Twenty years now?" I ask.

"Twenty-six next year. You know what that means though, don't you? You guys were together for so long it's going to take a lot longer than you want to recover from it."

"I'm not ready to let her go, Mom. I love her. I was going to marry her. I'm still not convinced that I won't someday," I respond, feeling my pocket for the small velvet box that was there. "What do I do?" I ask hopelessly.

"You keep looking. You keep searching. If you find her, you fight like hell for her. If you don't, I think you try letting her go. Whatever that looks like. If it's meant to work out with her, it will. Maybe she just needs some time and space right now."

"Okay, but what do I do with—"

"With all the pain?" she asks intuitively.

"Yeah."

"Write it down. Get it out. Put it in words somewhere. It doesn't matter if you send it to her or not. The letter isn't for her. It's for you, okay? Write down everything you want to say to her, you need to say to her. Then you try to move forward the best you can. Put one foot in front of the other, just do the next right thing."

"Anyone ever tell you you're pretty wise?"

"All the time." I can hear her smiling through the phone.

"Thanks, Mom."

"You're welcome. I love you, Kai. It's going to be okay, you know."

"How do you know?"

"Let's just say I have a sixth sense about these things. And really, there isn't any other option, is there?"

"Yeah, I guess not."

Later on my return flight home, I reflect on the past twenty-four hours. My spur of the moment decision to board a plane for North Carolina and my frantic search for Kendall. My fleeting glimpses of hope mixed with the impending feeling of dread. My father's obvious disdain and my mother's words of guidance. I'd been unsuccessful in finding her, leaving me feeling more defeated than ever. I could never quite figure out what I did right in my life to deserve Kendall. As a friend or a partner. But I also never thought I did anything that warranted losing her either. Not like this. Not without any fucking answers. I couldn't wrap my head around it. I'm not ready to give her up and I doubt I ever will be. Some piece of me will always belong to her.

I have my career to look forward to, but what is that worth, what does that mean without her? I guess I'm about to find out.

I take out a piece of paper from my carry on and begin writing.

Chapter 65

Kendall

THE ONLY WARNING HE gets is a text that says, "I'm coming over." Thirty minutes later, I'm standing outside his penthouse door pounding ferociously.

"Let me in, Kai, I know you're in there," I yell before knocking again.

I had finally bit the bullet and read one of Kai's letters. We've been working on our relationship, we're in a good place. *I can do this,* I reasoned. The letter was dated December 8, 2016. Roughly three months after I had moved to North Carolina to live with my Aunt Vicky. I quickly found out I very much couldn't do it, not without huge ramifications. His letter was endearing and heartfelt at times but there were also things that had been difficult to read and digest. I couldn't pin down my feelings, the pendulum swinging between grief and frustration, anger and relief. Even now, I'm feeling so many conflicting emotions I don't know where to begin. But the one I feel like I'm drowning in, really the only one that matters, is love.

He opens up the door groggy and confused. He's squinting at me trying to block the harsh light from the hallway with his hand. He's wearing boxers that might as well be painted onto his muscular body and nothing else.

"Ken? What's wrong? What are you doing here?" he asks, alarmed. I realize now how crazy I must seem, how completely insane this is. It was pouring when I left my house and I forgot an umbrella. The trek from my car to his apartment has left me looking like a drenched sewer rat. I swipe the arm of my damp sweatshirt across my face in an attempt to appear halfway decent.

"Can I come in? I texted you. Sorry about just showing up here."

"Of course," he replies, holding the door open for me and ushering me inside. We're standing at the entrance of his apartment right next to the sleek, modern open kitchen. I carefully pull the folded, handwritten letter out of my pants pocket. It had suffered the fate of a few raindrops, but still appears to be legible. We stare at each other for a few moments silently. His eyes flick to the paper in my hand and back to me.

"What's going on, Ken? What is that?" he asks, taking a step toward me.

"I read one of the letters you wrote me tonight," I admit. "It was the first one I've ever read."

"Ken, I wrote those a long time ago, I—"

"North Carolina." I blurt out cutting him off. "Did you come to North Carolina to look for me?" I demand.

"Of course I did." It's the certainty, the sureness of his words that cause my knees to buckle. It's fact, truth, an inevitability. They all blend together to tell me the only thing I really need to know. And that is that Kai wasn't going to let me walk away without putting up a fight. And he hadn't.

"Why?" I'm shaking now, my bottom lip quivering. Tears are falling freely from my eyes and I'm not even sure why. But I need to push through whatever this feeling is. He sighs, dragging his palm down his face.

"Because I missed you. Because I was heartbroken. Because I was fucking miserable without you and you just disappeared without a word." He's moved closer to me now, his mouth centimeters from mine. "We have the kind of love people only dream about. The kind of love that is worth fighting for. The kind of love that feels so good and hurts so fucking bad. The kind of love that breaks you apart and puts you back together again. So that's what I was doing, trying to put the pieces of us back together again. I was trying to figure out how we veered so far—"

But he doesn't get a chance to finish his sentence because my lips are on his. Kissing away his words, the pain, the heartbreak, the mistakes. There's only this, only us. The heat of his hands and the pounding of my heart. The desperation of our love. He gathers me in his arms, holding me tightly. I plant panicked, anguished kisses on his cheek, my lips skimming his jawbone and then I move to his neck and trail kisses along the column of his throat. I curl myself tighter into his embrace, my head resting against his chest.

You're perfect. I want to say. *I was so stupid and reckless all those years ago. I love you, I have always been in love with you and it runs deeper and burns brighter than it ever has.*

Every unbidden thought threatens to burst out of my mouth but somehow, I tamp them all down. All that comes out is a series of apologies.

"I'm so sorry. I'm sorry I wasn't where I said I was. I'm sorry that I lied. I'm sorry that I broke us. I'm just so fucking sorry," I cry. I don't know if I'm apologizing to him or myself. Probably both.

"Shh, it's okay, Ken. It's okay," he promises, kissing my forehead. His arms surround me. Steady and strong. Loving and warm. His solid chest pressed against my cheek is the only comfort I need. His voice an anchor in the storm. I'm still not entirely convinced I deserve him. But I love him anyway. I kiss him again, this time on the lips and it quickly becomes heated, passionate, *desperate.* I nip his bottom lip playfully and a growl erupts from his throat. He grips me underneath my thighs, lifting me up as my legs wrap around his trim waist. We're a tangled, chaotic, beautiful mess. Each of us trying frantically to get as much of our hands and lips on the other. I pull back from him breathlessly. I'm like a moth drawn to a flame and I'm ready to burn myself for him, ignite. Consequences be damned.

"Kai. I need you. I need all of you. I don't think I can wait any longer. I know we made a pact and we promised to wait, but we've been going to therapy and it does feel like we're making progress. And I know we're trying to uncomplicate things. But I've come to accept things with us are never not going to be complicated but they're always going to be worth it. If you still want to wait, that's okay, I'll respect whatever choice you make." I peer into his eyes and there's something firm and immovable there. It seems like a spur of the moment decision to throw sex into the mix and hope it doesn't destroy everything we've managed to repair. But it isn't, not at all. This moment has been quietly building, thrumming just beneath the surface since I first laid eyes on him four months ago. Since I walked away from him three years ago.

"Ken. I want this. I want you," he responds, clear eyed and confident. My heart starts racing, my pulse picking up speed. There is no going back after this.

"Are you sure?" I whisper.

"Yes. Fuck the pact," he confirms before crashing his mouth to mine. The four most glorious words in the English language. He backs me up until I'm planted against the wall, my feet off the ground molding my core to his. He starts rocking his hips into me and his hand glides underneath my shirt. The pressure, the friction is too much and not entirely enough. I want all of him. I want to feel him everywhere. I rip my sweatshirt up and over my head, my hair elastic coming free in the process. My hair falls in tight curls around my bare shoulders.

"Ken, you are so fucking beautiful," he whispers, my jaw in his hand.

"Mhm," I murmur, eager to kiss him again.

"I'm serious," he says.

"I know." I reach into his boxers to grip his length and start stroking him slowly.

"Fuck, Ken," he says, resting his forehead on my shoulder. "I'm not gonna last long if you do that. And I *want* this to last. I want to go slow the first time. Because I know I won't be able to later."

I'm distracted momentarily by the bright lights that compose the skyline outside his large picture windows.

"Kai," I murmur, "This view is breathtaking."

He nips my jaw playfully, trying to direct my focus back to him. "My view certainly is," he muses as he swipes his tongue from my collarbone to my chin. He has my undivided attention again.

"Respectfully, Kendall, the only view I'm concerned about is your breathtaking face while you come apart on my cock because I'm buried so deep inside of you, okay?"

Good lord.

Then he carries me—in between hot, intoxicating kisses—half stumbling half laughing to his bedroom.

When we were just hooking up before—when the pact was still very much standing—things were easy. Playful. But now that I'm standing directly in front of him, in nothing but my underwear, my nerves start to creep in. I have my hands crossed in front of my breasts, as if that could possibly help me now. His eyes scan the length of my body with longing and fervor.

"What's wrong? Where'd you go?" Kai asks, grasping my chin between his index finger and thumb and tipping it towards him.

"I'm just a little nervous I guess. You haven't seen all of me since before I had Akio and my C-section," I admit, twirling the end of a curl around my finger anxiously. His gorgeous sable eyes study me, rooting me to the spot.

"Did you forget our little shower excursion or when you had the flu?" he teases.

"I know but that was different. We were just hooking up before. This with you is..." I struggle to come up with the right words. *Daunting. Intimidating. Everything.*

"I thought we talked about this. I love your body, Ken. It drives me insane. As evidenced by the raging hard on I have right now," he smirks. He stalks forward, engulfing my body with his. The heat from his body rolls off of him in waves, igniting a flame in mine. His lips are on my throat, warm and patient, his right hand splayed across my lower back.

"You want me to beg? I will. I have no problem begging," he whispers. His other hand is gripping my neck while his lips glide over my shoulders and collarbone. He worships my hardened nipples with his tongue and teeth first. He kisses the smattering of freckles beneath my sternum, my stomach, my hips. It sends shivers careening down my spine. His mouth and hands move down down *down*. His touch cascading across my skin in a delicate, tantalizing dance. It makes my blood heat. I'm melting into a pool of lust. I'm certain I'll come before he's even inside me. He's kneeling in front of me now.

"You want me on my knees? I'm there," he murmurs, pressing his soft lips to the thin fabric of my underwear. *Holy shit.*

He slides his teeth over my clit and it's enough to rip a strangled keening cry from my throat. "Please, Ken, let me see you. All of you. Let me own your pleasure. I want to watch you unravel. Let me see this beautiful perfect body that gave us our son." His voice is rough, hoarse, pleading. He kisses my thighs, kneading them with his hands, his mouth dangerously close to where I need him most. Then he glances up at me, his dark eyes burning into mine before he tugs my underwear to the side and brushes his lips to my sex. All my fears, doubts, and insecurities float away on a cloud of lust.

"Please." That's all it takes. One word and his long capable tongue against my throbbing bundle of nerves. My desire for him explodes like a supernova. I move backwards onto the bed and drag his body on top of mine. My hand moves down to trace his chiseled abs and back into his boxers.

"Kai, why are you still wearing these?" I ask, yanking the thin material down his legs.

"I have no idea," he replies, unceremoniously shucking them off and over the side of the bed. Though he takes sweet, torturous time removing mine. Our mouths collide again with feverish, hungry kisses. He moves his mouth to my breast, careful to give each one the amount of attention it deserves. His tongue is slow and languid as it caresses my nipple.

"Kai," I whimper. "Please," I beg. I'm so close to the edge. I don't want this to end before it even begins.

"Patience, Ken," he says. He moves his hand down my chest and torso, over my abdomen, past my scar. He drags his fingers back and forth through my slick wet folds at an excruciatingly lazy pace. It's devastating, exquisite, torturous bliss. I bite my bottom lip to keep myself from shamelessly begging again. I think I might die in anticipation of his cock. *What a way to fucking go.* I bring my hand over his, urging him to go deeper and gasp as he slips two fingers inside me.

God yes. The ache at the apex of my thighs has been temporarily sated. But not for long. Because I know no matter how deliciously full of him I am, it's nothing compared to having all of him. His tongue slips into my mouth, gliding against mine while I moan into his. His fingers pulse deep and slow, coaxing, taunting, tempting my arousal.

His forehead is against mine, slick with a sheen of sweat when I hear him say, "I think we need a condom." It's strangled and gravelly. He's unraveling before me, this tightly wound, intensely focused man who almost never loses control, is coming undone because of me. I fucking love it.

"Mhm," I say. "I think you're right." Then he shifts off of the bed and I hear a drawer open and the distinct tearing of a foil wrapper. In a matter of seconds, his body is propped above mine, Kai resting on his forearms. I take the time to trace his tattoos with my fingers, running my hands down his carved biceps and roped muscles. I want to live forever in these moments with him. I want to freeze time, memorize him exactly like this. His sharply defined jaw, the slope of his nose, the searing passion in his raven eyes and every rugged plane of his body. He kisses me again as he nudges my entrance with his hard length.

"Is this okay?" he asks.

"Yes," I pant. He inches inside me slowly and I gasp again, partially from disbelief and partially from discomfort. He's thick and solid and incredibly huge. I forgot about the sheer size of him somehow.

And this is the exact moment I've been dreaming about for months, years maybe. I've fantasized about this alone in my bed with helpless, impossible want, the kind that could only be satisfied by him.

"Ken," he groans, "You're so fucking tight, baby." I shift slightly, trying to make space for him but I'm positive there is none. He tries to thrust but I know he can feel my body tensing up.

How the hell is he going to fit? He's probably not even halfway in.

"What's wrong? Am I hurting you?" he asks concerned.

"I think I just forgot what it's like to accommodate all of you," I admit sheepishly.

"Okay, what do you need me to do?"

"Just go slow, talk me through it. Please don't stop."

"I'm gonna push in a little deeper and I need you to take a deep breath. Try and make some room for me," he instructs. I do as he says, trying to relax my muscles. He does this a few more times, each time sinking further into me while I breathe deeply and spread my hips wider. What was once pain is now glorious, unrivaled pleasure.

"That's it, Ken. You're doing so good," he breathes into my temple.

I moan as he buries his cock inside me all the way to the hilt, clawing his shoulders. My hands traverse his traps and slide down his back. I don't even recognize the sounds I'm making. They're animalistic and raw. The praise, the fit, the feel of him is too much. My senses are overwhelmed, my nerves frayed and I still want him *closer*. My legs are hitched around his waist, my feet crossed at his back, my hips rising again and again to meet him, to chase this all-consuming high. I want to somehow bring him deeper but there's absolutely nowhere else to go. I consider, insensibly, asking him to remove the condom before remembering that was what landed us in this whole mess in the first place.

"Kai, I want you to fuck me like we used to, like I'm yours. Because I am...if you want me to be. I'm all in. Every part of me belongs to you," I tell him. And it's too late, the words are out there, tumbling out of my mouth before I can take them back.

"I do want that," he decides, thrusting inside me. Slow. Methodical. Heavenly.

"And are you mine?" I almost choke on the words. I coil one hand around his shoulder and bring my other palm to his stunning face.

"Kendall, I have always been yours and you have always been mine. We have always belonged to each other even when we didn't and time, distance, past indiscretions, the pain we've been through won't change that. I love you. I never stopped loving you and I never will," he promises.

A silent tear rolls down my face at the implication of his words. Our love has survived even after all we've been through.

"I love you so much, Kai. I've never stopped loving you, not for a second." I say breathlessly.

"Say it again," is his only response. His mouth is on my neck and I can feel all of him in every cell of my body. In the recesses of my heart, the expansiveness of my soul.

"Say what, that I love you?" I ask as he presses delicate kisses along the column of my throat.

"That you're mine," he whispers.

"I'm yours. Forever." Apparently, these words, these admissions, these promises are the last things holding us back. The limit of his restraint and mine has finally been reached. He rocks into me furiously, my thighs entwined around his waist. There's nothing better than this, I'm sure of it. This isn't just sex. This is the joining of our souls, the repairing of our hearts. It's unclear where he starts and I begin, the boundary undefinable. This is heaven on earth. And I'm reminded again that those pearly white gates, eternal peace, endless bliss, and enduring calm don't belong to a place. They belong to people. To us. *This.* These sacred ancient feelings and perfect togetherness. Our bodies fitting together like lock and key.

His head is nestled into my neck, his arms curled around my shoulders, pulling and tugging like I could anchor him. I'm sure there will be marks from his fingers there tomorrow. Good. He will have claw marks down his back to match.

"Harder," I beg. "Please, Kai."

He whispers sweet praise and unintelligible somethings into my skin while he slides home over and over, satisfying my every wish. He intertwines my hands with his above my head. He's filling me up, hollowing me out, creating infinitesimal space for himself with every thrust of his cock. Pushing me to the point of what my body can handle with every snap of his hips. He is quite literally stretching me to my limits.

God, how I want to be limitless for him.

I feel the orgasm start to build deep in my core and he's right there with me quickening his pace. Our lovemaking gets sloppy and hurried as we crest the edge of sweet blinding euphoria together. He grips my ass, angling it upwards and pushing impossibly deeper inside me. Then he hits that spot at just the right angle and I cry out in ecstasy. We're drowning in desire, in each other, freefalling together.

"Kai," I whimper as tears slide down my face. "I love you," I whisper almost imperceptibly. But Kai hears it. I'm in shock that we made it here after all we've endured.

We're us again. Us still. Us always.

"I love you," he says after kissing my forehead and again after he kisses my cheek. "God, I missed saying that to you," he admits. He repeats it over and over until it's the only thing I hear. Until it's imprinted in my skin and embedded in my heart. *I love you* as he smiles against my mouth and slips out of me. As soon as he does, I miss him. I want to tell him that I already feel empty without him. *I love you I love you I love you* as he burrows in next to me, pulling me tight to his chest.

He wanted to own my pleasure and he had, wringing out every last drop. I vow right then and there that it will never belong to anyone else ever again.

Chapter 66

Kai

S HE JUST SHOWS UP at my apartment at midnight out of the blue. I open my door and she's standing there, sopping wet. And I think to myself *I am completely gone for this woman.*

It doesn't take long for me to realize she came over here on a whim, much like my quest to fly to North Carolina in search of her. The letter that she's holding, I know it by heart. I had memorized every fucking line before I mailed it. I started it off cruel and bitter, heartbroken and angry.

I can't believe you fucking did this to me. To us. Don't I deserve some sort of explanation? Was our entire relationship a lie? How could you just walk away like it meant nothing? You're a coward, Ken, and whatever you're scared of, whatever you're running from, I hope it was worth it.

But the rest of it is an outpouring of love. My adoration for her.

I miss you the way the earth misses the sun's warmth in the depths of winter. If I'm honest, I think I'll miss you for the rest of my life. I feel so fucking empty without you. I keep trying to fill this hole inside myself with other things. But I know it's useless because the only person who completes me, complements me, knows the shape of my heart is you.

You are my entire world, my whole fucking heart. Every dream I could ever hope to have. I have never loved anyone the way I love you, as much as I love you, and I probably never will again. But I think I need to try and let you go. I'll love you today, tomorrow, forever, always. I'm scared that I'll never figure out how not to.

I didn't regret writing it, it helped me at the time, albeit marginally. But I regret the pain she probably feels having read it now, hours ago. *Would this always be our fate?* Living in a convoluted mixture of the past and present, doomed to bring up old wounds that would always somehow feel fresh? I hoped not.

But then her lips are on mine, sweet and calming. And I'm reassured that we can conquer anything, any challenge that comes our way as long as we have each other. I don't want her to bear this burden any longer, our downfall, the ruining of our previous relationship. And she needs to know she doesn't have to. I want to move forward with Kendall; I want everything with her. *All* of her. I'm about to tell her this when she's calmed down and I have her cradled against my chest. But suddenly we're making out again, our tongues fighting for dominance and it's clear we both have the same idea.

She tells me she wants to break the pact.

Thank fucking god. It's a miracle we even held out this long.

Our tongues are clashing, teeth clanging, our bodies vibrating with untamed lust. Before I know it, I'm pressing her into the wall and we're fucking with our clothes on. I'm so turned on and impossibly hard I think I might explode as soon as she wraps her dainty fingers around my cock.

"Fuck, Ken," I groan into her shoulder. A bead of precum leaks from my tip as she moves her hand up and down.

We bump into the wall, the couch, and an end table on the way to my bedroom. We're still kissing and laughing as I set her down at the foot of the bed. At some point, she shed her pants and shirt, leaving her in nothing but a small triangle of black lace already soaked in her arousal. She is a goddamn wet dream.

Fuck. She is perfect. Her dark curls falling down her back and around her shoulders. Her hazel eyes that give everything away. Her pink supple lips and her pert brown nipples. Her slender torso that's painted with freckles, eight to be exact. The soft curves of her hips alone make me weak. I want to grip them while she rides my cock, her perfect tits bouncing around wildly. But her hourglass shape and thick thighs are the stuff of fantasies. I want to wrap my hands around them while my head is buried between her legs.

And her face. Her hauntingly beautiful face. No matter how much I wanted to, I could never forget it. I'm relieved now that I don't have to. She is so fucking sexy I can't decide if I want to fuck her or taste her first.

I need to worship her body, cherish it, savor her. And I do.

You know the old adage, *you never forget how to ride a bike*? It's a little like that at first. Clunky and awkward getting used to the rhythm, the mechanisms, and each other's bodies again. But once we find our footing, it transforms into pure perfection. Like we had never separated, never stopped loving each other. And maybe we hadn't. Not truly. Maybe this, us, has always transcended time and distance. It's years of unfulfilled want and months of insatiable need unleashed in a matter of seconds.

There's nothing like making love to Kendall, fucking her. The woman of my dreams. Sinking into her again and again, my cock swallowed by her perfect pussy. Hearing her breathless sounds and cries of pleasure. Her internal muscles squeezing me, milking me dry until I see stars.

No one-night-stand or short-term girlfriend has even come close. There's something about being with someone intimately that knows all of you. The shape of your flaws and texture of your insecurities. Someone you have bared your soul to and who has willingly done the same for you. That intensity, that passion, that goes beyond sex. It's the kind of connection, the type of soul deep love that scares you shitless because you know without a doubt this is your person. This is the rest of your life.

This. Is. Everything.

Love that sets you on fucking fire. That's what I crave, what I've been missing all these years and I finally have it again with her.

***

T wo hours later, we're tangled together in my bed. Two sweaty, happy, exhausted bodies. We just had mind-blowing, earth shattering sex. The kind of sex that you reflect back on and think, *Was that real*?

She's lying in my arms, her naked back pressed to my chest, my leg wedged between her thighs. Her ass is teasing my semi hard cock. There's almost no part of me that isn't touching her. She's relaxed and sated and *mine*. I hear her breathing shallowly, softly. Not quite asleep but not fully awake either. She must feel me rustle behind her because she reaches her hand back to grasp my neck, her fingers stroking my face. Then she settles in closer to me.

Home.

This is home. *She* is home. I place my lips on her favorite spot right below her ear and let them linger there. I trace her throat, the hollow of her neck, her shoulder with my mouth, my arms tightening around her. I'm sure it would take a Herculean effort to let her leave this bed.

"Kai," she whispers.

"Yeah?" I pause, shifting behind her.

"You think we'd still be together if we had met today, at the supermarket or on a blind date or god forbid a dating app?" She laughs.

"Yes," I respond, without even thinking about it.

"How do you know?" she asks, stroking my forearm curled around her chest with her fingers.

"Because we're inevitable, Ken. It's not logical or rational. It just is. It's like trying to explain the moon's gravitational pull on the tides," I say, kissing her hair.

"So, you're comparing us to gravity?" she chuckles.

"Yeah, I guess so. What about you? Do you think we would be together if we met today?" She doesn't respond immediately.

"I think so. I hope so," she finally replies.

"How do you know?" I question with a hint of humor.

"Because my heart would just know."

"Know what?"

"You. My heart would recognize you, love you, find you any-where." And she's right, I know she is. It's sheer dumb luck that we grew up next door to each other. But even if we hadn't, I'd like to think fate would have intervened eventually.

I turn her face towards me so I can revel in her unbelievable beauty. I cradle her jaw in my palm, my thumb sweeping over her lips and her cheek, before finally resting on her chin. My lips are on hers and the kiss rapidly turns deep, passionate, and all consuming. I kiss her like she *is* gravity, the only thing securing me to earth. She grinds the seam of her ass against me, tempting me. I'm surprised she wants to go again already.

"Kai," she breathes. "I need to feel you inside me again." I'm instantly hard just from her words. I bring one hand to her clit, and circle it languidly while I drag the tip of my cock through her entrance. *Fuck me* she's already soaked.

"Fuck that feels so good," she moans as my hand moves faster.

"How good?" I press my lips to her throat and suck, swirling my tongue over her flesh.

"So fucking good," she rasps. "But it's not what I want," she admits.

"What do you want?"

"I want you so deep inside me that I feel you everywhere."
Jesus fucking Christ.

I need to put a ring on her. I need to marry this woman yesterday.

"Fuckkk, Ken," is all I can say. I don't waste any time. I don't have that kind of willpower—or any willpower—when it came to her. I clamp my teeth down on her shoulder while I ease into her. I go slow at first, letting her adapt to the tightness, the feel, the angle of me behind her. Her silken heavenly heat was made just for me. She's entirely at my mercy and I think that's exactly what she wants. I rock into her again and again, my cock thrusting into her core, my thighs hitting her ass. But then her nails are scraping the nape of my neck while I knead her tits. My tongue sliding against hers as she begs for *me*. We're moving together in sync. Her body had never forgotten mine and mine is more than thrilled to remember hers.

"More, please, Kai."

We're both feral, clawing at each other. Grasping for something, anything to keep us in the here and now. Anything that will make these fleeting moments last forever. My arms band around her tighter and tighter as I push up into her rough and fast. I'm pounding into her, bracing her body against my chest.

"You okay?" I manage to ask.

"God yes, I'm so close," she pants.

I'm moving so deep inside her, my pace rapid. I anchor her to me as I thrust home and bury myself deeper, bottoming out again and again. I hear the wet slap of our bodies against each other as we chase our orgasms together. I'm entirely sheathed inside her, lust drowning my cock when I feel her clench me tighter. Pleasure starts building at the base of my spine.

"Yes," she cries, "Right there." I feel her contract and pulse while she explodes around me. I pull out almost too late—her release of warmth and pleasure leaking out of her—as the orgasm barrels through me, starting in my balls and erupting from my tip in wet hot ropes. I paint her back with my come and probably hers and groan as the aftershocks course through my veins. The white-hot orgasm holds me hostage and my soul leaves my body for a few seconds.

Afterwards, I clean her up and we're lying together again, both on the verge of sleep. Her curls are tickling my chin and I hear the melodic *thump thump thump thump* of her heart as I watch her chest rise and fall. I glide my hands up and down her smooth tan skin. Kendall is my undoing, my salvation. My perfect piece of paradise. Her and Akio are every dream I could ever hope for.

"I'm not going to stop, Kendall," I whisper.

"What do you mean?"

"I'm not going to stop. Not until you have my last name. Not until I get to wake up every day next to you. Not until I know you both are mine to keep and you are exactly where you belong," I decide.

"And where is that?" she asks, drawing circles on my chest.
"With me, always with me." I whisper.
"Good," she murmurs.

Chapter 67

Kendall

Emma and I are standing around chatting in the children's area of the library while Akio and Maddox play with toy cars and dump trucks. Music playgroup had just finished and Emma is in the middle of gushing to me about her hot date with Jax. I feel him before I see him. His scent, earthy with a little spice, floats over to me. His confident looming presence hints at his arrival, sucking all the air out of the room. The timbre of his voice, deep and gravelly, travels over to me, tickling my arms with goosebumps. I don't quite understand the science behind pheromones, the reasons why my body reacts to his, and only his, like this. But I don't particularly care either.

"I think you should turn around," Emma states, eyes fixed on the man behind me. I do, already knowing exactly who I'm going to see and watch enamored as Kai makes his way to us. Every female gaze is locked on his towering frame, zeroed in on *him*. All the moms, librarians, and Ms. Candace included.

Kai is the kind of beautiful that makes necks snap and heads turn. He has that raw magnetism and blatant sex appeal that makes women weak with lust and drunk with desire. Over the years we've been together, I've witnessed smart, independent, strong women melt under his charm and forget their own name. They all fawn over him and I can't blame them. In college, our close group of friends and his teammates referred to it jokingly as the "Kai effect." I wish I could say I'm immune to it having dated him for so long and known him for longer. But I'm not. I don't think I ever will be. Because his true superpower—the thing that makes him undeniably mine—is his ability to make me feel like

I'm the only person in the room even though every single eye is trained on him.

"Hi," he smiles, hands tucked in his pockets. He's wearing dark blue jeans and a long-sleeved white Henley with a backwards Boston Bucks hat.

"Hi," I chirp, unable to contain my excitement and pure giddiness at him showing up here unannounced.

"I'm going to give you two a minute," Emma says gleefully before walking over to Akio and Maddox.

"What are you doing here?" I ask, taking a step closer to him. He coils his arms around me, my hands landing on his broad chest. We've developed an audience but I honestly couldn't care less.

"I missed you guys and I thought maybe Veronica needed to be knocked down a peg," he smirks, mischief in his dark eyes and my heart threatens to give out.

"You came here to rub our relationship in her face?" I whisper, scandalized.

"Yes, is that immature? Insane?" he asks.

"Mhm." It was diabolical, petty, totally unnecessary. *Un-fucking-hinged*. I love him more for it.

"So, should I just leave then?" he jokes, pretending to turn away from me. I grab his arm and spin him towards me, pulling him closer.

"No, definitely not," I shake my head while biting my bottom lip. He lifts me up, his arms hoisted underneath my thighs, so that we're chest to chest. And then he kisses me long and deep like he's just returned home from a goddamn war. Like I'm the first drop of water after a drought. Kai kisses the same way he fucks. Without holding anything back; with passion in his eyes and forever on his lips. It happens in slow motion this kiss, at least it does in my brain. My feet pop up wistfully like I'm starring in my very own romantic comedy, my arms swooping around his neck. And I think happily to myself, *I deserve this man who looks at me, touches me, cherishes me like I'm the greatest gift he's ever received*. Because that's exactly what he is to me. I'll never get tired of being kissed by him, like he's drowning and I'm his only source of oxygen. He groans against my mouth while I laugh and pull back from him slightly.

"This is not suitable for children. Let's keep it PG here," I whisper even though I want to do anything but that.

"Fine, fine," he acquiesces, pecking my nose and setting me down on my feet. Akio is bounding over to us in seconds.

"Kai Kai!" he squeals, running into his arms.

Kai lifts him up and spins him around twice. "Hey little man, I missed you," he says.

"I missed you!" Akio replies, draping his little arms around Kai's neck and squeezing him tight. Moments later, Veronica's blonde ponytail and made up porcelain face appear by my side.

"Kendall, can I talk to you for a second?" she asks.

"Sure."

"Go. I'll watch him for a few," Kai says winking.

She walks over to the large windows that look out into the courtyard of the library and I follow her. Veronica is clasping her upper arms and glancing down at her feet. She's definitely nervous. This isn't someone who has ever had to eat her words and subsequently swallow her pride. I'm certain of it. Kai's little stunt has accomplished its intended effect.

So then why do I feel so sleazy about it?

She clears her throat awkwardly. "I just wanted to say I'm sorry for what I said about you and Kai. I was obviously very wrong and he's clearly crazy about you," she observes quietly.

"Veronica, it's fine. It's not a big deal," I respond. Even though it had been, even though her hurtful words had stayed with me long after she uttered them.

"No, it's not," she admits, picking at her nails. "I get like that, you know? I had a hard time in high school. I was bullied pretty badly and I didn't have a lot of friends. It's not an excuse. I'm just trying to say that I learned early on the best defense was a good offense. Things only got worse in college and now I have a husband that barely speaks to me..." she trails off. "But anyways, I'm sorry."

For the first time, I see Veronica for exactly who she is. Someone who has tried and desperately needs to protect herself. Someone whose self-worth and confidence have been chipped away at so thoroughly, the only way she can rebuild it is on the backs of others. She isn't some selfish cruel bitch, at least not entirely. At one point, she'd probably been exactly like me—hiding in a bathroom stall listening and sobbing while other girls tore her apart. Or worse. And I know intimately those wounds don't always fully heal. What she needs from me isn't more anger or more hatred, more reasons to believe women are only out to get each other. What she needs and may not deserve is grace.

"Would you ever want to get drinks or dinner with me and Emma? Sometimes we get together outside of playgroup, you know, without the kids," I say smiling. It's real, genuine, inviting. Probably the first time I've ever smiled at her willingly.

"Sure," she replies. "I'd love that."

I don't envy Veronica, not anymore. And I won't be holding a grudge against her either. So many of us hide who we are, our pain, our secrets underneath a mask that we show the world. Everyone from time to time has to protect their hearts the only way they know how, with fangs and venom. But how many of us, when given the opportunity, actually admit fault, accept blame, and attempt to repair the damage? Veronica did. At least she's trying. And I suspect it's taken a lot to get her here. I certainly am not going to get in the way of that. It seems like more than anything, Veronica needs a friend and I'm in no position to turn one of those down.

When I return to Kai and sidle up next to him, he hands Akio back to me.

"How'd it go?" he asks, slinging his arm around my shoulder.

"Better than I thought it would," I say. He gives me a lopsided grin as the three of us walk out of the library together.

CHAPTER 68

KAI

O UTSIDE OF HOCKEY, THE arena where I shine brightest is loving Kendall, adoring her, and making sure she knows every day how much she means to me. All those things come naturally to me because she's just so *easy* to love and call mine. She always has been.

It's early May, a month after we broke our pact. Spring is in full bloom in Boston, flowers budding, greenery taking over, and the sun trying its hardest to break free of winter's icy grasp.

Spoiling Kendall and Akio has become one of my favorite pastimes and when I heard about the upcoming charity gala, sponsored in part by the Bucks, an idea began forming in my head. She deserves one night free of diapers and making dinner and caring for other people. One night where she can feel glamorous, dance, eat delicious food, and drink expensive wine. I've planned and plotted meticulously down to the very last detail, including having a dress tailored, hiring a team of makeup artists so she doesn't have to lift a finger, and enlisting her moms to help with childcare. In a shocking turn of events, Veronica offered to babysit Maddox and Akio until Kendall's moms could relieve her. Emma it seems is also going to the gala as Jax's official date. All that's left is the surprise, the grand reveal.

***

Kendall

> *I think Akio took Taylor's favorite toy by accident, a white plush unicorn.*

> *She had it yesterday when we all got together. Can I stop by real quick to check?*

> *She'll be a gremlin at bedtime without it.*

> *Sure. I don't remember seeing a unicorn anywhere though*

I RESPOND TO VERONICA'S text while rifling through my bag, before I enter my apartment with Akio. But as soon as I open my door, I know something is off. It feels like someone has been here, like their presence is still lingering, clinging to the air. But that doesn't make sense. The only person who has a key, other than my moms, is Kai.

Why would he be here without telling me?

Nothing looks out of place or disheveled, at least not in the entryway or kitchen. I pick up Akio quickly and check his room first, my heart rate skyrocketing as I crack the door open. Everything looks the same there, his bed unmade, his toys littering the ground. Maybe I'm just being paranoid. But then I reach my room and it's clear someone has been in it. There's a large garment bag lying on my bed with a note. This doesn't appear to be the work of a serial killer or burglar. Not that I have anything of much value to steal. I pick up the note written on off white thick card stock. It's in Kai's handwriting.

Thank fucking god.

Dear Ken,

I know the last letter I wrote you wasn't easy to read. Hopefully this one is. I live to love you. I love to love you and tonight, I want you to have fun and just enjoy yourself. I wanted to surprise you and sweep you off your feet properly. I hope I get to do it for the rest of my life. You are cordially invited to the Rayfield Memorial Charity Gala

as my date. I've taken care of everything. All you need to do is say
yes.
Yours Always,
Kai
P.S. *I can't wait to see you in that dress, but I'm even more excited to*
take you out of it.

Kai. Of course this had been Kai's doing, the romantic that he is.

I put the note down and unzip the white garment bag with nervous energy. And there, perfectly pressed, and no doubt professionally tailored, is a stunning Oscar de la Renta. My breath catches in my throat as I remove it carefully and admire it.

"Akio, can you go play in your room for one second, baby? Mommy just needs to make a phone call," I tell him, stunned and unable to peel my eyes away from the crimson dress. He scampers away to his room. The dress itself is a work of art. It's buttery soft, with off the shoulder straps and intricate red flowers crawling up the bodice. It has a slit on one side and it looks like it would hug me in all the right places—places I usually want to smother with Spanx. It's elegant, gorgeous, and I'm too scared to think about how much it probably cost. My heart's swelling in my chest, my hands shaky as I run them over the dress made specifically for me. This had taken a level of planning and execution I can't even imagine. For a second, I wonder, *Have I died and fallen into a Pretty Woman alternate universe?* That is the kind of statement this dress makes, the kind of unfettered power it wields.

I'm caught in my reverie when my phone starts buzzing in my pocket.

"Hello?" I answer.

"Hi," he says cheerfully and I can hear him giddy and smiling through the phone.

"Kai," I say, struck by a loss for words "This is too much..."

"It's exactly the right amount," he counters. "You had said you wanted to go to a ball or a wedding. But a fancy one. Somewhere we would have to get dressed to the nines. Where we could huddle in the corner and people watch and shit talk everyone. You wanted an unforgettable magical night full of extravagance. This is it, Ken. And you haven't even heard about some of the best parts yet."

He remembered. He did all this for me because I mentioned it one time. And I'm starting to understand there's nothing he wouldn't do for me. No limit he wouldn't cross, no wish that's too big. And don't I deserve that? Don't we all? A love that feels unconditional, uncontainable, that squeezes too hard, listens intently, and makes us feel seen and heard and valued.

Kai's voice cuts through my wandering thoughts. "Did you hear me? You haven't said anything in a while."

"Wait what?" I mutter as I pace around my bedroom like a caged tiger, expensive couture dress in hand.

"In a few minutes, Veronica is going to be there to pick up Akio. She's watching him and Maddox until your moms can take over," he informs me.

"Emma is going too?" I practically squeal with delight.

"Yupp. A makeup and hair artist will be at your apartment in thirty minutes. All you need to do is tell them what you want done. Emma too. And Jax and I will be there at 7:00 sharp to pick you both up," he replies.

"You've thought of everything," I murmur, stunned.

"I've thought of everything," he repeats. "So, is that a yes?" he asks, already knowing the answer.

"Of course it's a yes," I smile. "But how do I repay you, thank you for this? It's too much, Kai."

"You don't need to repay me. All I need is you and Akio and this life we're building together. That's all I've ever needed. I plan on spoiling you both forever."

"Okay," I reply as tears form in my eyes. "I love you, Kai Matsumoto. Thank you for being so good to me." But already I'm scheming up my own grand romantic gesture. One that would show him just how much I love him and how much he means to me.

"I love you, Kendall James. It's the easiest thing I've ever done."

Sometimes I'm in awe, utter disbelief that whatever gods exist out there decided to give Kai a beautiful face and an even more beautiful heart to match. But who the hell am I to judge the universe, higher powers, deities? They've intertwined Kai's path and mine many many times. They've given me the most precious gift in the form of my son. Maybe they are on to something.

***

H E SHOWS UP AT my apartment looking like sex on legs. Like he walked right off the cover of *Vanity Fair* and into my hallway. He's wearing a sharp midnight suit that's painted on him, tailored within an inch of his life, a crisp white shirt underneath accompanied by a black bow tie. His thick dark hair is slicked back, one tendril that refuses to stay put sweeping his forehead. His face is all hard angles—sharp jaw, chiseled cheekbones, and crooked scar contrasted against softer features, like his brilliant onyx eyes, plush lips, and sun-kissed skin. It's enough to make me wonder, *Will the sight of him ever not unravel me, consume me, obliterate me?* He looks good enough to eat, and I want to devour him. Jax is standing behind him like a sexy brooding bodyguard. But I don't give him any of my attention. Jax has the whole bad boy with a mysterious past vibe going for him. But Kai, Kai is breathtaking.

I. Can't. Take. My. Eyes. Off. Of. Him.

He is so unnervingly, infuriatingly handsome. And at this moment, all I can do is smile because he's mine.

CHAPTER 69

KAI

KENDALL IS STUNNING. A vision. Like so many times before and countless times after, it hurts just to look at her. I rake my eyes over her once, twice. It's on the third time I realize that no length of time would be enough. I could stare at her forever and still want more. If this fantasy is the last thing I see before I die, I think I'd be content.

Her curly hair has been straightened and pulled into a sleek bun that sits at the nape of her neck. She's wearing the diamond earrings I picked out and they send little fractures of light scattering across the wall. Her lipstick is a classic deep red, her cheeks two rosy, shimmering apples. Her makeup is natural and flawless, beautiful in an understated way, her bright hazel eyes framed by long lashes. Her almond skin is glowing, her chest and arms dusted with faint sparkles.

She is regal. Ethereal. I'm not worthy.

And the dress.

God help me.

I knew it was perfect when I saw it in the store. But nothing could have prepared me to see her in it. The way the red fabric hugs her curves and kisses her breasts. It caresses her shape, fitting like a glove. She is a goddess in red, an angel of seduction. And that tempting goddamn slit leaves nothing to the imagination. I want nothing more than to slide my hand underneath it and inch my way up her thigh until—

Jax clears his throat anxiously. I've spent so much time staring at her, ogling her that I don't realize how much time has passed.

"Um, should we like go in?" Jax asks awkwardly. Kendall and I break into laughter, both caught in the middle of eye fucking each other.

"Yes, come in. Please. We're almost ready," she replies, leading us inside.

I wrap my arms around her waist and bury my face in her neck, breathing her in. I don't care that other people are around. I don't care that we need to leave soon. I nuzzle her cheek, that spot just below her earlobe, pressing kisses to her throat. Then she kisses me soft and sweet, her tongue dancing with mine, and it's all I can do to remain standing. I kiss her back. It's deep and hungry, my hand cupping her head. Because she isn't the type to worry about smudging her makeup or messing up her hair. Because she is so goddamn beautiful. Because she is everything I have ever wanted. Because she's here and she's mine and I am never letting her go again. Her swollen lips curl into a dazzling smile as she sighs.

"Hi," I breathe, my forehead leaning against hers.

"Hi yourself, handsome," she whispers.

"Uh hello. You two do know there are other people around, right?" Emma quips as she breezes into the room in a pale yellow dress.

"Sorry guys. We're just excited," Ken replies.

"I for one am not sorry and I don't intend to stop on either of your accounts," I say without looking away from Kendall.

Twenty minutes later and fifteen minutes after I want to leave, we're finally in the car. The four of us are sitting in the back of a limo, drinking champagne, yelling over each other, and laughing our asses off. I know it's going to be a great night. I can feel it in the air, electric and charged and full of possibilities. The kind of night that stays with you long after it's over.

Chapter 70

Kendall

The thing about Kai is he doesn't do anything in half measures. He had remembered every detail of the dream date I talked about years ago, and he absolutely delivered. The Rayfield Memorial Charity Gala is held at the Boston Public Library. I've lived 15 minutes outside of Boston almost my whole life and never visited it. Standing in the foyer of the library and marveling at the gorgeous renaissance style architecture, marble walls, and soaring arched ceilings, I'm glad I hadn't. It made the night that much more magical.

"Come on," Kai urges, tugging my hand. I follow him with a smile wordlessly and sashay up the long steps behind him.

We enter the Bates room hand in hand and my jaw nearly hits the floor again. There's at least a hundred neatly set tables all decorated with tall flower centerpieces. Vivid blues and bright purples and softer pinks are mixed in with vines and greenery to create stunning bouquets that paint the circular tables in a sunset of colors. There are uniformed waiters and servers hustling back and forth between guests and the bar. The two bars stand on either side of the room, a few people lining up to receive signature drinks and glasses of top shelf alcohol. And right in the middle of the opulent hall is a fifteen-piece live band, a decent sized dance floor positioned right in front of it. Every person I let my gaze linger on is wearing an item of clothing that costs more than my monthly rent. Myself included.

Kai stares at me while I stare in awe at my surroundings. His fingers still woven in mine, he finally says, "Let's find our table."

Our table it turns out is in the perfect location, sitting equidistant between the band and bar, with easy access to the restrooms. Jonah and his date, Mindy, Jax and Emma, and two guests we have yet to meet are also seated with us. Jonah greets Kai with a hug and a slap on the back before he introduces us to his date.

Shortly after we sit down, appetizers and bread appear on the table followed by a fresh caprese salad. Kai's phone starts buzzing in his pocket aggressively. I watch as he pulls it out and ignores the call.

"It's just Aiden," he tells me unphased. "I'll call him back tomorrow."

"Did you ever figure out what was going on with him? When you said he was acting strange?" I wonder.

"Not really. Jenna had a little insight, but I think he has some deep gambling bets. Maybe some other stuff he's dealing with."

"Hmm," I murmur as I cut into my steak.

I'm at the bar waiting for my long island when I realize the bartender is staring at me. I guess glaring is more like it. His lips are pursed and his jaw is clenched like he tastes something bitter. If he grinds his teeth any harder, they might turn to dust. He shakes the drink tumbler, his cold assessing eyes never leaving my face.

"Is there a problem?" I ask, curious and emboldened. He stalks closer to me, slowly coming to stand at the end of the bar I'm perched in front of.

"Just wondering why a Black queen like yourself wouldn't choose to be with a Black king, that's all." The only reason this man does not have an imprint of my rings on his cheek is because he too is Black. Tall, dark, objectively handsome. As well as arrogant and incredibly stupid, I surmise.

"Excuse me?" I rear back dumbfounded.

"Did I stutter?" he presses and I feel like I might choke on my own saliva. Fury courses through my blood, hot and ruinous.

"No, I'm just appalled that you would ask that," I manage to reply. We'd been on the receiving end of distasteful comments and judgmental looks before. That wasn't new. But never, *never* has anyone deemed Kai unworthy, inferior. That spot had always been reserved for me.

Kai appears at my side a moment later. Kai, who encompasses my entire childhood. Kai, who fills me up. Who makes me whole, who loves me even when I can't love myself. Who forgave me even when I didn't deserve it. This man would go to war for me any day of the week and he has. Because what were the last three years we spent apart, if not war? It certainly wasn't peace. And this prick has the audacity to judge our relationship?

"Everything okay?" Kai asks, placing his large hand at the small of my back, sending little shivers of heat down my spine. The bartender clocks his movements, his eyes trailing from Kai's hand to my face.

"Yeah, everything is fine," I respond. "I don't think I'm in the mood for a drink anymore," I say, moving to turn around and pull Kai along with me.

"You know what, no. Everything isn't fine," I declare while abruptly facing the bartender. "Marcus here seems to think he knows more about our relationship than we do," I explain to Kai. I feel Kai's posture stiffen, his hand flex against my hip. Kai's gorgeous eyes flare with heat and I preemptively place a palm on his chest to prevent him from leaning over the bar and grabbing Marcus by the collar. Marcus proceeds to hold his hands up as if in surrender.

"Listen, I didn't mean anything—"

"I'm not really sure why our relationship is any of your goddamn business, why it's so insulting or unpalatable to you. But I have news for you: this man is my best friend, love of my life, and father of my child. And as far as I'm concerned, you can choke on our fucking relationship, okay?"

Who the hell did this guy think he was, that he could judge the worth of our love.

It wasn't the first time Kai and I had experienced something like this. But this is definitely the first time someone has been this blatantly aggressive about it. As if Kai and I being together is that hard to comprehend. As if we can't possibly belong together because he's Japanese and Hawaiian and I'm Black. It makes me feel like our relationship is wrong, even though I know in my bones everything about it is right. I am seething. People always needed a reason to destroy love in all its shapes, forms, and colors. That much hasn't changed. I'm not sure it ever will.

"Okay, I'm sorry," he mumbles.

"Come on, Kai," I urge him while tugging his arm to lead him away from the bar.

Desperately needing some air, Kai and I decide to take a stroll around the building and through the courtyard. We're walking along the edge of the fountain, his shoulder curled around mine. It's a perfect spring evening, warm with a slight breeze in the air.

"Doesn't it make you angry?" I ask.

"What?" he replies as if he and I were not just present for the same hostile exchange with the bartender.

"Other people thinking they know us or are relationship?"

"No, because I don't care if other people think we don't belong together. I know that we do. I've known since you came over to my house in hideous red overalls and chocolate brownie batter all over your face. From the moment you burst into my life and put your sticky hand in mine and said 'Hi I'm Kendall.'" He was right those overalls were hideous and Kai really really hates messes and certain textures. So the fact that he followed me willingly back then says a lot.

"Really," I chuckle. "You've known since then?"

"Yupp," he confirms bringing my hand to his and brushing a kiss over it. We walk a little further in silence. I wasn't going to let one asshole ruin my night. Kai is right. What other people thought was irrelevant. How we felt together mattered more. That's what mattered most. Judgmental bartenders and casual acts of racism be damned.

"Are you cold?" he asks.

"No, I'm okay." But before I can protest, his jacket is covering my shoulders.

"Just in case," he says softly.

"Kai, thank you for this. Not just the jacket but for everything. For always being exactly who I need," I whisper, turning to face him.

"You're welcome," he says, bringing his hands to cup my face. "Thank you for letting me and for being everything I need and more." I cover his hand with mine, leaning into his palm.

"There's something I've been meaning to say to you for months and for whatever reason I couldn't," I go on. "But I want you to know, I think you're perfect. You're smart and you're kind, selfless and loyal. You're the hardest worker I know and you aren't afraid to go after what you want. You love me and Akio exactly the way we deserve to be loved. And I just wanted you to know that for me you're perfect."

"Is that all?" he grins. His eyes are shining, his smile uncontainable. "You already know I think you're perfect, but I'll say it again if you need me to. As many times as it takes until you believe it." I put my finger over his lips to silence him, because he has already shown me every day how much he loves me, how much I mean to him. And I want this moment to be entirely about him.

"I love you so much, Kai," I say. He's about to reply but I shake my head with my finger still hovering on his mouth. "I know," I murmur.

His hand is gripping my neck, he's rubbing his thumb over my cheek, staring at me with the universe in his eyes and a thousand words on the tip of his tongue. And it feels like a love like this should be impossible. But it isn't. Not with him. It feels easy. Safe. *Right*. Like pancakes on Sunday morning, or curling up by the fire with a good book. Like hearing the hook of your favorite song or the smell of fresh rain in the summer.

He doesn't say anything—he doesn't have to. He kisses me with longing, ferocity, and passion just like he always has. His lips move over mine with the same intensity that he had when I was 17 and insecure and scared of what a kiss might do to us.

And I melt away into his arms.

CHAPTER 71

KAI

I PULL HER ON top of my lap at one of the high tops scattered around the massive fountain. My arms are curved around her waist, her long legs crossed over mine and that slit is tap dancing on my last modicum of restraint. We stay like this, my chin resting on her head and her body tucked into mine for a while. There's nowhere else I'd rather be. We don't have to say anything; there's no need to fill the silence with anything else other than our heartbeats.

It did bother me. More than I'd like to admit. People casting judgement on us, our relationship, especially when we had fought tooth and nail to get here. It took every ounce of control I possessed to not haul Marcus' ass over the counter and repay him for his hostility. But Kendall and Akio deserve better than that. And so do I. I'm not the same anxious teenager who excelled at sports but couldn't hold a conversation to save his life. Who bottled up his rage and panic with no outlet, except for her. I don't need Kendall to rescue me anymore. I'm not the same wounded, heartbroken man either, trying to repair himself by tearing through bars and women and starting fights just to feel something. I want to heal. I'm trying and that means examining the pieces of myself I don't exactly like, not just the ones she broke. The least I can do is think, respond before reacting.

My brain drifts off for a while and eventually I whisper, "Hey, Ken?"

"Mhmm?"

"Your laptop was out the other day while you were getting ready. I saw you were looking at night classes and different law school programs."

"Yeah, I've been thinking about it for a while," she admits, turning her face to look directly into my eyes.

"You have? Why didn't you tell me?"

"I haven't made any concrete decisions, and it never felt like the right time. But I thought with us being back together and you and my moms helping with Akio, maybe it would be?"

"I think that's great. I want to support you however I can."

"Really?" she asks, her eyes bright and hopeful.

"Of course. I could help pay for law school, you know. In fact, I want to." I smooth my thumb over her knuckles.

"It's too much, Kai," she replies, shaking her head. "I can't ask you to do that."

"You aren't asking. I'm offering. What if I helped pay for part of it or gave you a loan?" I propose. Not that I would ever let her pay me back but she doesn't need to know that.

"You're serious?"

"Very. I want to build a future with you and if that future includes you going back to school, then I want to help however I can."

"Just when I thought I couldn't possibly love you more," she muses, her lips tugging into a smile. "I'll consider it."

"Good. You should," I reply, pressing my lips to her forehead. "This slit is driving me nuts," I admit, kissing her cheek. I hug her tightly to my chest as I slowly move my hand up her thigh. I wonder if she's just as turned on as I am. She leans further into me, her breath hot against my ear.

"Lucky for you I'm not wearing anything underneath it," she purrs. *This woman is going to be the death of me.*

"Jesus Christ, Ken," I growl. "Are you trying to kill me?" She smiles conspiratorially, moving her hand over mine and guiding it higher. I'm about thirty seconds and centimeters away from pulling her behind a tree and slipping into her without a condom.

"What do you say we take this back to the limo for a brief intermission?" I suggest.

She kisses me on the mouth. "I thought you'd never ask," she replies.

***

WE EXIT THE LIMO flushed and flustered. I'm 150 bucks poorer but two mind bending orgasms richer. I paid the driver to take an extra-long smoke break and leave the keys with me. It was the easiest money I've ever spent. She smooths down her dress and fixes stray pieces of hair around her face while I adjust my shirt and tie. I know the image of Kendall riding me with only her heels on will live rent free in my brain the rest of night. Probably forever. Would she be thinking about the path I kissed from her breasts to her hips the rest of the night too? How I worked my tongue feverishly between her thighs until she begged. I hope so. We share a knowing smile as we saunter back into the gala.

CHAPTER 72

KENDALL

KAI AND I WALK back into the air conditioned hall hand in hand, my face warm from all the memories of where his lips just were. I get a drink from a waiter while Kai excuses himself to the bathroom. When I sit back down at the table, Emma locks eyes with me and gives me a devious grin. Somehow, she already knows about our extracurricular activities in the limo.

"Shame shame, I know your name," she whispers loud enough only I can hear. "You guys are the worst," she comments jokingly.

"Look, I can't help it that he is ridiculously attractive at baseline. In a suit it's just unfair really. No match for my traitorous vagina," I respond, taking a much needed gulp of water.

"You're probably right. There was a better chance of Jonah going home with his date than you two keeping it in your pants all night." I shove her arm playfully and we both start cackling. The night isn't even over and Jonah is already flirting with one of the male bartenders. At that moment, the band starts playing *Girls Just Wanna Have Fun* and we whoop and holler all the way to the dance floor. We sing the words loudly and somewhat off key into pretend microphones made from our hands and dance unabashedly for the next four songs. We get a few popular Drake songs, followed by classic wedding hits that morph into smooth oldies.

When Whitney Houston's *I Wanna Dance with Somebody* starts booming bright and upbeat, I look around for Kai. We used to love to dance to this song together. As if he could read my mind, two strong arms appear around my waist, his chin on my shoulder.

I worry about people who don't immediately get up and dance to this song, that don't feel the need to yell *I want to feel the heat with somebody* at the top of their lungs with their whole chest. Gen z could *never*. At this moment, I'm eternally grateful to be my authentic, nostalgic, unashamed millennial self. I pity those who can't feel its yearning in their heart or its ballad in their veins.

Thank god it would never be us.

"Want to dance?" he whispers in my ear. He twirls me, dips me, and gathers me in his arms as we shout the lyrics to each other. And I realize this song was made for people like us, two people who love each other so deeply, so unapologetically that it's impossible to deny we are soulmates. It's been crafted for moments that feel infinite and nights like this one that we wish would last forever.

Love is finding the one person you could spend the rest of your life dancing to this song with. And that person for me is Kai.

CHAPTER 73

KAI

WHEN I RETURN HOME, the door to my apartment is slightly ajar and there's noise coming from inside. *What the fuck?*

I quickly dial 911 while backing away from the doorway.

"Hello 911, what is your emergency?" a calm steady voice asks.

"I think there is someone trying to break into my apartment," I respond in a hushed tone.

"What's your address?"

"15 Grove Place, Charleston. I'm in the penthouse."

"Okay sir, are you in a safe location?"

"I think so. I don't know. I'm in the hallway."

"Okay, we're sending two officers to respond to the scene. I would suggest waiting outside the building or with a neighbor if you can. Do you want me to stay on the phone with you until they arrive?"

"No, that's okay. Thank you."

I should have taken her advice. I should have knocked on a neighbor's door. Then maybe I could have avoided dealing with a shitstorm I didn't want and wasn't prepared for. But curiosity, surging adrenaline, and an overwhelming need to protect what's mine forces me to creep into the kitchen and grab a knife from the butcher block.

I hear rummaging and loud thuds coming from my bedroom and stealthily move towards it. When I carefully and quietly set foot in my room, shock takes hold. *This is a bad idea.* My dressers have been ransacked, there are clothes everywhere. Deodorant, picture frames, a lamp and other loose items strewn across my bed. I'm even more confused when I realize I recognize the man currently digging through my walk-in closet.

"Aiden?" My voice is harsh and strained. I drop the knife and it clatters to the ground. "What the fuck is going on man?" He backs away from the closet, his hands up. He looks awful. Way worse than he did weeks ago. And giving him a once over I realize relinquishing my only weapon might have been a mistake.

"You weren't home," he stammers, hands on his head. "And you said I could crash here whenever I needed to. I was looking for something," he mumbles, running his fingers through his hair furiously. He starts pacing the room while he drags his palms down his face.

"I need money, Kai. I owe someone a lot of money. I don't have it and it's too much to ask anyone for. I thought if I could sell your Stanley Cup Jersey maybe I could repay part of the debt," he confesses.

"So, you broke into my apartment to steal from me? Are you fucking kidding me, Aiden? What is going on with you?" I yell. I take a deep breath, forcing myself to regulate my breathing before I do something I'll regret. "Do you understand how insane that is?" I press, my voice measured and calculated this time.

"I just need a second," he mutters while rushing to the bathroom. Before I can ask him anything else, the door is slammed in my face and I hear the click of the lock. I start banging on the door with my fist impatiently.

He needs a second? The asshole who just broke into my apartment? I want to kill him but I know those kinds of impulses aren't helpful right now and aren't going to get us anywhere.

"You need to come out here, Aiden. The police are on their way. I thought someone was trying to break in." I guess someone *had* broken in, it just wasn't the violent intruder that I assumed it was. He opens the door a fraction and it's up close I truly understand the shape he's in.

Grungy. Disheveled. *Desperate.*

This is bad. This is so bad. *And what the hell am I supposed to tell the police?* Not only had he been trying to steal from me, but he looks strung out. He's thin and pale, dark purple bags haunting his bloodshot glassy eyes.

Once upon a time, I convinced myself that I hated Aiden. Not because we fought over Kendall and not because I had deep misplaced anger over my mom's accident. But because I envied him and his golden life. His simple, uncomplicated functional family. I was much older when I reached the conclusion that every family is its own unique brand of fucked up. Every family has its secrets, trauma, and dysfunction. But it was much easier to hate Aiden for what I thought he had than myself for what I couldn't fix. I don't envy him anymore. I pity him, and that feels infinitely worse.

"Kai, I can't deal with the police right now," he begs. "I'm so fucking sorry. I'll never come here again. Please don't turn me in." He's shaking, worry seeping out of him.

I stare at this man, my best friend. The guy I grew up playing hockey and football with, who knows all my secrets, that I have probably punched one too many times. The same guy who won "best looking" in high school and could make any girl fall for him. Here he is in my apartment, begging for mercy and pleading for me to understand the situation he's in. I've never seen him like this. Small, panicked, broken.

What the fuck happened to him?

The plan starts taking shape in my brain before it's even out of my mouth.

"It's either jail or rehab," I tell him resolutely.

"No. No no no," he pleads, hands clasped together. He's crying now, wiping snot from his nose and tears from his eyes with his arm. "I can't go to rehab. I can't. They'll find me. I owe too much money anyways." This is my ultimatum and he's out of time and out of options.

"I'll pay your debt," I offer, my voice neutral and controlled. "But only if you agree to get on a plane tomorrow and go directly to a rehab facility."

He swallows, his Adams's apple bobbing in his throat. "Kai, I owe 50,000 dollars," he whispers, his dilated pupils locked on mine. At first, I think he's joking, that I heard him wrong. But his haunted face tells me all I need to know.

"Jesus Christ, Aiden," I scrub my hand over my jaw, contemplating the options. Not that there are many. If he goes to jail, he'll likely end up in the same position: trying to rob someone else, or worse. Rehab is the best place for him.

"I'll make up something to tell the police. I'll pay the debt. As soon as they leave, I'm calling your mom to make sure you get on the earliest flight to California tomorrow. And then I'm calling Jenna to make sure she meets you when you land. If this isn't rock fucking bottom man, I don't know what is. I'm not gonna bury you or forgive myself if I find you dead in a ditch somewhere. You. Are. Going. To. Rehab. You have to try."

He wipes his face again, straightens his spine, and nods. It isn't a lot, a glimpse of the man I once knew. But right now, it's enough. It has to be.

"Okay. These are bad guys, though, Kai. They have deep ties with the O'Rourke's. They might come looking for me even if I settle the debt," he warns, his voice shaky.

"I'll take care of it, Aiden. Let's get you cleaned up maybe. When's the last time you fucking showered?" I ask, crinkling my nose and trying to lighten the absurdity of this conversation with a little humor.

The police leave around 12:00 am. I told them Aiden was supposed to be staying with me for a few days but I forgot because my schedule was so hectic. I also fabricate a story about the mess in the apartment. They don't seem convinced, but they also didn't seem particularly inclined to fill out paperwork for me to press charges either. After they leave, Aiden showers, changes into fresh clothes, and falls asleep on my couch open mouthed and snoring.

My first call is to his parents. I relay the situation to his mom and ask her to get here as soon as she can. She is worried, on the verge of sobbing towards the end of the phone call, but promises they'd be here in the morning. Then I get a hold of Jenna. She's alarmed but not surprised. She clears her schedule for the next two days and reassures me that her and Amir will pick Aiden up from his gate and get him checked in to rehab. I'm relieved knowing Jenna will do whatever it takes to help him, to ensure he walks inside that building come hell or high water. All we can do is get him there, the rest is up to him.

The next couple calls I make are to rehab centers and addiction treatment facilities up and down the west coast. Aiden needs immediate help and some distance from all the bullshit dragging him under in Boston. I'm going to be hard pressed to find a place that's going to take him on such short notice even with the kind of connections I have. On a hope and a prayer, I contact the Betty Ford Center located in Rancho Mirage, California.

They have a spot for him.

***

THREE DAYS LATER, I'm sitting in a coffee shop with Kendall and giving her all the details about the situation with Aiden. Details that I've been too exhausted and distraught to explain over the phone. She sits in a chair across from me, picking at the lip of her iced coffee with lavender manicured nails, a nervous habit.

"So, you found him in your apartment trying to steal from you?" she whispers, leaning further into the table, her arms crossed on top of it.

"Yeah, he was looking for my Stanley Cup jersey to try and pawn it for money." For thousands of dollars and it probably would have sold for that, never mind that it wouldn't even have cleared his debt.

"Holy shit, Kai. That's terrifying," she comments, scanning my face. "But he's okay now? He's in rehab?"

"Yeah, Jenna said he was all checked in to a 90-day in-patient program. So, I think he's in the best place he can be for now." At least I want to believe he is.

"Okay but what about the money he owes and the people looking for it?" Right. Kendall isn't stupid or blind. She's put enough clues together to understand that whatever Aiden was involved with isn't good.

"I told him I'd pay it and I did." What I don't say is I settled the debt and then some. That I had secured a private carrier to deliver $80,000 in cash to low level workers and enforcers of the nefarious mob. That I hired private security detail to ensure this carrier wasn't harmed. That I had dipped my toes in something I probably shouldn't have but there's no going back now. I've waded into flames and I'm waiting to see whether I'd burn for it. I know engaging in any sort of illicit activity is grounds for expulsion from the league, reason enough to terminate me, and an easy way to nullify my 2.3 million dollar contract. I know this and I forged ahead anyway. Because I have my own debt to settle, my own sins to atone for.

"Why, though, Kai? You paid for his rehab fees and you're paying this debt. Why? I mean I know you were close with Aiden but this seems like a lot."

I sigh because I knew this question was coming and I don't know how to answer it, not completely.

"Because I'm the only person who can. Because I'm the only person close enough to him with the kind of means and capital to help him. And I refuse to play a part in his death no matter how tangential it is. You didn't see him, Ken, he was in rough shape. I couldn't just kick him out or turn him in."

"So, you think that will be the end of it then?" she hedges. *Do you think they'll let this go?* is what she's asking but not saying.

"I think so," I lie, taking my hand in hers and squeezing it gently. "Everything is going to be fine." Because I certainly can't tell her the truth. That I overplayed my hand in an attempt to right his wrongs. I'd given them $30,000 more than he owes hoping it would buy us safety, protection, but now I'm not so sure. I might have put a target on my back in an effort to save Aiden. They had more reasons now than ever to come after me and my net worth.

But there's also a part of me that feels partially responsible for Aiden's condition, his steep fall from the person he had once been. I hadn't held a gun to his head while forcing him to take drugs. And I hadn't dragged him to casinos and racetracks and dark seedy corners of ramshackle buildings to make bets he couldn't afford. I hadn't introduced him to the people he had unwittingly sold his soul to or been involved in the myriad of choices that led him to where he is now.

But I had encouraged him to gamble with me every once in a while. And a long time ago when we were young and stupid, I had beaten him so violently that I ruined the rest of his high school athletic career. I had destroyed any chance of him playing division one football or hockey. I put the nail in that coffin and unintentionally ensured his future didn't contain a multitude of paths. Maybe if things had been different, Aiden's life would look more like mine right now. So, no, I'm not directly to blame for his downfall but I feel dread trickling down my spine and the weight of guilt impaling my chest. And it compelled me to help him however I could. I couldn't fix things then but maybe I could save him now.

Chapter 74

Kendall

We're sitting in front of Magdalena for what is presumably our last couples therapy session. Or at least our last one for a while. She regards us for a few moments quietly.

"You two have done great work. I think you've made a ton of progress and some amazing breakthroughs. I think after today, I'd be comfortable seeing you both on an as needed basis if that's okay with you?"

"Sure," Kai says while I nod in agreement. But it can't be that easy, can it? You just sit on a couch and blab to a stranger about your problems and force yourself to be honest with your partner? And suddenly everything is resolved, all the hurt I've caused is magically fixed? But I know it's not that simple. That I'm painting what we've been through, everything we've endured to get to where we are now in broad strokes. We've done the challenging, heartbreaking work both inside and outside this office to make ourselves whole again. To make sure this relationship lasted this time.

"Is there anything else you guys wanted to discuss today? Any issues that have come up or things you're concerned about?" she wonders.

"There is something I've been worried about," Kai admits hesitantly.

"Okay let's talk about it," Magdalena acknowledges.

"We've talked a lot about our breakup and how it affected us. But I don't think you've ever really explained why you left," he comments, glancing at me. Sometimes I want to scream: *I gave you options. I gave you freedom. I sacrificed my dreams so you didn't have to*. But it's no use trying to rewrite the past, trying to make him understand I thought I was doing what was best for him. And even if that's what I convinced myself I was doing at the time, I know better now. And he deserves the truth, the whole truth.

"I mean you said it was because you were scared. Because you wanted me to have my career. But I know you and I know us and I know that's not the only reason. I think there's something you don't want to tell me. And whatever it is, I want you to know we'll figure it out."

Shit. He knows and it occurs to me that Kai is so strikingly perceptive and intuitive that he has probably known this entire time. He was just giving me the space I needed to process my own thoughts and feelings.

"I left for a lot of reasons but you're right, there's things I haven't told you, reasons I haven't completely shared with you." I pause, trying to gather my thoughts. "I thought we would be too much and not enough for you at the same time," I admit.

"Too much meaning?" Magdalena asks.

"A newborn right at the start of his career. Trying to juggle work and home and having a family when we were still so young. It would have been really overwhelming."

"Okay and when you say not enough, you mean?" She's staring at me expectantly, urging me to go deeper and I realize I want to. I need to get this—all of it—off my chest.

"I was his high school sweetheart. His neighbor growing up. And I knew he loved me—loves me," I amend. "I just didn't know if that was enough. Some part of me has always felt like I didn't deserve him. I was scared that one day he'd wake up and realize he could do better."

"Ken, you don't really think that, do you? That you aren't enough for me?" he asks, shocked and clearly hurt.

"No, not anymore. But I did think that for a while."

"Kendall," Magdalena cuts in "You were adopted, right?"

"Yes."

"And so this fear of not being enough. These insecurities, I would guess a fear of abandonment... Do you think you've had these feelings for a long time? Before you started dating Kai?"

"Yeah. I always felt like that about my family. My biological parents. If I'd been enough, wouldn't they have kept me?" I swallow thickly, tears burning my eyes. "Why couldn't they love me enough?" Even if no one had the answers and even if they didn't make sense, I needed to voice these questions. Because keeping them inside me for all these years hasn't done me any good. That kind of rejection, that kind of pain and loneliness. It never leaves you. It lives in your body and becomes a growing, feeding organism.

Kai turns to me now, resolve in his eyes and devotion in his heart. I know that look. He's gearing up to say something that would redefine me, something that would stay with me. Because that's just what he does. He loves me and he protects me and he reassures me. But perhaps more importantly, he knows exactly how I need to be loved.

"Maybe they did love you so much. But maybe they couldn't love you the way you needed them to. Maybe they wanted a better life for you than the one you might have had with them. Who knows. But what matters is that your family chose you. I chose you, and I'm going to keep choosing you for as long as you'll let me. The love that the people in your life have for you is immeasurable. It was never a question of you not being enough—because to your moms, to Akio, to me, especially, you are everything."

He reforms me somehow, reshapes me, makes me whole in places I didn't even know were fractured. I smile at him. It's warm and gracious, my cheeks streaked with tears. *Thank you thank you thank you* my heart sings.

But I have to know, everything. I have to keep going even if it hurts us.

"Did you want him, a baby back then?" I blurt out quickly, before I lose the nerve. He stares at me for a moment, contemplating. I need to hear him say the words.

"Yes, I wanted him. I've always wanted kids, you knew that. And I always wanted them with you."

"But I need to know specifically, did you want this baby, our baby at the height of your career?" Why I need to know his answer, feel the need to keep hurting myself I'll never understand.

"Yes." He's certain. Steadfast. Unwavering. He always had been. His eyes never stray from mine. It feels like a thousand knives piercing my chest, a vice around my heart. A physical blow to my stomach would have hurt far less. Because I realize now Kai loved hockey with every fiber of his being, but he loved me and Akio more. *How could I have gotten things so wrong?*

"Did you?" he asks, his eyes seeing more than I'm willing to say.

Did I? Have I ever been as certain about anything as Kai had been about every decision he has ever made?

"Honestly. I don't know. But I couldn't survive grieving the loss of him. That much I knew."

It's hard to say. As soon as I held Akio, I was positive. I would never love another thing on earth the way I love him. But before...the unknown, the waiting, the anticipating. The time between conceiving him and accepting him as a real thing, as my son. That time is so foggy to me. It's hard to untangle from everything else. Wrapped up in fear and anxiety. All those overwhelming thoughts threaten to take over again.

"What else? Is there more you need to say, Kendall? Things you've been holding on to that you might want to release?" Magdalena knows we're approaching a breakthrough. I can feel it like a chord pulled taut in the room, ready to snap with one revelation.

This is it. It's now or never.

"Before I left for North Carolina, your dad came to see me. He knew about the baby somehow—"

"What are you talking about?" Kai interjects. "There's no way my dad could have known about this, Kendall. He would have told me."

"Well, he did and he asked me not to tell you," I respond.

"He asked you not to tell me what? What is going on?" he asks, his panicked voice rising.

My head is in my hands now, tears streaming down my face. I stand up abruptly and start pacing the room. I feel hot, too hot, like my body is on fire and I'm breathing through a straw. There isn't enough air getting to my lungs. I'm on the verge of hyperventilating and Magdalena and Kai are staring at me with blatant concern and confusion, waiting for me to say something.

"Ken, what's going on? You're scaring me." A tsunami of shame, overwhelming guilt, and panic starts to rage wildly in my chest. I inhale deeply and blow out a stuttered breath. I say it with my back to him and my eyes closed. Because it's the only way I can say it. The only way that feels safe.

"Your dad offered me money to have an abortion. He told me even if I decided to have the baby, to keep the money and leave you out of it."

I turn back around to face them, and Magdalena's face has gone stark white.

"No," Kai looks at me incredulously. He's shaking his head, adamant that this did not happen.

"Kai, I'm telling you the truth. And I'm so sorry I didn't tell you sooner. But I didn't know how to tell you. I knew your reaction wasn't going to be good." He's sitting on the couch looking straight ahead, not making eye contact with either of us. Shock. He is in shock. His hand is covering his mouth while he shakes his head.

"No, no. He wouldn't do this. I mean, I know it's my dad and he's not the warmest guy. But he wouldn't do *this*. He loves me." He's staring at me now, awaiting confirmation. I think his dad did care about him in his own selfish, complicated way. I also know, all too well, that his father had done this terrible thing and that it could potentially destroy his relationship with Kai. Both things could be true and they aren't mutually exclusive. He looks younger now, terrified. Like the scared, angry teenage version of himself he had worked so long and so hard to banish. Like this information could break him. I don't want to break him and I don't want to lose him. Not when I just got him back.

"Perhaps we should all take a moment to just breathe, process what Kendall has shared," Magdalena suggests. For a second, I forgot she was even in the room. I sit back down on the couch, but Kai won't look at me and I don't blame him.

"I want both of you to take some slow deep breaths. In your nose and out your mouth, let's try and ground ourselves," she instructs. I do what she asks and so does Kai reluctantly. Inhaling deeply for four counts, holding my breath for seven counts, and exhaling forcefully for eight. Just like we've practiced. "Now Kendall, why don't you explain from the beginning what happened with Kai's father. Let's give Kai the opportunity to ask questions and clarify things."

I rub my hands together and start picking at my nails while I recount one of the most painful days of my life. "Kai and I had been arguing about my clinic appointment, for the abortion. He wanted to drive me and I wanted to go alone. His dad showed up later that day before the appointment. He said he knew about the baby—"

"Wait, how could he have known? I didn't tell him and I'm positive my mom doesn't know. She would have told me," he cuts in.

"I'm not sure, maybe he saw your phone or heard us talking. I have no idea. But he knew somehow. And he didn't want you to know that he came, that he knew about the baby. He said if I loved you, I wouldn't destroy your future or your career. He wrote me a check for 10,000 dollars, Kai."

He's looking at me, tears brimming his eyes. "And what did you do? What did you say to him?" he demands.

"I screamed at him to get out of my apartment. I told him I would figure it out without his money and he left. I never heard from him again. And I moved to North Carolina a week later."

"I just can't believe he would do something like this," he whispers while rubbing the back of his neck with his hand.

"Are you saying I'm lying? That I made up this entire story? Why would I do that?" I ask defensively.

"No, I just... I don't understand why he would do this. I can't make it make sense."

"It doesn't have to make sense for it to be true," I say quietly. "I'm sorry that you're finding out like this and that it took me so long to tell you."

"It wasn't your secret to tell," Kai observes.

"It wasn't exactly mine to keep either and I should have told you sooner. I didn't know how."

"Perhaps some of these thoughts and questions should be directed at your dad when you are ready to have that conversation, Kai. His reasons for doing things and motivations might provide some insight," Magdalena says.

"Okay," he replies. Although I know from experience and the way his jaw tightens, the muscle ticking, that this won't be a calm discussion. This will be confrontational, ugly, possibly violent. I shudder at the thought.

What have I done?

CHAPTER 75

KAI

SO, THIS IS IT. The thing she has been too scared to tell me. This awful, disgusting secret between us has finally been revealed. The one thing she knew could ruin us, ruin me if we give it enough weight and enough power.

How would we survive this? Could we survive this?

Our trust in each other is new, delicate, and vulnerable to threats. It's been dangling precariously on a tight rope and this confession sends it hurtling to the ground. Magdalena's calm, soothing voice interrupts my spiraling thoughts.

"So, how do you feel hearing this information, Kai? You two have done a lot to repair this relationship and work through difficult issues—especially regarding trust. What does that look like now?"

I feel broken. Betrayed. Seething. But I don't say any of that. I push it down and bury it somewhere deep. The same place my hatred and resentment for my father resides. *Am I angry at my father for his abhorrent behavior or upset at Kendall for shattering my trust again?* I can't disentangle those threads for fear that doing so would cause our entire relationship to unravel.

"I think I'm in a little bit of shock. I'm upset she kept this from me but I understand why she did. It was probably very painful for her to talk about and not something that's easy to say." I swipe my hands down my face in exasperation, struggling to find the right words. "My dad was never an easy guy to live with or understand. He didn't dole out affection willingly. And he never really cared about my breakup with Kendall. He ignored it almost like it never happened. I always thought it was weird, that it was simply him being him. Now things seem clearer though." I turn to Kendall so that I can look at her, really look at her. "Is this it? This is everything? There aren't any more secrets between us?" Not that I can take much more. I'm on the verge of losing my shit as it is.

She nods repeatedly, her entire being filled with remorse. "This is it. I'm so sorry, Kai. I didn't know how to say it and I didn't want to lose you. But I would understand if you couldn't forgive me for this."

The entire time I've been trying to play cards without a full deck, attempting to solve a puzzle when I was missing crucial pieces. For a moment, I'm surprisingly relieved. It must have been hard to carry this information for years, to feel like she couldn't tell me. She hadn't felt like she was enough for me; she was worried she would ruin my career and then my father came along and confirmed all her worst fears. She was young and pregnant, confused and distraught. So, she ran. Of course she did. And when she realized she had made a mistake, she didn't know how to undo it. For the first time since she resurfaced in my life, I have a clear picture of what happened all those years ago. I may not like it but at least I understand it.

I know exactly who to blame for this fucked up mess and it isn't Kendall. My father on the other hand still has to answer for his sins.

When we leave Magdalena's office, I don't even have to say anything to Kendall. She knows exactly where we're going.

"You can't kill him, Kai, you know that right? Your pretty face would not survive prison," she jokes but I know she's worried and she's right to be. The rage I feel towards my father is boiling over, about to reach a tipping point.

"I'm not going to kill him." Although I'm not sure who needs more convincing. I stop to face her and grab her shoulders "But I need to talk to him. I need to see the look on his face when he says it. I need to know why so we can put this behind us, okay?" I plead.

"Okay," she nods. "I understand."

When you strip it down to the bare bones, what are we to each other? Without the mistakes, the secrets, the heartache, the lies. Take the fact that we were high school sweethearts and had a kid together out of the equation. We love each other unconditionally and it defies logic and reason. We are perfect for each other in all the ways that matter. Toxic in all the ways that we can't control.

Lying about Akio's existence. *Toxic.* Keeping my father's dirty bribe a secret. *Toxic.* Embroiling us in Aiden's mess. *Toxic.* But what if we could find a way through it, and come out on the other side, start fresh? Without being bogged down by all this poison. I have to believe we can. I'm sure as hell not ready to accept the alternative.

CHAPTER 76

KAI

THE DRIVE TO MY parents' house is eerily quiet. I don't have the energy to talk and I think Kendall is terrified to say anything. It feels like we're a thousand miles away from each other. Blink 182's *I miss you* plays in the background softly as a foreboding ominous soundtrack to our present and future.

Don't waste your time on me, you're already the voice inside my head

I miss you, miss you

I pull into my parents' driveway and barely put the car in park before I'm racing to the door. Kendall remains in the car trying to decide whether she should come in or not. I find my mom at the kitchen table pouring over work documents.

"Kai, what a nice surprise, I didn't know—"

"Where's dad?" I demand, cutting her off. I need to do this now, before I talk myself out of it.

"He's in his office. Kai, what's wrong?" she asks.

"I just need to talk to him about something," I respond. But my dad joins us in the kitchen before I can go looking for him. He has his usual, impassive look on his face.

"Kai, I didn't know you'd be here today," he comments. At that moment, Kendall walks in the front door. To my father's credit, his fake smile doesn't falter, his body language doesn't change. The only tell is the feathered muscle in his jaw.

"Kendall, hi. It's so good to see you," my mom squeals. Kendall bends down to hug my mom as though no time has passed. She makes no move to acknowledge my father and before he can take this charade any further, I interrupt the niceties.

"What did you do?" I bark.

"What are you talking about?"

"You know damn well what I'm talking about," I snap, taking a few steps closer to him, seething with rage and hurt. I lower my voice to a whisper. "Three years ago, you went to Kendall's apartment. You knew she was pregnant. What. Did. You. Do?"

I knew he had done this without having to ask, without hearing him acknowledge it. Backed her into a corner and made her feel smaller and more insecure than she already had been. I knew because he had done it to me my whole life. And him coming to her with this offer was what tipped her over the edge. After all this time, she was the only one brave enough to tell me.

"I did what I thought was best," he replies coolly.

"You're a fucking coward," I say looking him directly in the eyes.

"Kai," my mom says firmly. "What is going on?"

"Anela, this is our business to deal with," my dad snaps. He swings his gaze to my mom and back to me quickly.

"Maybe it wasn't the right way to do things but I was trying to help you. Protect your dream," he reasons. *Protect me? Help me?* He is certifiably insane.

"You made a grave error, a catastrophic miscalculation. Hockey was my dream but it was only my dream because it was *yours* first. If you knew me, and I mean actually knew me, you would know that Kendall was really the only dream that mattered. Because none of this means anything without her, without them. You saw how I was hurting, how much pain I was in and you watched me suffer anyways. You had so many chances to tell me what you did and you chose not to. You did that."

"You're right. Maybe I should have told you. And that's on me. But you can't honestly tell me that married, pregnant, raising a kid at twenty two, potentially withdrawing from the draft, that that was your dream," he scoffs.

"That's not the point. It wasn't your decision to make. It wasn't your life and it wasn't only my future you almost wrecked; it was both of ours. I've spent my entire life afraid to mess up, trying to be perfect and live up to your expectations. The one time that something happened that was beyond our control you didn't even allow me the grace to come to you about it."

"Wrecked your future?" He laughs in disbelief. "Are you kidding me? You are where you are because of me. You only have your very lucrative, famous career because of *me.*" The leash on my restraint has been severed. I barrel into my father and pin him against the kitchen wall, his gray oxford shirt gripped in my hands. My breathing is erratic, my chest heaving.

I'm vaguely aware that both my mom and Kendall are yelling, but I can't seem to process any of it.

"I succeeded, I became everything I am *in spite* of you, your wrath, your excuse for parenting." I punctuate every word by digging my index finger deeper into his chest.

"Kai, stop, please. Just back up for a second," Kendall tugs on my arm, pulling me away from my father. I retreat two steps, but I remain firmly planted in front of him, trying to decipher the look on his face. I have never done anything like this. Confronted him, stood up to him, stood up for myself. I have never accused him of any wrongdoing and he has gotten so many things wrong.

"Will someone tell me what the hell is going on?" my mom demands. Kendall walks over to the kitchen table and motions for my mom to join her. I turn back to my father to see him running his hands through his hair nervously. He obviously doesn't care about ruining his relationship with me but he's worried about hurting my mom, that's one thing he can't stomach.

I scrape my hand over my jaw, my breathing labored. "You know there were times that it felt like Kendall was the only person that was there for me, supported me. Loved me despite feeling very fucking unlovable by you," I say quietly.

He's examining me closely, contemplating his next move.

"That isn't true," he replies.

"It doesn't have to be easy to hear and it doesn't have to be your reality for it to be true. But it is. That's what it was like for me." He doesn't say anything. He doesn't say that he loves me. He doesn't apologize and why would he? "You have one son who is afraid to tell you the truth and another that wants nothing to do with you. Nice work, Dad." I have spent my whole life working and competing for his love. Trying to earn his attention, time, and affection because it was never handed out freely. But if this is what it looks like, I don't want it. I don't need it.

I am *done*.

"Kai," my mother warns from her seat at the table. And I know she wants to stop me from hurting my father even more but I'm past the point of giving a fuck. I want to see him in pain, draw blood, and unfortunately, my older brother and his secrets would be collateral damage. I'm my dad's golden athlete but Ryo has always been his favored son, the brightest student destined to follow in his footsteps.

"What are you talking about?" he growls.

"Where exactly do you think Ryo is right now?" I press.

He scoffs in irritation, "He's obviously in California."

I huff out a dry, mirthless laugh. "He is in Thailand at one of my beach houses and has been for the last three months. He took a leave of absence from med school because he was having panic attacks and couldn't focus. And if you think for one second that you didn't have a hand in making him this way, you're in fucking denial."

My dad's face immediately crumples into abject horror, drained of its color. "No. No, he would have told me." He shakes his head in disbelief.

"Would he? Why would he think that talking to you would have solved anything? Anything short of perfection was unacceptable in this house. Jesus, we were terrified of even shitting the wrong way," I reply.

"That's enough," my mom declares firmly and I can hear her plea, *You've done enough damage, let it be.*

"Fine. I'm done anyways," I relent.

"I was trying to protect you. Everything I have ever done has been out of love," he reasons quietly and the worst part is, I think he truly believes that. I assume he's done but then he trudges on mercilessly.

"I wasn't the warmest dad, so what? I never beat you, neglected you. Never left you for days on end without food or water wondering when I'd be back. And I refused to let you grow up with less than you needed to survive. You three had a roof over your head, food on the table, and endless sports camps, recitals, and competitions. You lived in a fucking dream." I think he's so close to saying *my dream*, but he doesn't. I want him to admit it so badly, his bitter envy of the life he worked so hard to give us. "So I was a little cold, a little distant. What father isn't from time to time? I've given you and your brother and sister everything you could possibly need. And this is how you repay me?"

I hear all the things he can't say. *I gave you the life I never had, the one I always wanted.* And my dad had a hard life. I know that even if it was never said out loud. I picked up pieces and snippets over the years from my mom. He had to raise his four younger siblings mostly by himself. They grew up in what would amount now to a shack in relentless poverty. And it would seem that after his youth was spent nurturing them, caring for them, and protecting them, he didn't have any of that left over when it came to his own children. I couldn't exactly blame him but I couldn't justify his actions either. Not anymore.

Because what do we owe our parents exactly? What debt and for how long? For helping us survive and succeed in this fucked up world? And what do they owe us? Is it our burden to guide their inner child along a gentler path? Do we bear any responsibility for helping them heal the wounds and horrors they endured throughout their life?

I don't have those answers. I probably never will. I can make peace with my dad showing his love the only way he knows how. Eventually. But his blatant disgust and attack of my relationship with Kendall? Stabbing me in the back all while smiling in my face for years? The selfish cruel decision that could have resulted in me not having a son? I don't think I can forgive that.

"This might be the last time I ever speak to you. So, I'm going to ask you one more time and I hope you tell me the truth. Why did you do this?"

There's a panicked look in his eyes as they dart between me and my mom. "You have your own son now. Wouldn't you do anything to protect him to make sure his future was secure? I never wanted you to struggle the way I did." He *almost* sounds remorseful. I realize this conversation is about as close as I'm going to get to an apology because my dad doesn't have one empathetic bone in his body.

"I would never do something like this to Akio," I reply calmly. "I would never intentionally harm him or cause him pain. You don't do that to people you love, Dad." He stares at me wide eyed in horror, while the full impact of his choices catches up to him. What's that saying—heal so your children don't have to? My father didn't but I will. I will make sure Akio never feels the pain my father was quick to inflict on me and my siblings. That he never has to question whether he is loved or worthy or enough.

"This conversation is over. Come on, Ken, we're leaving," I tell them, striding towards the front door.

Once Kendall's hand is in mine, I turn back around to address my father. "I don't want you anywhere near me, Kendall, or our son. I don't want a single fucking thing from you anymore or ever again," I say, letting the door slam on our way out.

He probably didn't think he would lose me over this, that I would wage a war over Kendall. But he should have known I would burn down the whole fucking world for her, for them.

Chapter 77

Kendall

W E'RE SITTING IN THE parking lot outside my apartment in Kai's car. Usually, this is where I would ask if he wants to stay over, but I can tell by the tension in his shoulders, the rigid set of his jaw, and the excruciating silence that we'll probably be sleeping alone tonight. The humidity in the air is heavy and suffocating. There's only the console between him and I but it might as well be a thousand miles.

"I think I'm going to stay at my place tonight," he declares, eyes trained on the steering wheel. "I need a little time, a little space to think." He taps the wheel a few times with his thumb.

"Okay, I understand. Whatever you need." I bite my bottom lip, worry pulsing in my chest. "What if you can't forgive me?" It's so incredibly selfish, such a desperate question and still, I need to hear his answer.

"I will," he states definitively.

"But what if you can't?" I press harder. "And honestly, I wouldn't blame you if you didn't." I had just blown up his family, caused irreparable damage in a matter of minutes. I would under-stand if he hated me for that and couldn't move past it. It would crush me I'm sure, losing him a second time is not something I think I'd recover from. But there is a steep price to pay for my secrets, my lies. I just hope it doesn't cost us our future.

"Kendall, I will because there is no other option than us being together and staying together. There's no explanation for it other than I love you and we will find a way to make this work."

"Even if it's hard and painful and ugly?"

"Yes, even if it's all those things. I thought you understood by now that I am never letting you go again. You are stuck with me." He smiles, although it doesn't quite reach his eyes.

I'm not super hopeful but it will have to suffice for now. He deserves the time and space to process all this bullshit that I've kept wrapped up tightly for years.

***

WHEN I DON'T HEAR from him the following day or the day after that, the worry turns into full-fledged anxiety. Those two days go by at a glacial pace. I check my phone obsessively hoping he's texted or called but there's nothing. I'm completely checked out, knowing I won't be able to rest until I talk to him.

I start drafting at least ten text messages to him, but I never gain the courage to actually send them.

Hi how are you?

I miss you

Can we talk whenever you're ready?

I'm so sorry.

I can't be the one to reach out to him. I'm the one who messed things up, possibly beyond repair. He needed space and time even though it felt torturous to me. Every minute that ticked by felt like another nail in the coffin of our relationship.

Akio asking me to come play with him breaks through my turbulent thoughts.

"Mama, come play cars with me," he repeats and I realize I don't know how many times he's already asked me this.

"Okay baby, which color should I be?" I ask as I sit down next to him on his bedroom floor.

"You be green and I'll be blue," he declares.

"Okay," I say and offer him a half-hearted smile. That was about all I could muster up at this point. I could try to pretend for him at least. To be here, to be present, to be invested. Even though my mind lingered on Kai and every single mistake I had made in the last three years.

"Vroom vroom!" he shouts before crashing his blue monster truck into a yellow dump truck.

"Vroom vroom!" I echo.

After two more days of radio silence, panic starts to fester in my stomach. It works its way through my body, disrupting my nervous system until it becomes a boulder sitting on my chest, incessant insects crawling under my skin.

Something is wrong. Something is off.

He might be mad or upset but he would still talk to me. I know that much. He wouldn't just disappear.

Chapter 78

Kai

My father's betrayal, Kendall's secrecy, the dread that hovers like a shadow after trying to resolve Aiden's mess. They all close in on me at the same time. I don't know how to make sense of everything and I don't know how to keep the dark intrusive thoughts at bay. All the people I would usually turn to at times like this have let me down miserably.

I call Jenna while I drive around aimlessly but it rings three times before going to voicemail. Jonah hasn't responded to my texts, probably with his flavor of the week. And Jax is otherwise occupied with Emma. When I hop on the highway, I realize there's a car that has been behind me since I left Ken's apartment. A large black SUV. The same kind of SUV that surrounded the dockside drop area, where an anonymous middleman I hired exchanged $80,000 for what I had hoped was peace of mind.

Jesus fucking Christ, Kai, get it together. There is no one after you.

There is still one last thing I can turn to, a vice that has always been there for me when others weren't.

You know who didn't judge you, or ask questions?
Alcohol.

When I pull into Finnegan's, I watch breathlessly as the black car that's been trailing me pulls in too. *Fuck.* I exit my vehicle, but the black SUV remains parked and running a few spaces down from me. From my stool at the bar, I glance outside just as the car peels out and speeds away. Slightly relieved, I bring a glass of whisky to my mouth and for the first time in almost two years, I take a sip. The amber brown liquid burns my throat and scorches my veins. Soon, the stress and anger I'd been holding on to starts to evaporate from my body. I know I'll pay for it tomorrow, that the first things I'll feel when I wake up will be guilt and shame. Along with a nasty hangover. But that doesn't stop me, because I need relief at this moment more than I need anything else.

Two drinks and a little bit of wallowing later, I check my phone. Three texts from Kendall checking to make sure I'm okay. Five missed calls and two voicemails from my mother. I can't listen to those yet; I will deal with her a different day. Unsurprisingly, there is nothing from my dad. Jax finally responds shortly after 11:00; he said he was leaving Emma's and asked if I wanted company. I tell him it's fine. I don't really want anyone to see me like this anyways. I have blown almost two years of sobriety and my life is a mess.

After the bartender announces last call, I stumble out the front door to call an Uber. I might be in self-destruct mode but I don't want to die. I'm hovering with my face buried in my phone trying to keep track of my Uber's location. I sway a little, unsteady on my feet when I hear footsteps behind me. Before I can fully turn around, large thick arms wrap around my trunk and upper body.

"What the fuck?" I slur. "Let me go." He has my neck wedged in between his elbow, squeezing as hard as he can. Searing pain explodes in my neck as it becomes harder to breathe. Panic starts to set in while dots break out in my vision. I'm writhing and clawing at his arms, my feet scrambling for purchase. I fight with everything I can, trying to twist away from my captor.

NO, NO, NO. I refuse to fucking die like this.

I swing my foot back hard and connect with his knee. I hear the satisfying crunch of bone but his hold on me remains tight. A sinister voice growls in my ear, "You'll pay for that, motherfucker."

Then the attacker brings a cloth to my mouth and
everything
goes.
black.

CHAPTER 79

KAI

I OPEN MY EYES and immediately wonder whether I'm dead. But if I were dead, I don't think I'd feel any pain and I'm in so much of it. My head is throbbing and fuzzy, like cotton has been stuffed between my ears. It hurts to breathe, to blink, to exist. My chin rests heavy against my chest while I get my bearings. It stings and aches. I'm sure it's covered in bruises and cuts. My shirt is torn and soaked in blood.

I try to move my hands but they're being restrained by something. Zip ties maybe? I can't move my legs either. They are shackled to what I think is a wooden chair. And wherever I am is dark and dingy. The entire place feels musty and closed off, everything covered in a thick layer of grime. *Maybe I'm underground*? The floor feels wet and so do my sneakers. Glancing down and squinting, I realize the concrete is saturated, from a mix of my piss and blood.

Jesus fucking Christ. I'm going to die here.

In this dirty, disgusting shithole.

And just as I begin to slip into a panic attack, a rough hand grabs my jaw, yanking it upward.

"Nice of you to join us, pretty boy," the man sneers, giving me a menacing smile. It's the same disturbing voice of the person who attacked me in the parking lot. He slaps my face hard, making sure I'm paying attention.

"Where am I?" I mutter, turning my head out of his grip. I lick my bottom lip where blood trickles out, the metallic taste flooding my mouth.

"We can't tell you that. That would take all the fun out of it, wouldn't it, lad?" he speaks with a heavy Irish accent, confirming what I already know. I was right to be paranoid. There is no doubt in my mind that the man or men who kidnapped me are connected to the O'Rourke mob. I saw this coming. I just didn't want to accept it.

"What do you want?" I snarl, staring up at him. He's tall, maybe an inch or two shorter than me, with muddy brown hair and empty emerald eyes. He has a gun in a holster on his hip along with black steel-toed boots. Tattooed biceps bulge underneath his t-shirt. I could probably take him, or outrun him, but not in the condition I'm in. That's assuming I could even break free somehow.

"Listen mate, you thought you could fuck around with the O'Rourke's and we wouldn't come to collect?"

"I paid 30,000 dollars more than the debt. I would hardly call that fucking around," I respond. He moves quickly, even with his slight limp, taking a knife stowed in his pocket and bringing the sharp edge to the side of my face. He kneels in front of me, pressing it into my cheek.

"It wasn't your debt to pay, lad. And it wasn't your business to fuck with."

"But it's paid," I told him, trying to understand what this was all about.

"It's not about the money anymore, lad. We've been waiting for Aiden to pay his dues for years now. Do you know how much of our time he's wasted? And the boss doesn't like his time being wasted." I swallow, unable to form words. "The debt's been paid. But disrespect?" He clicks his tongue, dragging the knife down my cheek, a stain of blood following it. "That's a different kind of bill entirely."

"Please, I will give you whatever you want. Please," I beg. "Don't kill me."

"Don't worry, pretty boy, we aren't going to kill you. You're of no use to us dead," he says standing.

"So then what do you—what do they—want?" I sputter.

"You know, just a cool million."

The number lands like a punch to the sternum. A million dollars. I run the math before I can stop myself, liquidating my accounts, breaking my CDs early, bleeding out my retirement fund. The house in Thailand. Maybe then. Maybe.

"I don't have that kind of money liquidated right now," I say carefully. "That's not something I can pull up on my phone in the next five minutes."

He tilts his head, unbothered. "No one said anything about five minutes."

"I'm serious. That's... I'd need time. Days, maybe. To move things around without triggering flags."

"Flags," he repeats, like the word amuses him. "You're worried about flags?" He crouches down to my eye level and I can smell tobacco and something metallic on his breath. "Let me tell you something about your friend. Aiden's been borrowing from the boss for the better part of two years. Small amounts at first. Harmless, really." His mouth twists. "Then not so small. And every single time the deadline came, there was an excuse. Always a reason. Always next week, next month, just a little more time. Do you understand what that does to a man like the boss? What it costs him?"

I say nothing.

"Aiden wasted months of his time. And the boss?" He stands. "He doesn't forgive wasted time. That's the one thing you can't buy back."

"The million," I press, trying to keep my voice level. "If I get it to you, does that settle it? Is that the end?"

He laughs at that. like I've said something genuinely funny. "The money's just the opening act."

My stomach drops. "What does that mean?"

"It means the boss wants what's owed. And what's owed isn't just currency anymore." He walks a slow circle around me. "But we're reasonable men. Wire the money first and we'll have a conversation about the rest."

"And if I can't move it fast enough?"

He stops behind me. I can't see him and that's somehow worse.

"Then we start making calls," he says quietly. "There's a woman. Pretty. Dark curls. And a little boy—your son, yeah? Cute kid."

Every single nerve ending in my body goes cold.

"Don't," I say. My voice comes out lower and steadier than I feel, which surprises me. "Don't you fucking go near them."

"Then get us the money." He reappears in my periphery, moving toward the long wooden table where a leather toolkit is unrolled beneath a poorly lit swinging lamp. I can't make out exactly what's laid out on it but dread fills in every detail my eyes can't. He reaches for something small and electronic.

***

THEY DROP ME OFF blindfolded, barely conscious, hands tied behind my back, in an alley or abandoned street somewhere. My only indication of where I am the zip of cars and honk of horns in the distance. I hear quick footsteps approaching and flinch, nervous O'Rourke's men had come back. I can tell someone is kneeling down in front of me, and they gently remove the blindfold from my eyes. It's the first time I've seen the sun in days and it makes me want to weep.

"Hey it's okay, we're going to help you," a kind voice whispers. That's my last real memory before I wake up in the hospital.

***

I DON'T BREATHE A word of what happened to me to anyone. Not my parents, not the police or doctors. The only person that I think actually knows the truth, or some version of it, is Kendall. And she's been asleep at my bedside for the second day in a row.

I recount the fabricated story so many times that I want to scream. I tell them that I had been attacked, kidnapped, and beaten violently and returned somewhere near my apartment.

I didn't get a good look at them; they were wearing masks and they drugged me.

That's all I'm allowed to say. Those are my rehearsed lines and I stick to them like my life depends on it, because it does. Keeping my mouth shut ensures I keep my tongue and the rest of my body parts. Although I can tell from the heavy sedatives and the blinding agony in my knee that I'm in trouble. I would never play hockey again. I know that much. I wake up every couple hours in so much pain that my only option is to fall back into an endless drug induced sleep.

But my dreams have transformed into nightmares and so has my reality. Every time I close my eyes, I hear the crack of bone, feel the splintering of tendons and shredding of ligaments all over again. And Jesus, the blood. I'll never be able to unsee it. I relive the horror that gripped my soul every time he lifted the golf club and the roaring, explosive pain that followed. It was unescapable. It had reconfigured my DNA and seeped into the marrow. These wounds, this torture, will stay with me for the rest of my life.

It makes me wish I was dead.

Chapter 80

Kendall

I GET THE PHONE call five days after he dropped me off at my apartment and fell off the face of the earth. I knew even before answering the phone that something had gone terribly wrong. His mom explains what happened to him—without losing her shit somehow—and my heart shatters.

Abducted? Beaten?

What. The. Fuck.

She's still talking but my ears are ringing and my chest feels tight. I start rubbing my sternum to try and ease the ache. This doesn't *actually* happen to people that you know. This is the kind of thing that lurks in darkness, that people discuss in hushed whispers. The stuff of nightmares. The kind of horrifying stories that make headlines and are broadcasted on the five o' clock news. These are tragedies that happen to other people, but not yours. Not your person.

Not to Kai.

"Is he okay? Where is he now?" I hear myself ask as paralyzing fear coils around my bones. I'm definitely in shock, barely able to process her words.

This has to be some sort of mistake. Everything would be okay. He would be okay. He has to be.

"No, not really. He's in surgery right now for his knee. It will probably be a few hours. It's not good though. He needs you, Ken. I think he's going to need you more now than he ever has," she replies quietly.

I need to be with him as soon as possible.

"Okay I'll be there in an hour. Do you guys need anything?"

"We're okay. Just bring yourself, love." I try to wrap my head around the situation. How someone could do this to the person I love. Tears fill my eyes when I start thinking about how terrified he must have been, how alone he probably felt. All because he was trying to do the right thing by Aiden. I'm sure I'll kill him if he ever sets foot in Boston again.

Is he scared now? How severe are his injuries? Did he try and fight back? What happened after he was attacked? Did he escape or did they let him go?

The questions replay in my mind on a loop. Questions I need answered but don't necessarily *want* answered. I drop Akio off at my moms shortly after calling them and head to the hospital.

When I step inside his room, I'm relieved to find his father is nowhere in sight. A sterile cold smell mixed with antiseptic immediately assaults my nostrils. The room is small, painted in a pale blue with a couch on one side and a few hospital chairs scattered throughout. There's a tiny bathroom to my right and a whiteboard detailing Kai's care plan. Anela is perched in the corner sitting in her wheelchair and staring out the window, an absent look on her face.

"Kendall," she says, tears brimming her eyes. "Thank god you're here." I walk over and bend down to hug her, embracing her tightly. Maybe her strength and optimism would rub off on me somehow. Maybe I could absorb her pain if I hold her long enough. I'm not sure. I just know we both need each other.

Two hours pass and finally, Kai's dad enters the room, stopping short when he makes eye contact with me. He looks exhausted, disheveled, and uncertain about how to handle the situation.

"Kendall, I didn't know when you were coming. I can wait somewhere else," he suggests.

"No, it's fine. I think we're all going to be here for a while. We might as well accept that and get comfortable," I respond.

It's a temporary truce, a ceasefire so that we can all support Kai however he needs us to. And honestly, I don't even care about the issues with Kai's dad anymore. I just want him to be okay.

He nods and plops down in a chair next to Anela, letting out a long sigh. He hands a coffee to her silently and she thanks him. But her words are clipped and she doesn't spare him a glance.

Is it because the last time he saw Kai they had been at each other's throats? Or because he is now in a four-hour surgery that's taking over five hours?

I'm not sure. But their vibe seems off.

I'm so tired from stress, anxiety, and lack of sleep that I nod off while waiting for him to return from surgery. When I wake up, he's lying there immobile in the hospital bed and Anela is holding his hand.

He's okay. He's here. He's out of surgery.

But when I scan his body, I have to swallow the lump sitting in my throat to keep from sobbing uncontrollably. I'm afraid if I start crying, I will never stop. He is here but he is nearly unrecognizable. He definitely isn't *okay*. Both his eyes are purple and swollen. A large gash trailing from his hairline to his cheek. He has sizable bruises and cuts on his face, red welts circling his wrists, the skin around it chapped, broken, and tinged with dry blood. The presence of the marks indicating he was forcibly held against his will. And I knew that it had happened. But knowing it and seeing it are two different things. His left leg is elevated, his knee supported in some sort of bracing, metal rods poking out of either side. And these are only the parts of his body I can see. I'm too chickenshit to even consider the wounds that aren't visible. I can't open that box yet. He has an IV and lines running from his arms to a machine that administers medicine, a pulse ox resting on his right index finger. He's relying on a ventilator, and for some reason, that is what breaks me. It takes every ounce of strength I can muster not to crumple to the floor at the sight of him.

How is Anela suffering through this? How is she surviving right now? How is he?

I suck in a deep lungful of air and attempt to steady my breathing. I'm so fucking furious that someone did this to him but also grateful that he's alive. And I guess that's exactly what hospitals are, places of so many dueling emotions. Gratitude and anger, hope and heartache. Cursing the gods in one breath and praying to them in the next. I want vengeance, retribution. I want the blood of the people who had done this to him.

"His surgery went well," she whispers while I'm deep in thought. "I didn't want to wake you but he did good. He might need some smaller surgeries after this. And he'll be in physical therapy for a while. But he's going to be okay. He's only on the ventilator for a little longer until they are sure he's stable."

"Oh okay. Good. Sorry I wasn't awake when he came back," I respond quietly, shifting so that I'm sitting upright in the chair.

"It's okay. He knows you're here."

I give her a half smile and thread my fingers through his other hand delicately. I kiss his battered knuckles and tell him I love him and to never scare us like this again.

Later that evening, the ET tube gets removed but he remains asleep. The doctors say his body has been through so much trauma and pain that he will need to spend a lot of time resting.

Two days go by and eventually, Kai regains consciousness. With each passing hour, he appears to be a little more lucid. I stay by his side for those two days, only returning home to shower and check on Akio.

On the third day, I feel his hand shift next to mine. When I peer up at him, his eyes are open and the corners of his mouth are turned up.

"Hi," he says, his voice rough and gravelly from being intubated for so long.

"Hi," I breathe. "How are you feeling?"

"I've been better." He attempts a grin, but winces. He brings one hand up and runs it gently over the bruises and lacerations on his face.

"Kai, I thought—I didn't know what was going to happen to you," I blurt out. "I'm so happy you're okay," I whisper, tears in my eyes. And I know okay is relative, I know he isn't *really* okay. That he's been through something akin to hell, suffered through things that others might not have survived. But he's alive and that's enough.

"I know," he says. "Me too."

Chapter 81

Kai

"Hello?" I croak, my voice still hoarse from lack of use.

"Hey, it's me. How are you? Mom called and told me what happened but I can't get on a flight until tomorrow," Ryo explains, worry creeping into the edges of his voice.

"I'm okay. Feeling a little better after surgery." *Lie.* It's a complete lie. But I'm not really sure what I'm supposed to say to people.

"Yeah, but what the fuck happened?"

"Yeah, listen, I don't really want to talk about it right now—"

"Do the police have any idea who it was? Any leads?" he pushes and I know he won't let it go.

"Aiden owed some people a lot of money and I helped him pay the debt. That's all I know." He's silent for a moment, taking this in. I can picture him grinding his teeth and pacing back and forth.

"What kind of debt? And who did he owe? And why did you pay it?" He's spiraling and I'm in no position to answer any of his questions.

"Ryo, I don't want to get into it right now," I reply sharply. "But I'm glad you called. I'm selling my house," I explain without any preamble.

"Which house?" For a smart guy, he can be so dense, so fucking thick sometimes.

"The house you are currently living in. My Thailand house."

"Is someone after you for money? Is that what this is all about?" he asks, putting pieces together.

I ignore his questions while I try to get more comfortable in the hospital bed. "All that matters is that I'm selling it ASAP and you need to be out of there soon."

"How soon?"

"As soon as you can. Two weeks max," I reply, resting my head against the pillow and closing my eyes.

"Jesus, okay," he grumbles. I can hear him walking to the fridge and taking something out of it, the unmistakable sound of a beer can being opened. He takes a swig.

"I'm sorry about outing you to dad," I say.

"Yeah, nice fucking move, asshole. It's okay though, you saved me from having to tell him myself," he sighs. My life is a mess—everything is a fucking mess. But at least I can try to fix this.

"Still, I shouldn't have and I'm sorry. So, what are you going to do?"

"I don't know, maybe travel. Maybe give med school another shot. I haven't decided yet." He pauses. "Kai, how are you really? Don't bullshit me."

I swallow and pound my fist into my forehead trying to decide how much to tell him. "Pretty fucking bad," I answer. I hear him mutter something under his breath. He's trying to figure out how he can protect me from this pain, if he can protect me at all after this. Because it wasn't my father who had defended me to coaches that treated me like shit, or stood up to bullies on the playground when I was too scared to do it myself.

It was Ryo.

"What about hockey? Have they talked about a timeline for recovery?"

"My knee is fucked and so is my career," I respond without any feeling. Because that's exactly what it is, a fact. Not subjective, not an opinion. Fact. And I'm worried if I examine it with any emotion at all I won't be able to stop.

"Jesus, Kai. I'm sorry," he whispers.

"Don't ask questions you don't want the answers to, Ryo."

"I'll be there as soon as I can," he states. "Hang in there."

"I'll try."

Chapter 82

Kendall

Days go by and doctors and nurses shuffle in and out. We spend the time playing cards, watching reruns of *The Office*, and when no one else is around, snuggling together in the cramped hospital bed. He receives enough flower arrangements and fruit baskets to last a lifetime. They start to overtake the small room to the point where we have to give some away to hospital staff. His mom and dad visit every day, his sister and brother coming a few times a week. Jonah, Jax, and a few other teammates trickle in to check on him two weeks after his surgery. He perks up a little when he interacts with them, but I can't help feeling like he's trying to distance himself from me. Like there's something dreadful and unspoken between us. We don't really discuss anything real, anything meaningful, and I don't bring up the kidnapping or assault for fear of triggering him.

He's slipping away from me, I know it. And I don't know how to bring him back.

A few days before he is supposed to be discharged, I decide to bring Akio to visit him in the hospital. When I leave Kai's room, his dad is waiting just outside, leaning against the wall.

"Oh hi," I say sheepishly, pulling the door shut behind me. "I'm going to pick up Akio and bring him to the hospital to visit in about an hour."

He turns to me and starts wringing the back of his neck with one hand. His eyes remain glued to his feet for a few moments. "We'll make ourselves scarce then," he replies.

"No, I mean you can meet him, you both can. I just wanted you to have the heads up."

He studies me for a beat. "You would let me meet him after what I did?" he whispers, his voice low.

"Yes. Kai is going to forgive you eventually and I did a long time ago," I admit.

"I wouldn't be so sure. He's barely spoken to me since he woke up." But it's not on me to appease his dad and absolve him of his guilt. He needs to repair those things himself. When I remain silent, he sighs through clenched teeth. "I never did explain myself to you or apologize, Kendall," he says.

"No, it's okay. Really it's fine—"

"No, it's not. Please, let me just finish," he insists. And his dad has always been a man of few words—the fact that he had even spoken to me this long is telling.

"Okay," I acquiesce. Even though it isn't the time or place and even though I still have residual shame and anger from his actions. Because he doesn't deserve to be punished forever and he *is* Akio's grandfather.

"It was never about you. I was trying to protect Kai, his future. And I didn't go about it the right way. I know I hurt you, both of you a lot. I wish I could take it back. But I am sorry. I'm so sorry and I hope one day you'll allow me to be part of Akio's life. I'll do whatever is necessary to earn that privilege."

"Thank you. I appreciate that," I acknowledge. Right then, an alarm blares in the distance and a horde of doctors and nurses rush past us and toward the sound. I hold my breath as I watch them hurry by Kai's room. As soon as they turn the corner, a wave of relief passes over me.

How sick does that make me? How incredibly single minded?

"You know, once upon a time, I thought you were a threat to Kai, his undoing. That you would cause him to lose focus. But I realize my error now. You, Kendall, are his heart, *his* Anela."

I try to suppress a smile but it takes over my face anyways. This is high praise coming from him. Anela and Takura have always been deeply in love since we were kids. And it seems like that bond has only strengthened with time. I suppose it would have to in order to endure all the things they've survived together.

"You know, I'm not the only person who needs to hear these things. You need to talk to Kai," I urge him.

"I know. I will." He scrubs his hand over his stubble, pinning me with a serious stare.

"I needed the money," he says so quietly I'm not even positive I heard him correctly. I can tell there's more but he's trying to decide if he can trust me with it. "We were going to lose the house, after a malpractice lawsuit went south and I didn't know what else to do. Amy needed a deposit for college and I couldn't pay the mortgage. I told Kai I needed a loan from him shortly after he joined the league. He thought it was for home improvement projects."

"And you couldn't have told him all this somehow either before or after you approached me about an abortion?" I demand.

"No. Because all I had left was my pride and I couldn't give that away too." How alone and out of control his father must have felt to submit to that level of desperation. I see a trace of remorse and guilt on his face, two feelings I have never associated with Kai's father. How was Takura supposed to explain to Kai that he had failed him, that the power balance had shifted, that he was now responsible for cleaning up his father's mess? I still can't rationalize his behavior, but this does make it more palatable.

"So why are you telling me this?" I wonder.

"I just wanted you to understand it was never about you. It was my own stupidity and selfishness. And maybe it's easier to confess to someone I barely know than my own flesh and blood. You already hate me; you might as well know the full truth."

"I don't hate you." He doesn't say anything, just gives me a tight lipped smile. But then something strange and unnerving occurs to me.

"Why did you offer me money if you needed it so badly?" I blurt out. This is probably my only opportunity to get closure and answers from him, I might as well use it to my full advantage.

"I knew you wouldn't take it," he answers. Sure. Certain.

"How?"

"Because you're *good*," he emphasizes, a small smile forming in the corner of his mouth. "You always have been. I knew coming there and expressing my fears was probably enough."

"Will you tell Kai?" I prod.

"In my own time, yes. I think right now it's best for me to respect his wishes and keep my distance from Akio though. But I do want to meet him when things..." he trails off, struggling to come up with the words.

"When things settle a bit?" I offer. He nods.

"Thank you, Kendall, for listening to me," he says in parting before heading in to see Kai.

Chapter 83

Kendall

H OLDING AKIO ON ONE hip, I peer into Kai's hospital room. He's staring up at the ceiling blankly. *What is going on inside his beautiful head?*

What is he thinking?

As soon as we enter and Akio runs to his bedside, his entire demeanor changes. His face lights up immediately. He clearly needed this. We all did.

"Kai Kai!" Akio shouts, his little chin peeking above the hospital bed.

"Hey, little man!" Kai responds.

"We have to be careful, baby," I warn. "Kai is still healing and getting better." I pick Akio up and place him next to Kai and Akio wraps his arms around his neck. Kai's eyes blur with tears while he hugs him back.

"I missed you," Kai says, kissing his head.

"I missed you more," Akio challenges. Akio stares at him curiously, in wonder. The way only young children can. He brings his chubby little fingers up to Kai's face, where he traces the remains of cuts and bruises.

"Does it hurt?" Akio asks him.

"Not anymore," Kai responds, stiffening slightly.

"Were you brave?" Akio whispers. Kai clears his throat.

"I tried to be brave like Spider-Man," he answers, bringing his forehead to Akio's.

"That's really brave," Akio decides.

"Okay, why don't we read a book with Kai?" I suggest trying to change the subject for him.

"Yay!" Akio squeals. I remove a few of his favorites from my tote bag and hand them to Akio. While he contemplates which one he wants to read first, Kai mouths *thank you* to me over his head. I walk over to him and press a kiss to his cheek.

"You're welcome," I smile. "I'm going to give you two a little alone time, okay? Maybe get us some coffees." He returns the smile, his grin growing wide while Akio plops a book on his chest. And for the first time in weeks, I see a glimpse of the real Kai.

Chapter 84

Kai

I'M GETTING DISCHARGED TODAY. I'm finally allowed to go home. But most days, I wake up wishing they had killed me instead.

How fucking selfish is that?

I have PTSD I'm sure, just like after my first car accident. For which I've been given the name of a highly respected and sought after cognitive behavior therapist. But I have yet to make my first appointment. That would mean acknowledging and actively thinking about what happened to me. How I sat in my own filth, praying for death. And I can't do that, not yet.

I've met with local law enforcement multiple times. I've repeated my statement to probably a dozen people. They have no new information regarding my case and they reiterate that so far, they have no leads. Bad for them, good for me. They'll never find the building I was being held in and even if they do, the scene will be scraped of any DNA evidence. O'Rourke's men were careful, precise, meticulous. All the things you'd expect of loyal soldiers who murder and torture other people for a living. They would only be found if they wanted to be.

I've resorted to hiring contractors from a private security firm to be at my apartment around the clock, in hopes that it would make me feel more secure, more safe. That I'd be able to take a breath without losing my fucking mind. But safety is an illusion. Because if O'Rourke's men wanted to cut me up and send me in pieces to my family, they could and there would be very little that would stop them. Not the former military sniper I have on retainer or the two ex-navy SEALs I've hired as bodyguards.

I doubt I'll ever truly feel safe again.

***

"WELL, THAT'S THE LAST of it," my dad announces after carrying the rest of my belongings into my apartment. Him, my mom, and Kendall drove me home from the hospital today and helped me get settled in. I've been sent home with crutches, a walker, and three different prescriptions. I'm also required to attend physical therapy four times a week. There are severe limitations and restrictions that impact my day-to-day life. No putting weight on my bad leg, no heavy lifting, no showering without assistance. My life looks very different now; I don't know how to function in it. I'm not sure I want to and I don't really know how to ask for help either.

"Thanks," I reply. "I think I'm going to try and get some rest if that's okay," I say, moving to lower myself down to the couch. My dad braces my arm, trying to help me and immediately I snap at him. "I've got it, Dad." He holds his hands up and retreats a step.

"Are you sure, Kai? We can stay for a while. Make you dinner or whatever you need," my mom suggests.

"That's okay. I'm kind of tired." My body is fatigued, sluggish. Like trying to wade through quicksand. I could sleep for days and still be in a deficit.

"Okay, please call us if you need anything. I'll be back tomorrow to bring you to therapy," my mom reminds me.

"Okay, I will." They both hug me before walking out the door and I notice they both hug Kendall too. *That's interesting.*

After she closes the door shut behind them, Kendall takes a seat next to me on the couch.

"I can stay the night with you if you want. My moms can watch Akio," she offers, her eyes hopeful and bright. I hate that I'll have to crush it. That after everything we've been through, I would have to make her suffer more.

"That's okay. I think I just want to be alone," I respond, staring at my hands.

"Kai, what's going on in your head? You can talk to me, you know. Whatever it is."

"I think I need some time to be alone, Ken. I need space," I say softly.

"You mean like tonight?" she clarifies.

"I mean I think we need to take a break. I'm barely holding myself together. I can't make you a part of that."

"I want to be there for you. However you need me to be," she insists, gently laying her hand on my arm.

"I can't be with you like this, Ken. I'm broken. I need some time to figure my shit out," I explain. I'm clinging to a darkness, drowning in something I don't quite understand and I can't drag her down there with me.

"Then come to me broken. Let me help, let me heal you. We can heal together. Just don't leave. I won't survive it again," she says, desperation clawing at her voice. "Please, just come back to me. Come home," she pleads, her voice fractures on the last word. The corners of my eyes are wet but I still don't look at her, I can't. I don't want to hurt her and I don't want to lose her either. But I don't deserve her right now, not like this.

"Kai, look at me," she begs. I turn my head to see tears falling down her face. *Fuck.* "Please don't give up. Don't run away from us because things are hard and complicated and so fucked up."

I shrug out of her hold. "Why? Isn't that what you've always done?" My tone is accusatory and harsh, soaked with acid. And she doesn't deserve it. She didn't do anything wrong. I'm just so fucking angry at my life, how everything has gone completely sideways. I'm seething from the state of it. I don't know what to do with this gaping pit inside me and I don't have anyone else here to take the blows. She's the only one that can absorb my anger and somehow still love me.

She recoils like I physically slapped her and I might as well have.

"Kai," she whispers, hurt and anger flashing in her eyes. "That's not fair."

"I think you should go, Ken," I say, my voice the edge of a sharp blade. I've gone a step too far, I know I have. But I need a clean break. I need it to be done. At least for now. I want to draw the shades, crawl up into a ball, let my bed devour me and fall into a dreamless sleep. And maybe I'll come out of hibernation in a few days or a few weeks and this won't be happening. None of this would be real. My life wouldn't be ruined. Both my body and my mind wouldn't be shattered in a thousand fucking pieces.

Maybe I wouldn't wake up at all.

"Okay," she mumbles, rising from the couch and moving towards the door. I watch her wipe tears from her cheeks while she refuses to make eye contact with me.

"This isn't forever. I just think it's what I need right now," I whisper. She remains silent and quietly shuts the door behind her—leaving me alone with the numbness and demons.

I probably fucking deserve it.

Chapter 85

Kendall

"Okay," I hear myself reply.

Okay okay okay.

You know how if you repeat a word enough times it sounds warped, unusual, other worldly? That's how I feel walking out of his apartment, my heart obliterated and my body numb. I'm a little detached from reality. Like this is all a terrible nightmare I would eventually wake up from. He's been brutalized, traumatized, his world ripped apart. He's lost the career he spent over a decade trying to achieve almost overnight. That is too much for any person to handle and I don't want him to have to deal with it on his own. But I don't know how to reach him or get through to him like this.

I lean with my back against his front door, fingers gripped tightly around my mouth and jaw as wailing sobs shake my chest. The sounds I'm making are primal. Guttural. *Raw.* I haven't cried, truly cried, in a while. Not when I got the call from Anela. Not when I saw him for the first time after his attack. And just like that, the dam breaks loose. Hard, fast, uncontrollable. The kind of crying that makes your diaphragm ache and robs you of oxygen.

I knew this was coming, I could feel it. This divide that just kept growing and growing until it became impossible to cross. The distance, the separation, walls being put into place before I can even figure out what they're for.

Is he trying to keep others out or keep all his hurt and suffering in?

I'm sure it's both. Before all this had happened, I was envisioning our future together. A house, a dog, going back to school, marriage. Maybe another baby, one we had planned for. A life that we built around each other. A beautiful, chaotic, messy, wonderful life bursting with love. And now, when I think about the future, my stomach turns. Because I don't want it if it doesn't include Kai.

***

THE NEXT TWO WEEKS happen on autopilot. I stumble through them in a heartbroken fog that infiltrates my pores and tears at my insides. I keep my head down and stick to my routines. I drop off Akio at daycare. I go to work. I pick him up. I do exactly what I need to do to survive and nothing more. Finally, when I get home and Akio is asleep, I break out a carton of ice cream and let my emotions consume me for an hour while rewatching mindless television. An hour of sulking is all I get, that's all I allow myself. Because Akio requires structure and stability, and an emotionally available parent. Because the bills need to be paid and someone has to do all the things that need doing. I don't deviate from this norm, this script. I only open the Kai box for one hour a day. Anything more and I'm certain the walls will close in on themselves along with my heart.

It's not until a week later that Kai calls me. Three weeks of no contact, without seeing his gorgeous face, feeling his lips on mine. Weeks without hearing his voice. They go by in a similar haze. It's like trying to see without sunlight, trying to breathe without air. His absence annihilates me. I've been wandering around aimlessly with a cavity in my chest, missing the other half of my heart. By the time I pick up his call, I'm desperate for any scrap of him I can get.

"Hello," I answer.

"Hey," he clears his throat. "How are you?"

Miserable. Lost. Drowning.

"I'm okay. How are you feeling? How's your leg?"

"It's okay. Getting a little stronger every day." There's a short pause and then, "I miss you guys. I was wondering if maybe I could visit Akio soon. Or rather if you could bring him to me since I can't drive?"

"We miss you too," I admit. He's sacrificed so much. Everything. I'm not going to withhold the truth from him too just to save my pride. "I think we can make that happen. How about this weekend?" I suggest.

"Sure. Just let me know what time."

"Okay. Will your mom or someone else be there? I'm sure it will be hard to watch him and chase him around alone."

"Oh, you aren't going to stay?" he asks.

Is that disappointment I detect in his voice?

"I don't think I should, not when..." *Not when I can't touch you the way I want to. Not when you aren't really mine anymore. Not when the sight of you with our son is going to cause my heart to fracture even more.* "I just don't think it's a good idea right now," I finally say.

"Okay."

"Okay. I'll send you a text with better timing later this week," I respond curtly. There's so much I want to say, but I can't. *I feel like I'm dying without you. I haven't slept right in weeks. The ghost of us is haunting me. And I can't make it stop and I can't let it go because it's all I have left.*

"This isn't forever, Ken. I just think for right now it's best," he explains, reading my thoughts.

"I know," I reply before abruptly hanging up on him. He doesn't sound broken. He doesn't sound anything like the way I'm feeling. And I have the grim realization that the longer we spend apart, the harder it will be to find our way back to each other.

But for him, I can be patient. For him, I can try. He's waited longer than he ever should have for me. I could give him that same grace and understanding.

Chapter 86

Kendall

WE'RE STANDING OUTSIDE KAI'S apartment door, and I'm trying to summon the courage to knock. Akio stands at my side, his hand tucked in mine. It's the first time we've seen each other since we broke up.

Decided to take a break?

My stomach is churning while my heart rams into my ribcage. I can feel my pulse everywhere, a swarm of bees rioting at the surface of my skin.

"Let's go in, mama," Akio says. He swings my arm back and forth excitedly.

"Yupp, we'll just go right in," I mutter underneath my breath. *Just act like everything is fine for two minutes. You can do anything for two minutes.*

I knock a couple times while I swallow down the violent nausea. He opens the door and Akio sprints to him, nearly knocking him over. My eyes roam over him curiously. I'm immediately shaken by the state he's in. His shaggy hair is long, longer than usual, almost brushing his shoulders. And if I look closely enough, I see the tiniest slivers of grey. *Has he ever been grey since I've known him?*

He's sporting a five o' clock shadow and dark circles under his eyes. He leans on crutches while Akio hugs his good leg. Kai looks like he's aged a few years and lost at least 20 pounds. This thing is eating at him from the inside out, chipping away at his sanity and his composure. I wish I had the right words to say or knew how to help him. He didn't sound torn up about it all when I spoke to him on the phone a few days ago. But he *looks* worse, way worse than I imagined. He's deteriorating rapidly and concerned doesn't even begin to describe the ache in my chest.

"Baby, you need to be careful with Kai, okay? His leg is still getting better," I tell Akio.

"Okay, Mama," he says. Akio detaches himself from Kai's leg, runs into the apartment, and beelines for the couch, leaving Kai and I to stew in our awkward silence.

"Hi," he says. "You look good, Ken."

"You look different," I state. *Why the hell did I just say that?*

He bites the side of his lip, "Yeah, I know."

"Well, I should probably get going. Your mom will be here soon?" I ask, eager to spend as little time in his doorway as possible.

"Yeah, she should be. Are you sure you don't want to come in for a little bit?" He's looking at me with longing and hope. Like he needs me, wants me to say yes. The urge to help him, to protect him from whatever he's fighting, is at war with my self-preservation instincts. But I know this isn't him. I know the trauma he's harboring inside is to blame for the mess we're in now. I know it's in the driver's seat, both hands gripped on the steering wheel. He isn't in control. Not entirely.

"I have a few minutes before I have to get going. Until your mom shows up. Just to make sure you're good," I say, justifying it to myself more than I am to him.

He smiles, and for a moment, I think it's a real one. But only for a moment.

Akio is already settled in, toys sprawled on the floor, two books already opened on opposite sides of the living room. He's excited, and I'm excited for him. But I can't help but still feel weird about it all. We're here. Us. But we aren't really us. Not right now at least.

I follow him into the kitchen. He's moving around restlessly, filling a glass of water, setting it down without drinking it.

"How are you sleeping?" I ask.

"Fine."

The silence stretches between us. I open my mouth to try again but he beats me to it.

"I know how it looks, how I must look," he mumbles, avoiding eye contact with me.

"I didn't say anything, Kai."

"I'm going to figure this out, I promise, Ken." This statement should bring me some relief, that he wants to get better, but it doesn't because he's still trying to do this on his own. He's not letting me in.

Doesn't he know I would walk through fire for him, over and over? I would slay his demons alongside him? I would hold him up if he would just let me.

"I know, Kai, I just wish you would let me help, all I want to do is—"

"Yeah, well I don't need anyone's help," he snaps. "And I don't need to drown in everyone's pity either."

I hold his gaze for a moment, long enough to let him know the words landed. He looks away and I recognize a flash of regret in his eyes.

I don't fight it. There's no point arguing with trauma.

"I'll be back at 5 to pick him up," I say quietly.

I stop to kiss Akio on the top of his head on my way out. My body is moving faster than my brain, my feet shuffling backwards before I can change my mind. Kai hobbles behind the door and then closes it with a heavy thud.

His mom exits the elevator just as I'm about to step on.

"Kendall, it's so good to see you!" I wait a moment before getting on and bend down to hug her tiny lithe frame.

"You too. I just dropped Akio off. He's inside with Kai."

"You sure you can't stay for a little bit? I'd love to catch up with you."

"I would too. I just don't think it's a good idea right now."

She's silent for a moment, studying me. She takes my hand in hers and gives it a good squeeze. "Everything is going to be okay, you know, with you and Kai. You guys will figure it out. Just give it some time," she says quietly. Anela and her infinite wisdom. At one time, I considered her a third mom.

"You think so?" I wanted to believe her. I so badly wanted her to be right.

"I know so. He misses you," she insists. That, at least, I believed.

"I miss him too."

"I know, love. Just keep showing up for him, okay?"

"I'll try. I promise."

Chapter 87

Kai

After Kendall and Akio leave, it's just my mom and me sitting at the long farmhouse style kitchen table together. The three of us had just polished off an entire pepperoni pizza. She's staring at me with the kind of look only a mother can give. One that indicates she wants to say something, she's just waiting for the opportunity.

"Whatever you are going to say, just say it," I tell her.

"He's amazing, Kai. So much like you and not at the same time," she smiles. And he is. Akio is the best combination of both of us and yet entirely his own person.

"I know. It's all Kendall. She's been doing a great job with him," I comment.

"So have you," she observes. I haven't though, not lately. And that guilt feels like cement blocks attached to my feet.

"But that isn't what you wanted to talk to me about," I hedge.

"No, it isn't," she admits. "What happened with you and Kendall?" she pries.

"I just thought we needed a little space. That I needed some time to work through some things."

"And have you done that?" she asks, her eyebrows raised. "Worked through things?" She traces the top of her glass with her finger, patient and calculating.

"Well not exactly, but there's been a lot going on," I reply, slightly uncomfortable. I begin fidgeting awkwardly with the paper plate in front of me, ripping off little pieces and making a pile out of them.

"Mhm," she murmurs. "So, are you stringing her along then?"

"What? No, of course not," I huff, rolling a piece of uneaten crust in between my fingers.

"Do you still want to marry her?" my mom demands sharply.

"I'm not sure," I mutter, irritated at the direction of this conversation.

Couldn't everyone just leave me the hell alone and let me sulk in peace?

"Yes, you are. You're scared—that's different than not being certain or not knowing," she points out.

God, she's good. I suppose it's both a blessing and a curse how well she knows me.

I sigh, dropping the paper plate on the table and brushing the crumbs off my hands. "Yes, I still want to marry her."

"Then there's a hard truth you need to hear," she explains, crossing her arms on top of the table. "Marriage has many seasons, Kai. Hard ones and easy ones, long ones and short ones, ups and downs and highs and lows. Seasons of beauty and seasons of grief. Marriage is about carrying each other and loving each other through all of them."

I swallow because objectively, I know my mom is right. Kendall and I have been through so much together, we could get through this rough patch too. I just don't know how. I don't know where to start. And I'm scared she won't want all the broken, haunted parts of me. My damaged pieces and jagged edges.

"What if she can't love me like this?" I posit without looking at my mom. "I don't even like myself right now," I admit. I'm jaded, terrified. Leaving the house feels like a monumental task. So, I just haven't left...in weeks. I've stopped trying, stopped caring. And that paralyzing numbness is a slippery slope.

"She's the *only* one who knows how to love you like this. Kendall will meet you exactly where you are and love you more for it. You have always done that for each other."

"I don't want to burden her. To ask her to do that."

"Kai, I think she wants to carry you through this difficult season. And she can. She's much stronger than you think she is. She's just been waiting for your permission." She lets me chew on that for a moment. "I don't think this is really even about Kendall. I think this is about you," she surmises.

"I have nothing to offer her. I look around and I don't even recognize my life," I whisper, holding my hands out and palms up. I haven't admitted this out loud, not to anyone. And it doesn't change the circumstances, but I do feel a little lighter.

"You still have *everything* to offer her. She hasn't stopped loving you because your career path has changed. And of course you don't recognize your life. You went through something unimaginable and horrific. *You* have to create this new version of your life. You have to reinvent yourself and rebuild. You, my beautiful, brilliant son, have to rise from the ashes."

"And if I can't?" Because that's my fear, isn't it? Not just that I would lose Kendall. But that I'd lose everything. That I already *have*. This thing that's gnawing at me, this stain on my soul, would eventually swallow me up and spit out my bones.

My mom grins like she's privy to information I'm not. "Don't tell the others but you're my favorite and you're also the smartest."

I scoff. "I won't breathe a word because you'll deny it to the death. And I'm not the smartest, Ryo is. I've been knocked down, Mom, but I'm not delusional."

"You're damn right I'll deny it," she laughs. "Ryo might have the highest IQ but you are the smartest and most emotionally intelligent. He still has a ways to go in that department."

I snort in response because she's spot on.

"You can do this, Kai. You know why?" I shake my head. I glance at her, her eyes are bright and she's radiating love and warmth.

Thank god for her.

"Because you came from *me*. You forget I had to reinvent myself too, to rebuild all of it from the ground up. I had to fight tooth and nail for my miserable life and learn how to love it again," she explains, choking up a bit.

"You thought your life was miserable?" I ask.

She hesitates for a couple seconds trying to figure out her wording. "Not anymore, but yes, when things were at their worst. I did."

"I haven't forgotten, Mom," I respond my voice low.

I could never forget that day no matter how many times I've tried. *The sound of tires screeching, the crunch of metal and glass, the smell of burning rubber and acrid smoke singing my lungs. My screams penetrated the crisp winter air.*

"Haven't you?" she implores, her tone probably a bit harsher than intended. We don't talk about this time much, this period of her life and mine that's been drowned in shadows and ripe with suffering. It's a breeding ground for pain, turmoil, and instability.

And yet, here we stand. We've survived it.

"I had to learn how to navigate my entire environment in a wheelchair. To survive knowing I was the only person in most rooms that wasn't able bodied. To enter a room full of my peers, people who used to be my friends and know they pitied me. I had to give up my independence and rely on people way more than I'd like to. To fight that little voice in the back of my head that said dying would be better than the way I was living. I had to make peace with the fact that the first thing people notice about me is that I'm in a wheelchair. And I did it all with three young children."

"I know, Mom."

"Your life is very different now and that doesn't mean bad. It's just *different*."

"Yeah, I guess."

"I'm not going to pretend to understand what you went through and your lived experience. And I know you won't pretend to know mine. But what I'm saying is that it can be done. You *can* start over," she says, covering one of my hands with both of hers.

"How?"

"Well, let's start by cutting your hair. Maybe doing some things that would make you feel more like yourself," she suggests teasingly, reaching across the table to ruffle my hair. "But seriously, you have to live sweetheart and keep fighting for your life, as miserable and messed up as it may seem right now. You have to keep moving forward otherwise, this second shot you've been given will have been for nothing. You only get this one precious life, Kai. What are you going to do with it?"

***

I SPEND THE NEXT morning taking my mom's advice and trying to work through my massive to-do list. To start putting the pieces of my life back together. I go through my emails that have been piling up mostly from the team lawyers and director of PR. They want an official statement about my early retirement. What am I supposed to say—*I'm retiring because I had somehow gotten entangled in illegal gambling with members of the mob? That someone had tortured me, nearly killed me until I was crying for my mother?* Nope. I'm not touching that today. I have to start smaller. I elect to tidy my apartment instead, to the extent that I could with only one working leg. That at least feels manageable. I hobble around and throw away some empties, stray takeout containers, and get-well-soon flowers that have been rotting around my apartment since I returned home. This place is disgusting.

Then I research architecture programs and civil engineering graduate programs in Boston. All interests I might have majored in if my future hadn't been decided for me at a very young age. And that feels surprisingly refreshing, doing something just for me.

But, of course, my mind drifts back to hockey. The way it always does. I suspect it always will. Maybe I can't play anymore but I could coach. Minor leagues, professional teams—they all need coaches and assistant coaches. Who would be better equipped or trained to do that than me, a former NHL player?

CHAPTER 88

JENNA

I KNOCK ON HIS door feverishly. I'm in over my head here and probably way out of my bounds, but I'm sick of watching my two best friends fall madly in love with each other and then blow their relationship to smithereens the first chance they get.

I've had enough and haven't they?

"Kai, I know you're in there, let me in, god dammit!" I pound on his door again with my fist tightened.

Finally, it swings open and Kai, disheveled and unkempt, greets me with a hostile rough, "What are you doing here, Jenna?"

I grin sardonically. He looks surprised, but not angry. Which is *something*, I suppose.

"The better question is what the hell are you doing with your head so far up your ass, Kai? And thank god I'm here to help you pull it out," I quip.

"Nice to see you too. Please make yourself at home," he says sarcastically while I stomp into his penthouse apartment.

"What the hell is going on with you two? And what is that smell?" I ask, wrinkling my nose in disgust. He backs up a bit on his crutches, giving me a wide berth.

"Well, I haven't been able to clean that effectively with one leg and I'm sure you already talked to Kendall about what's going on between us," he answers. I venture further into his apartment, peering around with him on my heels.

"I have but I'm more interested in hearing your version," I reply, folding my arms and leaning against his kitchen island.

"Fine but can we sit at the couch or table? My leg is killing me."

"Lead the way." I follow him to his spacious living room that I'm sure at one point had been clean and organized. But there are glasses on the coffee table, boxes on his floor, loose clothes on furniture. He plops down on the couch and I sit in the leather loveseat. He's wringing his hands together nervously.

"Kendall and I are taking a temporary break," he sighs. "While I try and figure my shit out." He runs both his hands through his hair.

"Okay and how long exactly do you envision this break lasting?" I lean over and prop my chin on my clasped hands and elbows on my knees.

"I don't know."

"Right, okay. So how will you know when your shit is figured out? What's the indicator of that?" I'm not purposely trying to be a bitch or a thorn in his side. I just want to get to the root of all this. I'm tired of sitting on the sidelines.

"I don't know, Jenna, Jesus. If you haven't noticed, my life is a shitstorm right now."

Okay, I have to start easier. Softer. He's already in rough shape and he doesn't need me piling on. He needs support; we could figure out the rest after.

"Okay, well I think I can help with that," I say.

"How?" he eyes me skeptically.

"Let's start with your apartment. Get this sucker clean. And we'll go from there, start with smaller easy tasks and work our way up. Whatever I can help you with I will," I offer.

"I've been trying to clean it all morning but haven't made much progress... clearly. You'd really do that?" He seems unconvinced but it quickly transforms into pure undiluted relief.

"Of course I would. And let me restart because I feel like I came in kind of hot."

He smiles and it's small, almost undetectable, but it's there. "Yeah, you definitely did," he agrees with a halfhearted chuckle.

"How are you really, Kai?"

"Pretty fucking bad. I'm miserable and I'm afraid I'm going to lose her, Jenna," he replies.

"You won't. We'll figure this out," I say, trying to inject reassurance in my tone.

First, I clean his apartment and get rid of all the alcohol in it. Then I take out the garbage and tackle the mountain of dishes in the sink. I wipe the countertops and disinfect the bathroom, vacuum the floors, and put his room back together. When I emerge from his bedroom, he's on the couch, his computer perched on his lap.

"What next?" I say.

"I think I should go to an AA meeting," he whispers without looking up from his computer. I know this is hard for him, that some part of him feels ashamed even when he doesn't have to be.

"Okay, I'll help you find one," I suggest, pulling my phone from my back pocket. "There's one on Thursday in Griswold, 6:30 p.m.," I tell him. "You can Uber if you can't get someone to bring you." I message him the link and raise my eyes to his.

"Thanks." And he seems genuinely grateful. If I had to guess, Kai has probably spent the last few weeks fighting for his independence, trying to claim any shred of his old life that he could. Even though he very much needs all the help he can get.

"You're welcome. What else?"

"The Bucks have been hounding me about an official statement for my early retirement. I've been putting that off," he admits, lacing his fingers together behind his head and leaning back against the couch. I know he's trying to appear nonchalant, but I watch his jaw tighten, the vein in his temple bulging.

"Isn't that the director of public relations job? Tell them to draft a statement that you'll look over and edit if necessary. That's literally what they are getting paid to do."

"Right," he comments while opening his email.

After we Instacart groceries, make him an appointment with a therapist that specializes in PTSD, schedule weekly house cleanings, and research dog adoption events, we take a break.

"Kai, how's your mental health? How are you doing with everything that happened to you?" I wonder. We've put a dent in his to-do list and his apartment looks way better but we're still addressing symptoms of the problem—not the actual problem.

"You're a therapist and you seem to know me pretty well, despite us not talking all that often. So, why don't you tell me, work your therapy voodoo magic," he replies. He doesn't want to talk, fine. I can nudge him in the right direction.

"Are you having any thoughts about harming yourself?" I ask, hoping I'm way off base. His face stiffens. He works hard to avoid my gaze but he answers.

"You mean like swallowing an entire bottle of pain meds or wanting to sleep and not wake up?"

"Yeah, like that, Kai."

"Not as frequently as I was," he concedes.

"Okay, what about any PTSD? Do you have other intrusive thoughts, difficulty sleeping, flashbacks of trauma?" I mentally run through the list of symptoms we might see in people that have experienced significant traumatic events.

He nods his head. That's pretty much what I expected. But I hope for his sake, for Kendall and Akio's, and for everyone who holds him so close to their heart that we can get him through this. He *needs* to get through this but he can't do it alone. I make a mental note to contact his mom and ask if someone can check on him daily.

"Okay, I know you are seeing that therapist next week, but I think you also need to loop your regular therapist in. Are you on any antidepressants or anti-anxiety meds?" I ask, keeping my tone neutral and even. I want him to feel like he can divulge whatever he needs to, whatever is weighing on him.

"No, I haven't been on any since college."

"Well, I think you might need to consider it to help you get through the next couple months. Just something to take the edge off a little bit, okay? Think about it," I suggest. He needs a bridge, something to help him cross from this muck he's drowning in, to a possible future where *this* isn't all there is.

"Okay."

"Who else knows, Kai? About how bad this has gotten, the extent of it?"

"Just my mom. But I suspect my dad and Kendall have somewhat of an idea," he admits. His head hangs as he observes his hands.

"Listen, I'm going to give you a really harsh dose of reality tea and hope you don't choke on it. You need to let her back in, Kai. You need to let her help you and we both know you can't do this without her. And you need to start leaning on the people in your life that love you. We love you so fucking much and we want you here for a very long time." I don't want to push too hard or pressure him but I also am not willing to let him lose this fight. Kai needs to realize his people will have his back, lift him up, see him through this. Do all the things he has always done for them.

"I know," he says quietly. "I just don't know how."

"Just ask. Whatever you need, just ask. No one will blame you for needing help right now. I don't care if it's three in the morning California time, if you're freaking out and you're in a bad place. Just call, okay?"

"Okay."

"All the people in your life want to help however they can and they will. And as far as Kendall goes, she'll be here in an hour. And I don't care if I have to lock you both in a room myself until you make it right, but you guys will fix this." We might not have seen each other in a while, but I start bossing him around again like virtually no time has passed.

Another smile, a bigger one this time. *Progress.*

"Why are you doing this for me?"

"Because you're my friend. You've always been my friend, and that means something. I should have been there for you when she left and I wasn't. I ran to California, away from my problems. And I left a lot of people that I cared about behind. I'm trying to make that right."

"Thank you for being here, for helping me. And for calling her."

"You're welcome."

CHAPTER 89

JENNA

I OPEN THE DOOR and step out into the hallway, wrapping Kendall in a tender hug. I hope it softens the blow of everything I'm about to say.

"How's he doing?" she asks, worry etched into her features. She's tired and stressed; it's clear she hasn't been sleeping well for a while.

"He's not at his best right now. Not even close. He's broken and he's scared, Ken, and he feels like a failure, which we both know is new for him and probably the most terrifying." She nods her head, intently listening. "I'm going to tell you the same thing I told him. I'm going to give you a harsh dose of reality tea and hope you don't scald yourself on it, okay?"

She takes a step back, eyeing me precariously.

"What's that supposed to mean?" she demands.

"It means that I know you want to go in there arms swinging and have it out. And I'm telling you it won't end well if you do. That and he doesn't have much fight in him right now. That's not what he needs." I'm pushing, grasping at straws but it's imperative she understand the gravity of the situation.

"Okay," she looks at me tentatively. "What does he need?"

"He needs you to wrap him up in your comfort, your love, your security. He needs to know you aren't going anywhere and that you forgive him." The last part will be the hardest for her to swallow, I know that.

"I'm supposed to just forgive him just like that? Why? He doesn't owe me a conversation?" She scoffs in frustration. I take her firmly by the shoulders and peer into her eyes.

"Because it's Kai. Because he deserves it. Because he forgave you even when he didn't have to and even when it would have been easier for him not to. And because to be frank, the more pressing concern here is that he's drowning. He needs you, Ken. Think of all the times Kai has always—and I mean *always*—had your back and been there for you and Akio. It's your turn to show up for him. His entire future has been pulled out from under him. He can't suffer through that alone."

She has tears in her eyes and I know I struck a nerve. "What if we just have too much stacked against us at this point?" she wonders quietly.

"Ken, I want you to think about your life in 10 years. In 20 years. How do you picture it looking? What would be the safest option for you?"

"It seems like you already have an answer to your own question, Jenna. So why don't you just say it," she says, wiping away a tear with the cuff of her sleeve. She intended to be rude, but it's lacking all her typical bite and harshness.

"The easiest safest option for you would be to co-parent cordially with Kai. As friends. Maybe you stay at your current job, maybe you find one that's just as steady and financially secure but somewhere else. It wouldn't look very different from what you're doing right now. Maybe someday you find a nice guy that treats you well and fits into your life but not seamlessly. Not perfectly. Not the way Kai does."

"Or..." she presses.

"Or the other unsafe, wholly terrifying option would be to make things work with Kai. The man you've been madly in love with since we were 15. I don't think you want to settle. I think you want the option that scares the shit out of you. I wouldn't be here if I didn't think that. It's going to be messy and hard and it's probably going to feel like two steps forward and one step back a lot of the time but I promise you it will be worth it." She's crying big, relieved tears now as I take her hands in mine.

"How do you know?" she blubbers.

"How do I know?" I laugh. "The same way I know the sun is going to set in the west tonight and rise in the east tomorrow. The same way I know water is wet. You guys are soulmates, Kendall. Someone somewhere, cleaved a heart and a soul in two. You got one half and he got the other. You are two parts of the same whole. I don't have to tell you this. I know you know it. But if it helps, I'll say it anyways. You two together just makes sense; you two apart makes very little. I don't know how else to explain it. And I never really fit into our little trio, not the way I wanted to. But I wasn't supposed to either because what you two have is love. It's always been love. It used to make me mad, a little jealous. But I get it now that I have Amir, my missing piece. And I want that for you," I explain.

"I want that too. I want whatever option gives me Kai. All of him," she admits.

"I know you do babe. So, go get him. Help him fix this and make things right." I'm done meddling and playing matchmaker. How they move forward now is up to them.

Chapter 90

Kendall

K AI, THIS BEAUTIFUL, AMAZING dream of a man has proven to me over and over again just how much he loves me. He loved me even when it was hard, when it had been damn near impossible. Even when I didn't deserve it. He had loved me before we even knew what love meant or what it was. He has always loved me unconditionally and I know he will forever. It's my turn to show him there are no conditions, no limits to my love for him. That he is and always has been my home, my safe place, my peace, and my person. He's my soulmate in every sense of the word. That invisible thread that has connected us since we were kids has frayed but has not broken, and I know now it never will. It's time to start running towards that fact instead of away from it. It's time to fight for him the way he has always fought for me.

I walk into his room and find him slumped against the foot of his bed, staring at the wall. He's wearing nothing but hunter green boxers. His hair remains shaggy and now that he's shirtless, I spot scars I wasn't aware existed. He's still every bit as handsome, probably more so like this. Alone and vulnerable. Open and unencumbered with the pressure of having to please everyone around him.

"Hi," I say nervously.

"Oh hi," he looks slightly startled. "I uh, was trying to get dressed and I think I needed more help than I anticipated and yeah, here I am sitting in my boxers," he says with a dry laugh.

"Okay. Can I sit with you?"

"Of course."

He's on the floor, his head resting against his bed and I sit directly above him and start combing his hair with my fingers. Just like I used to when he was sad or stressed or nervous. His eyes close and he tilts his forehead so that it is resting against my knee. I don't say anything. I just keep weaving my fingers through his hair, making space for whatever he needs in this moment.

After an unknowable amount of time, I feel wetness on my leg. I look down at him, this man who is my entire heart, and he's crying, holding on to me like I could save him.

"I'm so sorry, Ken. I didn't know what to say and I didn't know how to ask for help. And I feel like my entire life is falling apart. But I don't want to lose you," he whispers between heaving sobs.

"You haven't lost me, Kai. I'm not going anywhere, okay?"

"I didn't know if you'd be able to love me like this. You deserve so much better." My heart breaks at his words, his uncertainty, his pain.

"Kai baby, look at me," I cup his face in my hands and bring his gaze to mine.

"I will *always* love you. I have always loved you. And I loved you way before hockey and completely independent of it, okay? I didn't fall in love with you because of what you can do with a goddamn hockey stick. I love you because of who you are and what you mean to me. You're the best partner and the most loving, adoring father. You're strong and loyal and fierce. You put 110% into everything you do. You're selfless and god, you're so fucking smart. I fell in love with you because even though you are intelligent enough to do anything, you chose the thing that would probably be the hardest and that would also make both you and your father happy. I love you more than life and you are *enough* exactly as you are, Kai Matsumoto. You will always be enough."

We're both crying now. He's kissing me through wet tears. It's panicked and hungry, desperate and raw. Like we have been apart for years rather than weeks. He's pulling me further into him, dragging me off the bed. I slide onto the floor and straddle his hips, trying to be mindful of his injured leg.

"You aren't getting rid of me again," I warn, pulling back from his mouth. "You're stuck with me. Whatever we do from now on, we do together. These are my terms, Kai, take them or leave them," I tell him, my voice sharp and certain.

"Okay. I'll take them," he nods, his forehead against mine. "I was so worried I would never get another chance with you, be able to make this right. I know how lucky I am. That's not lost on me. I'm grateful you're still here. And I'm not going to do anything to fuck this up. I'm not letting you go and I'm not going to do anything to jeopardize this," he promises. I don't know if I believe him, if I can fully trust him yet. But it doesn't matter because I love him and when you love someone, sometimes you have to offer up trust whether or not they deserve it, whether or not they give you anything in return.

"I know, Kai. I know," I whisper softly.

"I don't think you do. I can't lose you again. It nearly broke me," he admits.

"Me too. This thing we have, call it fate, soulmates, serendipity, but whatever it is, we weren't meant to live without each other. I sure as hell found that out the hard way and this part of me that needs you more than I need oxygen—it goes beyond logic, beyond reason, and I've given up on trying to shut that part of me up. I don't want to." God, I can't stop the word vomit now. I'm just blabbering, laying my entire heart on the line for him.

"So, we're soulmates?" he asks hopefully.

"Soulmates," I respond, kissing him. "Jenna explained it better. Basically she said together we make sense, and when we're apart, we don't."

"That tracks. Jesus, she's been fucking on one, huh?" he comments. But before I can respond, Jenna's blonde head appears in his doorway, hands covering her eyes.

"I believe you pronounced *thank you* wrong, Kai," she sasses and we both burst into laughter. It feels so good to laugh with him again. I roll my eyes and we say, "Thank you, Jenna," in unison.

"You're welcome. Now I'll be around for the next week or so, alternating between Ken's and my mom's if you guys need me. But it seems like my work here is done and I've been craving a pizza from Marchetti's. Feel free to resume whatever this is," she states, waving her hand in front of her, gesturing at us and grinning.

"Bye Jenna," we both shout. I press my lips to his again as soon as she's gone.

"Kai, I say this with as much love as possible, when was the last time you showered?" He isn't ripe, but he doesn't smell super clean either.

"Yesterday morning maybe?" The fact that he's unsure is enough for me.

"Why don't we do that first?" I suggest.

"I believe we were just in the middle of making up," he points out.

"I think we can manage both."

Chapter 91

Kai

S HE STARTS RUNNING THE bath and then comes back to my room to retrieve me. I lean on her, letting her guide me to the master bathroom, trying to keep most of my weight off my bad leg.

The steam settles around us like fog. She removes her shirt first, my mouth watering. Then she slides her bra off and shimmies her pants down her legs. *God, she's so fucking beautiful. How could I have been stupid enough to let her go?*

"Come on, handsome, let's get you in first." She carefully slides my boxers down and puts them to the side. Then she helps me sit down in the massive jacuzzi tub; the jets that are running have created a steady stream of bubbles. Her gorgeous hourglass shape disappears underneath the water as she makes her way toward me. Her lips are on my forehead, my cheek, my jaw. My skin is on fire with heat and tension.

"Please, let me love you, Kai. Let me take care of you," she murmurs. I nod because that's all I can do. She's here and she's naked and she still loves me. And maybe—just maybe—I could survive this, as long as I have her and her love to sustain me.

Her hands move slowly and gently along my shoulders, massaging my tight, weary muscles. Wherever her fingers go, her mouth follows. My traps, my upper arms, my chest. She caresses me with soft featherlight kisses, each time whispering "I love you."

It doesn't take long before my cock is aching for more of her, her touch, her heat. Her *everything*. She knows, she can feel the shift. Her hands inch down, sliding over my abs before grazing my pubic bone. Her fingernails lightly scratch my skin and I know

I've never wanted anyone the way I want her. On a cellular fucking level. The air feels carnal, electric. Like anything could happen.

"Tell me what you need, Kai. Whatever it is, I'll give it to you," she rasps.

"You. I only need you, Ken."

"I don't want to hurt you, your leg." She sounds worried.

"It's okay. I'll tell you if it's too much." Even though I wouldn't, I'd rather die before telling her to stop.

She moves slowly, her legs straddling my hips. She's holding the base of my shaft with one hand and positioning me at her entrance, her swollen clit pushing against my tip. She rocks her hips against me, and my head falls back against the tub.

"Goddamn, Ken," I growl.

"Is this okay?" she asks tentatively. She wants to be cautious, but I don't need caution. I need to fucking ruin her. I want to destroy her and make her whole at the same time.

"God yes," I say, moving my mouth to hers. Her tongue slides over mine like silk and she whimpers while she chases this friction we both desperately need.

"More Kai, I need more of you," she breathes.

"Me too." She places her palms on my shoulders while she lowers herself onto me. Her delicious heat swallows me inch by paralyzing inch until I'm entirely sheathed inside her and I swear I could die like this.

"Fuck, it's so good, *too* good." Good is too small a word to describe this. *Us.*

It's sweet sin. Violent, torturous delight. A beautiful fucking surrender. She looks down to where our bodies are joined.

"I can't move. I just want to savor this," she whispers.

"What?" I ask, pressing my lips to her neck.

"This, us. Being this close to you again and so fucking full of you."

Fuck.

I bring my mouth to her nipple, circling it with my tongue and tugging it between my teeth. I suck harder and let it go with a loud popping noise before I move to the other one.

"Jesus, Kai," she says, tipping her head back while I continue worshipping her body. She starts moving, unable to hold back.

Her arms are around my neck now, grasping me tightly while she sets a slow, euphoric pace. She rises up and then slides back down my cock again and again. I let her have all the control, take exactly what she needs. And she gives me everything in return. She peppers kisses along my neck, her mouth suckling, her teeth nipping while her tits bounce wildly in my face. I graze her ear with my mouth, whispering praise and sweet affection.

"I love you so much, Kendall. I'm sorry. I'm so sorry, baby."

Thrust.

"I'm sorry too for everything."

Thrust.

"Please come back to me," I beg.

Thrust.

"I never left."

I feel white hot pleasure coiling tight at the base of my spine. I bring my hands from her breasts to her hips, needing to feel all of her around me. Needing to hold on to something before I'm launched into the stratosphere. The love I have for this woman is breaking me apart and putting me back together at the same time. One arm snakes around her torso, molding her to me, pressing her chest against mine while I push up into her, as deep as I possibly can. I'm determined to hit that angle that makes us both frantic and delirious with pleasure. And holy fuck, it's a miracle when I do. I pump into her harder, the air filled with lust, the only sounds the wet slap of bodies, her breathy moans and my feral fucking growls. My knee would be screaming soon and I would pay for it later, but I don't care.

"Kai, I'm so fucking close," she cries, her legs locking tighter around me. Our pace turns brutal, her hips lifting and slamming back down on my cock. *Again and again.* She pulls on my hair while she digs her nails into my shoulder. My tongue moves against hers, her teeth snag on my bottom lip. Rough and greedy. Then I feel her walls shake around me, pulsing and squeezing until my eyes roll back in my head. She quivers with ecstasy. At the same time, my balls grow heavy and my release barrels through me. I feel it, *her* in my veins, my blood, my breath, my heart. In the shadowed depths of my anguished fucking soul. She's everywhere. She's everything. I'm a part of her and she's a part of me and there is no distinction between us. I swear we break a hole through time and space while the universe folds in on itself. I come inside of her while she dissolves around me and we sink into the aftershocks of our orgasms together.

She melts in my arms like warm honey.

Home.

"Home, you feel like home to me, Ken. You *are* home to me. And I'm so sorry I let myself forget that," I whisper, kissing her forehead.

"You're home to me too, Kai."

Chapter 92

Kendall

5 Months Later

"**C**ome on, Stella," I urge the sniffing dog to move along and find a place to pee on the busy sidewalk. She's a beautiful German Shepherd mix, that Kai, Akio, and I picked out together at a local dog adoption event. After his career ending injury, Kai had thought a lot about things he wasn't able to do while devoting his life to professional hockey. Having a dog was one of them and Akio and I were easily persuaded. Everyone needed to be on board since we are all living under one roof now. Akio and I moved in with him two months ago and it's been a great decision for all of us.

Kai and Akio have plenty of bonding time. He spends fewer days at daycare, and I don't have to stress about the costs of childcare anymore. I've since quit my job at the restaurant and reduced my hours at the law firm. On the days I'm not there, I'm freed up to continue working on my law school applications. I'm not sure I'll get accepted anywhere and most of the places I applied to are part time and online but I'm excited either way. I'm finally able to start thinking about my education again and options for *our* future.

Kai has taken so many steps to work on himself and our relationship too. We're still attending couples therapy as needed and Kai has weekly therapy sessions to help with the PTSD. He stopped drinking in September and has been sober ever since. He's enrolled in self-defense classes and while Stella might not be an official emotional support animal, she certainly acts like one. She fits into our little family perfectly and is completely in tune with Kai's needs. Slowly, things have started to get better and turn around for him and for us. He doesn't wake up throughout the night as much with nightmares or cold sweats. He can leave the house without having a full-fledged panic attack. He's had a lot of difficult conversations with his father over the past couple months and while their issues aren't entirely resolved, they've definitely improved.

I'm jolted back into the present when Stella drags me to a nearby tree to do her business. *It's so fucking cold.* This is probably the one aspect I hate about being a dog owner. Once she's done, I hurry her back inside our warm apartment building. I open the front door and she bounds over to the couch while I hang up my thick winter coat and scarf.

Akio is with my moms for the day and Kai is at an interview for a coaching position. I spent the morning cleaning and going grocery shopping, so I have the entire day to myself. After I watch a few episodes of *Parks and Rec* and make lunch, I throw in a load of laundry.

Two hours later, I'm putting folded clothes in the top drawer of Kai's dresser when I spot a box. Not just any box, a small black velvet box. That looks tiny enough to hold a ring. I open it, my hands trembling, terrified of what I'll find. Sure enough, there's a stunning princess cut diamond on a silver and gold band. It's exactly the kind of ring I would have picked out for myself.

What. The. Fuck.

Mindlessly, I move to the foot of the bed.

"Kai!" I shout. "Can you come in here for a sec?" I had heard him come through the front door only moments ago. He appears in the doorway a second later, glancing from the box in my hand to me.

"Kai, what is this?" I ask, even though I already know. Even though I'm well aware that the next few words out of his mouth would permanently alter my brain chemistry. He eats up the space between us, kneeling at my feet and placing his hands on either side of my hips.

"You know what it is. Why don't you ask me why I have it?" he responds, his dark eyes scanning my face.

"Kai, I don't want to play games right now or guess fucking riddles. What is this?" I demand. I don't even realize I'm crying until I feel wetness on my cheeks and tears slide down my neck.

"I bought it two weeks after I got drafted. I was going to wait to propose and then when you disappeared, I thought, if I could find you, fix things..." he trails off quietly. I'm positive there is no air getting into or out of my lungs. His admission hits me like a Mack truck. Like a ten-foot wave with a nasty undercurrent ready to drag me under. But this awareness doesn't drown me, this realization doesn't destroy me. I'm brought to the brink of madness, the edge of hysteria but no further. The kind of insanity caused only by the inability to be in the right place at the right time with the right person. A man who has been waiting for me for far longer than I knew.

No, this realization gives me life.

"North Carolina, you were going to propose?" He nods, splitting my heart and my soul wide open. "You still would have proposed after everything, after finding out about Akio?"

"I think it would have taken some time but yes," he says softly, bracketing his hands around my face. And I know with every fiber of my being this is the man I'm supposed to spend my life with. I think I've known it since I was 17. Kai, my oldest friend, the love of my life. The father of my child and keeper of my heart.

The only man that could worship my soul.

"And you kept it all this time?" I wonder, staring back into his onyx eyes, at my future, at *forever*. And it looks pretty damn good.

"I was waiting for you to come to your senses and find your way back to me. I knew it was only a matter of time."

Tears are streaming down my face, hard and fast now.

"I would have said yes, you know, in North Carolina. And if you asked, I would marry you tomorrow," I choke out through strangled sobs.

"What about today?" he asks, tears in his eyes.

I launch myself into his arms, knocking him over and we land on the floor with a mixture of laughter and tears. My hair falls in a curtain around his face and I start kissing him everywhere. His cheeks, his eyelids, his chin, his forehead, his lips. Any and every part of him I can get my hands on.

"Do you have any idea how much I love you, Kai Matsumoto? It's unquantifiable. The limit does not fucking exist. I am so stupidly, hopelessly, irrevocably in love with you. I always have been. And I don't want to spend another day of this life not married to you."

"Is that a yes?" he laughs.

"It's a hell yes." We're kissing again. It's frantic and demanding, hungry and hot. But before it goes any further, Kai's body stills as he pulls away from me.

"Wait wait," he says, his hands falling to my waist. "I had a whole speech planned. I wanted to ask you properly," he declares.

"Okay," I respond, sitting back on my heels. "Go for it, let's hear it." I grin. Because it doesn't really matter what his speech is. It's always been him for me. He could have proposed with the same ring pop he gave to me in third grade and I still would have said yes. But it means so much that he wants to get this moment perfect for me.

"Can you sit back down on the bed? I'm going to do this right," he explains, getting down on one knee and taking the open box in his palm. I obey his request and stare at him in anticipation.

"Kendall, I have loved you since I was fifteen. You said once that you thought we'd have a long love story, with twists and turns and ups and downs that will lead us to forever. And you were right because of course you were. There is no version of my life that is better without the both of you in it. I want you and him to have the life and love you have always deserved and I hope that you want that with me. You are my forever, my everything. Will you finally come home for good and marry me?"

Will you finally come home for good?

Somehow, these words are sweeter, more important, more *everything* than anything he has ever said before.

I whisper "yes" over and over, kissing him through tears. He slips the ring on my finger and it's a perfect fit.

It's just an ordinary moment during an ordinary day. It's not over the top or flashy. It's not Instagram worthy and doesn't need to be. It wasn't planned or executed flawlessly. It feels raw, honest, and real, just like us. The result of fate, timing, resilient love, and my obsessive need to stay on top of the laundry.

I realize, probably too late, or perhaps right on time, that for all the regular, mundane that is my life, *he* is the thing that makes it extraordinary. Kai is my once in a lifetime type of love.

Love that feels like home.

***

LATER, WE'RE CUDDLED UP in bed together, my head resting on my *fiancés* chest.

"I forgot to ask you after all the excitement, how did the interview go?"

He turns to me, pressing a kiss to my forehead. "It went really well. I should find out in a week or so. But I think I got it."

"That's amazing, baby! I'm so proud of you!" I squeal and I am. He's been networking, talking to previous coaches, doing a ton of interview prep for months, and it has clearly paid off. He interviewed for a few assistant coaching positions, both college and professional, but this one is a head coaching position for a growing NHL team. I know this is the only one he truly wants. But he doesn't seem super enthusiastic about this news.

"Yeah it is," he half smiles. *There's something he's not telling me.*

"But..." I press. For a long time, Kai had been so easy to talk to about his feelings, thoughts, fears. Ever since last June, getting him to open up has felt like pulling teeth.

"But what?"

"Kai, this is what you've been working towards. You just don't seem super excited about it..." I trail off.

"I got another offer for a job I barely remember applying for. It's kind of ridiculous but I can't stop thinking about it," he mutters.

"You didn't tell me that! Is it college or professional?" I ask, excitedly.

"Neither," he huffs, placing both hands behind his head and staring at the ceiling.

"Okay...so what's the position?" I wonder, even more intrigued. He turns to me and props his head up in his hand, resting on his elbow. He licks his lips and rolls his neck nervously but there is something in his eyes I haven't seen in a while. Light. Hope. *Optimism*.

"There is a failing youth hockey club in Toronto. They are looking for someone to take over as General Manager. They also need someone who can dig them out of debt and bankroll necessary expenses. I would act as a coach if I wanted to, manage finances, coordinate with the surrounding community, and organize and rebuild their club and youth teams. I would also probably be responsible for about a million other things."

"It sounds kind of crazy, but also exciting," I respond.

"Yeah?" he asks hopefully. He's looking to me for permission to dream this dream, to breathe life into this idea. He needs to believe that I think this is doable. And I do because I've come to learn Kai isn't capable of failure. It isn't in his DNA. He is wired differently, he always has been.

I nod aggressively, sitting up to a cross-legged position.

"Theres a catch," he states, stroking my knee with his palm.

"Okay, what's the catch?"

"Whoever buys this rink and takes over the hockey club has always lived in the house that is also on the grounds. And that house happens to be on a farm. A farm that comes with chickens, goats, and a few rabbits I believe and maybe some other miscellaneous animals." I think he's joking but his face lights up.

"Does it also come with a partridge in a pear tree?" I tease, but I can't help the smile spreading across my face. My heart rate starts gaining speed when I recognize exactly what this means for him, for our family.

A new beginning. A fresh start.

"Ken, this would be a massive undertaking..." he cautions, his wave of optimism starting to recede. "We'd have to move to Canada. We'd be responsible for an entire hockey club and a farm. We are very much *city* people. We don't know anything about farms," he postulates.

"Kai, I'm going to say something and before you say no, just don't say no, okay? Hear me out."

"Okay," he says, pinning me with a serious gaze.

"You have been chasing the feeling of perfection for as long as I can remember. This need to be great, to be the best, has been part of you since you were little. It's something I've always admired about you," I explain delicately.

"But..." he eyes me curiously.

"But even after you achieved your idea of success, surpassed it even, I know you still want more. You're still hungry for *something*. I don't know that you'll ever stop feeling like you need to be perfect. If the goalpost, this unattainable measure of success, will ever stop moving. And I think *this* opportunity to build something that's your own, that's entirely yours, could be good for you and for us. You've been chasing perfection your entire life. Maybe it's time to chase something else. Dream a new dream. Fall in love with hockey again. If anyone can do this, it's you."

"Maybe," he surmises quietly.

"You know we'll follow you anywhere. Whatever choice you make, we'll support you. I just think you should keep an open mind about it."

"Okay."

Kai is quiet for a while and I let him fade into his thoughts. I think he knows in his gut this is the right decision but he needs some time to process all of it, to arrive at that conclusion on his own. Not because I think it's a good idea or because it would be beneficial for our family, but because he wants it.

In my head, I'm already thinking about what Toronto will be like in the summer.

Chapter 93

Kai

MY DAD IS COMING over today while Kendall is at work and Akio is at daycare. It's only the third time I've been alone with him since everything happened last summer. We've talked a bit since then and come to somewhat of an understanding but there is still lingering hurt and frustration there. He is insistent and eager to meet with me and after almost dying, I've realized nothing in this life is guaranteed.

Around noon, he shows up in a long winter parka, carrying a bag of two greasy subs from one of my favorite restaurants. I open the door wider for him to come in and Stella immediately trots over to him. She barks loudly and aggressively, coming to stand between my father and me. But as soon as she sniffs his hand and circles him once, she decides he isn't a threat.

Not yet anyways.

"Hey, thought I'd pick up lunch. I hope that's okay," he says, handing me the bag and hanging up his coat.

"Yeah, that's great, thanks. We can eat while we watch the game if you want?" I suggest. He brushes snowflakes off his shirt and shakes out his hair while he stomps his feet on our welcome mat.

"Oh, okay. Sure," he replies. But I can tell he's disappointed. *Weird.* This has been our thing, our ritual even before my abduction and hospitalization. We rarely talk and when we do, we typically bond over sports. If there's something he needs to discuss, he would have to make the effort.

An hour and a half later, we're sitting on the couch watching the end of a college basketball game. He's on one end and I'm on the other. He reaches over to the remote and presses the mute button.

He swipes his hand over his face.

"I did want to talk to you about something, Kai. That's why I asked to come over," he finally explains.

"Okay," I respond, wringing my hands together. "What's up?"

"I want to know my grandson and I want to try and make things work with you, with us," he states nervously.

"That's a big ask, Dad. I don't know how Kendall will feel about that. We would have to talk about it." Which isn't a lie but it isn't the truth either. Kendall has been urging me to try and make things right with my father for months. She claims she has moved past everything and has forgiven him.

"How Kendall would feel about it or how *you* would feel about it?" he asks. So, I guess we're going there.

"I don't know, Dad. I'm trying to come up with a reason I would want you around my son and fiancée after you did the things you did."

He swallows and I can see something unfamiliar flicker in his expression.

Remorse? Guilt?

"I can certainly understand why you wouldn't want me around Akio or Kendall. I can't take back what I did. I will never be able to undo that. Even though I wish I could. But I can try to make it up to the three of you. And I am sorry for what I put you through. For trying to harm your beautiful family. There's no excuse for it."

My father has never apologized to me in my entire life. For a moment, I wonder if I'm imagining this conversation.

"And what about the years Kendall and I spent apart partially due to your decisions? The pain we both went through?" I press harder. "Because it isn't just about what you did. It's about the ramifications of your actions."

"I know. I realize that now. And I know I could have done things differently when you and your siblings were growing up.

Again, I can't change any of that, but I can apologize for it. I can try to make things right. And I am sorry. You were right. You don't do things like that to the people you love and I *do* love you and your brother and sister fiercely. I always have and I always will."

A tear slips down my face that I quickly wipe away. I shake my head, unable to believe the things I'm hearing. But this is real. He is here, admitting fault and attempting to make amends.

"You'll come to Sunday dinner with the whole family at least once a month. Mom, Kendall's moms, Amy, they'll all be here too," I tell him. His lips quirk into a smile and he seems surprised.

"Of course. I'll be there."

"You'll show up for him. Spoil him rotten. You'll love him unconditionally, without strings, without expectations," I demand.

The way you never loved me.

"I will. I promise. Thank you, son."

I nod, happy to have some of this weight taken off my shoulders.

"I want to tell you something and it is in no way a justification for my actions. But maybe you'll understand me a little better once you hear it."

"Okay," I wait for him to continue. He cracks his knuckles and brings his gaze to the ceiling. He wrings his hands over and over, the same way I do. Whatever he's about to say isn't going to be easy.

"When I was a kid, like twelve, my dad started to come home drunk, really angry. It just got worse and worse until he would come home every day belligerent. One day, he started to hit me. Some days it would be his belt. Some days his hands. It didn't matter as long as he got to unleash on something, someone. But I was the oldest so I took the brunt of it and tried to protect my mom and siblings the best I could." He pauses for a second, turning his back to me and hiking his shirt up over his head. His back is covered in scars, angry serrated misshapen raised blotches.

Jesus fucking Christ.

"Dad, I—"

"Let me finish, Kai. Let me get this out," he pleads. "When I was 15, I had had enough. I went through a growth spurt. I was almost bigger than he was. He hit me and I hit him back and I didn't stop until his face was almost unrecognizable. I told him if he ever came back, I would kill him and I meant it. He left that night and we never saw him again," he blows out a stuttered breath. "I always promised myself if I had kids, I would be better than my dad. And I was better than him. I never physically harmed any of you. But that's a pretty low bar. And it wasn't enough. I'm sorry, Kai."

"It's okay, Dad. I get it."

"No, Kai, it's not okay. I raised the three of you to be smart, driven, goal-oriented. I wanted you and Ryo to be protégés, mirror images of me. And thank god you aren't. You three are the best things that have ever happened to me, besides your mother. And I don't know why I spent so long trying to hide that. I think my mom always resented me because I was the reason my dad left. I was the reason we struggled to make ends meet. And because of that, I had to pursue a more stable career, not the one I actually wanted. I was never going to play in the NHL. It wasn't in the cards for me, but it was for you. I should have been happy for you. And for a long time, all I felt was bitter. We're supposed to provide the kinds of opportunities for our children that we never had. And all I ever did was envy you and for that, I am sorry, Kai. It was my pain to bear. It was never meant to be yours."

I understand it now. Not just his drive to push me and my siblings to be the best. Or his quiet, simmering hostility towards Ryo and me. Why I have almost never seen my father with a drink in his hand. Only on special occasions and even then, it was minimal. My propensity towards alcohol, my tendency to drink when I'm angry or upset, make a lot more sense now too. I would keep going, with no shut off valve until I woke up the next day with eight hours missing and unaccounted for. My dad's propensity towards violence—both physical and emotional—translated directly to my aggressive sometimes volatile outbursts. *Perhaps I'm a mirror image of him after all.*

"There's one more thing," my dad says, taking an envelope out of his pocket and holding it out to me. "I know you helped me with that loan when I needed it. And I also know whether you take that job in Toronto or not, you could use some extra cash flow. I want to give you this and I'm not accepting no for an answer."

I take the envelope from his hands warily and open it. Inside is a check addressed to Kendall and me for 300,000 dollars.

"Dad, I can't. This is too much," I admit quietly.

"Kai, I would have given this to you whether we talked or not. Whether you graciously allowed me to be part of Akio's life or you didn't. I want you and your family to have it. Start over if you want. Put it towards a house or that new job. Invest it or save it for Akio's college tuition. I want to do this. I can't do much but I can do this," he explains, emotion clogging his throat and tearing up a little.

A thought worms its way into my brain and sticks like glue, a thought that started materializing when my father first came clean to me about the loan he borrowed. *Maybe my father isn't just one thing*: evil and carnage, determined to fuck me and my siblings up as much as possible. Maybe he's a lot of things, only a fraction of which I understand. No one person is all good or all bad, I certainly believe that. There is a lot of gray in human nature.

"I don't know that I would ever be able to pay this back. I don't want to owe you anything," I answer shakily.

My father had done the best he could with what he had for his siblings and his children. It doesn't mean I forgive him and it doesn't mean what he did would ever be okay. Accepting his gesture could carry exactly as much weight as I let it. Maybe it just means that we're trying to work towards something better between us. Something honest. Real.

And that feels *good*.

"You don't need to. This is a gift. There are no strings attached. It is yours to do what you want with. You could choose not to speak to me for the rest of your life and I would still want you to have this." My father's voice cracks as he speaks.

I have never witnessed him cry. Not when Amy was born, not after my mom's accident, and not after my career ending injury.

This is a day of too many firsts. I nod again, lightheaded and a little shocked, and slip the check and envelope into my pocket. This gift he has given us is far bigger than money.

It's a clean slate. Freedom. The ability to dream again.

Chapter 94

Kendall

I ROLL OVER TO find a mishmash of bodies and limbs, both animal and human, tangled together in our king sized bed. Kai is lightly snoring with Stella pressed against his front. When we first adopted her, we tried to have her sleep in the crate. We quickly found out allowing her to sleep in our bed is better for her and especially Kai. Akio appears to be happily squished between me and Stella, his head now resting underneath my chin. He lets out soft little snores that mirror his father's.

How did I get this lucky?

I slip out of bed quietly, trying not to disturb anyone.

"Where you going?" Kai whispers without opening his eyes. He's adorable in the morning. His shirtless upper body and husky morning voice makes it difficult not to kick everyone out of this bed and keep him all to myself.

"I'm just going to start some coffee. You guys sleep a little longer, okay?" I say, rubbing his hand.

"Okay," he murmurs, wrapping his arm around Stella. I pad to the kitchen in my pink fluffy slippers and glance at the clock on our coffee maker. It's only 6:15. But it's also Christmas morning and there's still more work to be done before everyone wakes up.

I make up my coffee with cream and sugar and stare at our massive ten-foot Christmas tree. It's adorned in multicolored lights, silver and white balls, and a mismatch of homemade and store bought ornaments. A tiny red Akio handprint on thick paper that's framed by green popsicle sticks. A four inch metal hockey stick with the Bucks inscribed on it. Along with countless other trinkets that hang on the long evergreen branches.

After I finish stuffing Akio and Stella's stockings, light a candle, and put the remaining presents under the tree, I stop to admire the view from our penthouse apartment. It looks cold outside, but the sky is clear. Violet skies bleed into dark blue against the backdrop of the city. Weather reports for the last week have been promising a white Christmas, but I guess we'll have to wait and see. The street below is relatively quiet, only a few cars zipping by here and there. A bus stops to pick up a handful of people. Some look like they're headed to work, others have their hands filled with presents. The skyline of apartments and industrial buildings shine and twinkle with lights in the distance while Christmas music plays softly in the background. I sip my coffee and fold my arms across my chest while I listen to Nat King Cole wax poetic about *chestnuts roasting on an open fire*. I hum along to the lyrics, a feeling of peace settling over me.

I can honestly say that a year ago, I didn't think I'd be here. *Living with Kai. Raising our son together. Planning a wedding.* But I am so incredibly grateful that this is where we ended up.

While I get lost in the beauty of our home and the gratitude that fills my heart, I sense Kai walk up behind me. His strong arms curl around my middle and he rests his head against mine, his chin in the hollow of my neck. There's something about him hugging me from behind that makes my knees weak. I think it always will.

"Merry Christmas, Ken. I love you so much," he says, kissing my cheek.

"Merry Christmas, Kai, I love you," I reply, turning around and kissing him on the lips. I bring my hands to his face and smooth my thumbs over his cheek. "I love this life we're building together."

He brushes a kiss to my forehead and holds me tight against his chest. "Me too," he whispers. He no sooner finishes speaking and Akio and Stella come racing into the room. They are nothing but pure joy, excitement, and love. Akio collides with my legs and almost sends me toppling over while he shouts, "It's Christmas! It's Christmas!" And Stella begins jumping on Kai, barking happily with her massive paws on his chest. I run my fingers through Akio's hair and tip his tiny chin up to look at me.

"Okay okay, Merry Christmas! Who wants to open presents?" I shout as I gather him in my arms and spin him around. Kai takes him out of my arms and plants him on his shoulders while they circle the living room chanting, "Let's open presents!"

Three hours later, the Christmas morning adrenaline has faded and we're all on the tail end of a sugar high after having cookies for breakfast. We decide to get comfy and pile on the couch together. Akio falls asleep on Kai's chest, my head rests in Kai's lap, while Stella is snuggled up at my feet. There are half torn boxes, opened presents, toys, clothes and Spider-Man wrapping paper everywhere. We watch the remaining twenty minutes of *A Christmas Story* on TBS while we struggle to keep our eyes open. And right when the credits begin to roll, big white fluffy snowflakes start falling outside.

CHAPTER 95

KAI

"So, do you want to explain to me why you all of a sudden care about New Year's Eve and why the party you coerced me into throwing at our apartment had to be black tie?" I grouse while I pull into the underground resident parking lot.

She sighs, "We have been through so much in the past year. I just thought it would be nice to have family and friends over and host a party. Have all the people that love and support us in one place, you know?" Ken replies, her stunning hazel eyes gauging my reaction. I'm not sure how I'll ever be able to say no to her.

"Yeah, I guess you're right. I was fine ringing in the New Year with just the four of us. Quietly. In solitude and going to bed by ten," I tease. Slowly, over time, I've grown to love our small, steady, peaceful life and the comfort it brought me.

"Can you just try to have a good time?" she pleads before kissing my cheek and giving it a firm pat.

"I'll try," I grumble.

As soon as we open the front door, I know something is amiss. For starters, the kitchen smells amazing and there are people I don't know or recognize hustling back and forth between our bedroom, the living room, and the dining area. Our wide open concept apartment has been transformed into a...*wedding venue*?

I stare at Kendall in shock and awe, unable to process what I'm witnessing.

"Ken, what's going on?" I ask, my voice unusually high.

She swiftly drags me into our bedroom by my arm and shuts the door behind us. Her hands are clasped underneath her chin. "I wanted to surprise you with a grand romantic gesture. Our own little elopement ceremony. If you'll have me..." tears start building in my eyes. *This beautiful incredible intoxicating woman, I can't believe she's mine.* "We can also wait. If it's too much, we can just have a huge party tonight and continue planning like we have been. Honestly, no pressure," she stammers.

Jesus, she's nervous; she doesn't actually think I'd reject her, right?

"Of course I'll have you." I shut her up by taking her in my arms and kissing her long and deep, begging for more. "The party and black-tie dress code make a lot of sense now," I comment and smile against her mouth. My body is buzzing with uncontainable happiness and anticipation.

"Surprise!" she half whispers, half yells. "I didn't want to wait one more day to be your wife," she explains, rubbing her nose against mine.

"My wife, huh?" I smirk. *My wife.* She nods, shedding a few happy tears.

Our love had been resurrected from the ashes, forged from blood, tears, and sacrifices. Our relationship built and reconstructed over time. This life we're carving out together has been hard fought and hard won. And I can't wait to call myself her husband. My heart is thrumming with a wild, manic energy.

Never mind a ceremony, I want to consummate this marriage right here right now. She's wearing a red long-sleeved V-neck sweater that displays generous cleavage and skinny jeans that accentuate her *fuck me* hips. I pick her up swiftly, my hands gripping her ass and place her on top of the dresser. I step in between her legs and press myself against her, wanting her to understand how much I need her. How irresistible she is to me. I band one arm around her waist and pull her hips towards the edge of the dresser while the other tangles in her hair. I tilt her head back and brush my lips against her throat again and again.

"I need you right fucking *now*, Mrs. Matsumoto," I murmur, sucking on her pulse point.

"Tsk, tsk, tsk," she replies, wagging her finger. She leans back to look at me, her lips plump and swollen and her face flushed.

"I'm not Mrs. Matsumoto yet and there's still a lot of work to be done before the wedding," she cautions.

I groan dramatically. "Fine, fine. But I can't be held responsible for what happens after I see you in a wedding dress. A man only has so much restraint, Ken."

"Kai, as soon as we have some real time alone, I promise to show you just how *happy* I am to be your wife," she says, her voice low and sultry. Her tongue is warm and wet as she licks a path from my collarbone to my chin. Her teeth nip at my earlobe and tug sending shivers across my skin.

"Goddamn it, Ken, you aren't playing fair," I growl as I re-arrange myself in my now tight fitting jeans. She smirks mischievously, her bright eyes shining as she plants her palms on my chest.

"I love you, Kai, but you need to back up before the entire catering staff, florists, and planners hear us knocking boots."

"It's not my fault you're so vocal," I reply and trace her jaw with my nose.

"I think it's entirely your fault," she purrs, her breath hitching. I could feel how turned on she is. I know if there weren't thirty people behind our bedroom door, I'd be railing into her so hard she'd be begging, the dresser knocking against the wall and being emptied of its contents.

"Plus, it's bad luck to see each other on the wedding day," she adds, her tongue darting out to wet her lips. Kendall is trying to put space between us but her nails digging into my pecs and rooting me to the spot claim otherwise. Her brain is sending a message that her body is not picking up. But her dilated pupils, rapid pulse, and the goosebumps covering her arms leave no room for doubt. She may not want people to hear us but she definitely wants *me*.

She gives me a small shove. "Go on, I have to get ready and so do you. I'll meet you at the altar at 7. I'll be the one in white," she says smiling.

"Okay, okay," I retreat a step and hold my hands up in surrender. "What about a tux?" I wonder.

"All set. Jonah took care of it," she confirms.

"Rings?"

"Got those too."

"I haven't written my vows yet..." I say, starting to panic a little bit.

Why do I do that now— always look for holes? Why do I feel the need to shadow perfectly good things with doubt?

My therapist says it's part of the grieving and healing process. That eventually with time, I might be able to look at the world with more optimism.

"Well, good thing you have two and a half hours," she grins "But seriously, we can do our vows privately if you want. There's no pressure. This is *our* day. It's not meant to be stressful. Just happy. Only good things," she comments, squeezing my hand and giving me the reassurance I need. "Now go get ready, handsome. You're all set up in the guest room. Jonah, Ryo, and your dad should be here soon to join you."

No matter how many times I envisioned marrying her, dreamt about it, I never could have imagined this. Our home transformed into an elegant, winter fairytale, the promise of forever in every corner. Two rows of silken black chairs adorned with white bows make up the seating area. The makeshift aisle—our hardwood floors sprinkled with delicate white rose petals—gives everything an earthy feel. The altar is simple and understated, a small platform made of darkened wood. There's just enough room for both Kendall and me to fit. It's all framed by a white circular arch that has been decorated with sprawling flowers and greenery.

In two hours, I'm going to marry the woman of my dreams.

CHAPTER 96

KAI

I 'M FASTENING MY LAST cuff link when my father's salt and pepper head appears in my doorway.

"Um, excuse me, I'm looking for the groom," he jokes. I don't ever remember things being this easy with my dad. Light. Breezy. Almost refreshing.

"That would be me, I guess," I respond.

"You guess?" he replies, stalking towards me. This is when I would normally worry he would chastise me, scold me, cut me down. But he doesn't. "Alright, come on. Let me get a good look at you, son." I stand and do a theatrical spin, holding my hands out.

"So," I ask, slightly self-conscious. He brings his hands to my tie and adjusts it.

"There, now it's perfect," he comments. "You look sharp, Kai. I'm so proud of you."

I grunt in response. "I don't think I've ever heard you say that," I admit.

"Well, I should have said it long before now. Because I am. I always have been."

"Thanks, Dad."

"Are you nervous?" he wonders, planting himself on the foot of the bed.

"A little." *A lot. A whole fucking lot.*

"Don't be. Just focus on her. You two have always been meant to be together. Now you're just making it official, yeah?" I wasn't expecting my dad to dish out advice. I also wasn't expecting it to be helpful. But here we are, existing in the fucking twilight zone,

I guess. Before I can respond, Ryo and Jonah come laughing and bumbling into the room, each with a drink in their hand.

Jesus, what I would do for a stiff drink right about now.

Ryo stops short when he sees me. He claps his hands to my face, slightly buzzed already.

"You clean up well, Kai," he says. He pulls me in for a tight burly hug and claps me on the back. "Congratulations, man. I'm so happy for you guys. Although I don't know if I can leave this fancy hair to its own devices," he teases, putting me into a fake headlock that I easily slip out of.

"Cut it out, dick," I grumble, shoving him off me and running my hands through my hair.

"Congratulations, Kai. I'm happy for you guys," Jonah joins in. "Can't say I'm pleased about Kendall's plus one policy, but I still approve of her for you," he smiles wide.

"Jonah, you aren't bringing a one-night-stand or a booty call to our small intimate wedding. I stand by Kendall on that. Serious partners and spouses only." At that moment, my dad clears his throat and hands Ryo and Jonah glasses of champagne. He offers me a non-alcoholic beer. There's a pang in my chest when I realize there's a person missing. Someone I always thought would be by my side when I got married. *Aiden.* I push the thought away as quickly as it arrives.

"I just wanted to toast the groom," my dad begins. "May your marriage be long and prosperous, your hearts full, and your home happy. Cheers to you and Kendall." I smile at my dad—genuinely smile at him—while everyone chimes in with cheers.

***

I watch Akio walk down the aisle in a black suit that is almost identical to mine, holding Stella's leash and my heart bursts. He passes Stella to my mom and then comes to stand next to Ryo. The music changes and I know who's about to turn the corner from our long hallway. I feel blood rushing between my ears before they start ringing. My hands are beginning to tingle and tremble.

I could get beaten within an inch of my life but I'm too petrified to say my vows?

It feels like the world has been tilted on its axis while my breathing grows unsteady. But then Kendall comes into focus and everything shifts, the world is righted again because *she* is my center of gravity. *I love you,* she mouths to me. She's the most beautiful thing I've ever seen. The most precious thing I've ever loved. That's when I start crying hideous, heaving sobs. Ryo's hand is now on my shoulder to steady me.

He claps me once and whispers, "She's a vision."

She's three steps away from me now in a gorgeous silk dress with long lace sleeves. Her veil billowing behind her and her moms on either side, their arms threaded through hers. She's graceful, elegant, breathtaking.

Two steps away. I can see she's crying now too, her efforts to hold back tears just as useless as mine. Her makeup remains intact though and her face, like always, knocks the breath from my lungs.

One step away. I hug both of her moms and kiss them on the cheek. She's standing right in front of me, placing her perfect small hands in mine.

"Hi," she whispers.

"Hi. You ready?" I ask. She nods.

"Are you?"

"Ken, I've been ready to marry you since we were in third grade."

She smiles her perfect, golden smile that seeps into my bones like warm honey, and suddenly, nothing else matters. The officiant says a few words, providing an abridged version of our story, how we met, fell in love, and decided to get married. My sister and Jenna both do heartfelt, tender readings. But I don't hear, see, or notice anything but her. Then it's time for vows. The officiant looks to me and says, "Kai, you may now read your vows to Kendall."

I take the neatly folded piece of paper from my pocket, my fingers shaking and sweating and begin.

"Kendall, I knew as soon as I met you that I would never be the same. Once I experienced your bold and brave energy, with your wild dark curls and bright eyes, your smile that felt like sunshine on my face, I knew you would alter the course of my life forever. And so you did. I love to love you, I live to love you. It's a privilege and a blessing to be your partner and Akio's father. I'll choose you and love you in every lifetime we're together and I'll keep choosing you every day. And while this road we've had to walk to get here hasn't always been easy, it has absolutely been worth it. You are my best friend, you always have been and I'm so grateful that we became neighbors almost twenty years ago. I promise to love you every day. I promise to protect and provide for you and our family. I promise to keep you grounded and drive you nuts. I promise to nurture your dreams. I promise to always put you and Akio first. And I promise to always be your home, your safe place, and your person. You are every dream I could ever hope for. I hope you know how much I love you, today, tomorrow, forever. Always."

Chapter 97

Kendall

Kai has just read his vows and I'm crying just as hard as he was when I walked down the aisle. I wasn't sure if we'd ever make it here but I'm so happy that we did.

Kai. This perfect, handsome, amazing man. The best damn thing that ever happened to me was a goofy, shy, loving boy moving in right across the street from me.

He is filled with goodness and all the things I love. I remind myself to take a moment to appreciate the scene around me. Everyone we love is here. My moms are sitting in the front rows holding each other's hands and dabbing their eyes. Jax and Amir are here, smiling like lovesick puppies at Emma and Jenna respectively. Both of them stand to the right of me in midnight black chiffon dresses. Ryo, Jonah, and Akio stand to Kai's left. Broad, handsome, and beaming. Kai's mom is blubbering of course, and his dad is holding back tears. Veronica smiles at us from her seat next to her husband. The officiant turns to me now and lets me know it's my turn to share my vows with Kai.

I raise my eyes and tear-stained face to his and try to steel my resolve.

"Kai, my maid of honor said it best when she told me someone somewhere cleaved a heart and a soul in two and I got one half and you got the other. People may laugh or scoff at that. Maybe they don't believe in the power of soulmates. But I do. I think no matter what lifetime we're in, we'll always find each other. That there has been an invisible thread connecting us since we were kids and I'm confident that it's unbreakable. Untouchable. Unable to be explained but always felt and always there. We've been on the same wavelength, the same frequency for a long time now. You are the only person who knows the shape, the rhythm, and the words to the song in my heart. You are my greatest blessing, my heart, my comfort when I'm sad, my peace when everything gets too loud. My safe place to land. You and Akio are the best things that have ever happened to me. I promise to love you with everything I have, to take care of your heart and protect it fiercely. I promise to never bother you during a playoff game." I pause for comedic effect. "I promise to support you and your dreams, every endeavor you take on. I promise to be there for you and never take our love or life for granted. I love you and everything that you are, and I love you more each day."

He looks at me, his eyes shining and wet with tears. I bring my thumb to his cheek and wipe some away as I smile through my own. The officiant instructs us to repeat a few more things. We exchange rings excitedly and then he pronounces us husband and wife. Kai's hand is on my waist firm and warm, the other clasping my neck. He's staring at me like I'm everything, the very air he breathes. What his entire world spins around. And I accept it, believe it. What's more, for the first time, I know I deserve it.

He dips me to the floor and our mouths crash together. He tastes like forever, like happiness. Like every dream I've ever had unfolding all at once. He's the song I'll never get tired of singing. This kiss holds countless memories. It's love and hope and freedom and sacrifices. It's lazy Sunday mornings and gentle sunrises. It's the earth, the wind, the stars, and the moon. It's infinite and fleeting at the same time. It's pure magic just like the first time he kissed me in his parents' basement. It's his sweaty lips crashing into mine, after his first college win. It's the hot rapturous kisses when he's sliding into me over and over again. It's his hands on my hips and a peck on my cheek to let me know he's thinking about me. In this kiss we've lived a thousand lifetimes each with each other, each better than the last. It's everything we are and everything we have yet to be. It's the safest place in the world.

It's home.

Chapter 98

Kai

For the second time in less than a year, I look around and don't recognize my life. The difference is now it isn't suffocating me and it isn't pulling me under. My father is happy and present, loving on my mom and joking with my siblings. We're getting along by some miracle. Kendall is radiant, absolutely glowing in her wedding dress. She's beaming as she dances while Akio steps on her toes. We're married, raising a son together, and about to start a new life in Toronto. We're closing the door on this chapter and opening a brand new one. Everyone that we love and care about is here to celebrate us and root for our love. It's the kind of moment so sweet and so minute, yet utterly perfect you wish you could live in it forever. I can't believe this life is mine and that I get to live it with her. This path we've traveled has been paved with heartache, secrets, destruction. But it's also been filled with so many good things. I'm grateful that we finally found our way back to each other—that no matter what happens now or where we end up, no matter what lies ahead, I get to walk through life with her by my side forever.

I'm about to cut in between my son and Kendall and steal a dance with her when the one bodyguard I still have on security detail taps my shoulder.

"Boss," he says gruffly, his shoulders squared up with mine.

"Remy, you don't have to call me that. Just Kai is fine. What's up?"

"There's a man downstairs asking to see you. Claims he's an old friend. Says his name is Aiden," he responds.

The blood in my veins runs cold. I haven't spoken to Aiden in ages, not after everything that happened. Part of surviving is compartmentalizing and that means not thinking about what happened last summer every second of every fucking day. But as much as I hate to admit it, I have wondered how Aiden is doing. That my actions weren't in vain.

"Okay, I'll see him. Downstairs. Don't stray far," I instruct. Remy and I both get into the elevator and once the lobby doors open and I see him, I'm hit with a startling wave of relief. I thought it would be terror, anger, resentment. He crosses the foyer of my apartment building in a few strides.

"Hey," he says, wringing the back of his neck with his hand. "Jenna told me about the wedding," he admits.

"Yeah, she has a way of meddling, doesn't she?" I can't help but stifle a grin. Aiden looks good. Like maybe he finally got his shit together. A man beaten but not broken, thank god. He looks fit, trim, like he's gained some muscle back. His sandy blonde hair is short and styled and his dark blue eyes are clear. Filled with remorse and trepidation maybe, but clear. Which suggests he isn't actively using.

"Yeah. Listen, I'm sorry I just showed up here out of the blue and I don't want to intrude. I just wanted to say a few things and then I'll be on my way."

"Okay..." My eyes flick to Remy and I give him a brief nod, indicating everything is okay and he doesn't need to babysit us for this.

"I'm so fucking sorry man for what happened. For everything. I don't expect you to forgive me. But I *am* sorry. I didn't know it would be like that, that bad. I knew if they got their hands on me, they would hurt, likely kill me. I had too many bounties on my head. But I never thought..." he swallows, trying to compose himself. He stares at the ceiling, searching for answers, for words neither of us have, before bringing his gaze back to mine. "I'm so sorry, Kai, and I'll never be able to repay you for what you did for me. You saved my life, man. I've been clean for four months. I know it doesn't seem like a lot. But for me, where I was headed...it is."

"Aiden, it's okay. No one could have known what his next move would be. And I wouldn't be able to live with myself if I let you die. I made the choice. I suffered for it, but I made it. No one else." It wasn't easy and it didn't change anything, but it was the truth. No one forced me. I made the decision and I paid for it dearly. Some part of me knew I'd always be paying for it. But seeing him here, alive, healthy. Right now, that's enough.

"Thank you, Kai. I probably won't ever be able to thank you enough, not in this lifetime. I'll never be able to repay you for it," his voice cracks.

"That's okay. I'll let you keep trying," I smirk, attempting to lighten the mood.

"There's one more thing..." he admits, taking a step closer, his eyes darting around the room.

"Yeah?" I ask.

"When I was in rehab, I met a guy in there," he swallows and lowers his voice. "I can't tell you his name. But he was an FBI informant. He had spent three years on the inside with some of Ferrante's most loyal soldiers—"

"I'm not sure if I want to hear this, Aiden," I respond, the hairs on the back of my neck rising.

"Trust me, you do," he presses on. "He said things had been escalating in the past year or so. Fights, targeted attacks, crime rising in both Ferrante and O'Rourke territory. The last turf war and drug raid ended in a shoot-out. It was a fucking bloodbath. The whole thing was coordinated and staged by the FBI with the informant's help. I'm sure you saw bits and pieces on the news about it a few months ago."

I nod. I had seen it.

"Anyways, the informant said it resulted in a lot of arrests. He told me that almost everyone connected to the O'Rourke's, even lower level guys, are either dead or in jail. O'Rourke went into hiding but I'm sure he'll turn up soon. I just thought you'd want to know, maybe you'd have some peace of mind."

"Thanks," I reply, my mouth suddenly going dry. "You can come up, you know, if you want. There's tons of food, dancing..." I trail off.

"That's okay, I just wanted to talk to you." He offers me a small smile. "It's probably best if I stay away for the time being. You only deserve good things today. Congratulations by the way. I'm so happy for you guys."

Epilogue
3 Years Later

AFTER PRACTICE ENDS, I lock up the rink, exit through the back door, and make my way to the wall of trees that separates the hockey club from my house. I step over partially obscured roots and push long branches aside until I reach the trodden path that leads to our property. Spider webs glisten in the early evening sun, birds chirp and trill singing about the end of summer, and somewhere in the distance, I hear more woodland creatures scampering about. It's golden hour, my favorite time of day. Besides five a.m. skate. There's something about being the first person on fresh ice that hasn't been touched yet. Maybe it's that no matter what, you get to start again, have a blank slate every day.

Once I reach our backyard, I pause to watch a mother duck and her five ducklings swim across the pond leisurely. One duckling remains on the edge, probably too nervous to go in. I walk over to the pond quietly and bend down, giving him a gentle nudge with my hand. The mother swims over to him to make sure he gets in line. She stares at me for the briefest of moments as if to say *thank you*. I keep walking and round the front of the house. I can see them perfectly, my whole world, but they don't notice me yet. Kendall is sitting in a white rocking chair, our daughter on her lap. Akio is lying on his stomach, colored pencils and loose paper spread out around him, drawing a picture. Stella sleeps at Kendall's feet, curled up and content. My entire universe is in this wrap-around porch. Stella hears me first and in seconds, she's bounding off the steps, her paws landing on my chest. She's barking relentlessly, planting big sloppy wet kisses on my face.

"Hey girl, hey Stella, girl," I greet her, scratching her head and walking towards the front steps.

"Daddy!" Akio shouts, flying off the landing and into my arms.

"Hey bud, I missed you today," I say, ruffling his hair and sprinkling it with kisses.

"I missed you too! Can I go to practice with you next time?" he whines.

"This weekend you can, okay?" I respond.

"Okay," he grins. I put him down and him and Stella take after the goats and chickens milling about on the side of the house.

"Hey there, handsome, how was your day?" Kendall asks as she walks towards me in a yellow sun dress, our one and a half year old daughter in her arms. We've been married for almost three years. I've loved her for most of my life, and it never ceases to amaze me how beautiful she is.

How lucky I am.

I yawn, exhausted from a long day's work even though I spend my days doing what I love and would therefore consider it a stretch to call it work.

"It was good. The budget is going to be tight this year again," I respond, kissing my daughter's head and drooly adorable face as Kendall hands her to me. My wife burrows into my chest before she clasps her arms around my neck and lifts up on tip toes to kiss me. It'll never get old, her kissing me like I've been the only thing on her mind all day. Like no matter how much we see each other, it will never be enough. Like I'm the line of her favorite song, a story she never tires of hearing.

She sighs into my mouth. "I missed you, what's this about the budget being tight?"

"We need new uniforms for the juniors and seniors and another Zamboni...which means our bathroom remodel will have to be put on pause again," I tell her.

She smiles. It's patient, kind, and warm. "That's okay, we've suffered with one and a half bathrooms for three years. We'll be fine for a few more."

"Are you sure? We've been putting it off for so long."

"Of course I'm sure. The club needs it and that's more important, Kai," she decides, kissing my cheek.

"I'm sorry, Ken. I feel awful."

"Don't. Really, it's okay," she tells me, squeezing my hand.

While we aren't exactly hurting in the money department, we don't have unlimited funds either. That way of living is long gone. Kendall has a very generous salary at the firm she works at but she also does a lot of pro-bono work. She has the biggest heart and difficulty saying no to people. She graduated at the top of her class and began working at a small firm close to home that specializes in family law. She spends her days helping families fight for custody and prospective parents adopt children, and she loves it. She's put down roots in this place, found her footing and so have I. I've learned how to pivot, how to heal, what to prioritize and how to let go.

I've rebuilt the hockey program and youth clubs from the ground up. And I'm damn proud of it and what I've been able to accomplish since we moved here. People depend on me, look to me to solve problems, and I like being someone they can always count on. To fix things, create schedules, to ensure the club runs smoothly, that all positions are properly staffed and all the patrons are satisfied. Along with a hundred other unnamed, trivial duties that are not at all in my purview but somehow became my responsibility. And I like that too. That this job is like second nature to me—hockey being part of my blood, in the fabric of my DNA—but that it also comes with inconsistencies. Things that are so bizarre or unpredictable that you can't possibly make it up. Like figuring out how to safely move a family of bats living in the ceiling above the snack shop to a more ideal location without harming them.

I'm not rich anymore, not like I used to be. But it doesn't matter. We're rich in love. Smiles. Happiness. Peace. And a million small moments we wish we could freeze forever. And isn't that what it's all about anyways? How lucky are we that we have a life

so beautiful, so full and bursting with warmth and possibilities
that we get to fall in love with it all over again every day.

ACKNOWLEDGMENTS

THANK YOU TO MY husband, family members and friends for supporting me on this amazing journey of becoming a published author. I'm eternally grateful to my husband for building a business with me and for all the hours, work, and love you have poured into this novel. Thank you to my daughter for being a guiding light and source of inspiration. Thank you to my editor, Sana, for your tireless support and careful review of my novel. You have helped turn this book from a pipe dream into a real novel. Thank you to my mom and close friends that had the opportunity to read this book in its early stages. Your thoughts and feedback were invaluable.

A huge thank you to Alice Trijjet for designing this beautiful, romantic cover and for bringing my characters to life. Thank you to my PA Lynsey and my Street Team, for loving this book, hyping it up, and helping me bring it to a wider audience. Thank you to my devoted and supportive team of ARC readers, this book would not be possible without you either. And to all the readers who take a chance on this book and love it just as much as I do, thank you.

www.ingramcontent.com/pod-product-compliance
Lightning Source LLC
Chambersburg PA
CBHW020332180726

47991CB00020B/1269